Hailey Edwards writes about questionable applications of otherwise perfectly good magic, the transformative power of love, the family you choose for yourself, and blowing stuff up. Not necessarily all at once. That could get messy. She lives in Alabama with her husband, their daughter, and a herd of dachshunds.

Visit her website at www.haileyedwards.net

BAYOU BORN

Hailey Edwards

piatkus

PIATKUS

First published in Great Britain in 2017 by Piatkus

3 5 7 9 10 8 6 4

A CIP catalogue record for this book
is available from the British Library.

ISBN 978-0-349-41706-6

Typeset in Goudy by M Rules

Printed and bound in Great Britain by
Clays Ltd, Elcograf S.p.A.

Papers used by Piatkus are from well-managed forests
and other responsible sources.

MIX
Paper from
responsible sources
FSC® C104740

Piatkus
An imprint of
Little, Brown Book Group
Carmelite House
50 Victoria Embankment
London EC4Y 0DZ

An Hachette UK Company
www.hachette.co.uk

www.littlebrown.co.uk

For Michael, who nudges me stumbling
after my dreams when I'm too afraid to chase
them. And for Little Bear, who brightens
my world by simply existing.

I would also like to thank Tara Loder
for seeing potential in me.

CHAPTER ONE

───◉───

Fluorescent lights charged the short hallway with a buzzing hum that vibrated beneath my skin. The urgent swish as my polyester uniform pants rubbed together made me wince, but each fixture I passed under carried me nearer to sweet, sweet freedom.

Three steps, two steps . . . Almost there.

"Hey, Boudreau," John Rixton hollered at my retreating back. "I got something to show you."

Hanging my head on a soft groan, I pulled up short of my goal and clenched my fingers over dead air, the exit door still a foot away. So much for my quick escape. "I haven't fallen for that line since Joey Tacoma asked me to follow him behind the bleachers at my first football game."

"Will you come here if I swear not to peer pressure you into showing me yours if I show you mine first?"

Pursing my lips in consideration, I checked the time and decided I could afford to humor him for a few minutes.

"Promise you won't show me yours, period, and you've got a deal."

"Done and done." Not even the hard pass on a private family-jewel viewing managed to douse the glee that had him bouncing on the balls of his feet. "Come on, Bou-Bou."

I arranged my features into a cutting scowl that struck fear in the hearts of lesser men, usually those on the wrong side of a Mirandizing, and faced him. "Don't ever call me that again."

"Fine." He waved me toward the break room. "Just get moving."

Following a faint strain of tinny music, I paused beside him on the threshold leading into the blacked-out room. No fluorescent tubes flickered to life. Instead the area was lit by a single flickering candle. Not suspicious at all. "Do I have to do this?"

"Yes." He tapped the back of my boot with the toe of his to get me moving. "You really do."

Dragging my heels, I wandered over to inspect a cupcake of dubious origins. Definitely homemade. Its icing had gone flat from having been smeared on while the cake was still warm. Its foil-covered base had been used as a paperweight to pin open one of those fancy greeting cards that played music or allowed for voice recordings. I stood there a moment until the message looped back to the beginning in order to fully appreciate the torture being inflicted upon me by my friends and coworkers.

"*Happy birthday to you. Happy birthday to you,*" it sang cheerily. "*Happy birthday dear—*" here came the audience participation bit "*—woohoo, Luce! Luce as a goose! It's your birthday! Yeah! Birthday girl!*" That done, the card played on. "*Happy birthday to you.*"

After snuffing out the candle with a put-upon sigh, I chucked the chocolatey lump across the room into the wastebasket. The dull thud when it landed mirrored the enthusiasm with which it had been thrown. Picking up the card, I ripped out the music box and crushed it under my booted heel. Then I tore the card down the center and waited.

"Twenty-one seconds," Rixton crowed, flipping switches as he strutted into the room. "I win. Pay up, suckers."

The suckers in question ought to know better than to bet against Rixton. He was smart, he played dirty, and he knew me better than most anyone. Being partners did that to people, and we'd been paired up going on four years. Rising from their hiding places, the handful of other cops who treated me as a person instead of a sideshow attraction reached for their wallets with good-natured groans aimed in my direction.

"I baked that cupcake from scratch, you heathen." Maggie, dressed in a smart, white blouse smudged with blue finger paint and a swishy black skirt, reeled me in for a hug that made my ribs creak. She had serious muscle definition for a kindergarten teacher. Must come from wrangling six-year-olds all day. "Why are you an enemy of happiness?"

"You want happy, hire a clown." I kept up my grumpy façade lest the others figure out my core was one hundred percent marshmallow fluff. "Or slap red lipstick on Rixton. He's the next best thing."

"I heard that." He popped a rubber band around the thick wad of cash he had collected, mostly dollar bills, and tossed it to me, cackling when I caught the roll without taking my eyes off his. My reflexes amused him to no end. "The only lipstick you'll find on me comes straight from the Mouth of God."

Maggie choked on air. "Does Sherry know you call her that?"

"She's still his wife, so that's a no."

I screwed up my face at him. "Mouth of God? Really? You're lucky she doesn't sew yours shut."

"Why do you call her that anyway?" Maggie walked over and

toed the trash can as though she were mentally pro/conning going dumpster diving. Possible cooties versus guaranteed chocolate. Even I could do that math. But the fact she even considered mounting a rescue mission was telling. She had spent so much time enforcing the five-second rule that she might have actually started believing in honor among bacteria. "That's weird, even for you."

"Trust me." Cartoon hearts all but burst in his eyes. "If she ever put her mouth on you, you'd know how she got the nickname."

Pressing a fist against her lips, Maggie puffed out her cheeks. "I just threw up a little in my mouth."

She wasn't the only one left tasting acid. Granted, my reflux was one part TMI and two parts anxiety as my internal clock ticked down the minutes until midnight. Either way, I could do with a couple of Rolaids and a Pepto chaser right about now.

"On that note, I'm out." I waved to the room at large. "Thanks, guys. You're all the best. Each and every one of you. Don't let anyone tell you any different."

"Leaving so soon?" Maggie accepted a kiss from me on the cheek, an apology for not saving the cupcake for her, but I had a hard-ass, birthday-hating rep to protect. Plus, watching my greeting-card-fueled rampages had become somewhat of a departmental tradition. "You never want to hang on your b-day."

"We can do something tomorrow." I patted Rixton's shoulder, mostly in sympathy for his long-suffering wife. "All four of us."

"It's a date." He tapped my rubber-banded haul with his fingertip. "Your treat?"

"Make you a deal. Keep your grubby mitts off my cheeseburger fund, and I won't tell Sherry about the nickname." I thumped his knuckle when he faked having trouble letting go. "Old Sherry might have laughed it off, but Pregnant Sherry is hormonal and a teensy bit frightening."

"I'll remember this when we're naming godparents," he groused.

"Ignore him. Go home. Do whatever it is you do on birthdays that best friends aren't allowed to know about, despite the double pinky swear I gave in fourth grade to keep all your secrets." Maggie buffed her nails on her blouse. "A vow I have yet to break, thank you very much."

A groan eased past my lips. "Mags . . . "

"Don't *Mags* me. That old rotary phone was on the kitchen counter when I dropped off those cake samples yesterday. The ones my maid of honor is supposed to help me narrow down to a favorite? Then today, when I left the swatches for bridesmaid dresses with your dad, it was on the coffee table. That means *someone* is carrying it around with them like a security blanket. Kind of like they did when we were kids."

I spluttered a denial, but Maggie, being a teacher, was immune to both spittle and protestations of innocence.

"You spiral on your birthday, Luce. I would have to be blind or stupid not to notice, and despite what my kindergarteners think, I'm neither." The toe of her pumps started tapping, and had I been a student, I might have caved under her expectant stare. "You get twitchy the week before your birthday and start hovering over that relic like a bee waiting on a particularly ugly flower to open its avocado green petals. After your big day, you're back to normal, and it's back where it goes. Does it even work?"

"That old thing?" Heart thudding against my ribs, I forced out a laugh so tight it squeaked and inched toward the exit. "It's got sentimental value, that's all."

"Play you for answers." She held out her fist and waited for me to accept her challenge. "Real ones."

"I'm not going to rock, paper, scissors away my secrets." I bit the inside of my cheek. "Not that I'm admitting I have any worth winning."

Nose wrinkling like she smelled the lie on my breath, Maggie decided to let it—and me—go. "See you tomorrow, Lucey-goosey."

"How is that fair?" Rixton pouted. "I can't call you Bou-Bou, but she can call you Lucey-goosey?"

"Tuck in your bottom lip before you trip over it." Maggie flung out her arm, barring the door and corralling Rixton in the break room. "It's a nickname her dad gave her."

Grateful for the intervention, I mouthed *Bless you* then hit the hall at a brisk walk. I kept my head down, gaze trained on the grungy linoleum tiles, but I couldn't leave. Not yet. I had come this far, I might as well go the rest of the way.

Chief Timmons believed in a literal open-door policy, so all I had to do was stroll into his office and circle his desk to complete my birthday ritual.

A framed news clipping hung on the wall behind his chair, mixed in with the awards and commendations he'd received during his tenure. The article I'd come to visit had been printed fifteen years ago, and age had yellowed the paper. The caption read *Hero Cop Adopts Wild Child Foundling.* But the grainy portrait wasn't of a young girl wearing her Sunday best, long sleeves covering her arms despite the heat, her hair in ringlets, her tiny hand clasping the much bigger one belonging to the man who had claimed her as his daughter. No. The feature highlighted a feral child shown waist-deep in murky swamp water, hair matted against her scalp, her thin frame caked with muck that concealed her peculiar markings as she gnashed her teeth at a uniformed man, one Edward Boudreau, who extended his arms toward her.

This journalistic gem had been one of many such features responsible for launching Wild Child Mania, and the temptation to disappear it into an evidence locker under a false ID was strong tonight.

The chief had packed away the reminder during the nineteen weeks I'd attended the Canton Police Academy as a fresh-faced twenty-one-year-old on account of all the naked mud-wrestling jokes cracked at my expense. But he'd rehung it on graduation day in a special ceremony aimed at whipping the media circus that was sometimes my life. And here I stood, fifteen years from the printed date, watching the shrine to my otherness gather dust in its place of honor.

Maybe the hype wouldn't have escalated to this point if I hadn't been found in Canton, Mississippi. The sign posted on Peace Street calls Canton the City of Lights, but the description of "City of Lights, Camera, Action!", used on the town's website, feels more accurate. We're also called the film capital of Mississippi, and despite the small-town atmosphere and Southern charm oozed by the locals, some folks kept glitz and glitter in their eyes long after the film crews left.

I caught my reflection in the glass and winced. The woman staring back at me looked older than twenty-five, and there was nothing glamourous about her. Maybe it was the severe French braid tasked with keeping her unruly chocolate-cherry hair tamed. Or the weight of too many things seen churning storms in her sea-glass-blue eyes. Or maybe it was the fact I didn't know for sure she was twenty-five at all. Foundlings didn't exactly come with a manufactured date stamped on their heels.

"Happy birthday, Luce," I murmured to my mirror image. "Whoever you are."

I spun on my heel to leave as a partial seizure locked my knees and sent golden flecks crawling across my vision. Deep muscle contractions twitched through my arms and shoulders, chased by a localized burn that sizzled in concentric rings from my wrists up to my nape. As fast as it attacked, it retreated, and I sucked in lungfuls of air stained by the chief's favorite cologne.

Inhale. Exhale. Rinse and repeat. Easy as, well, breathing.

I shuffled into the hall, my feet weighing a hundred pounds each, and tugged the long sleeves of my uniform down my wrists until the fabric brushed the heels of my palms. Habit curled my fingertips over the cuffs to pin them in place. I held on so tight as I battled the receding tide of nausea, I winced at the sting as my fingernails bit into my skin.

At the other end of the building Maggie and Rixton chattered on as though no time had passed, their familiar voices carrying out the break-room door, and snatches of their conversation grounded me.

"Boo-boo? Ah. I get it. B-o-u. Not B-o-o." Maggie's snort rang out behind me. "Bou-Bou Boudreau sounds like a hooker name." At his offended gasp, she amended, "But a classy one."

"*Right?* That's what I'm saying." The squeal of his boots as they twisted on the linoleum was a familiar sound. He was dancing. Or trying to at any rate. Most of his moves resembled a plucked chicken in its death throes. "Slap me some skin, Magpie."

"That is *not* going to be my new nickname."

The sound of their good-natured bickering trailed me into the parking lot. I made it all of two steps before a buzz in my back pocket had me reaching for my cell. I read the brief text and put Dad's favorite swear to use. "*Sunday witch.*"

Don't get me wrong, I wasn't above using the alternative.

Once in a while an earnest *son of a bitch* really hit the spot. But Dad had raised me in grand Boudreau tradition, meaning there was a bar of soap kept in the medicine cabinet for washing dirty words out of clean mouths, and living at home again meant falling back on old habits.

Staring at the phone's screen didn't change the message. The echo of Rixton's laughter still rang in my ears when I forwarded him the bad news that our only lead on the missing person case dumped on our desks yesterday had dead-ended.

I loved being a cop, wearing the badge, making a difference. But some nights, like this one, when a case was a ticking time bomb, and it felt like I had a brick of C-4 strapped to my chest instead of a badge, I questioned what had convinced me that one person could make a difference in this world. The answer, of course, was more of a *who*.

Sergeant Edward Boudreau.

The blip of a siren had me turning as a dusty cruiser pulled in the lot and ejected two of my favorite guys on the force.

Speak of the devil.

"Hey, Dad." I propped my lips in a smile for him, then winked at the wiry black man beside him. "Hey, Uncle Harold."

Harold Trudeau wasn't Dad's brother by blood, but they had been partners for over twenty-five years, and that made us family. We all started walking at the same time and met on the sidewalk beside a sleeping anthill. I was average height in bare feet, but I had inches on them in boots. They blamed osteoporosis. Swore up and down if I'd met them twenty years earlier I would have had to tip my head back to meet their gazes.

But twenty years ago I hadn't existed. Luce Boudreau was a twenty-five-year-old woman with a fifteen-year-old identity.

"Hey, birthday girl." Dad hesitated a moment then wet his lips like he wasn't sure he wanted an answer to his next question. "You heading home?"

Home was a farmhouse situated on a few dozen acres outside town. After Dad suffered a transient ischemic attack last year, a mini-stroke, I had taken up residence in my old room. Someone had to keep an eye on him. Uncle Harold was a shameless enabler with a heavy hand when it came to mayonnaise.

"Yeah." I wrapped Dad in a hug meant to reassure. Not once had he ever asked me outright what I got up to with that old rotary phone of his, the one that hadn't tasted a live dial tone since the seventies. I had slept with it as a child and given it a place of honor on my nightstand as a woman, and that told him it meant something to me. He just wasn't sure what. "Be safe out there. Love you."

"Love you too, Lucey-goosey." He held on longer than he ought to have, and we both knew it, but I didn't rush him. His health scare had served as a reminder of how little time any of us have on this earth, and we seemed to have decided by mutual, unspoken agreement, to love each other that much harder until we ran out. "Call if you need me."

I murmured assurances that I would and extricated myself from his grasp before he noticed the cold sweat gluing my shirt against my spine.

"There's a checkpoint on Natchez Trace Parkway." Harold planted a kiss on my damp forehead. "Watch your speed on the way home, dumplin'."

"Will do." I waved them off then trotted across the lot. "Night, fellas."

Alone at last, I caved to the pressure mounting under my skin. I couldn't climb behind the steering wheel of my Bronco fast enough, punch the gas pedal hard enough, I couldn't freaking breathe until my tires skidded on the unpaved road leading home.

I sucked in a few of those calming breaths recommended by the self-help books Dad had dog-eared during what remained of my childhood. No dice. The next bolt of agony zinged from my nape down my arms, and my hands spasmed open around the steering wheel. I regained motor control through force of will, righting the Bronco before it bumped off the shoulder into a water-filled ditch.

I flicked my gaze to the radio display as the eleven dissolved into a twelve with two trailing zeroes. Gravel pinged the undercarriage as I hit our driveway. I parked in a spray of loose stones and stumbled out, squeezing the lock button on my key fob as I ran across the yard then leapt onto the low porch.

Briiiiiing.

"Hold on, hold on, hold on," I chanted under my breath. "I'm coming."

The blip of silence between that first shrill and the next had me blinking perspiration from my eyes. Quick as my shaky fingers allowed, I jammed house keys into their corresponding locks on the front door. Frantic by the third trill, I contemplated breaking a window on the fourth. The stubborn door swung open on the fifth, and I raced up the stairs to my bedroom. By the sixth ring, I had lunged for the phone on my nightstand and gripped the old-fashioned handset in a bloodless fist. I mashed it to the side of my head so hard I sealed the shell of my ear on the receiver. "Hello?"

Heavy silence roared until I got lightheaded from waiting. I couldn't breathe. I couldn't—

"Luce," Ezra husked, my name a benediction on his lips. "I thought you had forgotten our date."

And just like that, my world righted.

CHAPTER TWO

———◆———

The harsh rasp of his words abraded my senses and sloughed away the persistent ache in my arms and shoulders, leaving my nerves raw, my skin sensitized. Relieved tears washed the day's grit from my eyes as the throbbing receded. For the first time since waking, I unclenched my teeth.

"That's enough." I blinked to clear the golden flecks twinkling on my periphery. "I'm good."

"Don't fight me." The order lashed across my senses. "You need this."

As much as he did?

Before the peculiar thought took root, a second wave of power hit me low in the gut and shorted out my brain. Tingling awareness crashed over me, lifting me onto my tiptoes as though a part of me feared I might drown in his voice and struggled to rise above it. His energy surged, crested within me, then drained through my heels as my boots smacked the hardwood floor.

Impact buckled my knees, and I sagged onto the foot of my bed, flopping backward in a sprawl on the comforter where I shut my eyes for an unguarded moment and basked in the afterglow of my healing. Smoke tickled my nose, and I hoped it wasn't pouring out of my ears.

"You're getting better at this," I breathed against the cool, plastic receiver.

A pleased masculine sound bordering on a growl filled his end of the line in answer.

"It's like I'm going through withdrawals." Seizures, hot flashes, sweating, nausea, restlessness, all illustrated the portrait of a junkie. "I don't use anything stronger than aspirin. What could I be addicted to, do you think?"

He didn't enlighten me.

"The symptoms worsen each year." As though I were a long-time user surging toward an inevitable end. "Tell me what's wrong. Explain how to fix it. You must have an idea. It's your hoodoo that patches me up each time before I crawl out of my skin."

"No." Firm. Hard. This was his line in the sand. Always. It never budged, not even an inch. "You need me for that."

So much for unclenching my teeth.

"Yeah, well—" a bitter laugh lodged in my throat "—you make sure of that, don't you?"

That reliance chaffed worse than wearing wet cutoff shorts on a long walk home in the sweltering summer heat. I might be the junkie in this scenario, but he was my dealer, and I had no idea if what he dished out cured me or fed my dependency.

His low sigh tickled my ear. "I've upset you."

Seconds fraught with electric tension lapsed while I thought up and discarded possible responses.

"Forgive me," he breathed low. "I'll leave you to enjoy the rest of your night."

Slipping away. He was slipping away, and it would be another three hundred and sixty-five days until I feasted on the scraps of our conversation again. Ezra was the only lead I had on my real identity. I couldn't afford to let my anger off its leash. I couldn't risk spooking him. I had to keep him talking.

"Why did you?" I hated how much the answer mattered. "Call, I mean."

"You know why." A lick of wry amusement wiped away the sting of his denial. "The same reason you did eighty in a twenty-five zone to get home in time to pick up that phone you're cradling in your arms."

I glanced down and dang if he wasn't right. I had curled around the base like a child cuddling a teddy bear. How had he known? What kind of surveillance had he installed in my room that he could watch over me? Or was he reliant on tech at all? Our relationship was hardly normal. More like *para*normal. I had no idea of the limits of his powers. Who was to say they didn't extend to astral projection or some other metaphysical chicanery? I had long ago accepted that if the man worked magic through an unplugged phone, then he wasn't limited by the laws of physics like the rest of us.

"I can't help myself," I admitted after too long of a pause. I needed this, needed him. End of story.

I had no idea who he was, not really. Ezra was the name he had given me exactly once, his first and only mistake, and I had clung to that fragile lead on his real identity with bloodless fingers all these years.

Starting the September after I was found, he called each year on my legal birthday. My *found* day. The pain that morning had left me curled up in bed, so Dad let me stay home from school. Feverish, I'd drifted in and out of sleep for hours until I heard distant ringing. At first I thought it was a new symptom and ignored it, but its persistence urged me to my feet.

The sound originated in the attic, which Dad had forbidden me to enter after finding a black widow on one of the boxes of sheets he'd hauled down for me to use, but it kept ringing and ringing and ringing until I broke the rules to get relief. Eleven-year-old me had sobbed as Ezra shattered and remade her that first time. He had apologized over and over for the hurt while promising it was necessary, and I'd thought that made him my friend.

These days, though he was as good as his word and had perfected his methods, I wasn't as sure.

"Come inside." Despite the mystical possibilities, my gut told me he'd want front row seats for this experience. "Just this once give me what I wished for when I blew out the damn candle."

So much for falling back on old habits. *Sorry about the potty mouth, Granny Boudreau.*

"Don't ask for what I can't give."

Spinning the rotary wheel this way and that, I couldn't help pushing. "Can't or won't?"

"Sometimes the two are the same. Goodnight, Luce."

"Stay with me until I fall asleep." I fell back on our oldest bargain, the plea dating back to that first phone call. Rolling onto my stomach, I groped under the bed until my fingers brushed against a plastic case. I had pushed too hard, he was done talking, but I wasn't through with him yet. "In case the pain returns."

The olive branch dangled there for painful seconds while I hauled out the boxy yellow Geiger counter I'd borrowed from a friend who worked for the CDC from under the bed. Char blackened the sides of the unit, and the glass covering the dial had shattered. Great. That explained the smoke I'd smelled.

Its negative radiation reading, however, left me as stumped as usual about the nature of Ezra's magic.

Fabric rustled in the background as though he were making himself comfortable. "I shouldn't."

Triumph kicked my lips up into a fierce grin as I reached in my pocket for the voice recorder I used to make case notes on the go and positioned it near the mouthpiece. "But you will."

He let the ambient noise soundtrack he played in the background of all our calls answer for him.

One minor detail, one tiny slip-up, and I would have hunted him down and gotten my questions answered. He knew it too. And I'll admit I was flattered that he paid me the high compliment of respecting my determination enough to be wary of me. He had no idea the lengths I would go to in order to solve the mystery of him. Then again, maybe he did. After all, he hadn't fed me one scrap I could use against him in all these years.

Ezra. Do you know how many guys named Ezra live in Mississippi? In the US? In the world? Factor in its use as a surname too and . . .

A muffled *bzz bzz* hummed through my right butt cheek like I had bees trapped in my pants.

I set aside the recorder and reached behind me to palm my cellphone. The number flashing on the display was one I recognized. Rixton. He wouldn't call unless it was important, but I hesitated so long the call ended.

"I have to call my partner." I punched redial before Ezra could answer. "Will you wait?"

The noise droned on, reminding me of a chorus of box fans, which I took as a yes.

"Rixton?" I lay there, a phone held to each ear, one modern and mundane, the other old and otherworldly. As ridiculous as I must look, trapped between the present and the past, the contrast felt right. "Everything okay with Sherry?"

"Report came in ten minutes ago," he panted. "Body found in Cypress Swamp. Can't get to her. Something's in the water."

Dread glazed my spine, and I pushed myself up onto my elbows. "Like a gator?"

"Like nobody knows the hell what." A door slammed in the background, the radio chattering with updates from dispatch, and a siren keyed up for a run. "I'm en route." He hesitated. "You don't need to be here for this, but I figured you'd want to know in case it's our girl."

Our girl. Angel Claremont. Sixteen years old. Honor roll student. Taken on her way to pick up her little sister from the John W. Rosen Elementary School.

I worried my bottom lip between my teeth until I tasted blood. "I'm on my way."

I pocketed the cell, then ran one hand over my body conducting inventory. *Gun, badge, pepper spray, baton.* Carrying the old rotary phone under my arm, I scooped up the recorder then took the stairs at a clip. At the bottom, I turned right and opened the closet that hid Dad's gun safe, spun the dial and picked up a shotgun plastered in screamo band stickers from my misbegotten youth. Unable to prolong the inevitable, I shifted my attention back to Ezra.

"I have to go." Already my thoughts spun me away from him. "Never thought I'd say that."

Usually I was the one scrambling for ways to sucker him into extending the call.

"Be careful." A slight pause stretched before he added a gruff, "Please."

"Always am, but I'll be extra vigilant since you asked so

nicely." I lingered precious seconds longer while I worked up my resolve to sever our connection. "Until next year."

He didn't sign off, but then, he never did. I placed the handset back in the cradle and set the phone on the coffee table until it could reclaim its place of honor on my nightstand. On my way to the front door, I rewound the recording I'd made of our conversation, hit play and listened to static punctuated by my comments.

"You're good." I swept my gaze around the room like he might step from the shadows to accept the compliment in person. "You're real good."

I exited the house at a lope and scanned the bushes, but the floodlights mounted at each corner of the porch meant I had a clear view of the empty yard. Ezra must be close if he could see me through the window, right? But never close enough for me to get in my sights. After I secured the shotgun, I cranked the Bronco and headed toward the swamp. Not long after I turned onto Natchez, I spotted the whirl of red, white and blue lights. I pulled over when a siren screamed up behind me. An ambulance? The girl couldn't be ... could she?

I stomped on the gas until I reached the stretch of road congested by first responders, parked on the shoulder, then climbed out with my shotgun in hand. I greeted the officers I knew by name but kept my head down to avoid identification by those who might know mine thanks to my fifteen minutes of fame.

Just last month a fellow officer had asked to take a picture with Wild Child Boudreau when we both responded to the same domestic disturbance. Needless to say, I wasn't about to cheese it up with the guy while our victim cowered in a corner of her kitchen, blood smearing her lip where her husband had busted it in a drunken rage.

Celebrity sucked. Or was this notoriety? Maybe fame wore

differently for actresses or models, but when you're famous for being Swamp Thing Jr., people dehumanize you.

I already had enough questions about my humanity without folks adding to them.

"Rixton," I called out when I got close enough to spot my partner. "What have we got?"

"I've never seen anything like it." He lingered at the edge of an embankment that crumbled into viscous water dappled with bright green duckweed. Two pickups had backed as close to the waterline as the soft earth allowed. Spotlights mounted on their tailgates illuminated an area a good thirty yards from the shore where a body floated. "It's not a gator. Gators don't move like that. But it's so damn big, I can't think what else it could be."

Folks tended to forget that size records were broken for gators all the time. The current record-holder had been caught in Mill Creek, Alabama. At fifteen feet and nine inches long, it had weighed in at over eleven hundred pounds. This fella might be a contender for the title.

From here I couldn't tell gender or any other details of the victim, and I wondered if whoever found her had done so by accident. Gator-hunting season ended earlier this month. That didn't mean a poacher hadn't gone souvenir shopping and gotten more than he bargained for. "Is she alive?"

"We can't get close enough to verify. One of the EMTs swears he saw her breathing, but you know what hope and adrenaline does to people."

"Yeah." Hope was about as useful as an umbrella in a hurricane. "We're wasting time." The fact she was floating meant one of two things. She was alive, her lungs full of oxygen, or she had been in the water long enough for the gases built up during decomposition to make her buoyant. Either way, we wouldn't know until we got close enough to examine her. "We have to send someone out there. We got a johnboat coming?"

The Mississippi Department of Wildlife, Fisheries and Parks would send out a conservation officer if we requested assistance, but we didn't have that kind of time. Not when the girl had been in the water for an undisclosed amount of time, and not with a predator swimming in her orbit.

"Trudeau's putting it in the water over there." He pointed out a familiar rusty pickup parked on firmer soil. "Better move it if you want to catch a ride."

A smile bent my lips, and I patted his shoulder. The fact that Rixton hadn't called dibs meant Uncle Harold had shot down his request to ride along. Oh, he'd try the same with me, but I was onto his tricks. Plus, he'd always had a hard time telling me and my big blue eyes no.

"No, ma'am." Uncle Harold caught sight of me and practically made the sign of the cross to ward me away. "Your daddy would feed me to that thing if I let you get in the water with it."

"I won't be *in* the water," I wheedled. "I'll be in a boat. With you." I lifted my arm. "And this shotgun."

"The answer is still no, dumplin'."

The moment it hit me he was prepping for a solo launch, I set aside the shotgun and jumped in to help. "Where is Dad?"

"My place." Eyes downcast, he set about loosening the thick straps securing the aluminum boat to its trailer. "He's testing the pullout couch Nancy bought for the grandkids."

"Is he . . . ?" I didn't finish. I didn't have to, not with family.

"Nancy picked him up after you left. She settled him with a six-pack and one of her grandmother's quilts. He'll be fine. This year hit him harder than usual, that's all." He patted my cheek. "He'll be right as rain come morning."

Guilt soured the back of my throat, and I swallowed it down

along with the questions lining up on my tongue. My birth-day—no, my *found* day—beat Dad bloody inside for reasons I didn't fully understand. I don't know what he had seen in the swamp that night, what nightmares plagued him, but he had no issue with each of us celebrating in our own way. Me with the phone, and him with a good buzz.

"I should have sent him home." But I'd had other, selfish things on my mind. That damn phone call.

"Don't pick up that guilt. Set it down right now," he ordered me. "You know where he is, you know that he's safe. He could have taken a personal day, but he didn't. He wanted you to see he was dealing. Don't throw away a man's pride."

"Make you a deal," I started.

"No." This time he really did cross his fingers. "'Get thee behind me, Satan.'"

"Come on, Uncle Harold. The name's Luce, not Lucifer." I anchored my fists at my hips. "It'll be hours before Dad finds out about this, and he'll be nursing the mother of all hangovers by then. We're talking a good twelve hours before he's both conscious and sober enough to feel righteous when he gives me a come-to-Jesus lecture. This girl doesn't have that long."

"Goddamn pigheaded Boudreaus," he swore without heat.

Uncle Harold got downright blasphemous when he got his back up over what he considered tomfoolery.

A shrug twitched my shoulders. "I am my father's daughter."

"You remember that too." His sigh confirmed he had accepted the inevitable. "Let's go face down Baby Godzilla. Maybe I'll get lucky, and he'll eat me before your daddy hears tell of this."

A couple of nearby uniforms offered us a hand as we hefted the lightweight boat, carried it down to the sludgy water and slid it in between a pair of fat-bottomed bald cypress trees. I stepped in first, and one of the guys passed over my shotgun. The boat rocked under me, but it was a comforting sway. Most folks in the area kept a boat like this flipped hull-up in their backyard for weekend fishing emergencies. I accepted the heavy spotlight Uncle Harold passed me, the one he used for night fishing, and tightened the rugged clamps on a crimped section of the bow. A flip of the switch on its neck blasted the night with a thick beam I trained so it sliced through the other spotlights, crisscrossing over the body and illuminating the scene from opposing angles.

"I don't see anything," I muttered. "Maybe all the racket scared off the gator."

"And maybe we'll find all those barrels of gold James Copeland and his gang supposedly buried out here back in the eighteen hundreds," he scoffed.

We trolled within six feet of the body, then he cut the motor so we glided the rest of the way. I unhooked one of the plastic oars mounted on the inner wall and extended it over the water. Poking a corpse with a stick wasn't how I'd anticipated spending my birthday, but in this line of work, you learn to adapt. I got in a soft jab to her side, and her lips parted on a groan.

Corpses have been known to sigh as air is expelled from their lungs, but this close I caught the fine muscle contractions twitching in her eyelids.

"Hot diggity damn," I whispered, "she's alive."

"Praise God," he answered. "Let's bring that girl home."

Uncle Harold also fell back on his Southern Baptist roots when confronted with evidence of what he considered divine providence.

"How do you want to do this?" I twisted to face him. "Still no sign of the gator."

"Don't even think it." He fisted the back of my shirt. "You're not sticking your hands in that sludge."

I might have rebelled had a gentle wave not caused her left arm to give an involuntary bob under the surface. Metal glinted in the light, and I leaned forward despite Uncle Harold's weight tugging on me. Rose-gold stripes the width of a hair elastic began at her wrists and banded her arms. The rest of the intricate design was hidden by the depth at which her extremities floated, but I had seen enough to know the concentric circles traveled over her shoulders and across her back to join at her nape, a tattooed cardigan that wasn't ink at all. It was metal. Fine wire. An unclassified alloy.

Forget Ezra. This woman was like me. Our markings identical.

Ice pumped through my veins the longer I stared at her, and I embraced the diamond-sharp clarity in its wake. Cold detachment was my default setting whenever a situation at work spun sideways. The job was dangerous, and cool heads prevailed. Fear usually triggered this response, I learned that my first week on the street, and I was distantly aware that if I was shutting down then I must be terrified, even if I had ceased feeling the tremors. Gator or not, I couldn't lose her.

"Whoever this is," I said when I rediscovered my voice, "she's not the Claremont girl."

But the passing resemblance between the two explained why Rixton had been called.

A shiver in the water drew my eye, and my hindbrain zinged a warning through my limbs seconds before a crimson—*thing*— its scales a red so deep it edged into black, launched out of the water. I sat down hard, landing in Uncle Harold's lap as a blocky head surfaced, its meaty jaws snapping closed over the space where my head had been a fraction of a second ago.

"That was *not* an alligator." The quaver in my voice pissed me off. "That was— What was that?"

Ripples agitated the otherwise placid surface, and a gentle swell raised the level in a way that reminded me of how bathtubs overfill when you climb in one. But what the hell was big enough to disturb an entire corner of a swamp? Not the chitinous beast that had tried inviting me over for dinner. It had been massive, bulkier and more alien than any reptile I had ever seen, and yet ...

A sibilant hiss like steam escaping a tea kettle spiked the air, a curious thump as plated skin rasped against the underside of the boat, and I swiveled my eyes toward my uncle. He indicated the girl in the water with his chin, and bile rose up my throat imagining what had turned him so pale.

The girl had woken and angled her head a fraction in our direction. Pale eyes white-rimmed with terror rolled around in her head like rocks in a soda can.

"Run," she gurgled as murky water poured into her mouth. "*Run.*"

CHAPTER THREE

⸻⬩⬤⬩⸻

Aside from the fact running was a physical impossibility, what with the water and all, wild horses couldn't drag me away from this woman and the answers she might possess. Who was she? *What* was she? When had she been dumped? Where had she come from? How had she ended up in the swamp? Why had she been abandoned here? On and on and on to infinity.

I lifted my shotgun, braced the butt against my shoulder and watched for eddies around the victim. Gator skulls were thick, and gator hide was tough. I'd dated a boy in high school who hunted them with his brothers. In the way of guys desperate to impress girls, he'd explained in detail about the amount of skill required to hit what he called a kill spot at the base of their necks. Fire a bullet at the right angle, and it blasted straight into their brain for a humane kill. Or so he claimed.

But that thing wasn't a gator. Would the same rules even apply?

I was no slouch with a firearm. I had to qualify with my service weapon and a shotgun each year in order to keep my job. I could hit a bullseye, sure, but the idea of a kill spot being the size of a quarter *and* positioned behind the protection of meaty jaws made my palms damp.

The visual examination I had performed on the girl earlier indicated no obvious wounds, and there was no blood in the water. That was good. But hauling her out presented us with a couple of serious issues. I had no doubt that thing would get testy about us stealing its food and attack her or us or both. And johnboats weren't all that stable when two people attempted to haul a soaking wet third over the low rim. The last thing we needed was to end up in the water with her.

The purr of the motor turning over startled me, and I glanced back at Uncle Harold. "What are you doing?"

"We can't get her out without backup. Not without one of us getting injured. That gator—that *thing*—is too aggressive." His hand trembled on the tiller extension handle. "We'll put in that call to MDWFP and wait on them to dispatch a conservation officer with the proper equipment and experience to make this work."

I was already shaking my head. "The girl—"

"I saw her markings." He stared at my covered arms, recollection of my own banding clear in his gaze. "I want answers for you—for Eddie too—but the risk is too high."

"I can't walk away from this." I lowered the shotgun and twisted to face him. "If she dies, everything she knows goes with her. I can't let that happen."

"Well, that makes two of us." He lifted his chin. "And I outrank you, Officer Boudreau."

My lips had parted on a fresh argument when a high-pitched whine drew my attention as an airboat zipped from the direction of River Bend. A massive airplane propeller churned in a gleaming metal cage anchored to the stern and kicked up a damp breeze ripe with decaying vegetation and an earthy musk. Two men dressed in black tactical fatigues, their muscles coiled tighter than spring-loaded mousetraps, parked on a bench mounted in front of the cage. A third crouched on the bow with his head tipped back, nostrils flaring as though he was scenting the moist air. *Weird.*

"Who are these yahoos?" I murmured.

"No clue." Uncle Harold waited until they cut their engine, then killed ours, and yelled, "I'm Sergeant Harold Trudeau with the Canton Police Department. Identify yourselves."

"We're with White Horse Security out of Tupelo," the crouching man called back. His head swung toward me, the pink tip of his tongue peeking from between his lips as he inhaled. *Weirder.* "The Claremont family hired us to aid in the search efforts for their daughter."

I removed the flashlight from my duty belt and skimmed over their equipment. Their company logo was printed right there on the side of the boat. Most of their supplies were branded too, with the image of a muscular, white warhorse stamping its left front hoof. As I went to put away the light, the beam crossed over the face of the crouching man, who had shifted closer during my search, and I almost lost my grip. For a second I thought his eyes ... No. My mind was playing tricks on me. Still. I swept it in an arc, on purpose this time, but he had tucked his chin to his chest to avoid the glare.

"Are you licensed and equipped for animal control?" Uncle Harold asked, far too calm to have witnessed the same green reflection as I had imagined. "We've got a situation out here."

"Yes, sir." One of the seated men lifted a sleek, black shotgun in one hand and a gallon-sized, plastic freezer bag full of papers in the other. "We are." He toed the corner of a cooler strapped down with bungee cords. "We came prepared with bait, hooks and line, just in case."

"Call your credentials in to dispatch." He rattled off the number from memory. "Once I get verification, we'll talk."

The man who had yet to speak was the one who made the call. The guy with his foot still propped on the cooler pretended interest in the shore beyond my shoulder while sneaking glances at me. I was used to covert observation and caught him at it. He chuckled and shrugged like, *I'm staring, so what?* The first man was having trouble keeping his eyes to himself too.

What were the odds of a crew out of Tupelo recognizing me on sight? Sure, coverage of my initial discovery had gone nationwide, but that was old news. And yeah, a handful of stations outside our area had televised my graduation from police academy along with a human interest story cobbled together with soundbites and snatches of footage used without my or my dad's permission. But I couldn't shake the impression their interest in me was sharper than it ought to be.

A subtle vibration hummed through the soles of my boots, and I flattened my palm against the metal base. "What is that?"

The White Horse men kept mute, and not a one of them met my eyes. Behind me, Uncle Harold tapped his phone against his thigh like it might shake out the call he was waiting on. He'd felt it too, and he didn't want to analyze what might be large enough to send a growl bouncing off the bottom of a boat.

Careful not to lean out over the water, I wedged myself into the V near our spotlight and watched over the girl, whose eyes had closed after that brief spark of awareness. "We'll have you out of there in a jiffy," I promised in case she could hear me. "You're going to be okay."

The crouching man tilted his head in a catlike manner as though my behavior puzzled him.

Less than five minutes later, dispatch called with an all-clear, and Uncle Harold mopped his forehead with an embroidered handkerchief. "They're good." He cranked the motor. "Gentlemen, I thank you for your efforts. We'll await you on the shore."

I grasped his hand. "We can't just leave."

"You're welcome to stay with us," the quiet man offered.

The crouching man's lips stretched into a pointed smile. "There's an extra seat." He gestured to a shorter bench mounted behind and higher than where the others sat. "We'll make quick work of this."

Uncle Harold kept our hands linked. "Luce, I don't think—"

"I'll be fine."

The crouching man tossed me a rope, and I used it to reel us closer. The cooler man rose and aimed his shotgun at the water on one side of our boat, and the quiet man claimed a weapon from beneath his seat and did the same on the other side. They were covering me. "Keep my shotgun," I told Uncle Harold, jerking my chin toward the White Horse men. "I won't need it."

"Take care of my girl," he warned them. "Luce, I'll be on the tailgate waiting for you."

The crouching man reached for me. "Don't be scared."

"I'm not," I lied through my gritted teeth. I took his hands, and his long fingers slid under the cuffs of my shirt to finger the first of the metal bands embedded at my wrists. I snatched my arms out of his grasp, my pulse roaring in my ears. "Touch me like that again, and we won't need to use what you've got in that cooler for bait."

His eyes went heavy-lidded at the threat like I'd offered to strip naked and ride his thigh.

"Thom," the quiet man said, "don't antagonize Luce. You know the rules."

"Luce?" Uncle Harold hesitated.

"I have to do this." They could have been cannibals sharpening their knives and salivating, and I would have stepped into their arms with a smile if it meant saving this girl. "I'll be careful."

Turning my back on my uncle, I clasped forearms with the crouching man, and this time he behaved himself as he hauled me over the water and onto their boat. At least until his nose skimmed the column of my throat. *Weirdest*.

The quiet man emitted a displeased rumble of sound, and the neck-sniffer flowed back into his crouch at my feet. "I'm Miller Henshaw." He indicated the cooler man. "This is Santiago Benitez." He scuffed his boot near the crouching man. "Thom Ford you've already met."

"Thom's our tracker. Vanishes in the bush for weeks at a time." Santiago's dark, chocolate eyes flicked up to mine with a taunt in them. "He's half wild. Some might say feral."

Wild. Feral. Oh yeah. These guys knew who I was, and Santiago wasn't shy about letting me know it.

The thing about bullies is they tend to deflate when ignored, which is what I did to Santiago.

"We need to get her out of the water," I said to Miller. These guys had the muscle and resources to make it happen. "What's the plan?"

Smirking at Santiago's affront, Miller strolled to the cooler and flipped open the lid. The stink of whole, raw chickens left to stew in the sun almost bowled me over. "We're tossing these into the water. Soon as the gator heads after it, we're hauling up the girl."

Simple. Easy. I liked it.

Santiago abandoned his station and thrust his weapon into my hands. The weight of it made me cringe imagining the recoil, but these guys were built like brick houses. They could handle it. Santiago, who glared at Miller until he backed away from the cooler, lifted out the first of four chickens. He wound up his arm and hurled it. It made a loud splash when it landed, and the *smell*. Phew, boy.

Miller flipped on a spotlight mounted on a brace and panned the area. On the third sweep, he locked the base. "Got him."

Water churned, and two eyes breached the surface, their crimson reflection eerie but normal for gators. For that reason, I asked, "How sure are you that's the same one?"

"Positive." His tone left no room for argument. "Thom?"

Movement teased the corner of my eye, and I turned as Thom slipped into the water. "What the hell is he doing?"

"Saving the girl," Miller drawled. "That is what you wanted?"

"But Thom—"

"Will be fine," he assured me, returning his attention to the beast and Santiago's chicken flinging.

Thom reached the woman with an elegant breaststroke that sliced through the water. Sliding his arm around her waist, he reclined and used a one-armed backstroke for the return trip. The sight made my palms sweaty, and the shotgun slipped. The idea of getting in the water with that thing . . . Nope with a side order of nah-uh, never gonna happen. I returned the gun to the rack beneath the bench, afraid I'd fumble the thing and lose it to the swamp, then dropped to my knees and gripped the handhold for leverage. With Thom's help, I hooked one arm across the girl's chest and hauled her onto the deck. He hopped up beside us before I could offer him a hand.

"You're strong." He slicked damp hair off his forehead. "Soaking wet, that girl weighs a good buck thirty."

I didn't look up from checking her vitals when I said, "Adrenaline."

He made a thoughtful sound I figured was aimed at me until he wiped his fingers across her cheek. "This isn't Angel Claremont."

"No, she's not." The Claremont girl had family. She was normal. This girl—this woman—was anything but ordinary. "Does it make a difference?"

"Not to us," Santiago added cheerfully. "We get paid either way."

"Keep an eye out," Miller ordered. To me, he said, "Hold on."

I sat down, pulling her upper body across my lap, elevating her head, careful to avoid touching her bare arms, and braced my foot against the cooler to keep us from sliding. Halfway to shore, Thom placed his hand on my shoulder, and his grip was iron. I didn't rock even when Miller ran aground.

The EMTs rushed us in a flurry of activity. Lifting the woman and strapping her to a stretcher, they hustled her off to the waiting ambulance. Uncle Harold lingered near the tailgate of his truck waiting for the crowd to disburse, a cell pressed to his ear. Rixton lacked his patience. He stepped onto the airboat without waiting for an invitation, offered me his hand and hauled me to my feet.

"You okay?" The corners of his eyes were pinched. "I saw her arms . . . " He trailed off when he noticed the men flanking me. "Gentlemen."

"I'm good," I said, cutting him off quick. "We'll talk later. I'm heading to the hospital."

"No." He blocked my exit. "You don't want them connecting the dots any faster than they already will." He stuck out his arms when I tried dodging him. "Let me go. I'll keep you updated."

I seesawed between shoving him in the muck then bolting for my Bronco, and thanking him for having my back even though things in Luceville just got more bizarre. "Fine," I grated out. "We'll try it your way, but I want to know the instant she wakes."

Rixton tipped his chin at the White Horse Security guys. "Thanks for the assist."

"No problem." Miller spoke over my shoulder. "We'll be in the area until the situation is resolved." He reached into the box under his seat and produced a business card from the freezer bag where he kept his paperwork. "Call if you need anything."

I took the card, running my thumb over the embossed lettering. "I might take you up on that." I tapped the card against my palm. "Keep in touch. We all want the same thing, but Canton PD has jurisdiction. We don't need to step on each other's toes when we can learn to dance. Got me?"

"I'd be happy to keep you in the loop," Santiago piped up, "but fair warning. I've got two left feet."

"Night, guys." I cast them a wave then turned, pulling up short when Thom eased between me and Rixton. "Something to add?"

"No." He took a wet wipe from a packet Miller tossed him and cleaned the hand Rixton had used to pull me to my feet. "Just thought you might want one of these. Antibacterial. Don't want to get amoebas."

I accepted the wipe from the peculiar man and finished the job myself, tucking away the trash. Uncle Harold took my hands and helped me to shore, and Rixton landed beside me. The three-man security team reclaimed their original positions and motored back into the dark heart of the swamp.

"There's something off about those guys." Rixton stared after them.

"You caught that too?" The dynamic between the three men had been peculiar, the whole experience surreal.

"That one guy sniffed you." He cocked an eyebrow at me. "That's not normal."

"They told me he was a tracker."

"Trackers can be peculiar folk," Uncle Harold allowed. "We've got one in town that won't hang doors in his house because they make him feel confined."

I mulled that over, unable to put my finger on what bothered me about those guys. Other than their timing. They must have been listening to a police scanner, picked up the radio chatter then decided to announce their involvement by offering us assistance.

"I called your dad," Harold admitted after a pause. "Considering the girl . . . you don't need to be alone tonight. I know how protective you are of your privacy, so I figured you'd rather have him at the house with you than you join him at ours."

Gratitude welled in me. Thankfully it didn't leak out over my cheeks. "You're the best uncle, you know that?"

"I have the best niece." He chucked me under the chin. "She makes it easy."

"I've checked in with Sherry and told her where I'll be." Rixton glanced up from a string of texts on his phone. "I'm going to head on up to the hospital. I'll call when I've got an update."

"Keep Jane safe." Until she told us otherwise, that's who she was. Jane Doe. The urge to go after her, to be there when she woke, was a magnetic tug in my gut. But Rixton was right. Me showing up now was like inviting the circus to town. "I don't want her to vanish until I can question her."

"We'll get to the bottom of this." The strobelike effect of a camera flash had him shielding me with his broad back. "Go home before they scent blood in the water."

I nibbled my bottom lip. "I just . . . "

"I know," he said, and I knew he understood. "I'll ping some guys I trust, and work out a security detail so we have eyes on her at all times."

"Thanks." I ducked my head and wended my way through the dwindling crowd.

Sleep was off the menu for tonight, but first things first. I stank from the muck weighing down my clothes, and I wanted to scrub away the memory of those putrid chickens. As soon as I got home, showering off the sludge was my first priority. After that, I'd lock the doors and windows, turn on the security system and check the motion-sensor floodlights.

Rixton had made his point. It was the only reason why I'd let him go and agreed to stay behind when every instinct I had urged me to hold vigil at Jane's bedside. Once people got a look at her markings, they would start digging, and I was the first and only name they would find. My origin was about to be examined under a microscope. Again. Privacy would be a thing of the past. Not that I'd ever had much to begin with.

Happy birthday to me.

CHAPTER FOUR

⬥

Morning found me curled up on our battered leather couch under a light blanket. A Discovery Channel special on dinosaurs played on the flat screen television mounted on the opposite wall, providing me with ambient noise to drown out Dad's muffled snoring. Piles of scrapbooks, spiral notebooks and medical records documenting my first remembered year of life fanned across the cushions to either side of me and spilled over onto the coffee table where my laptop slumbered. I had spent the last several hours thumbing through my personal archives in the hopes some clue might jump at out me that explained my connection to Jane, but all I got for my trouble was the pinch of a stress headache.

Four hours ago, Rixton had checked in to assure me she was stable but had yet to regain consciousness. Again he reiterated there was no reason for me to put in an appearance, not until she woke ready to answer questions. And again, I heeded his advice. I didn't want to kick an anthill that left Jane to the swarm.

Heaving a groan at its weight, I hefted one of the fatter scrapbooks onto my lap and cracked the cover. A fifteen-year-old Luce stared up at me from the first page, her softball jersey smeared with red clay and her hair tucked under a cap. She balanced a trophy on her hip and wore three medals hung around her neck. Okay, so I might have been a tad competitive back in high school. I spared a wince for the boxes in the attic stuffed with plaques, medals, trophies and framed certificates. Fine, so maybe I had been a *lot* competitive back in the day. The high of victory had been slightly addictive to a kid without a past who was desperate to make her mark on the future.

I almost spit out my tea when the doorbell rang. None of the perimeter alarms had tripped to warn me company was coming. I leaned over the open book on my lap to peck at the keys on my laptop. Once the screen woke, I tapped into the live video feeds from various cross sections of the property and selected the front door camera. I half-expected the vultures to have landed earlier than expected, but the man dressed in a tight black T-shirt and tactical pants was no journalist. In fact, I was pretty sure a hunk of Woodall Mountain had chipped off during the night and rolled like a boulder onto my doorstep.

I pulled up the security app on my phone and pressed the intercom button, which activated a speaker mounted beside the front door. "Can I help you?"

"I'm here to speak with Luce Boudreau," he rumbled in a deep tenor befitting a half-man, half-mountain. A mantain?

Of course he was. "And you are?"

"Cole Heaton." His muscular shoulders bunched when he reached into a pocket. "I own White Horse Security Firm." He raised his ID to the hidden camera lens. He was good. Very good. Most people didn't notice it snug in the weathered molding framing the door. "I'd like to talk to you about last night."

Seeing as how I still felt a skosh guilty for not telling his guys upfront the woman in the water wasn't the girl they had been searching for, I figured I owed him. "Give me a second."

I slid the scrapbook off my lap and thunked it on the coffee table before stacking the rest of my mess on its bulging cover. My phone was the cherry on top. This way I wouldn't miss an update, and its presence discouraged sticky fingers. Folks might not think twice about flipping through scrapbooks left out in the open, but our society had evolved stringent *hands-off* cellphone etiquette. With my living room tidied, I stood and straightened my pinstripe pajamas. Cole had invited himself to my home. He deserved my limp ponytail and the fuzz of my unbrushed teeth. I opened the door and had to tilt my head back to meet his piercing blue eyes. He was taller in person. Really tall. And built like a freaking tank.

Black stubble covered his head, and his square jaw bulged as he ground his teeth. I suppressed a grimace at the state of his nose, which had been broken and reset badly multiple times. His left ear was worse. The top of it was missing, the shell ragged as though someone had gnawed on the cartilage. His hand, when he offered it to me, engulfed mine up to the wrist. His scarred knuckles resembled a losing tic-tac-toe board, and I had brushed my thumb across one of the raised marks before the impulse even registered.

"Ms. Boudreau." Glacier melt ran warmer than his voice, but a faint good ol' boy drawl gave it the potential for sweetness. Iced tea. That's what he reminded me of. Delicious but cold. *And always satisfying*, another supremely unhelpful part of my brain supplied. "Have I come at a bad time?"

Those frosty eyes slid over me from head to toe. I'd bought my pajamas in the tall department to get the longest sleeves possible, so the top was baggy but the bottoms fit. He couldn't seem to take his eyes off them. Was the contradiction of swaddling myself in yards of fabric while he sweated on the porch so odd? I kept our house subzero to compensate for my propensity toward wearing long-sleeved tops. Dad and I had long since acclimatized to the perpetual chill, but company often left early and with their teeth chattering.

I wasn't easily intimidated, every Goliath had his David, but this guy ... The weight of his stare as it lingered on the top button of my shirt, the pearly disc held on by a single ragged string, caused my stomach to flip like a stack of flapjacks and my nipples to harden against the soft fabric. I folded my arms across my chest, but he'd noticed my response to him. How could he not when I'd almost poked out his eyes?

"Now's as good a time as any." I nudged the door open wider in invitation, but I had to step back or risk him squashing my toes to fit in the entryway. I retreated until he was inside then bumped the door shut with my hip and flipped the locks. More than one person had invited themselves in when they'd met with no resistance. "Pardon the PJs. I'm off today."

"Your house, your rules." He prowled into the living room and planted his feet in front of what I jokingly referred to as my lifetime achievement wall. It was a collage of school portraits, team photos and some of my more impressive awards, including my state certification. "Your father must be very proud of you."

"Dad has never met an order form he didn't like." I insinuated myself between him and a reminder of the year my braces required so many rubber bands that I drank meals to avoid removing them. "But you didn't come here to talk about his Luce memorabilia collection." I herded him toward Dad's recliner. "What can I do for you?"

"What can you tell me about last night?" The springs groaned, and the wood base creaked while he settled. I hoped he didn't break anything. Dad loved that ratty old chair. "I've read Miller's report, but I'd like to hear your version of events."

"Your men aren't in trouble for lending a hand, are they?" I perched on the edge of my favorite couch cushion. "Our Jane Doe isn't the Claremont girl, but we couldn't have saved her without their help."

"Jane could have just as easily been our clients' daughter." He rolled his massive shoulders, fidgeting with a wide, leather, watch band that encircled one wrist, and even that casual movement made his seat groan. I noticed he wore a matching band without the timepiece on the other wrist, but it was none of my business if the guy enjoyed accessorizing. "I won't dock their pay for the supplies or the hours, and I won't bill the department either."

"I'm glad to hear it." Any lingering guilt at using them to further my own agenda evaporated. "So, about last night." I clasped my hands together. "My partner called and told me a body had been reported in the water. We're assigned to the Claremont case, so he got pinged." I summarized the rest, a shiver coasting up my spine at the mention of what the news had dubbed Super Gator, but I could have been reciting the alphabet for all the interest he showed. "That's about it. Jane was taken to the hospital, and I came home."

"MDWFP sent in a team to relocate the gator." A hint of amusement thawed his expression as his gaze touched on the television where the dinosaur documentary still played. "One of the witnesses claims it was a deinosuchus and wants the swamp declared a protected area."

"I was too busy not getting my head bitten off to get a good look at it." I rubbed the base of my throat. "From what I saw, I'd believe it was an actual dinosaur rather than the descendant of one before I agreed it was a standard American Alligator."

"It attacked you?" A growl pumped from his chest. "Miller's report didn't mention that."

"It happened before your men arrived." I curled my legs under me and closed one hand over the can of pepper spray I kept tucked between the cushion and the arm of the couch for emergencies. Cole, it seemed, had a bit of a temper. "I got so worked up when I realized Jane was—" *like me* "—alive, that I leaned out over the water. I understand the aggression, and I should have respected it more. The creature was protecting a potential food source."

"Call me if your investigation sends you back there." He made it an order. "That creature is dangerous."

"I appreciate your concern." That he assumed he had the right to boss me around rankled, but I wasn't about to snub a man willing to lend me his airboat. "I'll consider your offer if the time comes."

A chime filled the air, and I lunged at my phone. "This might be my partner." The text was indeed from Rixton, the message two words: Call me. "I need a minute."

"Take all the time you need."

I left him seated, then ducked into the kitchen, dialing Rixton as I paced. "Hey, what's up?"

"Got some updates for you." The rasp in his voice left me picturing him knuckling his eyes the way he did after long nights fueled by too much coffee. "Jane is stable, but her lids remain firmly in the down position. Buck relieved me at the hospital thirty minutes ago, and we've drafted Donaldson for third shift. They've both got your number, and they'll call at the first sign of trouble. Or the first hint of good news." His bleating yawn had me holding the phone away from my ear. "And lastly, though I'd hate for you to question my stamina, I'm not up for our birthday foursome today. Would you sew a voodoo doll in my likeness and stab it with needles if I wrote you a raincheck for tomorrow?"

"I can't sew, and I hate needles." They gave me the heebie-jeebies. "Besides, I would never do that to a doll. Put your face on it? That would just be cruel."

"Note to self." He spoke in a loud, clear voice that mocked mine when I used the recorder. "Ask Momma Ethel to sew Luce a Rixton doll for Christmas. It'll be the gift that keeps on giving. Anatomical correctness is a must. See previous statement about giving."

"You wouldn't dare." The nightmare image of a normal-sized doll with a life-sized penis attached set my eyelid twitching. "Your grandmother-in-law would have a coronary."

"She's been married five times and has her eye on the German widower who moved in next door." He chuckled. "Momma Ethel has seen more action than downtown Canton during a film shoot. Felt isn't going to be the vehicle of her demise. I predict it will be a younger man, and by younger I mean nearer the half-century mark, and the fistful of blue pills she spiked his drink with at dinner."

I turned my head against my shoulder to muffle my laughter before it escaped and encouraged him. Nothing stopped him once he got on a roll.

"Okay, I've got a warm bed and a hot woman waiting on me. See you tomorrow, Bou-Bou."

"Rixton—"

The call ended mid-cackle as he hung up on me.

"One of these days ..." Shaking my head, I tossed my phone on the table and strolled back into the living room. "Sorry about the interruption. Did you need anything else, Mr. Heaton?"

"Just Cole, and no." He rose in a fluid motion that should

have been impossible for a man of his size, and Dad's chair creaked with relief. "That's all I needed."

After ushering him out the door, I moseyed back to the table and dialed Maggie. She answered on the third ring. "Rixton can't make it today."

"Aww, shucks." She sniffled. "You can't see my face right now, but I'm tearing up at the idea of a girls' day out with my bestie."

I padded back into the living room, scissored my fingers through the blinds and watched Cole prowl to his vehicle, a massive SUV that would give other drivers on our backroads palpitations sharing the road with the gleaming beast.

"Unless . . ." She sucked in a sharp breath. "Is Sherry okay?"

Cole whipped around, perhaps sensing my eyes on him, and our gazes clashed. The smile that slit his mouth was grim and expectant, as though he had known I would be unable to resist spying, and all he'd had to do was wait for my curiosity to get the better of me.

"*Luce.*"

The volume of Maggie's shriek jarred me to attention, and I let the blinds snap back into place. "What?"

"Sherry," she enunciated clearly. "Is she okay?"

"Oh. Yes. She's fine." I shook my head to free it from thoughts of Cole. "Rixton's just tired. He put in sixteen last night."

"Hmm." Maggie drew out the sound into ominousness. "So, it's just us chickens."

"Cluck-cluck?"

"Excellent," she squealed, rattling my eardrums. "I'll be there to pick you up in thirty."

"Maggie, wait. I can drive—"

Too late. The call had ended.

I had to work on my people skills.

While I was in the kitchen, I jotted down a note for Dad and pinned it with a magnet to the fridge so he wouldn't worry. I tiptoed up the stairs and passed his bedroom door, not that anything short of a bomb going off would wake him, then changed into a long-sleeve T-shirt made from lightweight material, jeans and sneakers. I used an elastic to sweep my frizzy hair up into a bun, then grabbed my purse and headed for the front porch. Locking up and resetting the alarms took an extra minute, but I was used to the routine. With the house secured, I settled into a rocker to wait on Maggie.

The *meep meep* of a car horn snapped my eyelids open, and I leapt from the rocker, heart clogging my throat. "What the . . . ?" I reached for the gun at my hip on instinct and came up empty. "What'd I miss?"

"Looks like you partied too hard last night," Maggie called through the driver-side window of her sunshine-yellow Prius. "You were sawing logs when I got here. I considered asking you to build me a cabin while you were at it."

I wiped the crust from the corners of my mouth, ambled down the steps and climbed in on the passenger side. Slumping down in the seat, I let my head rest against the cool glass and savored the arctic rush from air vents she'd angled in my direction.

"Click it or ticket," she chirped helpfully.

I grumbled under my breath but did my civic duty by obeying the laws I was sworn to uphold.

"Are you sure you're up for this?" She drummed her fingers on the gearshift. "We can scratch the hen party if you'd rather wait until that pervy rooster is free. You guys have the same off days, right? Is he free tomorrow?"

Walking back into the house meant one of two things would

happen. Option one involved poring over all the dead ends I had collected until my head exploded, and no one wanted that. Brains were notoriously hard to scrub out of upholstery. Option two involved hatching a cockamamie scheme to get inside the hospital and putting Jane at risk. I chose option three.

"I need to get my mind off things." I made a shooing gesture. "Let's do this."

"Things? What things? Things that maybe happened last night . . . ?" she prompted, cutting a U-turn, then bumping us back onto the road where her small car at last gained traction. "Work with me here. I need deets."

I sat up straighter. "You haven't seen the news today, have you?"

"I gave up watching the news." Her lips flattened. "Too depressing."

She muted the soft jazz music pouring through her speakers, and the reason for her calmness hit me. "You've been listening to satellite radio all morning."

"I don't pay a subscription fee for nothing." She sneaked a quick glance my way. "Why? What'd I miss?"

I almost wished I'd kept my big mouth shut. Talking about last night would circle my thoughts around to Jane, and that was the last place my mind needed to go. But bottling up all my conflicted emotions had me feeling like a shaken two-liter soda ready to spew.

The best way to tell a story was to start at the beginning, so that's what I did. "Last night a woman was found in the swamp."

Maggie's grip strangled the steering wheel. "And?"

"She has the same striations in her skin as I do." The rest of the details burst out of me like Mentos mints dropping into Diet Coke, though I omitted references to the Claremont girl and our ongoing investigation. "I've wanted answers for so long. Now that it's—*she's*—finally here, I'm terrified."

"Who wouldn't be in your shoes?" Maggie reached over and squeezed my hand. "This woman might be able to tell you where you came from, what your birthmarks mean. Heck, she might be a relative. Did you think of that? What if it's genetic?"

As in passed down through a family.

As in I might have actual, living blood relatives.

People who were different . . . like me.

The instant the thought took root, I plucked it from my subconscious. It felt too much like a betrayal to the man who had taken me in and raised me as his own. I wanted my answers, yes, but a relationship with my birth family? That possibility twisted my gut into pretzels. Thanks to all the press, and my unique markings, I would have been easy to find if they had bothered looking. So why hadn't they?

Maggie coasted into a parking spot, and only then did I notice we had stopped in front of the wedding boutique where I had spent the better part of three weeks helping her choose between two fairy tale-worthy dresses that boiled down to "butt bow or no butt bow" to my untrained eye.

I suppressed a groan, but I'd asked for a distraction, and this definitely qualified as one.

"The plan was to trick you into cooperating with the seamstress for your final dress fitting and then rewarding you for good behavior with a birthday lunch." Maggie killed the engine. "But it's not every day you fish a maybe-relative out of the swamp. Let's skip the fashion show and cut straight to the grease. We can hit Miss Pansy's for burgers, fries and shakes, my treat."

A riot of jewel-toned gowns competed for attention in the glass display window, and I had no trouble picturing the bridesmaids who would one day fill those dresses shoving one another through the plate glass in pursuit of a bouquet and its promise of romance everlasting.

As much as I wanted to take the out I had been given, Maggie was right. It wasn't every day that I helped rescue a mysterious link to my past from the swamp. But it wasn't every day that my best friend got married, either. "How long will it take?"

"Fifteen minutes tops." She pressed the back of her hand against my forehead as though checking me for a fever. "Are you sure you feel okay? You're being so chill about all this."

I swatted her away. "Do you know what I want for my birthday?"

"Chocolate bars laced with fat-burning enzymes?"

"Ah, no. That would be what you want for your birthday. Me? I want to feel normal." Maybe for the last time now that Jane was in the picture. "Let's go be normal, okay?"

While Maggie gnawed on her bottom lip in consideration, I threw open my door. The second my sneaker touched down on the pavement, the hairs on my nape lifted. I scanned the courthouse square behind us and spotted a hulking black SUV idling at the curb across from a junktique store. The driver dipped his chin then flicked his meltwater gaze to Maggie when she appeared at my elbow before resettling his full attention on me. I rolled my shoulders as though I could shrug him off, but the man didn't blink.

Maggie wiggled her fingers at him then huffed when he ignored her. "Friend of yours?"

"That's Cole Heaton. He owns a security firm out of Tupelo." Hating to be the one who broke our stare-off first, I wanted Maggie out of his crosshairs, and that meant conceding victory to him. For now. "The family of a victim hired him to 'help' solve one of our cases."

"Ah. So he's an enemy." She winked. "Gotcha."

"Not an enemy." His team had helped me out of a tight spot last night. "More of a potential annoyance."

"Maggie," Mrs. Tacoma trilled behind us. "I thought that was you." Her lip curled so high over her gums she was forced to twist the expression into a smile at the sight of me. "Oh, and Luce too."

Long story short, the star quarterback, one Joey Tacoma, put his hands up my cheerleading skirt after a ballgame my sophomore year, so I brought my knee up and racked him so hard his eyes crossed and stuck that way. Or at least that's how Maggie retells the story.

No means no. Full stop. And when your dad's an overprotective cop who insists his daughter master basic self-defense, my *no* was more of an *oh hell no* with talking points that included using my kneecap as punctuation.

"Come on in, girls." Mrs. Tacoma managed to include me in the invitation without choking. "I have iced lemon water if you're thirsty."

"Last chance to escape," Maggie whispered when she caught me checking out the SUV again and stuck out her fist in an offer to play me for it.

"And miss out on this?" Turning my back on Cole, easier said than done, I figured if Mrs. Tacoma could fake cheer then so could I. I grabbed Maggie by the shoulders and shoved her into the relative privacy of the shop. "I'm *so* excited to see how my dress fits after those alterations."

Maggie turned her strangled laugh at my obvious lie into a coughing fit that sent the proprietress bounding after a glass of the proffered lemon water and gave us a moment alone.

"You are the worst liar." She swiped her fingers under her eyes. "Seriously, I would believe a scam email over you. Not even one of those intricate advance-fee scams. I'm talking penis-enlargement pills here. That's the level of your game."

I growled at her, showing teeth. She countered by sticking her tongue out at me.

Maturity was overrated.

"Here we are." Mrs. Tacoma returned on a breeze smelling of mothballs and fruitcake and pressed a cool glass into Maggie's hand while shoving a voluminous dress bag at me. "You can use fitting room one."

I bit my tongue on a comment about us being her only customers. Why did the room number matter when there was no one else here? But I thanked Mrs. Tacoma, which sent Maggie into another fit of coughed laughter, and entered the room earmarked for me. I gagged when I opened the door, understanding why this torture chamber had been selected. The cubicle was as spotless as the rest of the shop, but the reek of spoiled milk set my eyes watering. The metallic undertone convinced me a shopper must have tipped over a bottle of formula on the carpet, and the spill went rancid before its discovery.

Pride is a burden, and I carry mine around like those women who stuff tiny dogs in their purses.

After filling my lungs to capacity, I rushed through changing and met Maggie near a trio of floor-to-ceiling mirrors. She wrinkled her nose but took one look at my flushed cheeks and didn't ask. I stepped up on the raised dais and took my place centerstage while the bride looked her fill.

Maggie beamed at me with such joy, I had to find somewhere else to look. "You're gorgeous, Luce."

"You have to say that." I peeked at my reflection, her tennis shoes sticking out from under the dress and the sunlight warming the red highlights in her messy bun. "You picked out the dress. Of course you think she looks nice in it."

"Not *she*, not *her*." Maggie came to stand behind me and rested her chin on my shoulder. "*You.*"

Our eyes met for the briefest of seconds, and I grimaced at the slip. She stepped back, and I cut my gaze toward the figure in the mirror like this was all somehow her fault. No. Not *hers*. *Mine*.

"Fine," I grumbled. "*I* look nice in it. Better?"

Phrases like *dissociative amnesia* and *depersonalization disorder* had been murmured in soft voices across my hospital bed once the doctors realized my memory stretched back minutes instead of years. They postulated that my lack of an identity cornerstone might explain why I had trouble connecting with the person who looked back at me in the mirror.

The former was public knowledge. The latter, I usually hid better than this. But Maggie would have recognized my internal struggle with or without the verbal cue. She had known there was more to me avoiding this gauntlet than simple vanity or old grudges.

"Better," she allowed. "Now if only I could get you to believe it."

"Ah. Here we are. Any of these laces would make a lovely veil." Mrs. Tacoma drifted out of the back with a binder straining to contain its samples and shoved it in Maggie's hands before she deigned to notice me. "The cut flatters your figure. Are you sure you don't want the sleeves adjusted?"

"Nope." The fabric hit just below my wrists, right where I liked it. "I'm good."

"Maggie—" Mrs. Tacoma began in a huff.

"The maid of honor is meant to stand out," Maggie steamrolled her. "The sleeves make a statement, and since Luce is the one wearing the dress, her comfort is the most important factor, right?"

"Well . . . " Mrs. Tacoma waffled, losing ground quickly. "Of course you're right, dear."

With the inspection done, I left them conferring over complementary bridesmaids' gowns while I changed back into my street clothes. The last soundbite I heard came from Mrs. Tacoma as she urged Maggie not to stress over the cost of the dresses she chose since her taste was so exquisite the girls were sure to reuse them.

Mmm-hmm. 'Cause that's ever happened in the history of sateen.

Eyes watering from the offensive smell, which hadn't improved upon airing the changing room, I raced through swapping out my clothes then left my gown hung on the interior of the door so Mrs. Tacoma had to fetch it in person or risk an awkward explanation to Maggie about why that one gown of the half dozen destined for her bridal party stank to high heaven.

Fifteen minutes later, we stepped out onto the sidewalk and into the sunshine. Maggie charted a course for Miss Pansy's that required us to cross the street and pass the spot where Cole had parked earlier. A quick scan of the area turned up no SUVs or broody security-firm owners. Not that I'd hoped to see either. I was just being cautious.

"Are you going to explain that funky smell?" Maggie plucked at my shirtsleeve, which, along with the rest of my outfit, smelled more like baby vomit than fabric softener thanks to their short stay in the changing room. "Or do I have to supply my own explanation?"

"We're about to eat," I deflected. "Trust me. You don't want to hear this before that happens."

"I wouldn't have used her shop if I'd gotten a choice." She thrust out the book of lace samples and mimed throttling the cover to illustrate her point. "You know that, right?"

"Your mom has been tight with Mrs. Tacoma for a long time." The Tacoma and Stevens families had both attended the same church for generations. "It was natural for her to want to toss business at her friend."

"The thirty-five percent discount didn't hurt," Maggie snarked. "Don't get me wrong, I'm grateful my dress is one less expense checked off the list, and that my folks believe in supporting local businesses, but the way she treats you is unforgiveable."

"I can deal. It's only a few more months." I shrugged. "Besides, I kind of admire the death grip she's got on her grudge. I hurt her son back when I was a kid and therefore off limits. Now I'm an adult, and she's enacting all the petty revenges she's dreamed up over the last nine years."

"Money isn't everything, and her son was an asshole. There's no way you were the first girl he lured under the bleachers with those big, brown eyes. You were just the first who fought him off."

I was about to agree with her when my cell chimed with a text message. I whipped it out and swiped the screen so fast Maggie stepped back on reflex. Catching herself, she inched closer and checked to make sure no one else on the sidewalk had spotted my lapse.

"Careful," she warned softly. "What if that guy was still hanging around?"

Fingers trembling, I jabbed in a quick response then grabbed Maggie by the elbow. "Can you drop me at Madison Memorial?"

"The hospital?" Understanding dawned, and she clutched the book to her chest. "That was Buck?"

"Yes." I swallowed the lump in my throat. "Jane Doe is awake."

CHAPTER FIVE

Maggie shut down my plans to storm the castle and forced me to lower my metaphorical sword. A quick call to one Valerie Burke, the school nurse at John W. Rosen Elementary School, where Maggie also worked, gave us the inside scoop.

Valerie, it seemed, picked up shifts on the weekends at the hospital to earn extra money, and she claimed the vultures were already circling Madison Memorial. One whiff of my presence would send them divebombing to pick my brain like a ripe carcass for tidbits about Jane. That was how we ended up parked at a Blue Hippo gas station two blocks from the medical complex.

"This will work," Maggie assured me. "Valerie is good people."

Squirming in my seat, I kept my mouth shut. I didn't like dealing with unknowns. Especially when the variables were people I hadn't met to evaluate.

"That's her." A tentative smile formed on her lips. "Let's do this."

Valerie was all smiles as she exited her minivan and aimed a wave at us. A plastic grocery store bag swung from her fingertips, a metronome indicating the level of her excitement, and all I could think was how much I wanted to snatch it from her hand and duck into the bathroom to change.

"You're really her," she said, sounding starstruck. "I heard around town you'd joined the force like the man who—" She snapped her mouth shut before compounding her faux pas. "I meant to say like your father."

"I really am me." I resisted the urge to tug my sleeves lower. The way Valerie stared at my arms left me twitchy and eager to get this done. "I appreciate your help. I would appreciate it more if you didn't mention this to anyone."

"Not even my husband?" She tugged on her earlobe. "It's just that he's big into cryptozoology, and he's always been fascinated by your case."

A monster hunter was interested in me? Tabloids had called me an alien a few times, but a monster … That was new. Maybe I ought to send him a cast of my feet as a thank you for his wife's help.

The sharp intake of Maggie's breath heralded an avenging angel taking wing, and I almost felt sorry for the woman. Almost.

"Thanks for all your help, Valerie." She placed herself between me and the woman she now viewed as a threat instead of as a friend. "We have to scoot, but I'll call you later. We can do lunch next week and discuss those immunizations pamphlets you mentioned."

"Do you think I could get just one…?" She reached in her purse, retrieved her phone and waggled it at Maggie. "My husband will never believe me without proof. Pics or it didn't happen, you know?"

"I asked for this favor as your friend," Maggie said in a tight voice.

"It's fine, Mags." I waved her off and took my place next to Valerie. The sooner I fed the troll, the sooner she would give us what we came for and crawl back under her bridge. "Do the honors?"

Maggie accepted the phone, framed the shot and glared over the screen at Valerie. The other woman's excitement caused her to miss the death of their friendship in Maggie's eyes, but I saw it, and my heart squeezed at being the cause. "Three ... two ..."

Valerie flung her arm around my shoulders like we were old pals and hammed it up for the camera while my flesh crawled under her hand. She formed a gun with the fingers of her free hand, then blew across the tips like she had bagged and tagged one of the mythical beasts her husband played at hunting.

Gooseflesh rippled up my arms in a stinging wave. Once my voice reached my ears, the words diffused, as though they had traveled lightyears in order to reach this moment. "I don't like to be touched."

The thumping of my pulse grew deafening. Maggie rushed forward, her lips moving on soundless words I was past hearing. She pried Valerie off me, slapped the phone across the woman's palm and marched her to the van. Not until after the driver-side door slammed shut in a fit of temper and the vehicle dipped out of the lot did I realize I had taken a step toward her parking spot.

"Are you okay?" Maggie moved to touch my hand but stopped short. "You look ... odd."

"I'm fine," I mumbled, still staring in the direction the van had gone. I rubbed my arm where Valerie had touched me until the sting of violation lessened and dragged my gaze to

Maggie. "I just—People still manage to surprise me. Not in a good way, either."

"Go change." Maggie pressed the bag into my hands. "I don't know how much time this bought us."

I let her shuffle me off to the bathroom where I traded my jeans and top for peach-colored scrubs. Valerie had included a light jacket made from coordinating material, though its deep wrinkles convinced me it been living in the bottom of her locker at work since the weather turned hot. I emerged and let Maggie tug down my hair and finger-comb it into a curtain of soft waves that fell around my shoulders. I never wore my hair loose. Even Dad would do a double take before IDing me.

"Come on." She jogged to her car, and I followed. "Let's make this snappy."

Part of me expected the local skunk ape—or whatever they'd dubbed the bigfoot rumored to live in Cypress Swamp—enthusiast club to be camped out and awaiting our arrival at Madison Memorial. But it seemed Valerie had been content with her photo.

We parked in the back of the lot, and Maggie exhaled, her hands flexing open and closed around the wheel. "Do you want me to go in with you?"

Thanks to her job, Maggie knew a gaggle of parents, grand-parents and other assorted student relatives. Going out with her was like being the plus one of a minor celebrity in its own way. Everyone knew her or knew someone who knew her through their kids or her parents. Inconspicuous, she was not.

"It's probably best if you don't." I held the door handle in a death grip. "You don't have to wait. I can get a ride home."

Maggie pinched my thigh, and I jumped. "And miss the recap? Are you crazy?" She gestured to a box on the backseat.

"I have papers to grade. I can keep myself occupied. Take all the time you need."

"Here goes nothing."

"Or everything." She said what I had been thinking. She leaned over, opened the door and shoved until I worked up the courage to exit the car. "Call if you need an extraction. I can fake an exploding appendix, you know, cause a distraction."

Huffing out a laugh, I shut the door and set out for the front entrance. As much as I wanted to duck my head, that would draw attention. So I set my shoulders back, kept my chin high, and walked in like I owned the place. No one looked twice at me. No one stopped me. Scrubs were their own kind of camouflage in this place. I hit the bank of elevators, rode up to the third floor and wandered around until I located the correct room. I stood there with my palm flattened against the wood for so long an actual nurse came to check on me.

"You must be new." She cocked her head at me. "I'm blanking on your name, but you look so familiar."

I offered her a bland smile. "I just have one of those faces."

"Maybe so." She lowered her gaze to where my nametag ought to be and wrinkled her forehead. "What did you say your name was again?"

My lips parted to deliver the first lie that popped into my head—*Valerie Burke at your service*—when the door opened under my hand.

"I thought I heard voices." Buck glanced between us. "Everything okay out here, ladies?"

"I came to check on the patient," I blurted, and both of them glanced at me.

Buck's mouth fell open when he looked at me, really looked, then he snapped his jaw shut and stepped aside so I could enter the room. "I've been expecting you."

The actual nurse started to protest when he cast her a dazzling smile. "Thanks so much for your help earlier. I thought I would die of thirst before my relief got here. You're a peach."

"I brought you a refill." She offered him a foam cup. "Call down to the nurses' station if you need anything else. I'll be here until midnight."

"I'll do that." He winked before shutting the door on her pinkened cheeks, then he turned and flashed his dimples at me. "Hello, *nurse.*"

"You said Jane was awake." I shoved him aside and drank my fill of the slight figure propped up in the hospital bed, tubes snaking over her face and slithering down her arms, her fair skin as pale as the starched white sheets tucked under her. "Has she spoken?"

"She was awake when I called you, but they aren't sure it's going to stick." He kept his voice low. "She hasn't spoken, but she appears to understand what's being said to her."

I passed a hand across my mouth to keep my warring thoughts contained.

"I'll give you two a minute alone." He reached for the door. "You were smart to play dress-up, Boudreau. I had to unplug the room's phone. Otherwise it rings off the hook. The press has gotten wind of her, and you don't want them to pick up your scent while they're at it."

"Thanks, Buck."

After he exited the room and the door snicked shut, I approached the bed. Jane wore a standard hospital gown, the short sleeves exposing her bare arms and the rose gold ribs that matched mine down to the spacing. I reached for the thin sheet, intending to tuck it under her chin and hide her arms from the curious. It was what I would have wanted. But her eyes snapped open and latched onto me.

"Hi." I cleared my throat and tried again. "I'm Officer Luce Boudreau."

"You . . ." she whispered " . . . where there."

"You remember." That had to be a good sign. "How are you feeling?"

Jane gave a weak shrug in answer.

"Can you tell me your name?" I inched closer so she didn't have to strain to see me from the corner of her eyes. She had yet to turn her head, as though it were too heavy to shift on the pillow. "Do you remember how you ended up in the water?"

No answer, but her fingers twitched. No. She was curling them. Asking me to hold her hand.

The automatic response—*I don't like to be touched*—never made it past my lips.

Her right palm flexed open again, and I slid my left across hers. She laced our fingers in a steady grip and raised our joined hands until the topside of her forearm brushed the underside of mine. The metal in our skin struck, and a harmonious chord resonated in the quiet between us, as though we were tuning forks testing our pitch against one another.

A lukewarm wave of energy lapped against the distant shores of my mind, the sensation at once alien and yet familiar, the ragged contrasts so marked as to make me question if the sensation left in its wake ought to be labeled as pleasure or pain.

"What was that?" I tugged on my hand, but she held fast. "What does it mean?"

A shuddering gasp parted Jane's lips in the faintest hint of a smile, but that small exertion—whatever it had been—caused her eyes to droop, too heavy for her to prop open another minute. Her muscles relaxed in a cascade until her arm hung suspended by our joined fingers. Careful not to brush metal against metal a second time, I lowered her arm to the mattress.

"Jane?"

Her chest rose and fell in even sleep.

"I'm going to let you rest." The longer I stayed, the higher the risk for us both. And I had to get out of here, had to process what had just happened. "When you wake, if you want to see me again, tell the officer on duty. He knows how to reach me. They all do."

Jane didn't stir again, so I exited the room and left the same instructions with Buck. I hit the elevators, my skin paper-thin; fragile in a disturbing and familiar way. Lost in the possibilities, I didn't sense the danger until the sliding doors locked me in a metal box with a predator.

"It's dangerous for you to be here." Cole kept to his corner of the elevator, which didn't mean much when he could stand in the middle and brush his fingertips against either side. "The press got tipped off about ten minutes ago about a woman matching your description who stole scrubs from an employee's unlocked vehicle then proceeded to impersonate a nurse to gain admission to a restricted area."

Valerie. That little twerp. Covering her tail in case I got caught.

"I had a plan." I set my jaw. "Looks like that plan needs to change."

"I can help with that," he offered.

"Why?" I situated my back in one corner and faced him. "Why are you here and why help me?"

"I'm here for the same reason as you, I imagine. Members of my firm helped facilitated Ms. Doe's rescue. I have a vested interest in her welfare." He didn't look at me, just watched the numbers ticking down to the lobby. "I have an SUV waiting in the employee parking deck under the hospital." I didn't ask how he'd made that happen. "You fill me in on Jane's condition, and I'll give you a lift home. Sounds like a fair trade to me." He cut his eyes toward me, his lips twitching at one corner. "You can call Ms. Stevens and tell her that her services are no longer required."

"How did you—?" I vibrated with rage. "You followed me."

"Yes or no." He lifted his chin, drawing my attention to the countdown. "Do you really want to explain how you got those scrubs or what your interest is in Ms. Doe?"

"Yes," I bit out from between clenched teeth.

His wide palm smacked the grid, and the button for the first floor went dark. A circle marked with a P, I assumed for parking deck, illuminated. This time he didn't bother retreating to his corner but stood his ground, crowding me without meaning to, invading my space just by existing.

The doors opened on a shadowy concrete tomb I'd had no idea existed until this moment. I had taken a step before Cole swung one of those tree trunks he called arms out and barred the exit. While he scanned the area, treating me as a civilian and as a liability, I considered facing the vultures to escape a solo car ride with him.

"We're clear," he pronounced, shoving off the doors as they whirred in distress over their inability to close, and left me to match my strides to his. We reached his black SUV, and he stopped. "This is me."

"Yeah, I saw you in it earlier." I climbed in once he unlocked his behemoth. "Canton is a small town, but it's not so small that we should keep meeting like this."

Cole didn't rise to the bait. He strapped in, waited until I had done the same, then turned over the engine and cut a sedate path out the exit into the more familiar parking lot at the rear of the facility.

"You can drop me at the Blue Hippo the next block over."
There. That sounded polite. Ish.

"I can drive you—"

"*No.*" I strove for calm while my nerves jangled from the
strange resonance that still vibrated through my bones. "No
thank you." I shot my ride a text. "Maggie and I have unfin-
ished business in town."

Cole didn't need to know that business involved stuffing
my face with all the greasy junk I had banned from the house.
Burgers, fries, onion rings, milk shakes … All items on Dad's
forbidden-foods list. All items I needed stat so I could drown
my worries in canola oil.

"Yesterday was your birthday."

I waited for the other shoe to drop. "And?"

He rolled a shoulder, and I swear the car dipped to one side.
"Happy birthday."

"Thanks, but it's not really my birthday."

"That's why you don't care if your friends celebrate it a day late."

The way he said it, with zero inflection, as a known fact, had
me tasting blood as I bit down on my tongue in an attempt
at civility. The guy had helped me out twice now, and I owed
him. To pay him back, I would give him a pass on his invasion
of my privacy.

"Oh, look. There's Maggie." I didn't wait for him to turn in
to the gas station. I jumped out when he yielded to a pedestrian
on a crosswalk. The glass whirred down behind me, and he
glared through the open window. Backing toward the parking
lot, I threw up my hand. "Bye, Cole."

He did this thing with his lips, twisting his mouth into a
vicious curve that wasn't a smile—a silent snarl maybe? Either
way, it looked much better from across two lanes of traffic than
it would have from across his console.

A horn blared behind him, and he was forced into traffic. I watched until he vanished out of sight then trotted over to Maggie, who was busy shuffling papers and cleaning out the passenger seat for me. A red pen balanced over her left ear, and I didn't mention it even after she put her other supplies away.

"Maybe we should consider upgrading Cole's friend status," she said when I opened the door. "He did you a solid back there. One minute I'm grading papers, minding my own business, and the next a news van almost rear-ends me getting into position by the front doors."

"We can thank Valerie for that, I'm sure." I shifted my hips and pulled a highlighter out from under me. "Cole said someone called in a tip about a stolen nurse uniform and gave them my description."

"I had no idea she was married to a fanatic." She pulled out into traffic and aimed us toward Miss Pansy's. "I'll make sure the uniform gets washed and returned."

"Mags, stop beating yourself up over it. You'd never let a crazy within spitting distance of me on purpose."

"I keep replaying it in my head, and it looked so bad." She winced. "Really bad. Like a setup. Like I had traded favors with her. I would suspect me if I were you."

"Canton is a small town. Our friendship is common knowledge. It's more likely she put herself in your path, you absorbed her into the Maggie Collective the way you do, and she abused that trust."

"The Maggie Collective?" She scoffed. "What am I? The Borg?"

"No. You're a good person with a robust social circle thanks to the school, the church and your parents." The Stevenses belonged to that rarified class best known for being rich, the origin of their wealth so shrouded with the mysteries of time no one outside their family could pinpoint where their vast fortune had originated. "People take advantage of your kindness to exploit your connections."

"Okay, okay. I get it. I'm a sucker. Write it on my forehead already."

I rolled the highlighter through my fingers, tempted, but tossed it on the backseat.

"We've got company." She ogled the side mirror. "Maybe *friend* wasn't the right word. Maybe we should upgrade Cole to *stalker* status."

"What?" I twisted in my seat, and sure enough, the grill of his SUV filled the rear window. "Sunday witch."

"We should head to a public place, right?" She stomped on the gas to put a gap between our bumpers. "Confront him there?"

Confrontation was one word for what I was about to do to him.

Five minutes later, Cole still breathing down our necks, she cut the wheel and angled for a spot in front of Miss Pansy's. I sprang from the car before it stopped rolling, causing Maggie to curse behind me, and marched over to Cole as he threw his SUV into park. He lowered his window, braced his forearm on the lip and kicked up one of his eyebrows, the one I was just getting around to noticing was bisected by a faint scar.

"What is it with you and jumping out of moving vehicles?" Lines bracketed his mouth. "Were you a stunt woman in another life? Do you want to kill yourself?"

"What is it with you tailing me everywhere I go?" I returned with equal ire. "You've been my freaking shadow all day."

"Small town," he said flatly.

"I want you gone by the time we finish our lunch, or I will call this in. You're on the job? Great. Congrats. I wish you the best of luck. But I'm not. Not today and not tomorrow. See, there are these things called days off, and I'm making use of mine."

"By stealing a pair of scrubs and infiltrating a hospital to visit Jane Doe incognito."

"I borrowed them, thank you very much." I sawed my teeth until my jaw popped. "Goodbye, Cole."

I seemed to be saying that a lot. Too bad he was refusing to hear it.

Cole braced his wrist across his steering wheel like he had nowhere to be in a hurry. "See you around, Luce."

Maggie leaned out her window. "We're not eating at Miss Pansy's today, are we?"

"Nope," I snapped, rounding her car and sliding back in my seat. "Drive through it is."

She uttered mewling noises in the direction of the restaurant, but I couldn't shake the sensation of Cole's eyes between my shoulder blades or Jane's soft voice and resonating touch. And Ezra. Where did he fit in all this? Now that the shock was wearing off, I had to face the similarities between what Jane had done and what he could do. I had no name for what had passed between Jane and me. A knowing. A recalibration. A centering. Something primal tied to the metal under our skin. Something more intimate than what Ezra and I shared and yet . . . and yet . . .

Pressing my cheek against the cool glass, I let it numb my chaotic thoughts.

We hit the golden arches, which cost me serious friendship cred. Maggie was forced to drown her sorrows with a vanilla sundae she dumped over two apple pies. And no. She didn't offer to share.

We crashed at my house, watched sappy movies and decided

on having an honest-to-God sleepover since Justin Sheridan, her live-in love muffin and husband-to-be, was out of town on business. I had just started digging for the pump that went along with the air mattress we used for guests when a light flipped on upstairs.

No junk food in the house was my bright idea, but I'd broken that rule into chicken nugget-shaped pieces tonight.

Maggie and I scattered like cockroaches back to the dark living room where we hosed the air with a vanilla lavender aerosol. We bundled up our trash, ran it out to the can at the end of the road, then rushed back inside to brush our teeth and gargle. We had just collapsed on the couch when Dad walked past. Hair smashed flat on one side, he wore boxers, one sock and a T-shirt. We froze, clinging to each other, waiting to see if he sniffed contraband in the house, but he only grunted what might have been a greeting on his way to the downstairs bathroom. Once the water turned on, we exchanged loaded glances, then burst into giggles like we'd been tossing back vodka shots instead of mouthwash.

Even with it being just us chickens, as Maggie would say, it was still the best unbirthday I'd had in years.

CHAPTER SIX

———◆———

The next morning I woke with the rotary phone tucked in the bend of one elbow, its plastic body warmed from contact with mine. Heat stung my cheeks, and I braced for Maggie's teasing, but the deflated air mattress pancaked on the floor told me she had already left for work.

Strumming my fingers over the rotary dial, I lifted the handset and pressed it against my ear. Perfect silence greeted me. "Jane is like me." I expected no answers. Not from the phone, not today, not when Ezra was never where or when I needed him most. "What does that make you?"

I startled when my cellphone rang and dropped the handset, almost clocking myself in the face. Mouth gone dry, my brain attempted to warp the modern ringtone to fit the *briiiiiing* I was so desperate to hear. A second of disappointment was all I allowed myself before rolling over and palming my cell where it rested on my dresser.

"Rixton." I returned the old phone to its usual spot. "Let me guess. You're standing me up. Again."

"We need to talk." He pitched his voice low. "Not over the phone."

A chill walked down my spine. "Where do you want to meet?"

"Let's do it in public, somewhere close to my place."

"What? No joke about doing it in public?" I sat upright, heart pounding. "This must be serious." I scooted to the edge of the bed. "Where is good for you?"

"Sherry's craving peanut butter froyo. I figured we could meet up at Hannigan's, the three of us."

"That works." I shucked my pajamas and started rooting through drawers for clean underwear. "Are you sure Sherry ought to come?"

"Try and stop her. I dare you. And Luce? I spotted a news van on Main Street. Pretty sure he got lost on his way to the hospital since cell service is crap in town. His wouldn't be the first GPS to lose its signal and guide a driver off the beaten path, but he might be trolling and hoping to get lucky."

"What time?" Frozen yogurt wasn't, as far as I knew, a breakfast food, but then again, I wasn't pregnant. I just hoped Sherry wouldn't bring pickles from home to use as garnish. "Hannigan's doesn't open until noon."

"Let me check with the boss." Rixton muted the call while they hashed out their schedule then came back on the line. "Sherry has an acupuncture session in Madison at one she refuses to cancel. Her migraines are getting worse, and weirdly enough jabbing her with needles is the only treatment that's alleviating the pain."

"Try being married to you," she yelled from a distance. "Then we'll see how many migraines you get."

"Travel wipes her out." Rixton spoke over her. "She'll need a nap before we meet you."

"I might be carrying a baby, but I'm not a child. I don't require scheduled naptime."

"Baby," he soothed, "you woke up an hour ago, and your lids are already heavy."

"Who's heavy?"

"Holy mother of— Shit." Footsteps pounded. A door slammed. *Click.* Rixton must have locked it behind him. "Damn that was a close one. Okay. You still there?"

Fists pounded on the door.

"Be out in a minute, hon," he called to his wife. "Potty time is private time. You taught me that, remember?"

Her muffled roar made me grateful I was neither pregnant nor married to Rixton.

"How about five?" Rixton tapped the receiver. "Hey, Bou-Bou, I'm talking to you."

"That works." Assuming either of them survived the fallout from the bathroom door opening. "See you guys then."

"Luce." His warning tone snapped me to attention. "Watch your back."

"Will do." I ended the call, then dialed Maggie. I owed my partner-in-crime thanks for going above and beyond yesterday. But instead of rolling straight into voicemail as usual when I called during school hours, I heard the smoky jazz lullaby of her ringtone below me. She must have left it downstairs. "Well crap."

I made a mental note to swing by the school and drop it off after I met with the Rixtons, then dressed in jeans, boots and a flowy peasant blouse with billowing sleeves in a floral pattern. I scrounged a frayed elastic and raked my fingers through my snarled bedhead, or I tried to, but detangling the frizzy mass proved impossible. *Ponytail it is.* Wincing at the tug against my scalp, I bent my stubborn hair to my will.

I pocketed my phone, and then hit the stairs. A quick search of the downstairs revealed Maggie's cell on the bathroom vanity. Dressed and ready, I settled in at the kitchen table with my laptop and started digging through updates on the Claremont case. When the words started blending on the screen, I flipped over to the local news and monitored it for snippets about Jane.

Late afternoon found me bleary-eyed, with a stiff back and a hankering for a cool treat to offset the summer heat baking the grass in our backyard into crunchy, brittle nubs that stabbed your soles when you dared go barefoot.

After shutting down the laptop, I drifted into the living room and lifted my keys from a cup hook by the front door. I locked up behind me, pausing until the steady blip of the alarm's green dot winked at me.

The drive into town blurred, the mental haze clearing in time for me to snag a coveted parking spot in front of Hannigan's. I was punching the lock button on my key fob when I spotted Rixton and Sherry walking my way. Based on their matching goo-goo eyes, and the way their linked hands swung like a pendulum between them, they must have kissed and made up since we talked.

Acupuncture must be some good stuff.

"I planned on returning the DVDs you lent me, but John has forbidden me from carrying anything heavier than a paperclip." Sherry tugged on his arm. "Unless he's already sitting down and wants a glass of tea."

"Liar, liar, maternity pants on fire." He swatted her butt, and she took the hit with a gleam in her eyes. "That's not true, Luce. Don't believe a word this woman tells you, unless they're compliments about me. Those you can take to the bank."

Guess that meant naptime was code for ... Yeah. *That*. So much for my acupuncture theory.

"You married this?" I hooked a thumb at him. "What were you thinking?"

"I wasn't." She rubbed her stomach. "I was drinking."

"I took her to Vegas and got her sloshed on fruity drinks, popped the question, then dragged her before an ordained Elvis before she changed her mind."

"That is exactly how I don't remember it." Sherry arched an eyebrow. "Like not at all. I woke up the next morning in bed married to him." She elbowed him in the ribs. "What did you put in those drinks anyway?"

"Nothing illegal." Rixton dropped a lingering kiss on her lips. "In most countries."

"Get a room." I didn't have to fake my gagging. "Aren't married people supposed to stop having sex?"

"That's not how it works, no." He slipped his wife tongue that had her squealing and fighting him off in a fit of giggles. "The more I have of her, the more I want. And being the brilliant man I am, I put a ring on it, so she's mine. Plus, she's pregnant, and she puts out a lot. Like a *lot*. And she gets kind of violent. About everything." He waggled his eyebrows at me. "Have you ever tried angry sex with a pregnant lady? It will change your life, I guarantee."

Even when my mind dipped into the gutter, I was still soaring in a penthouse suite compared to their permanent address on TMI Lane.

"*Johnathan*," she squeaked. "What's between you, me and my hormones is our business."

"Luce doesn't mind," he assured her.

"Luce does mind," I contradicted him.

"Let's get that froyo." Sherry ditched him to hook her arm

through mine. "The sooner we find something to stuff in his pie hole, the sooner quiet and reason will be restored."

"Sadly, I came here to talk to him." Hannigan's was a family-owned frozen yogurt bar, and its décor was best described as "unicorn vomits rainbow on white canvas". I followed Sherry's lead as she selected the biggest cup on offer, then swirled in peanut butter frogurt. She topped that with crushed peanut butter cups, peanut butter drops, halved peanuts and a pump of warmed peanut butter. Who was I to deviate from a theme? I even paid the bill out of respect for her creative genius, and okay, so Rixton had to buy his own. "We'll have a moment of silence while he slurps down his swirl, then it's down to business."

"I brought knitting to entertain myself." She patted a bag slung over her shoulder. "Playing beard for your covert meeting beats sitting around the house under a magnifying glass."

A swirl of warm air caressed my cheek, and a twitch started between my shoulders. I glanced across the shop, closing my lips over the spoon as another patron joined us for a cool treat. I choked on a peanut butter drop, and Sherry leapt to her feet, as much as any woman nine months pregnant can be said to have leapt, and Heimliched me.

"I got it down," I wheezed. "Sherry, stop. No. I'll hurl if you keep socking me in the gut."

"Are you sure you're okay?" She took a bottled drink from the wall cooler and made sure the cashier added it to Rixton's tab. "Drink this." Her gaze slid past my shoulder. "What got you so . . . ? Oh. Wow."

Once I could breathe again, I shoved off the table with my palms and moseyed up to the new customer. "Got a sudden craving?"

Cole stared down his crooked nose at me. "Something like that."

"You're following me again." I locked down the urge to squirm under his gaze. "Why?"

He selected two of the largest cups and started filling them.

"You can't ignore me when you're literally the size of an elephant in the room. I see you. We all see you." I cut in line ahead of him and blocked his path. "Why. Are. You. Tailing. Me?"

"You're paranoid."

His cool dismissal sent heat blasting into my cheeks. Was I paranoid? Yes. Was I paranoid about him following me? No. Yesterday had proven he had an agenda. But what? I wasted precious seconds vacillating and lost the hottest edge of my temper. Or I thought so until he scooped peanut butter drops into both his cups.

"You can't even come up with your own flavor combination," I spluttered. "You *are* stalking me." I gripped his forearm, and I might as well have been groping a boulder. "Is that why your men just happened to be in the right place at the right time?"

Note to self: It's not paranoia if they're really out to get you.

"My men received a tip and went to investigate." He kept studying me from under dark lashes. "I can't help they found you instead. We are working the same case, after all."

"Is there a problem here?" Rixton sidled up next to me. "Luce?"

"This is Cole Heaton, the owner of White Horse Security." I noticed I was still holding onto him and jerked my hand back to my side. "Cole, this is my partner, Detective John Rixton."

"How do you two know each other?" Rixton asked in a lazy Southern drawl. "You weren't on that boat, Mr. Heaton."

"No, but he was at my house the next morning." I had zero qualms about throwing Cole under the bus. He was so freaking huge the crash would probably wreck it instead of plowing him down anyway. "He wanted to ask me about Jane."

"Pay for your food and join us at our table," Rixton ordered him. "We'll talk there."

Since I hadn't taken my eyes off Cole, I hadn't noticed the two teen cashiers gawking at the altercation. One had a phone in his hand held at chest-height like he might be filming. Not good.

I smiled at the boys, and then rejoined Sherry at the table. "That man is—"

"Built." She fanned herself with a napkin. "Is all that muscle for real? Maybe you should bounce quarters off his abs to be sure."

"Stop drooling." I snatched the napkin and pressed it to her lips where it stuck on a daub of peanut butter and hung there. "You're a married woman."

"My ovaries are otherwise occupied," she said, spitting off the paper, "but there's nothing to stop yours from exploding."

"Except that he might be one of those newspaper-clipping nutso stalkers obsessed with me," I huffed.

"On a scale of one to ten," she mused, "how big of a deal-breaker would it be if you found a scrapbook with a lock of your hair glued to a page in the front seat of his ride?"

"That would be a one hundred." Though I might be tempted to compare scrapbooks, if such ones existed, before reducing his to ashes. "Are your hormones that out of whack?"

"Hmm?" She mimed squeezing his buns and snapped her teeth in their direction. "He's so bitable."

"You'd chip a tooth."

"Dentures aren't only for the over-sixty crowd anymore." She spooned up her frogurt. "Hmm. I wonder what Rixton would think if I could pop out my teeth when I—"

"*Sherry*," I squeaked. "He's my partner. I won't be able to look him in the eye after hearing you fantasize about gumming his sausage. Can you take that mental picture back please?"

"Who's gumming sausage?" Rixton dropped into the seat next to hers. "Whose sausage is getting gummed? And can I volunteer?"

"Y'all are insane." I dropped my face into my hands. "And you're breeding."

"That makes it sound so dirty." Rixton nudged my foot with his. "Say it again."

"Please stop." I laughed through my embarrassment. "I can't even with you two."

The grating of metal chair legs against tile floor brought my head up in time to watch Cole join us. He sat beside me, naturally, and crowded me with his bulging muscles. I considered elbowing him to give myself room but worried I might shatter my funny bone in the process, which would not be humerus. He looked ridiculous with the hot pink spoon fisted in his hand, and I couldn't tear myself away from watching him scoop up that first bite.

"It's good," he announced upon noticing my rapt attention. Humming in the back of his throat, he took a second bite and then a third. "Very good."

"You've never had frogurt?" I cocked my head at him. "Yet more evidence you're a stalker."

"You flatter yourself." He cut his eyes my way. "Do you have many such admirers?"

An unladylike snort escaped me. "Wouldn't you like to know?"

His tongue darted out to lick his lips. "I asked, didn't I?"

A frown gathered between my brows when he did it again. He had asked me something?

Sherry pinched my thigh, and I jumped. The mountain

demolished his dessert, but his eyes twinkled. Oh, how they twinkled. Fine. So the fact his upper lip was fuller than the lower one had intrigued me. Next time I gawked I would be subtler about it.

No. Bad Luce. There would be no next time. What would be the point when he'd leave after this assignment ended? Not that I was thinking that far ahead. Argh. I had totally been thinking that far ahead.

"Rixton?" I diverted my attention to my partner. "You invited him to join us for a reason?"

"White Horse took over security for Jane Doe this morning." Rixton wiped away his jokester persona with a napkin across his lips. "That's what I wanted to tell you, Luce. The PD won't assign her an official security detail unless her life is endangered, and we know they set the bar too high on that. We can rotate out volunteers, but that won't ensure continuous coverage, and it's a stopgap measure."

"Funny how you neglected to mention you were visiting a potential client when we bumped into one another in the elevator," I grated in Cole's direction. "What business is Jane of yours?"

"I follow the money." He stacked his cups—both emptied—when I had yet to take a second bite. "I'm mercenary that way. I got an offer to protect her, and I took the contract. End of story."

Call me crazy, but I didn't believe a word out of his incredibly distracting mouth. "Who's paying you?"

"Divulge a client's personal information?" He clicked his tongue. "People don't stay in business long if they let beautiful women talk them out of their secrets."

The compliment set my cheeks tingling. Oh, he was good.

"Could her family have put up the money?" Sherry reached for her husband's hand. "They must be worried sick about her."

"Her prints aren't in the system, babe." Rixton brushed a knuckle across her cheek. "She's unidentified, a Jane Doe, and that means no one—not even her family—knows to look for her here."

I stirred my froyo until the ribbon of peanut butter dissolved, leaving me with a goopy mess too mushy to eat. Or maybe the topic had cost me my appetite. Did Jane have family? Would they come for her? No one had ever claimed me, but I had been a child. She was an adult. She might have a husband or kids of her own out there searching for her. They would want to put this nightmare behind them once they found her. Maybe put me behind them too. I couldn't let that happen. I had to learn what she knew.

"I have to go." I stood in a rush and my chair wobbled. "I need to see Jane again."

"I'll escort you." Cole shot out his arm, his fingers tangling in the curlicue detail of the seatback, righting the chair before it clattered to the floor. "I'll handle introductions and let the crew know you have clearance to visit as often as you wish."

An escort inside would spare me the cloak and dagger routine. A girl could only bum so many sets of scrubs. Besides, look how well that worked out last time. I might as well have faced the vultures considering how Valerie had rung the dinner bell for them before I escaped the hospital.

"I don't see any strings attached." I waved my fingers through the air, miming a search for spider webs. "I can feel them, but I don't see them. Yet."

"I'm a patient hunter." The corner of his lips twitched. "The best-laid traps are the ones you don't realize were there until they close behind you."

A sultry breeze ruffled my shirt, but I dismissed the new patron in favor of keeping my eyes on Cole.

"Ms. Boudreau," a man called. "Are you Luce Boudreau?" I turned at the sound of my name, like an idiot, and that was all the confirmation the reed-thin man required. "What do you know about Jane Doe? Is it true she was discovered in the same swamp where Edward Boudreau found you fifteen years ago?"

"Go." Sherry pushed me toward the door. "We'll handle him."

What happened next blurred around the edges. Rixton stood to run interference. He hesitated a second to tell Sherry to stay put. I was striding toward the door, Cole on my heels, when the newcomer fisted the sleeve of my top. It was wide-neck and elastic, and his yank pulled it off one shoulder.

The neckline snapped taut and caught under my bra cup, exposing my entire left shoulder and most of my arm down to the elbow.

The shock of the violation, the stunned incomprehension that a strange man had laid his hands on me, locked my muscles until all I could do was stand there and gape. *Did that just happen? Is this real?* It was such a nightmare scenario for me, being exposed in public. Amnesia swept through my muscle memory, the trauma wiping away all those years of self-defense classes. One move had stripped me of my armor at the worst possible time and left me a victim. Again.

A feral growl ripped me out of my head, and I jerked up my top. The asshat had torn the fabric, so I tucked the ragged material under my bra strap. I spun at the sound of shattering glass and found Cole holding the man a foot off the ground, one of his large hands wrapped around the guy's windpipe. The other hand had yanked the camera from his grasp, and his huge booted foot had stomped it flat. The breaking glass was courtesy of a framed picture Cole had bashed the man's head through. Blood speckled the mat surrounding a dollar bill from Hannigan's opening, the first one they'd earned.

For a good ol' Southern boy, the guttural words pouring out of Cole's mouth, pressed flush against the reporter's ear, were not in any way comprehensible. Another language definitely. German maybe?

I crossed to him when it became obvious no one else was brave enough to get between the furious titan and the target of his wrath. Rixton had shielded Sherry, and he wasn't budging until the situation was contained and his wife and child were safe. "Cole?"

"He touched you," he snarled. "Exposed you."

"Can you put him down?" I rested my hand between the slabs of muscle between his shoulders. "The cops will be here in a minute." I had no doubt Mr. Hannigan had mashed his panic button. "Let them take care of this guy."

Choking sounds interspersed with sobs had me lifting my gaze to the reporter. Cole caught the man looking in my direction, and the vibration in his chest deepened until the man whimpered and crushed his eyes shut. A second later, the tang of ammonia filled the air. The guy had pissed himself, and that was the only reason Cole turned him loose and took a step back. Lip curled, he glowered at the guy.

"There are parts of the swamp that have never been seen by human eyes," he told the man. "Touch her again, and I'll give you a guided tour."

The guy curled in a ball, hands covering his face, and rocked until sirens blared in the distance.

Aware I was taking my life into my hands, I tugged on Cole's shirt until he angled his body toward me. I was a country girl, and I knew all about not getting between a predator and his prey. But I needed Cole to greenlight me with his crew, and that couldn't happen if he was in lockup. "That was an extreme reaction, don't you think?"

"No." Muscles fluttered in his jaw. "I don't." He hooked his index finger and tapped under my chin until I looked all the way up at him. "What if there hadn't been witnesses? What if he hadn't stopped there? What if he hadn't come alone? Do you think his friends would have helped you? Or stopped filming? No matter how long you screamed?"

"I would have snapped out of it, okay? He surprised me. The attention has gotten rough before, but no one has ever . . ." I fingered the torn edges of my shirt. "I wasn't ready for him to put his hands on me. I will be next time."

"We need to leave." He lowered his hand. "The cops are almost here."

"I am a cop, remember?" I thumped my chest with my closed fist. "Plus, you kind of Hulk-smashed this place. There are repercussions for that sort of thing."

"You expect me to hang around and answer questions." He made it sound like I'd asked him to donate a kidney then offered to cut it out with a butter knife and no anesthesia. "I have a spotless record precisely because I avoid both those things."

"How about this?" I walked him backward with a palm flattened against his rock-hard chest then applied slight pressure on his shoulder until he sat in the nearest chair. "I'll stay here and hold your hand so the big, bad cops don't scare you."

Cole extended his arm, palm up, and waited for me to make good on my promise.

"I didn't mean that literally." But I put my hand in his and let the fold of his fingers swallow me up to the wrist. Lifting a concrete block one-handed might have been easier than bearing the full weight of his hand, his arm, when he relaxed into my grip. Biceps trembling, elbow joint aching, I didn't complain. How could I when he hadn't so much as peeked at my bare skin? He must be curious about the markings. He was in this up to his neck. Yet he had tossed aside a prime opportunity to evaluate me, to compare my banding to Jane's, and I respected him for that. "I don't get you, Cole, so give me some pointers. Should I thank you for defending my honor? Or would that only encourage your caveman tendencies in the future?"

Quicker than a rattler striking down a field mouse, he swung his head toward the reporter. "He put his hands on you." His lips peeled from his teeth, and a low sound pumped through his chest that made my fingers itch to flatten my palm against his back once more. "He's lucky I let him off with a warning."

Well, that answered my question. Wrap his hips with animal pelts, pass the man a club, and Cole would be a Neolithic dream come true. Good thing I wasn't sleeping much these days.

CHAPTER SEVEN

———◈———

Feral cats showed more kindness to stray dogs than Cole showed my fellow officers, his words full of hiss and spit, but he had sheathed his claws for me. For now. Oddly proud of myself, I felt as though I had tamed a tiger to eat from my palm. Cole gave a concise statement to Officer Landry, one of Dad's fishing buddies, and if the older cop objected to Cole rubbing his thumb over my knuckles like worry stones, he didn't let on.

Oh yeah. He was *so* tattling on me once he got out of here.

The reporter, Moses Franke, shivered like a Chihuahua while giving his account and chose not to press charges. Had I been in his shoes, with Cole sitting three feet away, I wouldn't have had the balls to cry foul either. I wasn't as forgiving. Accidental public urination wasn't enough of an apology for me. Charges, they were getting pressed.

"Mr. Hannigan is not one of your admirers." Free at last, Cole eased open the froyo shop's front door and scanned the sidewalk while using his body as a shield against whatever had caused his forehead to pucker. "Four eye-witness accounts, and he still attempted to shift the blame onto you."

"He's never liked me much." Yet another reason why I rarely came here and never alone. "I had a gum-chewing problem as a teen, a nervous habit. He blamed me for what he called the 'slobber graffiti' under his tabletops." The funny thing about Mr. Hannigan was he seemed like an okay guy on the surface, but he never forgot I had crawled out of the swamp, and he never let me forget around him either. "This is the latest in a long string of attempts at banning me from his establishment for life."

Having a cop for a dad, even as a grown woman, served as one heck of a deterrent against discriminatory shenanigans. Mr. Hannigan wanted the law on his side before he made a move, and this latest incident might actually give that to him.

"You should have told me." Cole glanced down at me. "I wouldn't have paid him."

Cole had arranged for a wire transfer to cover the exorbitant "estimated" cost of repairs, tacking on extra to cover Mr. Hannigan's mental anguish caused by the destruction of a beloved keepsake—the framed dollar bill.

"You and your bank account made quite the impression on him." I attempted to peer around Cole. He shifted to make that impossible. Since I didn't have any rock climbing gear handy, I couldn't very well scale him to discover what held his attention. "He'd probably be thrilled if you became a regular."

"That won't ever happen," he murmured.

I chose to view his declaration as one of annoyance and not of solidarity. I was no less suspicious of him, no less annoyed with him, but I'll admit I was flattered. The guy had defended my honor. Who did that? No one these days. Certainly not for me. Never for me.

"Can we get out of here?" The stares on my back were starting to make my skin prickle.

"Channel 8 News is out there." He angled his face in my
direction. "Their van boxed-in your Bronco. The reporter is
practically oiled up and sliding across your hood." A steady
rumble moved through his chest, and this time I did place my
hand on his back to feel the vibrations, to prove I wasn't crazy.
"We'll take my SUV to the hospital. I can give your keys to
one of the crew, and they can drive your Bronco home. That
work for you?"

"Let me notify Rixton." Rixton, who had informed Landry
he would be taking his wife home, and if he wanted their
statements, he could come get them. "He'll worry if he spots
the Bronco, but I'm not here."

"You're smart to tell him where you're going and with who."
Amusement tugged at his lips. "I wouldn't trust me either if I
were you."

"Sure you won't reconsider telling me who hired you to
protect Jane?" I folded my arms and waited. "That would go a
long way toward earning my trust."

"Trust will come in time." He made it sound like a foregone
conclusion. "Do you have everything you need?"

"Yeah." I checked my top, tucked in the fabric where it had
come loose, all the while hating there would be photos of me
emerging from Hannigan's in a ripped shirt after the altera-
tion. That wouldn't be good for Dad's blood pressure. "Let's get
this over with."

"Here." He gripped the bottom of his polo and tugged it over
his head. He wore a plain, black undershirt, but the motion
untucked the thin fabric from his pants and exposed a glimpse
of ridged scarring over hard muscle. "Put this on."

"Thanks." Walking out in Cole's shirt was adding more

fuel to the fire, but I would rather burn than expose my secrets to the masses. I shrugged into the polo and grinned at him. The hem hit right above my knees, and the short sleeves hung past my elbows. I held my chin up when he went to button the black discs he had left undone at his throat with surprisingly nimble fingers. "You're kind of a beast. You know that, right?"

The sight of me sporting White Horse gear—his gear—had elicited a pleased rumble from him. Typical guy response. I think they came hardwired that way. Now his slow perusal came to a screeching halt as my words registered, and he mashed his lips together. "I know."

Considering how Valerie had all but called me a cryptid, and how that made me feel like a dirt sandwich, I cringed at the name-calling. Of all the accusations I'd made, this one alone seemed to truly bother him.

"Hey, I meant you're a big guy." I gripped his wrists and squeezed to get his attention. "Not literally."

The tension in his shoulders eased. "Is that a problem?"

"Are you offering to sit on the couch watching football and drinking beer until all this—" I dragged a finger down his defined abs, inviting the warm shiver that followed "—turns to pudge if it is?"

"My body is a weapon," he admitted, watching me with rapt attention. "I can't afford to let it go to . . . pudge."

"Is security work that dangerous?" His expensive taste in toys proved his firm had done well for itself. Landing contracts with people like the Claremonts had to be lucrative. "Or is your appearance a deterrent?"

"Both." A flicker of motion caught his eye, and a black SUV with a bright White Horse logo pulled up to the curb. "That's our ride."

"That's your SUV." The odds of two such beasts prowling our streets was slim. "Who's behind the wheel?"

"Santiago was due for a grocery run, so I got him to drop me off first." Reaching for my elbow on reflex, he drew back at the last second. "Where am I allowed to touch?"

"My hands." I didn't waste breath asking how he knew I was touch-averse. He saw everything with those meltwater eyes. "I avoid contact on my arms and shoulders."

He took my hand like it was his right and led me into the maelstrom. Channel 8's cameraman rushed us, and the reporter trailed him shouting my name. Lights flashed. More pictures for me to gather and scrapbook later. More photos for me to scan while I waited for the tug of recognition in my gut that said *Hey, that's me.* Had I been alone, I would have ducked my head and ran, but Cole waded in, and I bobbed behind him. Surprise, surprise, no one jostled me. Word traveled fast. They wouldn't touch me today, a small gift, but their memories were short, relentless hunger driving them, and I would be fair game again tomorrow.

We reached the SUV, and Cole yanked open the door. He placed his hand on my hip and guided me inside before scooting across the bench seat and slamming a barrier between us, the bright lights and raised voices.

"Nice shirt." Santiago met my gaze in the rearview mirror. "Does that make you an honorary member of the crew?"

"Drive." Cole punched Santiago's headrest. "Take us to Madison Memorial."

Santiago grunted once in his boss's direction, then glided into traffic.

I let my head fall back against the seat and blew out a sigh. "Thanks for getting me out of there."

"You're welcome," the men said in tandem, and Cole scowled as Santiago tacked on, "Life's never dull around you, is it?"

"I like dull." I fastened my seatbelt. "Life just didn't get the memo." I felt Cole's eyes on me and turned my head toward him. "Who's covering the hospital?"

"Portia Cannon," Santiago answered for him. "She's got legs for miles and ain't picky whose hips she wraps them around. Ain't that right, boss?"

A heavy silence descended over the backseat. Oh. *Oh.*

"Thanks for oversharing." Guess he'd noticed the handholding and decided to put a stop to that. I could have told him not to bother, that I wasn't interested in climbing Mt. Heaton, but I saved my breath. "You could have given me relevant information—height, weight, hair color—but you do you."

A mental picture of how Cole's bedroom might look, outfitted with ropes, harnesses and carabiners popped into my head. The absurdity of it all forced out a snort that had Santiago squinting at me. Pleased to have gotten under his skin, I ignored the surly driver, picked up my phone and started damage control.

I texted Dad and Uncle Harold, skipped Maggie since I still had her phone, then read Rixton's reply.

He led with an update on Sherry, who was napping, then let the other shoe drop. We were off the Claremont case. The girl's parents had thrown their weight around and gotten the case reassigned to the FBI office out of nearby Jackson. I didn't blame them. Their access to superior resources gave them an edge we lacked, and the longer she remained missing, the slimmer the hope of bringing her home alive.

Dad responded with four words—also expected—*We need to talk.*

Uncle Harold replied with a row of emojis I translated as "smiling while a four-leaf clover and a dog eats cake in a church." Or maybe he meant he was a lucky dog because he was in church eating cake? A potluck maybe? His grandkids were trying to make him hip to their lingo, but so far all their efforts had accomplished was making me feel old and in need of a translator.

"Here we are." Santiago pulled under the portico. "You want me to park or circle?"

"Circle," Cole decided. "Keep an eye out. Make sure we weren't followed."

The doorlocks popped, and I exited the vehicle. Cole got out and paced around the vehicle, peeling off the White Horse logos where he found them, then tossed them in the trunk along with several other interchangeable magnetic signs stuck together in clumps. Below those, metal gleamed. License plates.

I fingered a square marked with Tombigbee Electric Power Association logo. "Do I want to know?"

"No." He closed the hatch then pounded his fist twice against the glass. "It's best if you don't."

Briiiiiing.

The trill of an old-fashioned rotary phone lifted gooseflesh down my arms, a Pavlovian response that set my pulse sprinting like a thoroughbred through the starting gate at Churchill Downs.

Turning away, oblivious to my near-heart attack, Cole unclipped a thick, black phone from his belt and pressed it against the side of his face. "What did I tell you about dicking around with my ringtone, Santiago?"

The panicked breath trapped in my chest released in a dizzying gust. *Get it together, Luce. Millions of people use that ringtone. All things old are new again. You can't jump out of your skin every time you hear it.*

"You've been taken off the Claremont case. It's been reassigned to Special Agent Farhan Kapoor of the FBI."

"What?" I startled out of my daze. "How can you possibly know that? I found out five minutes ago."

"Is it my fault?" Cole put away the phone and glowered down at me. "Are you being punished for what happened earlier?"

"No." I cobbled my stray thoughts into a cohesive whole. "We're a small department. Rixton and I are good at laying the groundwork. We conduct interviews, track leads, call hospitals and morgues in the surrounding areas and get the ball rolling, but we don't have their training or access to their resources." I twitched a shoulder. "I won't lie. It burns. We get a twenty-four-hour window, if we're lucky, before these cases dissolve in our hands. We've had our turn. It's time to bring in the big guns."

He worked his jaw like he wanted to disagree but set about clearing a path through the stragglers camped out in lawn chairs. Slushies from Blue Hippo filled many a drink holder, and the scent of microwave burritos and nachos heavy on the jalapenos peppered the air.

"Gah." I entered the hospital and tucked my nose against my shoulder when the disinfectant tickled me into a sneezing fit. "Do all hospitals smell the same?" I wiped my watery eyes on my sleeve, at once wishing to return to the bean-and-cheese-scented portico. "Burnt Lean Cuisines and bleach."

He skirted me and headed for the bank of elevators. "Have a grudge against hospitals?"

"Doesn't everyone?" I kept it light. No need to explain the months and months of testing I'd undergone while doctors attempted to solve the riddle of my banding. Dad had checked me out against the advice of my doctors when their attempt to remove the one nearest my elbow resulted in eventual regeneration. Metal was not an alloy produced by the human body. I shouldn't have regrown the missing striation, but I had inside of a week. "It's got to be one of the more common phobias."

"She's on four now." He ushered me inside the booth when a bell chimed and mashed the button for the fourth floor. "We arranged for a private room, and her medical bills are covered."

"That's generous." My reflection scowled at me from the mirrorlike chrome doors, and for once I agreed with her before smoothing the irritation off my face. "Your client must have deep pockets."

Faint creases lined the corners of his eyes. "You'd be amazed how deep everyday people can reach when a loved one's life is on the line."

"So you're in security for the money." The scowl reemerged.

"Yes." His tone dared me to challenge him. "Why did you become a cop?"

"Not for the paycheck," I shot back.

"Is that why you still live at home?" He towered over me. Towering was kind of his thing. "Can't afford your own place?"

"Not that it's any of your business, but Dad had a health scare last year." I dragged my upper teeth over my bottom lip. "I chose not to renew the lease on my apartment and moved back home so I could keep an eye on him." I tried not to think about Jane when I said, "He's all the family I've got."

The doors slid open, and I stepped into the hall before he landed another barb.

"Her room is this way." His fingers brushed the back of my hand but didn't latch on. "You brought ID?"

I patted my jeans pocket. "Always."

We rounded the corner, and my knees threatened to lock. A tall, blonde, dressed in what I was coming to regard as the White Horse uniform, stood with the long legs Santiago had promised crossed at the ankles. A foam cup with a bendy straw sticking out of the top sat at her feet, and someone had drawn flames like you might expect on a muscle car up the sides with a red pen. A Rubik's Cube whirled in her hand, and she kept her head bent over it, the tip of her tongue peeking out of her mouth while she manipulated the puzzle to completion.

"Portia." Cole sighed.

"One second." Three more twists of her wrists, and she took a bow, the finished cube sitting on her open palm. "Ta da!"

He lifted the toy for examination. "Where did you get this?"

"A kid three doors down. His older brother is kind of a dick." Her lip curled. "Gave it to him and promised if he solved it by the time visitation rolls around tomorrow that the doctors would let him go home."

"You're not supposed to interfere," he murmured, returning the trinket.

"Do as you say, not as you do." She looked straight at me. "Right?"

"Hi." I thrust out my hand. "I'm Luce Boudreau. I thought you might want an introduction to the person you're talking over."

"I'm Portia." She curtseyed, and it wasn't a half-bad effort either. "It's a pleasure to finally meet you, Luce Boudreau. You're shorter than I expected."

"Well, you're exactly what I expected." I winced at how that sounded then gestured toward her legs. "Santiago said—"

"Oh, I can just imagine what Santiago told you about me. Let me know if this comes close." She spun on her heel in a dramatic turn and fainted against Cole, pinning the back of her hand to her forehead. "Oh, Cole, it's simply been too long since you last ravished me." She fumbled in her pocket and produced a wrapped spork probably scavenged from the cafeteria. "Here's a spoon. Eat me up with it."

With a put-upon sigh, he took one calculated step back, and she hit the floor on her tailbone. "Behave."

"Do you really think I'd tap that?" she asked me from her seat on the linoleum. "He has no sense of humor, he's my boss, and he's larger than some small countries." She smoothed her hands down her curves. "It's this body, isn't it? It's so hot guys leak brains out of their ears even when I'm in uniform. Or maybe especially when I'm in uniform." A slight frown plumped her lips. "I'm going to miss that."

This body. What was that supposed to mean? It sounded almost like something I would say, but clearly Portia was at home in her skin while mine sometimes felt more like a rental. Vanity maybe? I almost asked why she would miss her own body, it's not like it was going anywhere, but I didn't have time to pry open that can of worms when I had bigger fish to fry.

"I'm just here to see Jane." I held up both hands, palms out. "It's not my business who's tapping what."

"Santiago is just pissy because I felt him up one night after a few beers. I got nowhere. Seriously. I've held stiffer homemade noodles. Uncooked ones. We're talking raw dough." She scoffed. "His revenge is telling anyone who'll listen that because I made the mistake of wanting him to scratch my itch that one time that I have claws in all the guys."

"Pretty sure they make a cream for that." I cringed away from her frankness. "Lucky you, you're in the right place to get a prescription."

"You're so cute with your blushing and your manners." She mimed pinching my cheeks. "You have no idea how much I'm loving this." She made a frame with her fingers and squared it up on my face. "Let me savor this moment."

I took a careful step out of arm's reach and backed into Cole. "Is weird a résumé requirement for you?"

"You have no idea." Leaning over Portia, he opened the door to expose Jane resting comfortably under the covers. "Step over her." He toed Portia's thigh. "Or on her. I don't care which."

"Excuse me." I stepped over Portia, who was still grinning at me, and approached the bed. Cole was a warm wall at my back as I drank in the sight of her. "There's more color in her cheeks today. Maybe she'll feel like talking."

"Are you hoping she has answers for you?" The heat of him enveloped my spine. "I can promise she has none you'll want to hear."

"My whole life people have looked at me and talked about me like I was a prize-winning science fair project. That reporter today? Do you know why he did what he did?" Clenching my fists, I kept them balled at my sides. "He did it because he doesn't look at me and see a person. I'm a *thing* to him." I couldn't bear to look back at Cole. "You saw me when he ... you didn't stare like the others, but you must have seen." I swept a hand out toward Jane. "Look at her. We're the same. For the first time ... " My shoulders hunched. "Please, don't smash my hope."

"I apologize." He retreated. "Take all the time you need."

Years of longing for a connection, any connection, to my past tightened my throat when I might have thanked him for wanting to spare me from the razor edge of hope that so often cut those who wielded it.

Cole shut the door behind him, and a muted conversation struck up in the hall.

I soaked in the gentle wave to Jane's hair, the dark lashes resting on her cheeks, the gauntness of her jaw. I too had been little more than skin and bones when Dad found me. But I had been around ten or eleven, as best as the doctors could tell. Jane was closer to my current age.

"Who are you?" I asked the question of the quiet room. *And who does that make me?*

Jane didn't offer me an answer. She didn't so much as flutter an eyelash.

An itch started under my skin the longer I remained in the room, not the pins-and-needles pain that assaulted me each year on my birthday, but a lesser irritation. Time and time again, I had to wrench my gaze from her bare arms by reminding myself how much I hated when people stared at me.

The better part of two hours slipped past before I started feeling like a creeper and decided it was best if I went home. The reassignment of the Claremont case meant I had no pressing business for the rest of the night. I wondered if Santiago would mind stopping at the local Thai place for carryout so I didn't have to cook. I wasn't in the mood, and Dad couldn't boil an egg. Not unless you wanted it rubbery enough to pass for a bouncy ball.

Leaving Jane behind, I reentered the hall and bumped right into Portia. "Where's Cole?"

"He went to handle your clearance with hospital security." She plucked at the front of my shirt. "Tell anyone who asks that you're consulting for White Horse."

I readjusted the fit. "I'm not going to lie."

Laughter exploded from her, and she bent at the waist. "You *slay* me."

"Leave her alone." The quiet order bounced off the blonde, who kept hooting. "Are you ready to go?"

"Yeah." Nothing about the past two days felt real. The super-gator attack, finding Jane and meeting Cole and his peculiar crew, all of it had a dreamlike quality. Tomorrow I might wake up to discover it had all been imagined, that wishes didn't come true when you blew out candles. "Would you mind making a pit stop before you drop me at home?"

"That reminds me." He held out his hand. "Keys." I passed them over, and he tossed them to Portia. "Drop Luce's Bronco off at her place."

The mischievous curl of her lip disturbed me. "How does Portia know what my Bronco looks like? Or where I live?"

"It's black," he continued on as if I hadn't interrupted, "and it'll be the only vehicle parked at Hannigan's at that time of morning." After a pointed look at me, he added, "I'll text the GPS coordinates."

I anchored my fists at my hips. "You're almost as good at covering your ass as you are at being an ass."

Portia launched into peals of laughter again.

Cole only smiled, but its duration made me squirm.

"Newsflash, Cole," Portia sing-songed behind him, rapping her knuckles on the back of his skull. "Fire is hot."

The oddness of her statement broke our stalemate. "What's that supposed to mean?"

"That people don't change," he told me, bitterness a tang on his breath. "That no matter how many times you stick your hand through the flames, you'll still get burned."

Unsure what any of that had to do with me, I shrugged. "Pretty sure they make a cream for that too."

Portia's belly laugh bounced off the walls and ceiling, and she dabbed her eyes with her shirtsleeve.

Maybe I would invite her in for breakfast when she swung by to drop off the Bronco. We could bond over egg-white omelets with low-fat cheddar cheese, and she could explain why she found everything I said or did hilarious. Sure, I liked to think of myself as funny. Who didn't? But today I hadn't been trying. Yet I could barely string two words together before her face split in a grin. Of one thing I had no doubt. She wasn't laughing with me; she was laughing *at* me.

CHAPTER EIGHT

―――――◆―――――

I was mulling over the menu at Thai-Thai For Now when my cell rang. I checked the caller ID, frowned and walked to a quiet corner of the bustling restaurant. Cole shadowed me, but I had given up on the expectation of privacy around him. "Justin. Hi. How was your trip?"

He wasted no time on pleasantries. "Have you heard from Maggie?"

"No." I winced at the sudden weight of her forgotten phone in my back pocket. "But that's my fault."

"Your fault how?"

"We had a girls' day out yesterday, a late birthday thing, and she ended up staying over last night. She left her phone in the downstairs bathroom this morning, and I meant to drop it by the school, but I got sidetracked."

"We were due at my parents for dinner twenty minutes ago." Crickets sang in the background. He must be standing on their back porch. "She didn't come home from work today."

"Have you checked with Pilar? Was the big K4/K5 powwow this week or last week?" I tapped the menu against my knee. "Those ladies get competitive with their monthly hall themes. Could she be holed up in her classroom with her Cricut?"

"That was last week," he said with the conviction of a man invested in his partner's life. "This isn't like her, Luce. Maggie would have called if she was going to run late."

A kernel of ice budded in my heart. "What do you need?"

"I'm not sure." A door closed, and the nature sounds hushed. "Where are you?"

"I'm in town." I ignored Cole when he crowded me. "I'm ten minutes from the school. Less than that if I drive instead of walk. Want me to go bang on some doors?"

"I don't want to put you out." His frustration only galvanized me. "Are you sure you don't mind?"

"Maggie is my best friend." I caught Cole's eye and started walking. "Anything you need, I'm your girl."

"Good. Okay. Thanks." He exhaled softly. "You check the school. I'll make some calls. I'll start with Pilar and work my way down to her parents."

"Keep calm. I'll touch base with you within the hour." Justin ended the call sounding less harried. "Looks like I have one more stop to make." I found Cole lurking behind me. "This is where we say goodnight."

There existed within me a wellspring of clinical detachment I could access during emergencies. Once I tapped into that place of cool logic, it shut down my fear and panic and squeamishness. It allowed me to function with a clear head and postpone the emotional fallout until later. Now, for Maggie's sake, I grabbed hold of that Zen with both hands.

"Where do you need to go?" His gaze tagged the road leading

to the school. He must have pieced together the location based on my end of the conversation. No one's hearing was that acute. "I'll take you."

"You've done enough." I took stock of my surroundings through that clear lens, and the worry retreated another few centimeters. Hannigan's wasn't that far, but Cole had already passed my keys off to Portia, and the spare had been lost to the depths of the couch months ago. "I can't afford to pay you to babysit me. I'll have to weather the revival of Wild Child Mania on my own." As usual. "Might as well start now."

"A man assaulted you earlier. You're not going anywhere alone." Dusk had fallen since we entered the restaurant, and a blanket of stars waited beyond the bruised clouds to roll across the sky. "You can't afford to pay me enough *not* to babysit you if you're dead set on walking."

Red lights flashed in my periphery, and the SUV rolled back before Cole finished barking at me.

"Where do you two think you're going?" Santiago glared at my empty hands. "And where is my order of kanom gui chai?"

"Your chive cakes will have to wait," I informed him, then started walking.

"Cole. You're not serious. Fuck." He smacked his open palm against the door then pointed at me. "This SUV turns into a pumpkin at midnight, princess." He looked at me, really saw me, as if he viewed me from the opposite end of that same frigid lens. A flicker of emotion I might have labeled as fear twisted his features before he dialed up his bravado to cover the slip. "You and your glass slippers better get clip-clopping if you want to make the deadline."

"We're walking." Cole snapped his fingers. "Follow at a distance. Keep an eye out for—"

"Don't tell me how to do my job." He jabbed the button to

raise the window with one hand and cranked up the radio with the other. Through the glass he mouthed, *Tick tock*.

"Are we walking?" Cole swept his gaze over me, searching for whatever Santiago had glimpsed, but he didn't flinch away from what he saw. "Or should I call him back?"

I set out down the sidewalk, the ice in my chest expanding and contracting like a living, breathing thing, and I didn't check to see if he followed.

Five minutes later, Cole gripped my hand to stop me. He crossed to the next cement square and squatted over a dark spill on the sidewalk. He faced away from me, but his back expanded as though he were drawing air deep into his lungs.

"This is where the Claremont girl vanished," I said in case he didn't recognize the area. Passing on the ride with Santiago meant we ended up walking the exact path she had taken that fateful day. Perhaps the decision had been a subconscious one on my part, meant as a goodbye since she was no longer mine to find. "She was last seen by a classmate who lives in the Dunleavy Apartment Complex."

The brick buildings hunched together across the street, about fifteen minutes away if you stuck to the sidewalk.

"This is fresh blood." Another shift of his broad shoulders, one I caught on the edge of my vision. Had he dipped his fingers in the liquid to test viscosity? Scented it to be sure maybe? I shifted my weight forward, and caught the glitter of moisture on his fingers. I rocked back on my heels, shook my head. He must have used a wet wipe, cleaned his hands. It's not like he would have licked his fingers. "Who do you want to call?"

"How sure are you someone needs calling?" The yellow beam of the SUV hit me across the cheek. "We can't know it's human."

The noise he made in the back of his throat disagreed with

me, but I wasn't ready for what it might mean. Fresh blood near where the Claremont girl had been taken. Fresh blood on a path Maggie walked daily, which she had no reason to stroll at night. None.

A fresh wave of soothing coolness yanked me back from the precipice and focused my mind.

"I need to get to the school." I stepped into the road and around him. "Can Santiago call . . . ?"

"Are you determined to make honest men of us all?" A wisp of humor laced his words.

I couldn't find it in me to crack a smile. Not until I had laid eyes on Maggie. Not until this ice block in my chest thawed.

Cole stood and gestured the SUV to the curb. He crossed to Santiago, who lowered his window, and they exchanged words that resulted in Santiago piercing me with a scowl I was starting to recognize as his default expression around me.

"He's calling the police," Cole informed me. "He'll wait here for them to preserve the scene."

A jerky nod was all the thanks I could offer before my feet wrested control of my body away from me, and I broke into a steady jog aimed at the kindergarten wing of the John W. Rosen Elementary School. Most of the classrooms sat dark and empty, but a few lights gave me hope. I coasted to a stop at the rear doors leading to the parking lot where the buses lined up and pounded my fist against the locked metal door. No one answered. I jumped a chain-link fence that cordoned off a cluster of air-conditioning units and approached one of the lit windows. I banged on the glass until a sour-faced man frowned down at me. He cranked the window open a fraction and pursed his lips.

"Hi there. I'm Luce Boudreau with the Canton Police Department." I pasted on a winning smile I didn't feel. Swallowed by

Cole's enormous shirt, I must have looked more like a kid than a cop. "I'm also a friend of Maggie Stevens."

"Jeremy Hendricks," he answered with reluctance. "I'm one of the first-grade teachers. Is there something I can help you with, officer?"

"Maggie didn't come home from work today. Her fiancé became concerned when she broke dinner plans with him and called me. I was hoping you could let me in to check her classroom. I want to make sure she didn't lose track of the time."

"Maggie left hours ago." His expression softened a touch. "One of the other teachers—Robert Martin—backed over a stray. Maggie was walking to her car and saw it all. She scooped up the dog, and Robert drove her to Rice Animal Hospital."

Hope, that most useless of emotions, closed tight fingers around my throat. The blood on the sidewalk . . . Maybe the dog had run from them after being injured. Cole could be wrong about it being human. Except the staff parking lot wasn't on that stretch of road. There were a few spots, yes, but Maggie didn't often park at the curb. The walk was too far for the spiky heels she loved wearing.

"Thanks for your help." I pulled out my wallet, thumbed one of my business cards and passed it to him. "Call if you think of anything else or if you see her before I do."

"I hope you find her soon." He accepted the paper rectangle through the slit and tucked it into his front shirt pocket. "Maggie's got a big heart. She's a favorite around here. I can't keep my kids from popping back into her classroom for hugs."

"One last question." I couched it as an afterthought. "Robert Martin. Do you have a number where I can reach him?"

"No. Sorry. He teaches three grades ahead of me. Our paths don't cross often."

"Okay." I waved. "Thanks."

I was slower going over the fence this time. Cole offered me his hand, but I swung my legs and jumped without assistance. We'd had a fence three times this height as part of the obstacle course at the academy. Chain link I liked. Plenty of hand and footholds. It was the wooden privacy fences that got you.

"Do you want a lift out to the animal hospital?" Cole fell in step beside me. "We can use my SUV and Santiago can catch a ride from one of the others."

"Let me call Justin first." I dialed him. "Hey, did you have any luck?"

"No one's seen her." Metal clanged in the background. Had he thrown a pan in the sink? "People don't vanish into thin air."

I rolled in my lips to keep the cop in me from admitting that sometimes, yeah, they did. Instead I passed on what Mr. Hendricks had said about the dog and the emergency trip to the vet. "Has she ever mentioned Robert Martin to you?"

"The name doesn't sound familiar, but I know the other K5 teachers best." He pushed out a sigh. "You know what a softie Maggie is. She would have jumped into a car with Freddy Krueger if it meant saving an injured animal."

"Rice Animal Hospital closes at five." Dad and I had used the same clinic for his ancient lab, Yeller, until she passed from old age. "The closest emergency vet is about forty-five minutes away." Also a fact I knew thanks to Yeller and her tendency to eat pennies. I held out my phone, checked the time. "It's eight o'clock now."

During the school year, it wasn't unusual for Maggie to stay well past the three-oh-five bell. She sanitized the classroom, commiserated with the other teachers or babysat stragglers whose parents couldn't pick up their little ones on time due to their work schedules. Say she left at five, her usual, then the forty-five-minute drive there and back plus the time required for the vet to tend the dog framed up a reasonable window of time. But my heart pounded so hard it threatened to bruise my ribs. I couldn't shake the sensation of impending doom.

Justin must have been running the same mental calculations as me, because he interrupted my thoughts. "This could all be a big mix up." His punch of relief nauseated me, because it hit me square in the gut for an altogether different reason. "She might be on her way home."

Maybe. I hoped so. But why hadn't she borrowed a phone and left Justin a message warning him she would run late? There might not have been time in the moment, but after? Martin must have a cell. Who didn't these days? Say his battery was dead and they were too frantic to charge it during the drive. Okay, well, the clinic had a landline phone. No battery required. No spotty coverage worries. No reason for her not to pick it up and dial home.

I scuffed my toe on the concrete. "Maybe."

"Thanks for your help, Luce. I'll call when she arrives."

Please let her arrive.

"You told him the truth." Cole dipped his chin, watching me tuck away my phone. "It's not your fault people hear what they want."

"Speaking of hearing, what big ears you have, Grandma. The better to stalk me with, I presume?" He didn't take the bait, so I massaged my forehead. "I want to check the lot before I go."

He swept out his arm indicating I should lead the way. I crossed the grassy lawn and strolled under the awning until we reached the parking lot. Maggie's sunshine-yellow Prius sat beneath her favorite tree.

"I don't like this." I circled the car but didn't touch it even to test the door handle so fingerprints could be lifted if necessary. "Maggie forgets things, but she isn't thoughtless. She would have called if her plans changed. Why not borrow a phone to call Justin or use the one in the main office?"

"I can trace Robert Martin," Cole offered.

"That's okay." I rolled my head on my neck. "I'll run him down at the station. Tomorrow, I guess."

"I'm right here."

"Kind of hard to miss you." I glanced over at him. "You're like a baby mountain that got tired of where it was planted and invested in a nice pair of boots to go adventuring."

"That's not what I meant." He anchored his hands at his hips. "I have resources at my disposal. Why not use them?"

"I have my own resources, but thanks." I patted his elbow. "I've already told you I can't afford you." I cocked my head at him. "I'm not even sure why you want to help. Where's the angle?"

He didn't protest having one, which assured me I would cut myself on his one day soon.

"Can I request one last favor?" He nodded that I could, and I trespassed on his hospitality. "Can you drop me off at the station?"

"You're going to file a missing person report."

"Yes." The prospect drained me until I had no energy left to contemplate what this might mean. "Justin is going to realize she may not be coming home soon. I can't give him much, but I can give him this. The quicker the report is filed, the sooner the search can begin and the sooner I can access full departmental resources to help locate her."

"I'll drop you off and ask Miller to get your keys from Portia. He can bring the Bronco around for you."

"That would be perfect." I cut a path for the SUV, which had been joined by a cruiser. The ripple of the lightbar, usually a welcoming beacon, locked my knees, and I lost all motivation to walk the rest of the way. Once I spoke to another cop about Maggie, it was real. She became a file on someone's desk, a stack of papers to flip through. "This is one time I wouldn't mind ducking out on the cops."

"Let me see what I can do." Phone in hand, he started texting. "This will only take a minute."

Sensing his dismissal, I drifted a short distance away and began pacing. I had counted on the ride to the station to digest what this meant. Canton was a small town. The fact Maggie worked at the same school as Angel Claremont's little sister had meant nothing. Until Justin's call. Until the blood on the sidewalk. I prayed the latter got dismissed as part of the dog incident, but what if it didn't? What did that mean for Maggie?

A horn honking snapped me from my thoughts. I don't know how long I'd been standing on the curb, but Cole had already made himself comfortable in a black SUV identical to the one up the road. Thom sat behind the wheel of this one, and he finger-waved at me.

I got in beside Cole in order to avoid Thom, but he tracked my progress and grinned like the Cheshire Cat, all bright teeth, when I opened the door.

"You smell nice." He sniffed the air. "Cole's scent is all over you."

Fire zinged up my spine, thawing me further, but I kept the heat out of my cheeks. "Um, thank you?"

He nodded his satisfaction, then faced forward and made a U-turn to avoid the lightshow up ahead. I was dreading the ribbing I'd get entering the station dressed in Cole's shirt when Thom wrenched the wheel hard to his left. My head cracked against the window to my right, and my ears rang. Fireworks rocketed behind my eyelids, and the world exploded in a shower of agony as the vehicle screeched to a stop. Everything hurt. Nothing worked. My eyelids kept slipping lower and lower.

"No ... hospitals," I murmured. "I won't go back. I won't ..."

A bellow rose from the seat beside me. More of that harsh language flowed between the front seat and the back. But I was having trouble focusing, their conversation half English and half unknown, too fluid for me to cup in my hands.

Briiiiiing.

That damn ringtone followed me into oblivion.

CHAPTER NINE

———◈———

"Ms. Boudreau." A cold metal disc pressed against my chest as the congenial voice droned, "Ms. Boudreau, can you hear me?"

"*Luce.*" A fierce growl laced with command splintered my head. "Wake up."

"No." I pried open my eyes and squinted at the pockmarked ceiling. "No ... hospitals."

"This isn't a hospital." The first speaker solidified into a middle-aged man with thinning hair. "This is a private clinic."

Pulse hammering in my ears, I swatted away his hand. "Don't touch me." I braced my palms on the table and pushed upright while my body protested going vertical. "Just ... don't."

"He didn't examine your arms or your shoulders." Cole shuffled the doctor aside so that he dominated my field of vision. "I carried you in, and I stayed with you the whole time. I never let you out of my sight."

Stupid, grateful tears welled in my eyes. "Thank you."

"I called your father. He's on his way." His gaze lingered on my damp cheeks. "Can you lie back down for me?"

"I don't . . ." My elbows buckled and went out from under me. Cole lunged forward, caught me in his arms and lowered me as softly as a whisper. "I meant to do that."

"I'm sure." Amusement glinted in his eyes, and I traced the crinkles at their corners. The fine lines vanished at my touch, and he firmed his lips. "You hit your head pretty hard."

A distant part of my brain rebelled against me wasting precious time. I had been on my way *somewhere* to do *something* important. The urge still clawed at me, but I couldn't remember what I had been doing, and my icy calm had abandoned me. "What happened?"

"Thom swerved to miss a deer." He arranged a wafer-thin pillow under my head then withdrew. "You hit the right side of your head on the window. You've got a concussion."

That all sounded scary, so I pushed those worries aside. "Dad's on his way?"

He checked the cheap, plastic wall clock. "He should be here any minute—"

"*Luce.*"

"—now," he finished. "Thom, lead Sergeant Boudreau back."

Shuffling noises sounded behind me. Thom had either been standing watch at my back or in the hall. I couldn't tell. My sense of direction skewed to one side, and, without Cole's touch anchoring me, I gripped the edges of the table to keep from rolling off onto the floor.

"Relax. I won't let you fall." Cole made it a promise.

"*You.*" Dad choked out the word. "Get away from my daughter. I can handle things from here." Dad interrupted my line of sight. "Baby girl, what have you gotten yourself into this time?"

"A car wreck," I told him matter-of-factly. "A kamikaze deer got me."

"Is that so?" He aimed the question at Cole. "A deer?"

If Cole answered him, I didn't hear.

"Daddy." I rolled onto my side. "I think I'm going to . . ."

Gut heaving, I emptied the contents of my stomach onto his boots.

"Is it safe to move her?" he asked the doctor. "Can I take her home?"

"Home is the best place for her. She's shaken, a little woozy and nauseated, but stable." He passed a note over me, a prescription maybe. "Seek medical attention immediately if her condition worsens."

"Thank you for your help." Dad clasped hands with the doctor, then jerked back, his face purpling as Cole slid his warm hands under my back. Dad gripped the front of the much bigger man's shirt. "What the hell do you think you're doing?"

"I'm carrying her out to your truck." Cole tucked me against him with a possessive growl. "Are you going to fight me over this or get the door?"

Thom materialized at my elbow, and his lip curled at my father.

"I'll get the door." Dad pointed at Thom. "You stay right where you are, Thomas."

I must have gotten hit a lot harder than I thought, because it sounded like my dad had just called Thom by his full name. The incident at Hannigan's would have made the rounds by now, so I figured Dad knew Cole's record like the back of his hand. But Thom hadn't been there. How could Dad know him? Unless he had pulled files for all of White Horse's people. That was a Dad thing to do.

Thanks to the thousand-pound gorilla clapping my

throbbing head between his cymbals, I nuzzled the space between Cole's pectorals and shoved all that nasty logic business into the back of my head for later dissection.

The men didn't exchange another word until Cole had me propped up on the passenger side of Dad's pickup. That all changed once the door shut. Dad was madder than a wet hen, and Cole didn't look far behind him. They kept their voices too soft for me to pick up the particulars, but neither man looked pleased when the confrontation ended. Cole ignored my dad while he cleaned off his boots, his stare a cutting, vicious thing.

He didn't want to let me go. I could tell. I don't know how, but I could. That protective streak of his kept popping up when I least expected, and ... it was nice. Maybe that's why it made me so suspicious.

"What aren't you telling me?" I settled in and let my eyes shut. "You and Cole have history, don't you?"

"We'll talk tomorrow, after you've rested."

"Promise?" Of all the things I might forget about tonight, this was not one of them.

"I promise." He patted my knee. "Now rest."

I scooted closer and curled against his side, resting the good side of my head against his shoulder. "Okay, Daddy."

CHAPTER TEN

━━━◆◆◆━━━

Morning sucked. Hard. It was bright and loud and shiny. And bright. *Really* bright. So bright it felt like the sun was standing over my bed drilling into my temple with a sharpened ray of light. I sat up and immediately wished I hadn't. I dry-heaved a couple of times, but my stomach was empty. Thank God. The inside of my mouth already tasted like I'd been making out with Rixton—which is to say a horse's ass.

A few minutes of sitting up did wonders for my sour disposition, and I swung my legs over the edge of the bed. I hadn't noticed, but I wore the same clothes from yesterday. Jeans encased my legs, and Cole's oversized shirt hung off one shoulder. His scent wafted around me as I moved, and I shucked it over my head to escape the reminders of last night.

The thought of food set my stomach roaring as I made my way to the bathroom. I was too woozy to go through the motions of showering. Instead I sprayed dry shampoo into my hair, fluffed it, then peeled off my clothes and bathed my face and upper body in the sink. I changed into clean underthings, pulled on fresh jeans, then tugged a long-sleeved T-shirt over my head. I transferred the contents of my pockets into my new pants. Feeling refreshed, I went in search of Dad.

I found him sitting in his recliner with the tablet I'd bought him last Christmas balanced on his lap and a special on the unexpectedly vicious nature of hippos playing on the TV in the background.

"I like reading on this thing. The large font—it is called a font, right?—is easy on old eyes." He tapped a few buttons. "But I miss the smell of newsprint." He rubbed his fingers together. "The way it blackens your fingertips."

Nostalgia was one of Dad's favorite stalling tactics, and I wasn't falling for his tricks. "How do you know Cole?"

"Straight to it," he grumped. "Your mind has always been a steel trap. Made fibbing to you nearly impossible when you were little." He waved me into the living room. "Sit down or else you can't jump up and yell at me properly when what I have to say lights a fire under you."

"Okay, I'll play along." I sat in my favorite spot and curled my legs under me to prove I was too mature to hop up and down and scream at my own father in a tantrum. "Lay it on me."

"I know you know where I ended up that night." He must have meant on my birthday. "I didn't mean . . . I didn't want—I *don't* want—you to worry about your old man." He set the tablet aside. "I was flipping channels on the TV at Harry's when the show I was watching cut to a breaking-news segment."

Yep. He meant my birthday. I linked my hands in my lap and waited.

"I caught a glimpse of the woman you helped retrieve from the swamp." His chest expanded on a deep inhale. "I saw her arms, the bands." He gusted out a sigh. "What are the odds of her being found in the same swamp with the same markings? It has to mean something." He dragged his gaze to mine. "You had to come from somewhere. Babies aren't found under cabbage leaves, and young women aren't discovered under a film of duckweed either."

"You saw her arms on TV." I pressed a hand to my lower stomach. "I'd hoped with the darkness and the distance . . ."

How many others recalled the early photos of me exposed the same way? How many of them would make the same leap as Dad? We had identical markings. I had seen them for myself. What did they mean? Where did we get them? Unless . . . was Maggie right? Had we been born this way?

"I saw the logo for the security company," Dad continued, "and I googled them. Did I say that right?" I nodded that he had. "I called the number listed on their website and asked to speak to the man in charge. That man was Cole." He flicked his wrist. "He and I met and came to an agreement."

"Wait a minute." I stopped him right there. "*You're* the one who hired White Horse to watch Jane Doe?"

That explained not only the top dog's appearance on my doorstep but also his willingness to play chauffeur. Not to mention Dad's noticeable absence. He had been hiding from me.

"What was I supposed to do?" He set his shoulders back, ready to stand in the face of my anger. "It was all over your face what she meant to you." He plucked at a loose string coiled on his armrest. "You were too young to remember the worst of the media frenzy when you were found." I didn't correct him. He believed I had been spared by virtue of my age, but eleven was plenty old enough to recall the height of Wild Child Mania. "I knew that if I'd seen her arms that others would have too, and I wasn't as careful of you at first as I should have been. There are pictures documenting your markings. I trusted those doctors to keep them confidential. I was a fool for believing the diplomas on their walls made them good and honest men."

"You did the best you could." More than anyone else would have done in his shoes.

"Are you very mad at me?" He stared at my toes, as though that was as high up as he dared look.

"For blowing your retirement fund on Jane? Yes." I stood and crossed to him, kneeling on the floor and encircling his waist with my arms. He leaned forward into the hug. "For protecting me like you always have? No. I didn't buy you all those Father of the Year shirts for nothing. You earned them."

He dropped a kiss on the top of my head then pulled back when I winced. "How's your noggin?"

"Sore." I sank into lotus position on the rug. "It feels like a mule kicked me in the temple."

"I called the shift office." He peered down at me, stern Dad Face in the on position. "I explained what happened and faxed over the note and contact information for the doctor who saw you last night. You're on sick leave for forty-eight hours. You've got time built up if you need more after that."

Seeing as how my head felt like a rung bell, I didn't fight him over a mini-vacation.

"How are Cole and Thom?" A vague memory tickled the back of my mind. "I heard them talking. At the clinic, maybe? That must mean they're okay."

"They're both fine." He smoothed his hand over his shirtfront.

"Are you sure you're not holding back?" I scrunched up my face. "You're worrying your middle button. That's your tell. What haven't you told me?"

He scraped his nail across the plastic disc. "I also retained Cole's services on your behalf."

"On my ... *Dad*. You hired a bodyguard for me?" My soul shriveled at the thought even while I relaxed a fraction. This I could process. This I could handle. A decent guy defending me out of the goodness of his heart? Now that had been odd. Muscle paid to protect me, well, that fit my worldview just fine. "That explains a lot actually."

The persistence. The protective streak. The violence on my behalf. Acceding to my requests. No wonder Cole had played so well with me. He had been paid to keep an eye on me, and what better way than to cart me around and pretend curiosity in my pursuits?

I was such an idiot for not piecing it together sooner. Even Maggie had befriended me because of my reputation. She'd wanted to be a lion tamer that year and figured I was good practice. Though my lack of body hair, claws and fangs had initially disappointed her, my willingness to jump through hula hoops in her backyard while she cracked the frayed end of a jump rope at my feet redeemed me in her eyes. She'd charged kids a dollar each to watch the show, and we'd used the money to eat froyo until we got so sick we barfed until our toes curled in the bathroom at Hannigan's.

Huh. On second thought, maybe *that* was why the old coot hated me so much.

"I fired him." Dad jutted out his chin. "His second night on the job, and you land in a clinic with a head injury." He crossed his arms. "He can keep the contract on Jane Doe until other arrangements can be made, but he is *not* to interfere with you."

As much as my pride stung, I rallied a defense for White Horse. "You can't blame Thom, who was the driver and yet has managed to escape your ire, or Cole for a deer jumping in front of the SUV. We live out in the country. Wildlife takes out vehicles all the time."

He muttered something under his breath that I let pass in the interest of allowing him to vent.

The house phone ringing cut his tirade short, and he scowled at the receiver cradled on the wall in the kitchen. Cell coverage tended to be spotty out this way, so we kept a landline phone for emergencies. Usually the only calls that came through were telemarketers or the job. I stood and followed him. I hadn't eaten breakfast yet, and I wasn't in the mood to cook. "Cereal and milk it is."

"Luce."

"Hmm?" I got down my favorite bowl. "Is that work?"

"It's Justin Sheridan." His forehead puckered. "Do you feel up to talking to him?"

"Sure." I accepted the handset and reached for a box of sugary flakes. "Hey, Justin. What's up?"

"I wanted to thank you for filing the missing person report last night." He sounded raw. "I wasn't ready to face up to it, and I would have cost us time."

"What are you talking about?" I cut a glance at Dad. "I didn't file any paperwork yesterday. I was off." The first half of his comment caught up to me. "Who's missing?"

"Are you okay, Luce?" A note of doubt plucked my ears. "You don't remember?"

Ice spread in a sheet down my spine, and I shivered where I rested my hip against the counter. The pain in my head worsened, and I hissed as my brain throbbed. "I was in an accident. I have a concussion." The chattering of my teeth drew Dad's attention. "It's all hazy after . . ."

"Oh God, Luce," he breathed. "Why didn't you mention it sooner? Are you all right? Do you need anything?"

"Answers." I gritted my teeth and accepted Dad's help sitting at the table. "What happened?"

"Maggie didn't come home last night."

The phone slid from my numb fingers and clattered across the floor. Needlelike pain jabbed my scalp as a haze blurred my eyes. Faint echoes—memories?—swirled up from my core, hit the roof of my skull and shattered open.

Mountainous rocks jutted from the barren earth, the peaks capped in ice and dusted with snow. A silken caress down my spine had me searching the open skies for the male responsible. I tipped back my head, a grin on my lips, and locked gazes with eyes the perfect crimson of a ruby's heart.

Hot tears filled my eyes, and a blink sent them rolling down my cheeks. I clawed at my hairline as a wave of dizziness crashed over me, the strange landscape blurring, and my head dropped like a stone. My forehead bounced off the wood, and the lights went out.

"Ms. Boudreau." A frigid disc touched the skin over my chest, and my eyelids fluttered as an affable voice nudged me toward consciousness. "Ms. Boudreau, can you hear me?"

"No." Throat dry, I coughed when I tried to swallow. "Hospitals."

"This isn't a hospital." The words swept déjà vu over me. "This is a private clinic. I'm Dr. Leon Norwood. We met last night after the accident. Can you open your eyes?"

I cracked them open to find a middle-aged man with thinning hair hovering in front of me with a pen light aimed at my forehead. The second our gazes met, he jabbed me in the eye with the beam. An ice pick to the temple would have hurt less.

"Your concussion appears to be more serious than originally suspected." He thumbed my bottom eyelid and pulled it down. "I could diagnose the full extent of your injury if you would allow a few minor tests."

"No," Dad answered for me, "she doesn't want them."

MRIs, X-rays, ultrasounds. Been there, done that. Got the IV tracks in my arm to prove it.

"Your father tells me you've got a case of retrograde amnesia." He explained before I could ask. "It means you've forgotten a block of time prior to your accident. From what Mr. Boudreau explained, it sounds like you're missing three to four hours."

I swallowed to wet my throat. "Will they come back?"

"Long-term memories tend to return in bits and pieces as people heal from head injuries. It's perfectly normal for glimpses to return out of sequence, so don't panic if what you recall doesn't fit the version of events you've been told. It will take time for your brain to sort out the puzzle of what happened. Don't try to force it. Let it occur naturally."

"Will those glimpses include ... other things?" The bite of frigid wind still chapped my cheeks. "Scenes that don't ... " I made a vague gesture. "Can the memories reorder themselves into something new?"

"It's possible you might interpret them that way." He reached for a pen. "Are you experiencing fractured memories?"

"No" seemed like the best answer to the curiosity sparking in his eyes. "I need Cole." I bit the inside of my cheek. "What I meant is that I need to talk to Cole."

Dad glowered at me, not pleased by the slip-up.

"I was with him last night. That I do remember." I swatted the hovering doctor away and pushed upright. "He might have the answers I need."

"Dr. Norwood just said not to force the memories." Dad gripped my shoulder to steady me, his fingers light and not in contact with the metal under my skin. "You need to rest."

"I'm not forcing the memories." I rubbed the heel of my palm into my eye. "I'm acquiring new ones. He can tell me what happened. Then I can let it go."

"You've never let go of a thing in your life." He sighed. "Whoever said daughters are a father's delight must have meant a father's demise."

"You know you love me." I curved my hand over his weathered one. "I'm not actually trying to kill you."

"That's what scares me." He removed his hand and let me test my steadiness. "Think how much faster it would go if you put any effort into it."

I chuckled, and it made my head ache worse, but the pain was minor when it eased the worry pinching Dad's face.

"I can't rest while Maggie's out there alone." Guilt at having forgotten her even for a moment pressed on my chest until my lungs burned as if a lace of ice fringed them. "She's my best friend."

"Did you hear me speak? No. You didn't." He huffed in a resigned way. "What's the point? Might as well be talking to a fencepost."

Dad took my elbow in a light grip. I slid off the table and checked to make sure I could stand on my own before stepping out of his reach. He didn't take offense. He understood. And he kept close enough to catch me should my stubbornness send me crashing face-first onto the tile.

We passed through the empty waiting room, and I sneezed so hard I lost my balance. The musty air tickled the back of my throat, the scent reminding me of rooms closed up for too long between uses. What sort of doctor practiced out of a clinic like this one? Casting stones was out considering my hang-ups with hospitals and lack of trust in doctors in general. For Cole to trust him, Dr. Norwood must have had as much reason to hide from the medical community as I did. There was an odd comfort in that, a shared secret almost.

Outside the sun glared bright overhead, and sweat pearled on my forehead. It must be nice to wear tank tops or short-sleeved shirts in public. Guarding my privacy almost suffocated me in the Deep South humidity.

"Heard you wanted to talk to me," a deep voice rumbled from my left.

"Cole?" I spun to find him leaned against the siding not a foot away from me. "How did you know?"

"Dr. Norwood texted me." He straightened to his full height. "So here I am."

"Texts might travel at the speed of light, but men don't." I crossed my arms over my chest. "What are you doing here?"

He nodded a reluctant greeting to my dad before focusing on me. "Would you believe I was in the neighborhood?"

"No." I took a stab in the dark. "Let me guess. You were still playing bodyguard, despite Dad firing you, and followed us out here. A less charitable woman might call that stalking. Oh, wait. I already have. Repeatedly."

Teasing him came harder today than it had yesterday. Knowing where we stood, knowing what motivated him, had given me perspective. And if my chest ached a little, well, it was only what I deserved for forgetting. I ought to thank Cole for the reminder.

"I called him," Dad admitted. "I'd never even seen this clinic before last night, and I wasn't exactly here to absorb the décor. I wanted the same doctor to take a look at you, but I got here, and it was so dilapidated, I decided to verify the address." He poked his finger through a hole in the siding. "How is this place not condemned?"

"It's camouflage." The examination room had been spotless, the equipment well maintained, the man soft-spoken but capable. "His patients must have their reasons for avoiding the hospital." I took Cole's measure. "What's your excuse?"

The edge of his lips curved. "I'll tell you mine if you tell me yours."

"I didn't invite you here to flirt with my daughter." Dad angled himself between us. "Actually, I didn't invite you at all. You gave me the confirmation I needed over the phone. Why are you here?"

"I wanted to check on Luce." His gaze found me over Dad's shoulder.

"I fired you." Dad made a slashing motion with his hand. "She's no longer your concern."

"Can we go somewhere and get some breakfast?" I appealed to the nurturer in Dad. "My stomach would settle faster if it had some food in it." I rested my head on his shoulder. "Besides, I wanted to talk to him anyway. His nosiness saved us the hassle of hunting him down."

"You're a terror." He tweaked my nose. "I suppose you might as well be a terror full of maple syrup."

Grinning up at him, I caught the peculiar expression tightening Cole's face before he smoothed it away. There and gone so fast, if I had to name it, I would have called it envy.

The drive to the local Waffle Iron took ten minutes. We met in the parking lot and entered in a cluster like old friends. The waitress showed us to our table, and Cole slid in beside me before Dad could wedge himself between us. I smothered a laugh that earned me side-eye from Dad. It was probably a good thing they'd broken off their arrangements. Cole enjoyed needling his employer way too much for any kind of working relationship to survive between them long-term.

After we'd placed our drink orders and been handed menus, I twisted in the booth to better see the man beside me. "So, here we go. I don't remember last night. Words I never thought I would say to a guy's face." Dad's scowl cut deeper while Cole managed to look amused. "Or ever. I don't drink and date. Or really drink. Or actually date."

Dad nodded with satisfaction that I had given the correct answers.

Leaning closer to Cole, I begged, "Feel free to stop me from rambling at any point."

He picked up the laminated menu and started scanning. "What do you want to know?"

"I remember visiting Jane Doe, but the rest is hazy." I selected a straw and started picking off its wrapper. "Though I did wake up with a killer Thai craving."

"We stopped for takeout at a Thai place in town. That's when Justin Sheridan called." He outlined the rest of the evening, and I tucked away every scrap of information. He gritted his teeth through the retelling of the accident and ended on a wholly unexpected note. "Since you were incapacitated, I took the liberty of reporting your friend as missing on your behalf."

"That was you?" The straw rolled from my fingers. "I figured her parents must have gone down to the station after Justin told them she was missing."

"I owed you." Cole had faced down cops and paperwork— two of his least favorite things—for my friend. For me. He shrugged like his thoughtfulness didn't matter, when it meant more than I could put into words. "I should have taken better care of you in the first place."

"Now you sound like Dad." I accepted my drink straight from the waitress and speared it with my straw. "Mother Nature was at fault. Not you."

The rest of our breakfast passed without a hiccup, and Cole paid the bill, much to my father's protests. I hadn't lied about the food. It did settle my stomach. It centered my thoughts too. I had all the pieces, or most of them, and they were sliding around in my head searching for interlocking corners. We left at the same time and stopped outside the restaurant to make our awkward goodbyes.

"I need to swing by the station." I had expected pushback from Dad, but Cole beat him across the finish line with a resounding *no*. "I want an update on Maggie's case." Chances were good Rixton and I had been passed over for that assignment due to our friendship with her. That left few choices, none of which satisfied me. I wanted a hand in her case, conflict of interest or not. "I need to follow up with Robert Martin too."

"You're on sick leave," Dad reminded me.

"Then I'll go off sick leave." I already had my phone in my hand. "Let me check in with my partner first."

Briiiiiing.

Chills blasted down my spine, and I shivered. I really wished Cole would change his ringtone. But if I asked him to outright, the first question that popped out of his mouth would be *why*? And the only answer I would give him was *just because*. I wasn't about to expose even more of my soft underbelly to him. I shifted away to give him privacy to answer his phone and bumped into Dad, whose face had gone bone-white and whose eyes carried a darkness I glimpsed only one night out of the year.

"What's wrong?" I gripped his elbow and guided him onto a bench. "You look like you've seen a ghost."

"Maybe I have." He blinked at Cole a few more times, shook his head, then scrubbed his face with his hands. "I didn't sleep much last night. I'm due for a nap."

"Okay." I waved goodbye to Cole, who didn't look pleased about me slipping away while he was otherwise occupied, and walked with Dad to his truck. "Let's do that."

Dad really must have been knocked for a loop. Otherwise he never would have fallen for my dutiful daughter act. His parental instincts always told him when I was faking. He remained distant on the drive home and went up to his room when we got there. I waited a half hour, until I could hear his snores from out in the hall, then palmed my keys off the kitchen counter where Dad must have left them after Portia swung by this morning.

"Sorry, Dad." I trailed my fingers across the back of his recliner on my way to the door. "But Maggie is my friend."

And I had too few of those to give up on even one.

CHAPTER ELEVEN

‹———◆———›

Conversations stuttered and died after my arrival at the station, a lull so profound it was obvious my coworkers had been gossiping about me prior to my arrival. Now that I was here, their wagging tongues had gotten tangled and tripped them. A few managed a wave. Most couldn't meet my eyes.

Me, I was numb to the offense. Or so I told myself. I was more curious if the chatter was about Jane Doe and me, as I'd overheard one man intimate we were runaways from some bizarre swamp cult, or if the curious looks were the result of Cole's interlude with the reporter. Or both.

I bumped into Rixton in the break-room, donut in one of his hands and a cup of coffee in the other. "My, aren't we feeling clichéd today?"

"What are you doing here?" He slapped his open palm on the table in an invitation to join him. "You're on leave. I saw the paperwork this morning."

"Rumors of my death have been greatly exaggerated," I deadpanned.

"Your dad isn't prone to exaggeration. He said you were in a wreck last night and got your brains rattled." The paper cup protested as his fist tightened around it. "He banned me from visiting you at the house, and he strongly suggested I not call either."

"Maggie," I said.

"Maggie," he agreed. "I respect the hell out of your dad, but that was dirty pool. You're my partner, and my friend. I deserve to be there when you need me."

"I'll talk to Dad."

"I assume since you're here and he's not that you've broken out of prison, aka your house, and that your dad has no idea where you are."

"Nailed it in one." I pushed spilled sugar granules around on the cracked Formica. "Tell me what you know so far, and make it quick. I can't stay here long. It's the first place he'll search for me."

"The blood collected from near the school?" He raised his eyebrows to make sure I was following along. I rolled my hand until he got the hint and continued. "It's human. It's type A. Maggie's blood type. DNA results will take a couple of weeks."

"So not blood from the stray." I drew a swirling pattern with my fingertip. "Did you follow up with Robert Martin?"

"No, I didn't." He crammed the rest of his snack into his mouth then washed it down with steaming joe. "Not our case, remember? They gave this one to Dougherty and Buck."

"Slip of the tongue." I had anticipated the case being handed off, just as I'd known he would keep a hand in until Maggie was found. So I pushed. "What about Martin?"

"Dougherty interviewed him this morning. He admitted to backing over a dog, almost pissed his pants thinking the owner had brought charges against him. He corroborates the story you were told. Maggie saw it happen, rushed over and scooped up the animal, and he offered to drive her to the vet. The local office was closed, so they headed out of town. He claims they spent the better part of an hour there but left after the animal's condition was considered stable. He dropped her off at the school around seven forty-five, then went home to bed."

"Witnesses?"

"The vet's receptionist, Jennifer Stanley, confirmed a man and a woman arrived together. Maggie insisted on paying the bill, so her name was on file but not the man's. Ms. Stanley was shown a photo of Martin and positively identified him. And get this—" he leaned closer "—Maggie asked to use their phone. Ms. Stanley believes the party she called didn't answer. She couldn't make out what was said, but she got the impression the conversation was one-sided."

"Has Dougherty pulled their phone records yet?" I huffed out a breath that sent sugar swirling. "We've got to nail down that voicemail."

"He's cutting through red tape as we speak," Rixton assured me. "I offered to sharpen his scissors if he needs help."

"Good." The mention of scissors had me picturing Maggie making victorious snipping motions with her fingers across the edge of my palm the last time she beat me at her favorite game. Massaging the ache behind my breastbone, I drummed my fingers on his wrist. "I almost forgot. I have her phone. She left it at my house that morning. Dad must have pocketed it last night."

"Ask him to drop it off when he signs in." Rixton's expression grew thoughtful. "I don't know how much use it'll be to Dougherty and Buck since she lost it prior to ..." His lips mashed together. "Still, I'd rather we had it than didn't."

My thoughts exactly. "Anything else?"

Rixton did me a solid by ignoring the catch in my voice. "Ms. Stanley estimates Maggie left with Martin around seven."

"The school would have been deserted at that hour. Do they have any overnight security?"

"Nope. We loan out an officer during school hours to the high school, but not to the middle school or the elementary. However, the proximity of the elementary to the high school means the premises are often vandalized during football games. They have a decent security system in place. I believe Mr. Druthers, who owns the home security company off Handover Street, donated the equipment."

Thank God for free advertising. "When do we get our hands on the footage?"

"*We* don't." He dusted his hands. "But I hear Dougherty will have a copy by the end of business today."

"What's with the resistance I'm sensing here?" I leaned forward. "I know you want in on this too."

"Chief Timmons was asking around about you today. He heard about the tiff at Hannigan's, and he's got his bloomers in a bind. You know how much he loves the press. I get the feeling he's sizing you up to be a sacrificial lamb to earn some goodwill in the papers. We've got two open missing persons cases, and that doesn't happen in a town this size. Not to mention Jane Doe. People want answers, and he doesn't have any. The Claremonts are vocal about wanting their daughter back, and they've got nothing on Maggie's folks once the shock wears off and they get organized."

The fact that Maggie's parents let Justin do all the talking for them where I was concerned hadn't slipped my notice. They had never approved of our friendship, but I'd hoped they would overcome their prejudice for her sake. Snubbing me despite my affiliation with the department told me loud and clear they weren't interested in my help. Too bad they were getting it whether they wanted it or not.

"I wondered when the chief would be ready for his close-up." I propped my elbow on the table and rested my chin in my palm, pretending the slight from the Stevenses didn't hurt. "Speaking of Jane Doe, I found out who hired White Horse to guard her." He didn't blink, and a red haze shrouded my vision. *"You knew?"*

"I suspected." He ducked his head. "This week kicked you in the lady-junk, and I didn't want a spot in line. Plus, your dad is a crap liar, so I figured you two would have it out soon and you obviously did."

"He paid Cole to shadow me." I savored Rixton's apparent shock. Guess he hadn't put two and two together, which made me feel better for sucking at the same math. "That's why Cole went ballistic at Hannigan's."

"No offense, Luce, but I doubt money had anything to do with his reaction. You don't manhandle a woman in front of any man with a soul and expect to strut away without consequences. You sure as hell don't rip off a woman's shirt for a peek and snap photos you plan to publish later. I would have ripped the guy a new one if Cole hadn't lost his damn mind and almost done it for me."

Any argument I made past this point would make it sound like I cared what Cole thought of me. Sure, he had a white-knight complex that explained his choice in logos. And yeah, he'd held my hand that one time for so long my arm went numb. And okay, so I might have an excess saliva problem around him. But he had been paid to look twice at me, and I had trouble getting beyond that. Good thing I had more pressing matters than worrying about a guy with one foot already across the county line.

"A little bird told me the Feds will be rattling some chains later today," he said, lining up his shot and tossing his empty cup in the trash. "Kapoor is swinging by to pick up the hard-copies on the Claremont case."

"I'm guessing we've been cut off cold turkey on that front." I hadn't been a cop long enough to forge my own contacts within the FBI, and Dad milked his sparingly since working for such a small department hadn't given him many opportunities to rack up favors higher up the food chain either. "If Dougherty proves a connection between the two incidents, Maggie's case will be absorbed into their investigation."

A knock on the doorframe had us both turning. This was a common area, but the trainee had obviously not wanted to interrupt an intense conversation.

"There's a guy at the front desk." He pointed over his shoulder. "Says he's here for a meeting with Officer Boudreau."

"You've got to be kidding me." Rixton chuckled under his breath. "This I've got to see."

He jumped to his feet. I was slower to follow, and not just because of my head injury. The trainee waited on us to join him then led the way up front. Skin prickling from all the unwanted attention, I suppressed the urge to rub my hands up my arms.

One of the girls from dispatch caught my eye, shot me two thumbs up and mouthed, *Yum.*

"I didn't know tall, dark and mountainous was such a turn-on for so many women." I kept my voice pitched low, but Cole turned as though he had heard me. "He ought to smell like pine boughs or mountain streams."

"Do you hear yourself?" Rixton quirked an eyebrow at me. "It's like you're spouting the script for a men's body wash commercial. Do you like this guy or something?"

We reached the desk before I formulated a response, and

the trainee vanished behind a stack of boxes. Poor kid. He was scanning old case files into the new system. I remember those days. Good times. No. Actually, they weren't.

"Hiya, stalker." I waltzed right up to Cole. "How can I help you?"

"You drove yourself here."

Despite the fact he had made it a statement, I couldn't help asking, "Your point?"

"You blacked out this morning. You're suffering memory loss." He loomed over me. He seemed to enjoy that. Looming. He stuck out his hand. "Give me your keys."

What?" Rixton attempted to join in the looming, but he lacked the height for it. Plus, I had seen him wearing Sherry's panties once on a dare. After that, a guy loses the intimidation factor. And my respect. "Is that true?"

"Yes." No point in denying it when Cole looked seconds away from patting me down until I jingled. "I drove thirty-five the whole way here. It's fine."

"It's not fine." Rixton's expression soured. "You've got to take better care of yourself."

"Maggie needs me," I growled. "I can't sit on my hands and hope someone else brings her home."

"No one's asking you to do that." He jabbed a finger at me. "But you've got to use your head."

"She can't use her head." Cole stared down his nose at me. "She almost cracked it open last night."

I spluttered as the guys ganged up on me.

"Luce, please," Rixton pleaded. "Let me drive you home. Don't want to go there? I'll drop you off with Sherry if your old man's smothering you."

"I'll take her home." Cole made it sound like a foregone conclusion. "I'm sure her father's looking for her by now."

"I'm not a kid. Don't treat me like one. You're not getting paid to paddle my ass and drop me off on the porch. Oh wait. That's right. You got fired. You're not being paid at all." A growl rumbled through Cole's chest that turned heads in our direction. "I take the coddling from Dad. He's earned the right." I drilled my finger into Cole's chest. "You haven't."

"I can get Donaldson to drop you off," Rixton offered. "Give yourself twenty-four hours to rest."

"The first twenty-four hours are the most critical." He couldn't argue with me there.

"You're no good to Maggie like this. Do you think she'd want you to kill yourself searching for her?" He softened his voice. "I'll keep you in the loop. Updates every two hours, I swear. Tomorrow, if you're stronger, then we'll hit this hard. Together. Deal?"

I glanced between them. "Do I get a choice?"

"No," they said together.

"Were you dropped off?" I sighed in Cole's direction and accepted the inevitable. "Or is someone waiting on you?"

"I told them I'd catch a ride." He didn't rub it in my face that he was right. But he sounded so sure he would get his way I wanted to kick him in the shin. "I'll drive you home, if you'll let me."

If. That was the biggest concession I was likely to get from him. "Fine." I dropped the keys into his palm. "Rixton, you're a traitor, and I expect a text from you in two hours on the dot."

"Love you too, Bou-Bou." He danced out of reach of the punch I swung at his face. "Testy, testy."

"I'm going to murder him one day," I confided in Cole on our way to the Bronco. "He's going to call me the right nickname at exactly the wrong time, and I'm going to poison his donut or cut his brake line. Oh! Or I could drop him in a vat of acid."

Except, knowing my luck, he would survive, wake up believing he had super powers, and then use the experience as an origin story for his inner supervillain. As flattering as having an arch nemesis might be, I didn't have time for monologuing with one. Also? Sherry deserved better than to be damned to a lifetime of laundering unitards. Especially considering the aforementioned panties incident.

"No, you won't." He opened the passenger-side door for me. "You're a cop to the bone. You wouldn't do anything to jeopardize your career."

Alone in the car, I admitted to myself that he had a point. I did love my job. I loved Rixton too, in the way little sisters must love big, overbearing brothers. Dad's heart would break if I got brought up on murder charges, and prison was not kind to fallen officers. So, when the time came, and Rixton uttered the last Bou-Bou that broke this camel's back, I would just have to make very sure I didn't get caught.

Knuckles rapped on the glass, and I frowned at a man of average height with tan skin, dark hair and the eyes to match. His smile was all boyish charm, a stark contrast to his serious outfit. Black tactical pants bloused over his gleaming boots, and a flak jacket zipped over his T-shirt. I absently wondered if Ranveer Singh, the famed Bollywood hottie, had a younger, more bullet-resistant brother.

"Ms. Boudreau?" He lifted his wallet and flashed me his badge and ID. "Can I have a moment of your time?"

Aware Cole had frozen in his tracks at the hood of the Bronco, I lowered the window. "Sure." I studied his credentials and decided to prod his ego a bit. "What can I do for Agent Farhan Kapoor, FBI?"

"Special agent," he corrected without losing his grin. "Actually, I'm the SAC on the Claremont case." The Special

Agent in Charge took my hit to his credentials on the chin. "I believe I have you to thank for laying the groundwork for me. The file you compiled saved us a lot of time."

"You can thank my partner while you're at it." I jerked my chin toward the station. "He's at his desk."

"John Rixton." The name rolled off his tongue without a hitch. "He's got an excellent record, a few commendations. I saw at one point he was interested in a job with the Bureau, but he withdrew his application. How did you two end up together?"

This was the first I'd ever heard of Rixton showing interest in the Bureau, and I could tell from the way Kapoor watched me digest the information that he'd meant to tip me off balance. Well, mission accomplished.

"His previous partner was killed in the line of duty." The statement came out hard, raw. "He was given two weeks to grieve, then was stuck with a green kid fresh out of the academy. We've been together ever since. The end." From the corner of my eye, I noticed Cole's slow prowl closer to the agent. "Now that story time is over, what's the real reason you stopped me?"

"I heard a friend of yours who worked at John W. Rosen has gone missing." He gentled his tone. "I was hoping you might give me a heads-up if you think the case is about to land on my desk."

"Luce was in an automobile accident last night," Cole rumbled. "She sustained a head injury and is in no condition to do your job for you."

The venom in his voice drew me up straighter in my seat. Interesting. Did this mean the FBI had stepped on White Horse's toes in the past? Kapoor in particular? I couldn't see the two working together. Not when Cole had already proven he did not play well with other authority figures.

"I'm sorry to hear that," Kapoor murmured and passed me a

card from one of his many pant pockets. "Call me when you're feeling better."

"Sure." I skimmed over his info, including his private line written on the back in fresh ink. "I'll do that."

He turned on his heel and left, tossing me a wave over his shoulder as he vanished into the building.

Cole watched him leave before joining me in the Bronco.

"What's his deal?" I thumped the card. "Is his name worth the paper it's printed on?"

"He's good at what he does," was all Cole had to say about that. "What you said back there—" He toyed with the vents until cool air blasted us both. "You replaced Rixton's partner?"

"No. People are irreplaceable." My chest caved at the idea of losing Rixton. "We almost killed each other the first six months. He resented me, told me I'd gotten where I was because of my dad, because of my . . . celebrity. He called me . . . " I cringed to remember those early fights. "But I was determined to prove I'd earned my badge, and I knew I'd lucked out with Rixton. He's got a brilliant mind, and he's all heart. After all these years, it still matters. It all still matters. Some cops go cold, but he gets hotter with experience, more determined to do all he can."

Cole blinked at me a few times, a twitch in the skin between his brows. "I would never have guessed that based on how close you are now."

"Yeah, well." I shrugged. "One day I was in town picking up groceries. There was this guy, Donny, the town drunk. He checked out ahead of me, and we walked out together. His buggy clinked the whole way to the curb. He reeked of cologne, like he'd drank it to mask the liquor on his breath. He didn't bob or weave. His steps were even, like he'd counted each one from the door to his truck. I had no reason to stop him, but I couldn't let him go.

"I stood there beside the Bronco, keys in hand, wondering how much he'd already had to drink, how long it would be before we got called about him streaking past Orville Baptist Church." I waved a hand. "Anyway, this brunette bombshell was strutting through the parking lot, deep in conversation on her phone, not paying attention to her surroundings." I snapped my fingers. "It happened that fast."

"He hit her."

"Nope." I hooked my thumb toward my chest. "He hit *me*. I saw him about to cream her, and then I was there. Right there. I shoved her out of the way, and took the full impact. I was lucky nothing was broken. I was just bruised up for a few days."

"That was lucky," Cole agreed too easily. "But what does that have to do with Rixton?"

"The bombshell was Sherry. She was on the phone with Rixton when it happened." I sank into the seat. "She didn't know who I was, didn't even know I'd been assigned to him. Six months, and he hadn't mentioned me to her once. She was pissed he wasn't dealing with his grief, pissed at how he lets the what ifs eat him alive, and she was pissed at me for letting him get away with stonewalling me."

"You three faced me as a unit at Hannigan's," he mused. "Now I understand why."

"Sherry was the glue that held us together until we stuck." I adjusted my vent to give my fingers a task that wasn't picking at my nails. "There's nothing I wouldn't do for her or for Rixton."

Or for Maggie.

The last name went unsaid, but Cole nodded as though he'd heard, as though he understood loyalty.

I liked him better for it, even if he had proven his could be bought.

CHAPTER TWELVE

———◆———

Halfway into our trip, Cole's phone trilled its trademark *briii-iiiing*, and I reacted too late to stop the full-body shudder that worked through my limbs. Since the ringtone hadn't been his choice, maybe I could sweet talk him into picking a new one. One that didn't lodge my heart in my throat each time I heard it.

Each *briiiiiing* landed in my ears like a hammer on an anvil, cracking open my façade.

Oblivious to my scheming, he answered with a gruff, "What now?" His grip creaked on the leather of my steering wheel. "I see." He cut his gaze toward me. "We're on our way."

"Change of plans?" I toyed with my seatbelt to curb the urge to shake the information out of him.

"That was Miller. He showed up to relieve Thom and noticed Jane Doe's got a nasty shiner and bruising down one side of her body." A cold glint lit his eyes. "No one entered that room without an escort and a damn good reason for being there. Jane wasn't left alone with any member of the hospital staff, and my people don't leave their posts. Staff bathroom breaks are handled in Jane's room, and food is sent up to them."

"Could the injuries be self-inflicted?" I scraped my bottom lip with my teeth. "We don't know why she was out in the swamp, and she hasn't remained conscious long enough for a psych eval. We can't afford to make any assumptions about her mental health without information to back up the supposition."

"Just like that?" He couldn't help but crane his neck at me. "You're not going to implicate my crew?"

"Um, no offense, but if your crew bungles a protection gig by beating the crap out of your client, you deserve what's coming. All that media attention? You don't want that. No one wants that. Inviting it would make your crew stupid for being reckless, and that would make you an idiot for hiring them. You're a lot of things, Cole, but dumb isn't one of them."

"High praise coming from you."

"There's also the fact that Dad hired you. Do you honestly think he would have done that if he hadn't dug so deep into your background he could tell me at what age you potty trained? Hey, eyes on the road." I rapped my knuckle on the windshield to get my point across. One near-death experience was one too many for me. "He would have called in favors to investigate your crew too. That's not saying people can't hide smudges on their records." Cole's disbelief at me asking him to wait for the cops at Hannigan's told me any public records only scratched the surface of his operation. "More than that, Dad's been a cop for a lot of years. His friends have been too. If he thinks you're competent, and since you managed to part the man from his wallet, I'm saying he does, then I'm not wasting energy casting shade at your crew."

His lips dipped at the corners. "You're too trusting."

"You are the first and probably last person to ever say that about me." The list of people I allowed into my inner circle was short: Dad, Maggie, Rixton, Sherry. Not a whole lot of room for error in there.

"Records can be doctored. Files can be lost. Images can be manipulated." Softer, he said, "People lie."

"Oh, I don't know." I couldn't resist teasing him. "Haven't you heard? Jails are full of honest criminals."

"Why do you do it?" His thumbs traced the leather stitching. "What about the job appeals to you?"

Cole hadn't outright mentioned my foundling status. He'd skirted it once or twice, and that was as near as I wanted him getting to my past, but I could tell him this.

"Dad is part of the reason. I admire him, always have. The job didn't shape him into the man he is, but he fits the mold. I wanted to fit it too." I wanted to belong, and the department had seemed like a big family to me that only required a piece of paper to join. I had earned my certification, but it wasn't the golden ticket I had imagined it to be.

"And the other part?" He pressed like the answer mattered to him.

"The first emotion I can recall experiencing in my life was terror, and I've never stopped being afraid." Of who I was, what I was, of learning the answers at last and then having to live with them. "I don't let it dictate my life anymore, but it's always there. The only thing that ever made it better was, again, my dad. When I had nightmares, I would climb on his lap. Even though I was too old for him to baby, he would rock me in his recliner until I fell asleep. He was always in uniform. He worked a lot of overtime back then to compensate for his instadaughter." Never once had he uttered a complaint or made me feel like a burden, even one taken on gladly. "I came to associate feeling safe with the press of a cold metal shield beneath my cheek. The badge is a talisman. As long as I'm wearing it, I'm . . . okay. Safe."

Cole's knuckles whitened as his fingers clenched, but he didn't speak.

I wasn't sure what to say either. I didn't open up to people easily, but Cole had a knack for prying answers out of me.

The tension lingered until I felt obligated to fill the silence.

"What about you? Most guys I know in security are either ex-cops or former military. Am I getting close?"

"I've served," he said cryptically. "The skills I learned are best suited to this line of work. I don't have a calling. I don't take comfort from the job. I have bills, and this pays them."

Each time I asked about his work, I got the same answer. It was a sore spot for him, but I couldn't imagine why that might be. He was a success from my point of view. But then again others might say the same about me.

We didn't talk again until we reached the fourth floor. A hospital-issued security guard stood across from Miller, and the two men appeared deep in conversation. Thom exited Jane's room as we approached and waved us over, ignoring the new guy who brought a radio to his lips.

Once inside, Thom crouched on the floor, craned his neck and sniffed the air.

I edged around him while he did whatever it was he was doing and approached the bed. Jane had one hell of a shiner, and her jaw was swollen. Dark bruises spread down the left side of her throat and vanished beneath her hospital gown. I tightened my jaw to keep from snapping demands for an explanation when it was obvious we had none.

"When did this happen?" I examined her for other signs of disturbance and found grit on her soles and on the sheets near the foot of her bed. "Do you see this?"

"I do." Cole walked the floor, staring at the gray-flecked linoleum squares. "There's some residue here too. It's crunching under my boot." He mirrored Thom's position and swiped his finger in a line, then lifted them to examine. "Grit this small and pale makes me think sand. Thom, call Portia down here with a kit. I want samples of this and scrapings from the bottoms of her feet."

"We should call the station and report this." I left the cover folded above her ankles. "Either she's sleepwalking or—Honestly? That's all I've got. How else would she have grit on her feet?" I faced Thom. "Who found her? How was she discovered?"

"Miller heard a thud, went in to check on Jane and found her sprawled on the floor. He called me, and since I was in the lobby, I came right up to help secure the area while he reported the incident to the hospital's chief security officer."

"Thom," Cole prompted, and the man stood and left.

"I wonder what's up there." I tilted my head back. "Looks like a standard drop ceiling. Those aren't sturdy enough to hold substantial weight. No one could have crawled across it, climbed down and beat her with a sock full of quarters, then left the same way." I smirked at him. "There goes my ninja theory."

"Not many people think to look up," he observed with approval.

I debated offering him a confidence, then decided it was in his nature to dig to the root of a problem, the same as it was in mine. He would have sought out articles about me before accepting Dad's offer, and he would have seen most of the images that filled my scrapbook online. Leaving me no secrets worth keeping. Save the one.

"I have newspaper clippings of me sleeping in a hospital bed, curled up around a teddy bear one of the volunteers sewed. The angle meant it had to have been taken from above." I scanned the ceiling one last time. "That picture meant enough for someone to belly crawl and violate a child's privacy. People are more entitled now than they were a decade and a half ago, not less. I wouldn't be surprised if we discovered similar images for Jane online snapped courtesy of a drone hovering at the window or a nurse wired for video."

His firm lips mashed together. "That's why you fought so hard against going to the hospital."

"One of the reasons." The other being Dad had hammered it into my head I had to avoid them at all costs. As peculiar as I was on the outside, I had quirks inside too. Ones my doctors had taken a keen interest in, ones Dad had refused to allow them to verify. "Mostly I hate hospitals." Worried every time I walked into one I might be hauled down to some secret basement laboratory never to be seen again. "Doctors aren't my favorite people either."

Thom reappeared with Portia in tow before Cole pressed for more details, and relief swept through me.

"Hey, lady cop." She carried a bag over her shoulder and dropped it on the floor with a thud. "Good to see you again." She cozied up to me with an air of expectation. "So what have we got?"

"Good question." I checked with Cole to make sure he was cool with me giving one of his people orders. He didn't bat an eye. "Can you grab a sample off her feet and maybe one off the floor? Do we have a way to make discerning a pattern easier? I'd like to know if she got up under her own power and where she went."

"There's only one way out that's not through that door," Thom murmured, and we all glanced at the window.

"We're three stories high. That window won't open." I crossed to it and hesitated with my hand above the thick black trim. "Can you dust this for prints? Hers are in the system now. We can check for a match."

"Sleepwalkers have said and done many a bizarre thing." Portia set to work, and we all stepped back to give her room. "I read about this one case where a guy dressed for work, drove himself to his law practice, then fell asleep behind his desk. A paralegal found him wearing a sundress and made up like a hooker the next morning. He blamed it on sharing a closet with his wife." She wiggled her eyebrows. "Except there were pictures of her, and she was a wee thing. No way was that dress hers. The makeup was too dark for her complexion too, but it worked for him. You ask me, the guy's subconscious basically outed him as a crossdresser."

"Are you saying her subconscious told her to beat the crap out of herself?" I studied the room again. "What would she have used? And what about the sand? There's none between here and the parking lot. She had to have picked it up from this floor. Someone must have tracked it in."

"We can't test the soles of every person who's been in here. For one thing, it would take forever. For another, most people wouldn't agree to it considering we're not cops, and they don't have to play nice with us. Particularly when we're attempting to nail someone for assault." She flipped the cover over Jane's feet when she finished. "What would it prove anyway?"

"You're right." I massaged my forehead, the right side of my head throbbing, and conceded the point. "I'm going at this from the wrong angle."

But the only other option involved Jane letting herself out

the door, one guarded by a White Horse guard, and I didn't see that happening. The IV pole alone would make a stealthy escape impossible. Not to mention the fact she hadn't been conscious long enough to form full sentences, let alone plan escape routes.

"Are you in pain?" Thom crowded me, our arms almost brushing, and canted his head. "Your scent is off."

"Could you do me a favor and not smell me?" I was all too aware I hadn't taken an actual bath this morning, just hit the hot spots with a washrag. I didn't want a guy sniffing out things deodorant was meant to conceal. "Why don't you give Cole a workup and tell me what he ate for breakfast?"

Thom set off to do just that when I caught his arm. "I was joking." Mostly. "Just respect my personal bubble." I held out my arms to my sides and turned a circle. "All of this is *me* space. It's polite to keep outside someone else's *me* space."

"*Me* space," he repeated and took a healthy step back.

"That's perfect." Maybe I ought to open Wild Child Boudreau's Finishing School, cash in on my fame while teaching others as socially awkward as I once was the lessons in conformity hammered into me by the public school system. "Thanks."

Commotion at the door resulted in an eruption of medical personnel flooding the room.

A tall man with slicked back pewter hair dressed in a white coat paled at the sight of Jane's battered face. "I need to examine my patient and document her injuries." Two nurses flanked him. "I have to ask you to leave."

"Ms. Boudreau will stay in the room with Ms. Doe." Cole ignored the man's flushed cheeks. "Until we're certain of the extent and cause of her injuries, my client would prefer Ms. Doe not be left alone with hospital personnel."

The doctor's face turned a mottled scarlet. "Are you implying misconduct on our part?"

"I'm just doing my job." Cole spread his hands. "Same as you."

"Who, may I ask, is your employer?" The man whipped out a pad with his name stamped in gold at the top and a fountain pen that cost more than most shoes I owned. "I would like to speak with him myself."

"Sergeant Edward Boudreau." Cole pulled one of Dad's business cards from his pocket and passed it to the doctor. "Make sure you tell him how dinged up Jane is now compared to when she was entrusted into your care."

Snatching the card, he made a show of slashing notes with his fancy nib in his specialty ink.

"I've got to meet with a potential client in twenty minutes," Portia announced as she snapped her kit shut and joined us. "Do you want to keep this just in case, or should I take it?"

"I'll drop it off at home," Thom offered. "I'm headed that way to pick up supplies."

"Works for me." Portia saluted Cole then spun on her heel. "Guess I'll catch you guys later."

Thom prowled after her into the hall, leaving Cole and me to face down the syringe-slingers.

"I'll wait outside." His gaze raked over Jane, then swung his head toward me. "Right outside."

"We'll be fine." I flicked my wrist. "I promise to give a full oral report on our way home."

Cole grunted but shuffled into the hall, closing the door behind him. I crossed to Jane's good side and stood watch while the doctor examined her. Her breathing hitched when his fingers grazed her ribs, and the instant he touched the band near her wrist, her eyes popped open, malice whirring in their depths.

"Don't touch me," she snarled, her fingers curving into talons.

Having had my fair share of bad reactions after waking to find medical personnel huddling around me, I could hardly blame her for lashing out at them. It's what I would have done—had done—in her shoes.

"It's okay," I soothed. "They're just here to check out the bruising down your left side."

Her head whipped toward me. "Luce?"

"Hey, you remembered." I gripped the rail to keep me anchored. "Can you tell us what happened?"

"I don't . . . " Wrinkles gathered between her brows. "What happened?"

Where to start . . . "You were hurt." I kept my voice calm. "You don't remember?"

The white around Jane's eyes grew more pronounced as her gaze tagged each person in the room.

"Ms. Boudreau," the doctor chastised. "You're upsetting the patient."

Faster than I could snap at him, Jane's eyes rolled back in her head, and her spine bowed as a seizure gripped her. The nurses swarmed, shoving me aside until my back hit the wall, where I stood until they stabilized her before sliding out the door to join Cole in the hall.

"How is she?" he asked without missing a beat.

"Stable." I massaged my temples, pressure throbbing beneath my fingertips, the headaches so much worse since the accident. "I pushed her too hard."

"You're trying to help," was all he managed in response.

But deep down, I worried he saw what I was beginning to understand too. That Jane might start associating me with the vultures if she kept waking to find me hovering the second her eyes opened. Had she truly slept through my previous visit? Or had she faked sleep to avoid the avalanche of questions she sensed would snow her under if I caught her awake?

Our stealthy escape was ruined when I kicked over a foam cup, and clear liquid fizzled across the tiles. Miller, noticing the mess, waved us on behind his back and continued to argue with the same security guard. With him stationed at the door and the medical staff inside the room, they could hold down the fort without us.

My phone chimed on the ride down to the lobby. I checked the screen and groaned.

"Rixton says two of the homeowners from the Marsh Landing subdivision have reported 'monster alligator' sightings. The PD is blaming the news coverage for the paranoia. They have no plans to investigate but will pass on the information to MDWFP." I scrolled down further. "One homeowner claims they have proof. Bloody footprints on their driveway."

"Trophy hunters might have flushed out a gator." His thoughts echoed mine. "That would account for it being so far from the swamp. As for the blood, a bullet might have grazed it."

The subdivision was a long walk from the swamp, and a good distance from the nearest marshy area too. Gators were territorial. Only the introduction of a larger predator would send one scrabbling for cover in a subdivision. For the first time since rescuing Jane Doe, I recalled the bizarre rise in the water level that had rocked our small boat. The super gator we saw wasn't large enough to cause that displacement. Were there two of them? More? The beast we saw had to come from somewhere, right? Gators laid clutches of twenty to fifty eggs. Did that mean we ought to expect eighteen to forty-eight more complaints?

"Have you heard an update from the MDWFP about the super gator?" I made a grab for my keys in the parking lot. No surprise, I came up empty. Prying them out of Cole's fist would require a chisel and hammer. "I doubt the department checks back with them. It's not our jurisdiction."

"I'll have Thom make the call." He loaded me in my Bronco, hopped in beside me and rested his arm along the back of my seat. "You'll just sneak out to look at those prints if I don't take you, won't you?"

"Yep."

"I can't talk you into going home and napping?"

"Nope."

"Why are you interested?" His voice dropped an octave. "Do you think it's connected to the Claremont case?"

"Maybe," I admitted, as my stomach dropped into my toes. "I hope not."

One gruesome angle remained that no one had explored. Gators, as a rule, weren't man killers. They didn't waddle up sidewalks, pick out tasty morsels, then drag them back to their swampy lairs. They were ambush predators, preferring to ID potential quarry while submerged, leaving only their eyes and nostrils above the waterline. Plus, the distance was too great from the school to any decent hiding place. At the time the Claremont girl vanished, kids were loading buses and car riders were waiting on their parents to pull around the loop. A student or faculty member would have heard her screams, would have witnessed the attack. There would have been blood. Lots of it. Smears. Drag marks. *Something.* But Angel Claremont had vanished into thin air when help had been one cry away.

Still, these sightings meant we had to give credence to the grisly possibility that these super gators might be to blame.

"Did you see what Thom hit last night?" There was more

than one way to bloody an animal. "I heard it was a deer, but did you see it?"

His pause lasted longer than a simple yes or no required. "No."

"Is it possible he clipped a super gator? They're cathemeral, both diurnal and nocturnal." *Location, location, location.* Too many coincidences in a confined space. We were missing something. "We were in the right area."

"Anything is possible," he agreed with reluctance, and I got the strangest feeling he was holding back on me. "I can have Thom swing by the subdivision with the kit. He can't have gone too far." His sigh heralded defeat. "We can take samples and document the scene before it's disturbed."

"Let's cross our fingers the PD was the only phone call the homeowners made." I relaxed as he shifted into drive. "The last thing we need is a local hoping to cash in their fifteen minutes of fame."

CHAPTER THIRTEEN

The Upton family lived in a house identical to three others we'd passed on the way to their address. The subdivision was new, the landscaping vibrant-green despite the heat thanks to the liberal application of sprinklers, and every road past the front gate was as smooth as a baby's behind. That wouldn't last long. The heat and damp would have the asphalt cracking in a year or so, well after the last plots were sold to eager up-and-comers.

"The natives are restless," I murmured as we turned onto a cul-de-sac brimming with activity.

"Are you sure you want to go out there?" He parked at the curb of the nearest house and let me make the decision. "Is it worth playing twenty questions to get your answers?"

"Maggie is out there somewhere." I sucked in a deep breath and pushed out my anxiety. "She's worth this and more."

"Okay." He glided forward. "We do this your way."

The crowd parted at our arrival only to seal around us once

the engine died. My breathing hitched at the press of faces near the glass, but I tamped down the building panic and shoved open the door before I thought better of it.

"I'm looking for Mr. Upton," I said to the nearest body. "Can you point him out to me?"

"He's the one standing on the lawn holding the hose." The young man swept his gaze down me before settling on my face. "Watch out. He's paranoid someone's going to crush his stupid Bermuda grass."

"Thanks." I ducked my head then spun away from him. "I appreciate the warning."

Hands trembling at my sides, I pulled myself together. Expectation the crowd would recognize me and turn had me nauseated. It had happened before, and I figured it would again. Just hopefully not today. But the sight of these tracks put folks in mind of the super gator in the swamp, which reminded them of Jane, who reminded them of me.

Fifteen years of friendship is worth a few minutes of discomfort.

Squaring my shoulders, I set out for the driveway using my best all-business cop walk. A single *excuse me* passed my lips before Cole eased in front, acting as a cowcatcher to scoop the curious out of my path. I rested my palm flat against his back in thanks, his strength a comfort, and he shivered.

We broke from the herd, and I eased around Cole, figuring a badge might put Mr. Upton at ease. His lip curled at the sight of me. Before I could raise my ID, he took aim, cranked his wrist and loosed a pressurized stream of water at my face. A snarl ripped through the air behind me, and then Cole was there, lifting me off my feet and spinning us around, hunching over me so that he took the brunt of the impact on his shoulders. Icy water poured down his back, dribbling down his front to wet me, and fine mist sprayed the back of my neck.

"Canton PD." I held up my badge. "Lower your hose."

Cole's laughter hummed against my spine, more felt than heard. His grip loosened as the deluge dried up to a dribble, and his lips brushed my cheek. "Bet you've never said that in an official capacity."

"I've never been assaulted by a man wielding a hose, no." I hesitated. "At least not in public."

"Canton PD? Aw, *hell*. I saw you get out of the Bronco and thought you were more gawkers." Mr. Upton flung aside his weapon of choice. "Mindy, grab some towels!" He picked his way to us wearing cleats strapped over his tennis shoes. For aerating the soil maybe? "The crowd was getting rowdy, and I was trying to preserve the scene for you like they do on those police TV shows."

"We appreciate that." A quick examination showed I was dry except for a strip down my back that had poured over Cole's shoulder onto me. "Sorry to show up unannounced." I inserted myself between Cole and the source of his annoyance. "I was in the area and figured I could document the tracks in case MDWFP is interested in them later."

"Hi there, officers." A short woman jogged up to us wearing the same cleats over her flip-flops. "Here you go. Fresh from the dryer. I tumbled them to warm them up for y'all."

We accepted the towels and patted our faces dry then Cole moved on to blotting his arms.

"Do you mind if we take a look at the tracks?" I assumed the couple had been tiptoeing around their yard in an effort to keep off the concrete of their circle driveway. "We'd like to take some pictures and collect a sample of the residue."

"It's blood," Mrs. Upton told me. "You should have seen it earlier. It's mostly brown now from the sun baking it, but it was bright red this morning."

"We need to be sure, ma'am." Cole gave up on getting dry and passed back his towel. "If the animal is wounded, we need to be prepared for its aggression."

"Of course." She held the damp terrycloth to her chest and peered up at him. "The clearest tracks are over here."

"Hey," Mr. Upton barked. "Get off my lawn." He chased off the cackling teenager who'd dare breach the line, then resumed his position in the center of the yard with the hose in his hands. "You won't be laughing when I call your father with a bill for damages, Leeroy."

Tuning out the neighborhood drama, I joined Cole and Mrs. Upton. I'd noticed a few partial tracks lower on the driveway, but she was right. These were flawless. And they were massive. The wound must have been fresher when these were made, the bleeding freer. I could have popped off my boots and lined them up heel-to-heel lengthwise inside the print.

"Five toes, three claws." I snapped a series of photos with my phone. "That means a front leg was injured. See these slight points on the first three interior fingers? This is the left paw."

"How do you know so much about gators?" Cole took a few pictures of his own.

"I watch a lot of Discovery Channel." He didn't need to know I'd also nursed a crush on Steve Irwin, the Crocodile Hunter, for years. "Dad is big into educational television."

A car door slammed, and the crowd shifted in anticipation. Thom shoved through them, bumping shoulders and knocking one guy over who didn't move fast enough. I swung my head toward Mr. Upton, who took aim, but hesitated once noticing he held my attention.

"He's with us," I called and waved for Thom.

He strolled up the driveway, managing not to step on a single track without appearing to avoid them. He reached me and knelt, our elbows almost brushing. I shifted my weight, but he shuffled aside before I could move.

"*Me* space." He set the kit down between us. "I remembered."

The urge to pet him came out of nowhere. One did not pet grown men in praise for learning a new trick. But there was something about Thom. Perhaps it was his animalistic qualities that kept me puzzled as to how to react to and around him.

"Would you care to do the honors?" Cole asked as he *drip, drip, dripped* a safe distance away. He wiped his eyes, then flicked the water from his fingertips. "Thom isn't qualified for evidence collection."

"Sure." I cracked open the kit and did a double take at the high-end equipment. This stuff was so much better than the supplies I kept in an old metal ammo box in my trunk. "You guys have some mighty nice toys."

Thom fingered a glass vial. "Have you ever thought about working for the private sector?"

"Not really, no." I removed a folding metal ruler and placed it beside the cleanest imprint, then took another series of photos to show their length and width. I located a box cutter and used a packet of alcohol wipes to sterilize the blade, before scrapping flecks of dried blood onto a small piece of paper I then folded and tucked into an envelope. I didn't get much, but experience told me it would be enough. "Thom, can you put on this glove and collect a few blades of grass from that patch for me?"

"Oh dear." Mrs. Upton swayed on her feet. "Not the Bermuda."

Thom prowled into the yard in search of a saturated clump while I cleaned up my area and placed the samples in with the others taken from the hospital. I dusted my hands, noticing how gritty my evidence was, and examined the area.

"There are a few more prints near the cookout pad on the

side of the house." She wrung the towel in her grip. "We just had the pavers laid. We haven't even put the grill out there yet."

"Would you mind if I had a look?" I stood and followed her to a six-by-six pad of red brick pavers set in a herringbone pattern. Sand pushed up through the cracks, and a wheelbarrow full of the stuff sat to one side. A few yards away, on a tarp resting on the neighbor's side of the property line, heaped a mound of sand flattened by a recent rain. "Can I take a sample of this?"

Relieved I wasn't going to violate their sacred food prep area, she nodded. "I don't see why not."

I jogged back for another envelope and dropped a few pinches in before sealing it closed. A smaller print, this one with four toes, indicating a rear leg, made me pause. I took a picture of that too and then went to check on Thom. I had copies of the report Mr. Upton had called in, so I didn't need to question the couple further. They hadn't seen the animal, only what it had left behind in their yard.

The first thing I spotted when I rounded the corner of the house was Cole lowering Mrs. Upton to the concrete. Her legs had gone out from under her. Her husband wasn't in any better shape. He sat on the lawn, smashing the grass under his butt as he recoiled from a horror concealed by their minivan. Knowing I would regret this, I eased around the second vehicle and found Thom appearing confused as he held up an entire square of sod he had ripped from the earth.

"I didn't pull that hard." Turning his face into his shoulder, he sneezed as he offered it to me. "I tugged on a few blades, and the whole thing came up in my hands."

"It's fine." I carried the chunk of sod back to the kit, plucked a few promising blades then presented the square to Mr. Upton. "I am so sorry the tech got overzealous." Tech was a stretch, but we needed to cut and run. "He didn't mean to damage your beautiful lawn."

The poor man cradled the Bermuda patch against his chest. "Are you finished?"

"Yes, sir." I gestured for Cole and Thom to follow. "We'll leave you to, ah, perform triage."

We walked to my Bronco together, and I had my fingers on the door handle when someone tapped my shoulder. I suppressed a shudder and turned to find the same teenage boy who had pointed out Mr. Upton aiming his phone at my face.

"I thought you looked familiar. You're that girl they hauled out of the swamp when I was a baby." He kept his hand steady. Not a picture. He was filming me. "Your dad's a cop too, right?" He grinned at me in open curiosity. "Do you remember your parents? Your real parents? Where did you come from anyway? Is that girl in the hospital your sister? Are you runaways from some freaky cult?"

Cole reached over my shoulder, plucked the boy's phone from his hand, then hurled it at the pavement so hard the screen shattered. The hard shell bounced four times before spinning under the Bronco and staying there.

"Hey! That's my phone." The boy dropped to his knees and crawled under my vehicle to retrieve his device. "My parents are going to kill me. They just paid for an upgrade."

"Your parents love you. They won't kill you." Cole gripped my hips and lifted me into the vehicle. "I don't have those problems."

The kid paled and stumbled into the throng of onlookers, many of whom had no doubt recorded the entire incident. Sometimes I hate modern technology. Mostly on days ending in Y.

I waited until Cole had safely navigated us out of the subdivision to say, "Thanks." I adjusted the air vent to keep the chill off my damp skin. "For humoring me, and also for smashing that guy's phone."

"He's lucky it wasn't his face," he grumbled.

"I would have had to arrest you." I patted his forearm. "Assaulting a minor is a major offense."

He grunted in my direction. Clearly we needed to work on his sense of humor.

Flashing lights in the rearview mirror had me leaning over to check our speed, but Cole was within the posted limits. "What in the world?"

He coasted to a stop on the shoulder of the road and placed both hands on the steering wheel in clear view while I twisted around to get a look at the cop as he exited his vehicle. Ignoring the surly driver, Buck trudged through the high grass to reach me. He tapped on the window and waited for it to lower before leaning his forearm on the frame.

"Hey, Buck." I shoved him out of the vehicle. "What's up? We weren't speeding, my insurance is current and I renewed my tags back in February."

"You weren't answering your phone." He rubbed his nape. "Thought you'd want to know . . . " He loosed a frustrated noise. "We found a leg out on Barnes Road."

"A leg?" A stunned moment lapsed while my thoughts reordered themselves. "As in a *human* leg?"

"Well, it wasn't a turkey, if that's what you're asking." He dropped his arm. "Female, if the size is any indication."

"How fresh?" I forced myself to ask like I was talking about a slab of meat and not a person.

"Fresh." His lips pursed. "No decay."

My palms went damp. "How?"

"Animal attack as near as we can tell at this point." The radio perched on his shoulder squawked. "I have to get back.

I saw you pull out of Marsh Landing and figured you'd want to know."

"My cell must have died back there." I rubbed my palms on my thighs. "It's been getting a lot more action than usual the past few days. I'll get it charged. How long ago was the leg discovered? Has the scene been cleared?"

"About four hours ago. We cleared out about thirty minutes ago." He eased back a step. "Are you heading up there?"

Cole rested his wide palm on my thigh, and I jerked my gaze to his. Had another man done it, I might have taken it as a possessive gesture intended to stake his claim on me in front of a male he viewed as competition, but that was probably all the Discovery Channel talk catching up with me.

"It's not far," I told him. "About five minutes." Close enough one of the super gators roaming the subdivision could have hightailed it over there. "Are you going to drive me, or can I drop you off somewhere first?"

"You're not driving anywhere." He noticed the position of his hand, snapped it back to the wheel, then turned a snarl on me. "You're pushing yourself too hard."

"I have to do this. Please, Cole. Help me out here, and I'll go home and nap." I held my three middle fingers flush, then touched my thumb to my pink finger. "Scout's honor."

He eyed my hand with skepticism. "You were never a scout."

"You don't know that."

"There was no portrait of you wearing a Girl Scout uniform at your house."

"I forgot you saw my lifetime-achievement wall," I grumbled.

"This is the last stop," he warned. "I mean it."

I saluted him and then twisted back to find Buck chuckling under his breath.

"Thanks for the update. I appreciate it." I folded down my

visor and lifted a plastic gift card branded for a national coffee chain. "There's five *bucks* left on there. Go wild."

"Bucks because my name is Buck. Ha. Never heard that one before." He accepted the gift as payment for my pun. "I heard about the accident. I'm glad you're okay." He sized up Cole as he spoke. "Be careful out there. Call if you need anything."

"I will." Silly as it might be, it warmed my heart to know that Buck had my back. That was more loyalty than most offered me. "Thanks for volunteering to stay at the hospital with Jane Doe. That was—Thanks."

"No problem. Consider it a birthday gift." He patted the side of the SUV. "Now you can't say I never gave you anything."

Buck strode toward his patrol car, and we let him leave before Cole made a three-point turn to get us headed in the right direction.

"He's a good guy," I told Cole between directions a few minutes later. "He was in my class at the academy." His molars continued to seesaw as they had since Buck popped in on us. "He dated another girl in our group."

"You don't owe me an explanation."

"Maybe not," I mused, "but you've stopped grinding your teeth."

He did that growly thing under his breath and parked on Barnes Road. We got out and didn't have to look far to find the crime-scene tape strung between black tupelo trees where the sidewalk ended.

"What are you hoping to find that the others missed?" Cole ducked under the yellow streamers and entered the patch of forest. "The leg was found here."

"How do you do that?" Thom might be the Wild Man to my Wild Child, but Cole had his quirks too. "You're like a blood-hound when it comes to, well, blood."

"The ground is soft." Beyond this clearing, marshland waited, the only reason this stretch of trees hadn't been bulldozed to make room for yet another development. "See the ring of boot prints? People circled this area." He pointed out the center of the ring. "The leg must have been discovered there. No impressions."

"It was placed there for someone to find." This close to homes with kids who no more listened to their parents' warnings about not exploring the woods than I had as a child meant it was only a matter of time before the gruesome token was discovered. "There's very little blood. Whatever happened, it didn't happen here."

"This doesn't feel the same as the other incidents. The Claremont girl and your friend were taken with care that no one noticed when they went missing. This is the opposite. It feels desperate. It's a bid for attention."

I wasn't much for profiling, but I had to agree with him that the killer—how else did you come by a whole human leg?—was baiting us. "Do you think we're going to be finding the rest of the parts over the next few days?"

"It's possible. It depends on the reason for the kill and the purpose behind revealing it to us."

"An animal attack, that's what Buck said." I measured the distance from here to the water in my head. "It doesn't fit. There would be paw prints in ground this mushy, drag marks, slides. But there's nothing like that."

Cole pinched a leaf between his fingers and studied its veins. "Gators aren't this aggressive toward humans."

The way he said *humans*, so emotionally divorced from the word, sent a shiver up my spine. "How much longer do we have on those results from your lab?"

"It takes about sixty hours for results to get fast tracked through the system."

"That's still got the PD beat." Thom had asked me if I'd ever considered working in the private sector. I hadn't seen the appeal then, but I was seeing it now. "It takes weeks ... months sometimes."

"Do you want to take samples from here to add to your collection?" He stood and dusted his hands. "Should I fetch the kit?"

"We should talk about expenses. Your time is worth money, and I've been hogging you for days." I had a healthy savings account, another benefit of living at home. I would gladly invest in the hunt for Maggie. "Not to mention the tests you're running on my behalf." I stared up and up at him. "Invoice me when you settle on a figure, okay?"

Rather than answer, he strode back to the Bronco. For a guy who worked in security, who I was dragging deeper down the rabbit hole of police work, he wasn't pushing to charge me for all his billable hours. Rich people stayed wealthy by not spending their money. The same rule applied to seemingly well-off entrepreneurs. Yet he was tossing his time, his money, into the fire every minute he spent with me. Unless ...

"Do you require clients to pay a retainer?" I asked when Cole returned. "Am I burning through Dad's? Is that why you haven't shaken me down for all the work you've done?"

"Yes." Cole worked his jaw until it popped. "You're still on your father's tab. Satisfied?"

Not really. "You will bill me if I go over?"

"I'll invoice you if that's what you want." He opened the kit and passed over gloves. "Should I charge you for these too?"

"Why the attitude?" I set about collecting samples. "You're running a business, not a charity."

"You were wrong about me." The tendons in his neck

strained. "It's not always about the money." A dark flush swept over his cheeks, and he stalked off deeper into the woods.

"Wait." I sealed up my baggies, tossed my gloves and went after him. "Talk to me."

A growl pumped through his chest.

"*Cole.*"

The sound of his name brought him up short, and he paused in front of an ancient oak strung with brittle vines, but he didn't face me. "I never planned on charging you for any of this." His hands flexed at his sides. "You've been helping us with Jane and the Claremont case. I wanted to repay the favor."

"You don't owe me anything." I brushed my fingers against his. "I would have done this for them with or without you picking up the tab."

"I know that now."

"You don't have to sound so grumpy about me finding out." I pried his fist apart and slid my palm against his as I scooched close enough to glimpse his profile. "I'm glad you told me. It gives me a chance to thank you." I raised up on my tiptoes and pressed a kiss to the underside of his jaw, as high as I could reach without his cooperation. "Thank you."

His fingers contracted once around mine before he released me and shoved his hands in his pockets.

"I like you." I'm sure the tree he spoke to was very flattered. "But this—you and me—can't happen."

"Is the problem my dad being a client?" Conflict of interest was an understatement for how entangled we had become over the past few days. "Or me being an ex-client? Or my connection to Jane?"

"Yes." He latched on without specifying a qualifier.

"Okay, I can respect that." We each wrote our own code of ethics, and it was up to the individual to uphold them. "How about we call it even up to this point? No more freebies, okay? And maybe, if you need my help, I should work with one of the others instead."

"All right," he rasped, voice tight.

"Good. Okay. We're agreed then. We each go our separate ways." Except we had ridden together. "Starting tomorrow."

"Tomorrow," he agreed, the strain ratcheting his shoulders tighter.

"There are still a few hours left in today." I released an inward groan the second the words passed my lips. We stood yards from where a human leg had been recovered, we were knee-deep in an investigation without any authorization whatsoever to conduct our information gathering, and I was basically asking him out on a date when a relationship was off the table. "You know what? Never mind. I was way out of line. Forget I asked."

Slowly, he angled his body toward me. "What did you have in mind?"

"We could get takeout and go back to my place." An entire colony of fire ants must have been dumped down my nape for how bad it stung. "I'm not hitting on you." Except maybe I was a little. "I'm peopled out for the day, but I wouldn't mind some company."

Hello, contradiction.

"We could watch a movie or play a board game." I had a few calls to make to assure myself the ball was still rolling in Maggie's case even if I wasn't the one behind it pushing, but that was all the energy I had left in reserve. "Or maybe we could sit on the porch. The mosquitoes aren't too bad yet."

"You're asking me out on a date." A line appeared between his brows. "To eat, and watch television?"

The adorableness of his utter confusion was the only thing that kept me from snatching back the invite.

"Dinner and a movie is a classic combo. It's basically the definition of a date." I shoved him, which popped my wrist but didn't threaten to topple him any more than a breeze might level a fortress. "How do you not know this?"

"How many other men have you invited home with you?" His soft voice promised violence.

"That's a personal question." And I had no time for guys who looked down on women with sexual histories. As anemic as mine was, I still owned it. Another part of me sighed with relief at having pinpointed a flaw, a solid reason for being glad tonight was a one-time deal. "I don't recall asking you how many women you've invited back to your place."

"None." Cold. Flat. Dead. The word had no pulse. None. The man was serious. The mountain was admitting to never having been conquered.

Sweet baby Jesus.

CHAPTER FOURTEEN

Inviting a guy back to my place came with one huge drawback that was normally an asset. Dad. He would be pissed at the way I'd handled him earlier, tucking him into bed, then darting off without leaving so much as a note behind. He wasn't the type to call and ream me out over the phone. No, he stewed in his anger until it bubbled out of his pores.

"We don't have to go through with this." Cole sat beside me in the Bronco, both of us staring up at the front of the house. We had been parked in the driveway for a good five minutes while I studied which lights were on in what rooms while attempting to divine my father's whereabouts and mood from them. "I can call for a pickup."

"I'm a grown woman." I clutched the DVD rentals to my chest. A steaming bag of Thai carryout sat between my feet and perfumed the air with curry. "I can pick my own friends and make my own decisions."

Yes, it had been reckless to get behind the wheel in my condition, but fear drives desperation. Sometimes literally.

"Do you need this?" Cole reached between the seats and produced a small paper bag from the convenience store filled with nickel candies for Dad. A peace offering. Fine. Okay, a *bribe*. "You can breathe into it."

"You are no help." I snatched it from his hand. "Come on. Let's go face the firing squad." We got out and strode onto the porch together. I tested the front door, expecting to find it locked, but it swung open under my hand. Proof Dad was waiting for me. "Dad?"

"In here," he called from the kitchen.

"Hi." I lingered in the doorway with Cole a massive shadow behind me. "How are you feeling?"

Dad took a sip of his coffee, earning himself a moment before he answered. Once he set the mug on the table, he seemed to have come to a decision. "Better." His gaze hadn't stopped boring into Cole since we entered, and there was a weary set to his shoulders, a grimness in the twist of his mouth that set me on edge. "Cole and I need to talk."

"Dad—" I began.

"*No.*" The word lashed out at me, left me raw and stinging, his temper an exotic beast I had rarely glimpsed. "Cole, you and I are going for a walk. We're long overdue for a chat."

"He's right." Cole met his stare. "We should talk."

"Dad, it wasn't his fault." I couldn't let it go. "I drove myself to the station—"

"Cole." He stood and rinsed out his mug. "I'll meet you outside."

Our guest left on silent feet, a marvel considering his size, and I was left staring at Dad's bunched shoulders as he braced his palms on the edge of the sink.

"I was standing in the hall outside your bedroom the first time I heard that old phone ring, and I know it's called for you every year since on your birthday."

"W-what?" I almost swallowed my tongue.

"I paid a guy to take it apart and check for transmission equipment. I thought maybe it had been wired by some industrious bastard looking to get a story using you. When that dead-ended, I tried tracing the calls and got nowhere," he continued, huffing out a laugh. "People thought I was crazy. *I* thought I was crazy."

"You're not crazy. Or you're not alone in your crazy." I rubbed the sting from my nape as I recalled the myriad ways I had tried and failed to accomplish the same goal. *Like father, like daughter.* "Last month I bummed a Geiger counter off a friend and used it to test my room before, during and after the call."

"And?" He chortled. "Any luck?"

"None." I was on the verge of explaining why I had considered radiation as a possibility, but Ezra was a secret I had kept to myself for so long, I wasn't ready to share him yet. Not even with Dad. "I'd call it magic, but I'd rather learn I was radioactive, honestly."

It worked out well enough for Spider-Man.

"We're taught from a young age that magic is for books and movies." He pulled himself upright and looked at me with such pride it made my chest hurt. "Yet here you are. You're special, Luce. A gift. I've always known you were more."

Magic.

Special.

More.

I cringed away from the labels before they stuck. I was *other*. I had long ago accepted that. How else could I explain those calls? Or my arms? I didn't have special powers. I was just marked.

Was that magic? Or biology? And why would Dad bring up those things now when we usually worked so hard to ignore them?

"We never talk about the calls." I focused on that rather than on me. "I figured it was easier if you pretended they didn't happen. What's changed?"

"Cole's ringtone." He tapped the side of his head. "Hearing it was like getting struck by lightning."

"Yeah." A movie slid from my arms, and I bent to retrieve the case from the floor. "It spooked me the first time I heard it too, but Cole isn't responsible." I spoke over Dad's argument. "The caller is powerful. His magic, for lack of a better word, is in his voice every time we speak. Cole is a commanding presence, but he's just a man. There is no *zing*."

"Are you sure?" Dad searched my face. "I can't shake this feeling . . . "

Cops trusted their guts, and no argument I made was going to talk him out of believing his.

"Is that why you asked him to walk with you?" I sorted the movies into a neat pile. "You're going to grill him?"

"I want to hear his intentions from his own mouth." He made no apologies. "Having Cole in the house is like being in a dark room with a hungry tiger, and I'm wearing a raw steak tied around my neck. The tiger might not kill me getting at the steak, but it wouldn't feel bad if it did either."

"Is it okay that I brought him here?" I stopped fidgeting and really looked at him.

"Just be careful." He pushed away from the counter. "The way he looks at you . . . " He kicked a chair leg on his way past. "I'm a man, and I've given women that look often enough I recognize it."

"*Dad.*" I covered my hot cheeks with my hands. "He doesn't want a relationship with me."

Cole had made that much plain. This wasn't a date-date. It was more of a . . . friend date. Platonic even.

Except for that whole excess-saliva thing.

"That's what worries me." His voice carried from the living room. "Guys like him never do."

The door shut, and I got to work fluffing the pillows on the couch. That done, I arranged the containers of food, then set out glasses, filled them with ice, and then fetched the tea pitcher. Cole had chosen an action movie I'd been meaning to watch, and I loaded it first in case Dad opted to stay and chaperone until time for him to shower and dress for work.

I dropped onto the couch, took a sip and crunched on an ice cube.

Cole was not my mystery caller. I would know. Sure, they might both have deep voices. And yeah, Cole did growl. A lot. More than any man I had ever met. The caller tended to rumble and let his silences speak for him too. That was the thing. His silence. He spoke so little and so rarely that comparing the two men was like trying to identify an unfamiliar song used in the background of a movie. A couple of chords, a few words, that was all. A snippet. A taste.

As much alike as they might be on the surface, Cole lacked Ezra's magnetism. He was solid and fierce and powerful, but his was an earthy kind of appeal. Not the crackle of otherness that raised my arm hairs and wrung my gut into knots.

Speaking of knotted guts. . . Worry for Maggie beat under my skin in time with my heart. The quiet house provided no white noise to block out the frantic mantra playing on a loop through my head.

I will find Maggie. I will get her back. I will punish those who took her.

I had polished off half my drink attempting to clear the

lump in my throat when the front door opened. "Did you boys enjoy your walk?"

"Your dad showed me the woodshed." Cole twirled a bit of green between his fingers. "I noticed he has a sharp ax, a sturdy shovel and plenty of acreage."

"Oh, wow." I slow-clapped for Dad. "You really pulled out all the stops." To Cole, I explained, "Usually he doesn't imply his willingness to chop up prospective boyfriends and bury them on the property until the second or third date. You must be special to get the white glove treatment."

"Very funny." Dad folded his arms across his chest. "Cole and I have come to an understanding."

I raised an eyebrow. "One that involves death, dismemberment and backyard burial?"

"That's for us to know and you to find out if he hurts you."

The urge to roll my eyes twitched in my lids, but my headache prevented me from indulging.

"Are you going to join us? We stopped at Thai-Thai." I sank back into position and left it up to Cole if he wanted to sit beside me or in Dad's recliner. "There's plenty to go around."

"I can't. I have to shower and shave." He checked his watch. "Harry's picking me up early so we can grab a bite at the deli before our shift starts."

"Hmm. That's industrious of you." I tucked my legs under me. "I thought you had to be on the clock to get the discount."

"The uniform is all that counts." He dusted his hands together. "Harry called ahead to be sure the new manager hadn't changed things."

"I figured." I clicked my tongue at his retreating back, then returned my attention to Cole. "You've heard of extreme couponing? Well, those two could do a show for cops on how to ferret out the best food in town at the lowest prices with the highest discount."

Though the deli was one of the few takeout spots Dad was allowed to eat at with any regularity these days thanks to their heart-healthy menu options.

Most restaurants in town offered discounts for on-duty officers as a thanks for their service and as an enticement to keep a police presence in their establishments. Cops don't make much money, and patrol makes it hard to pack lunches and take breaks. Getting a hot meal with a smile and a side of conversation at the cost of a PB and J was sometimes the highlight of an otherwise disheartening shift.

Cole humored me with a fleeting smile that as good as said he had one foot out the door.

"You aren't staying, are you?" Needing a barrier between us, no matter how flimsy, I bent my legs in front of me, wrapped my arms around them and then braced my chin on my knees. "You can leave with your manhood intact, if that's what worries you. Braver men than you have been cowed by the woodshed."

"This was a mistake." Meltwater eyes fastened onto me. "There are things you don't know about me that make this . . . a bad idea."

"You could always tell me," I hinted with zero subtlety.

"No. I can't. I'm not sure I would even if I could." He rubbed a hand over his bristly scalp. "I called Santiago before I came in. We're driving the samples from today straight to the lab to trim down the wait time for the results."

"Oh." I flexed my toes, suddenly deep in thought about when the last time was I'd had a pedicure. "That makes sense."

"Luce."

"We don't stand on ceremony around here." I located the remote and hit play on the movie. "You can show yourself out."

Cole left without saying another word. Boots thumped down the porch. Boots thumped up the porch. Down. Up. Down. Each footfall an accusation. I imagined his pacing shook the house. The floorboards, which were twice my age and temperamental, groaned in protest. I tiptoed toward the bay window, then cursed. Someone had cracked the blinds. We never slitted those. Dad must have been watching for me and made an exception. Meaning Cole would have spotted me had he not been stomping off in the opposite direction.

Quick as a whip, I bolted for the couch where I dug into my plate and gave the movie my full attention. Mostly. Focusing was hard with him making so much racket.

Good grief. Was he *that* impatient to leave? Worried I might follow him out and invite him in again if he didn't rush away? Fat chance of that happening. I would gnaw off my own hand before using it to twist open that doorknob.

Tonight had been a whopper of a mistake. Clearly the guy had deeper issues mixing business with pleasure than I'd realized. Good thing I was off the Claremont case. Until a concrete link to Maggie was established, if such a connection surfaced, that meant he and I had no reason to socialize outside of hospital visits to see Jane. Though I had yet to see him on sentry duty. Maybe I'd get lucky and avoid him all together.

A low purring sound underscored a fight scene in the movie. Must be one in the fleet of SUVs White Horse owned. Unwilling to mute the TV, I strained my ears but didn't hear a door open or shut. I gave him ten minutes to get gone, then killed the movie and melted into the couch on a groan.

"It's for the best." I gathered the food containers and shuffled off in search of my laptop. I planned to set it up at the kitchen table and get some work done while shoveling in a double portion of gang massaman. Maggie's phone rested on the placemat next to my charging cord, and I trailed my fingers over its hard case. "Cole was a distraction. A *big* distraction. A distracting distraction."

As far as resources go, he sure came in handy, though.

By the time Dad popped his head in to say goodnight, I was too full to move but determined to plow through Cole's portion. Waste not, want not. I didn't want it, but I wasn't letting it go to waste like the rest of my night. Dad had the good sense not to ask where Cole was or why he had left. He also didn't appear too surprised to find me alone, so there you go. Mission accomplished.

"Do me a favor? Drop this off with Dougherty or Buck." I tossed him Maggie's phone. "That way the techs can comb over it, and her family can sign it out after if they want it back."

Wary of my pleasantness, he left in a hurry before I decided to get mad at him for spooking Cole.

Still, I wasn't all that irritated with Dad. And I couldn't work up a good head of steam over Cole either. He had already made up his mind about us—or the lack thereof—before I put my moves on him. Basically he had passed on us, and I had served him up a heaping helping of Luce regardless. No wonder the poor guy hadn't asked to take his food home with him. He'd lost his appetite.

Dad made me promise to lock up after him and reset the alarms, and I agreed without complaint since it forced me to stop wallowing. In theory. In fact, I wallowed for about an hour after he left. Had smoke not been curling off my scorched taste buds at that point, it might have taken me longer to summon the motivation to stand. I downed the first glass standing in the open doorway of the fridge. The second I carried with me into the living room to sip while I activated the security system. I pulled up short in front of the bay window, the open blinds drawing my attention. A menacing darkness tainted the shadows on the porch. They all stretched taller, darker than usual. All the super gator talk must be getting to me.

I twisted the blinds closed on a shudder then returned for the final standoff between me and the fifty thousand peppers they must have used in the curry sauce. I made it to the kitchen when the planks on the front room groaned. Old houses settled at night. That noise I was used to. But this was similar to how the wood had protested beneath Cole's weight.

I turned back to the living room, slowed my breath and strained my ears for hints about my visitor. A low hiss poured under the front door, and I forgot to breathe. Slowly, the protesting planks, the clack of nails, crept toward the bay window. I had my phone in hand a heartbeat later and made good time reaching the closeted gun safe.

"Something is on the porch," I said in lieu of a greeting while I loaded my weapon with shaky hands.

"Stay inside and keep away from the doors and windows," Dad barked. "Wait. What do you mean some*thing*?"

"You know how there's been a rash of super gator sightings?" I waited for him to confirm he'd been keeping up with the news. "I have a bad feeling—"

An explosion of glass tinkling onto hardwood startled a scream out of me. Where the bay window used to be, a reptilian *thing* as tall as a freaking pony shook the ruined blinds off its head. I backed slowly into the kitchen, tagging and dismissing possible escape routes. The front door was out. The path upstairs was blocked. That meant my only avenue of escape was through one of the windows. From the backyard, all I had to do was . . . Damn it. I double checked my pants. No keys. Cole must have hung them by the door on his way out. The Bronco was useless without them.

"Dad," I whispered, "it's in the house." Its roar shook the picture frames on the walls, and I swallowed to moisten my throat. "I have to go now. I need both hands." Uncle Harold shouted over my dad in the background. "I love you, Daddy."

I muted the phone and shoved it in my back pocket. Bracing the butt of the shotgun against my shoulder with one arm, I fumbled behind me at the nearest window with the other, locating and twisting the lock. I raised the sash, cursing at the noise, then kicked out the screen. A hiss rose behind me, and cold sweat glued my shirt to my spine. Panic drummed a tattoo against my rib cage, but fear kept hold of the reins. The icy calm I had come to depend on failed me. And then it was too late to find my chill.

The super gator was in the room with me.

I didn't give myself time to think. I raised the gun, shot out one of its vulnerable eyes, and leapt through the open window. The drop wasn't far, but the bushes weren't kind. Limbs scratched my arms and tore at my legs through my pants. I shoved the branches aside, got my feet under me and ran. Where to go? Our nearest neighbors were miles away, and that thing moved like lightning. Even half blinded, I was no match for it on my own. The shed was a wash. If it could knock out the bay window, it could warp the steel siding. The only choice I had was to run for the woods.

A furious shriek dumped adrenaline in my veins. Behind me glass shattered and a meaty body thumped to the ground. Its pitiful cries told me two things. I had hit where I was aiming. *Thank you, indoor range.* And it was pissed. Super pissed. Someone-just-exploded-its-eyeball-in-its-head pissed.

A stitch lit my side on fire, and I sucked in a sharp breath. I really ought to buy a treadmill. If I survived this, I was totally buying a treadmill. I pushed harder, faster, until I hit a dense patch of clover, chicory and cow peas. A food plot Dad maintained for the deer. That meant I was in the right area. I hadn't been down here in months. I had no idea where he'd set up his tree stand this time.

After several frantic minutes of searching his favorite spots, I located his new perch. I gauged the distance from the ground to the seat to be around twenty-five feet and decided it was as safe a place as any for what might be my last stand. My last stand. In a tree stand. *Ha*.

Oh, God. I'd heard about this. Gallows humor.

I was so going to die.

CHAPTER FIFTEEN

———◆———

Tree stands remind me of heavy-duty lawn chairs on the best of days. Ugly and flimsy came standard, and most setups left you exposed to the elements. The small platform attached underneath the seat as a footrest was hardly a deterrent. Not that most hunters had to worry about deer fighting back. At least its thick nylon straps provided some stability, and I would feel better with the trunk at my back. Since we were on private property, and Dad was getting to the age where putting it up and taking it down was a hassle, he mounted his in a permanent fashion and kept it covered with a tarp when not in use.

To reach his lookout, you had to use climbing sticks. The inch-square metal tubing ran like a spine from a foot off the ground all the way up to the seat. Every few feet a hand/foothold, about six inches of square tubing, branched off to make climbing easier. That was the general idea. It might have worked too if my palms hadn't been so sweaty they kept slipping off the ends, or if my knees hadn't been jelly, or if I hadn't been forced to tuck my shotgun under my arm to make the climb in the first place.

Leaving my back exposed inundated my thoughts with nightmare scenarios of being attacked from behind, dragged into the woods while I kicked and screamed, until the super gator devoured me in a single gulp. No. Wait. Gators thrashed and twisted to tear their meals into bite-sized morsels.

Not helpful, brain. Not helpful.

I cleared the first section, paused to free the straps, then kicked the metal spine to the ground. I did the same with the second portion. Three more remained, but I didn't want to screw myself if I ended up having to abandon this location and left them in place.

Dad was en route with backup, but I had no idea how long it would take for them to arrive and locate me. Until I saw lights or heard sirens, I was on my own.

I finished the climb, crawled into the chair and drew my first clear breath since I'd heard the bay window go. Fear had turned my arms as limp as overcooked noodles, and I rested the shotgun across my lap while I got my pulse under control. Tempted as I was to call Dad, there was no use tormenting either of us with false comfort. Plus, I didn't want the noise to attract the super gator. The stink of my fear would make following my trail easy enough. No point in waving a glowing phone screen under its nose too.

When my heart stopped clogging my ears, the first thing I heard was nothing. The forest held its breath, even the crickets tucked in their forewings. One ballsy frog croaked but the sound choked off, and I imagined the guy sitting next to him smacking him upside the head like, *Really? You want that thing to eat us next?*

A steady rumble, the rustle of a low body brushing the earth, a twig snapped beneath a heavy foot.

I had been found.

I lifted the gun and strained to see past the gloom. I wished I hadn't. The super gator was bigger than I remembered. More horse than pony. I hoped the angle was playing tricks on me. Eyes glittering in the moonlight, it entered the wooded copse and huffed a wheezing sound resembling laughter.

Sweat stung my eyes, and I wiped my face on my sleeve. That was the head injury talking. Bad enough a prehistoric relic had waded out of the swamp. I wasn't believing it enjoyed a sense of humor too.

The thing panted whistling breaths, its body built for bursts of speed and not for endurance. Now that it had me treed, it took its time circling my hideout. A hissing rattle vibrated its throat, and it scratched at the bark before hefting itself upright and sinking its front claws deep.

"Shoo. Go away." Panic lifted my voice an octave. "Go find yourself a nice, fat deer. They're high in protein, and they taste so much better than people. Seriously. You should try one and then report back."

Nothing I said or did made any difference, and I had too few bullets to fire them until presented with a possible kill shot.

Through sheer determination, the beast managed to climb a few feet before its weight hauled it back down to earth, leaving furrows raked into the trunk. I almost cheered until it bunched its muscles. Typical gators could jump up to five feet from a dead stop. This thing wasn't normal. I was guessing it could manage twice that if not three times the height.

Brain, we really need to chat about this factoid obsession of yours.

Town wasn't that far. Help could be here in fifteen minutes, maybe twenty. I'd hiked at least ten minutes to get to this point. A half hour. All I had to do was last thirty minutes, tops. I could do that. I gasped when the creature made its leap and snapped its jaws so close its fetid breath closed the distance. Each reset took it a minute, but it kept trying, gaining altitude with each lunge.

I was eyeing the limbs above me, debating their ability to support my weight when a grating rumble poured through the air, vibrating my bones. The thing aborted its next attempt and wriggled back a step. *No, no, no.* One was bad enough, big enough. There couldn't be two out here. The growl causing the metal beneath me to hum projected from a throat a lot bigger than the one I'd been staring down a moment ago.

The gun wobbled in my grip. I held on tight and tried again to find my calm, but my nerves were shot to hell.

What was that noise?

Then I didn't have to wonder.

"Son of a bitch," I breathed.

A second monster prowled forth, this one the cured ivory of aged bones. Moonlight caressed its faceted scales, glittered in its leonine mane and illuminated immense racks of branching antlers. The creature married the serpentine lines of a Chinese dragon with the sturdy arms and thickly muscled thighs of a European dragon. Its tail ringed the clearing, a whip of impossible length, and its graceful neck arched as it studied me through crimson eyes peering from a feline visage. I allowed myself a second or three, maybe five, to admire its regal beauty before terror set the muscles in my legs quivering.

Nope. Not happening. Not real. This was not real. Dragons weren't real. This was a stress-induced hallucination brought on by my head injury. I must have jarred my brain again when I hurled myself out the kitchen window. Was that part even real? Had any of it happened? Or was I home in bed sweating out the nightmare to end all nightmares?

The dragon—and it was definitely male—positioned himself

at the base of my tree, lowered his head and hissed through teeth as long as steak knives. The rattling noise it made had me leaning over the edge of my seat, peering down for a better look at the membranous folds it shook and puffed out to make itself bigger.

Wings.

It had wings.

Stick a fork in me, I was done. I was no princess, and this tree was no castle. The dragon wasn't guarding me. He was about to hand the super gator its ass and then flitter up here to gobble me up like a children's book gone horribly wrong. A frantic part of my brain shouted I should lift my phone and snap a picture to warn the others when they found my cell instead of my body, but I couldn't lift a hand. I was paralyzed. All I could do was watch and make my peace.

The super gator, pissed at the interruption, lunged at the dragon. Its teeth slid right off the thick scales covering his body. In retaliation, the dragon whipped its tail around and cracked the gator on top of the head. The gator roared its fury and charged again. The dragon, seeming bored by the confrontation, let the gator inside its defenses, then raked a gleaming talon down its side, gutting it from shoulder to hip.

Blood perfumed the night, and the dragon inhaled with delicate sniffs. Dazed by the promise of fresh meat, it didn't appear to notice the gator backpedaling into the shadows. The dragon lifted its front paw and licked its talons, cleaning itself the way a cat might. Only when he was spotless, the white of his scales flawless, did he turn his attention to me.

An inquisitive hum left its throat, and he waited as though expecting an answer.

"Hi, big guy." I wet my lips. "I'm pretty sure you're just the brain damage talking, but thanks for getting rid of that gator. Maybe you could not eat me, and we could both call it a night?"

The dragon twitched his tail, but I had no idea what he wanted. Except maybe a Luce kabob. A short growl later, he tightened his wings flush with his spine and sank his claws into the bark. Nimble as a jaguar, he climbed until his head hung at my eye level. Intelligence sparked in his gaze as he studied me, and white mist huffed from his wide nostrils. He angled his neck so as not to gore me with his impressive racks, then coiled his tail around the trunk, curling the spade-like tip around my ankle.

"I don't understand." Why speaking to him felt so natural, why I half-expected an answer, I had no idea. Brain damage. Had to be. Compared to dreaming him up in the first place, what was imagining he could talk too? "What do you want?"

Head the size of my torso, each tooth the length of my hand, he was no housecat for all that his mannerisms reminded me of one. A slivery tongue swiped across his muzzle, and the chill of his breath as his mouth opened made me shiver.

"I don't want to hurt you." I tightened my grip on the gunstock. "Let's hope you feel the same about me."

The gun was a comfort object at this point, the equivalent of a blankie for me to cuddle while I told myself everything was going to be okay. Figuring why the hell not, I might as well enjoy myself in the seconds before I became dragon kibble, I reached up and smoothed my hand across his wide brow. The beast cringed away from me, as though it feared my touch more than the weapon braced across my thighs. I was still marveling at the velvety softness of his antlers when a siren squawked in the distance.

The cavalry had arrived.

"You need to go." Shooing a dragon with a utensil drawer for a mouth seemed like a bad idea waiting to happen. "You hear that, boy?" I flashed back to the days of when I'd had a pet to talk to, though Yeller mostly ignored anything not gelatinous and sliming out of a can. "Those are my people, and they're good people, but they're worried about me. They're going to think you're the bad guy here."

The dragon's English must have been rusty. Instead of high-tailing it out of there, he flexed his claws as though kneading the tree behind me.

Out of ideas to save him, I lifted the gun and aimed it between his eyes. "Please, just go."

A huff of breath blasted my face as he sniffed the barrel and jerked back, eyes wide in alarm.

"I don't want to hurt you." I wasn't sure that I could, even to save myself. "I don't think you're real, but I can't live with you being harmed even in a dream."

A rasp of rough hide against fabric sounded as he unwrapped his tail from my ankle and then from around the tree. He didn't climb down the way he had come but flared his wings and leapt to the earth. A forlorn expression lit his eyes as he stared up at me one last time.

I was holding his gaze when the first shot hit its mark, and red blossomed on his chest.

"*No,*" I screamed. "Don't shoot. He didn't hurt me."

The dragon staggered, scraping at its torn flesh with a clawed hand, and tears filled my eyes. Through them I spied the glint of rose gold bands encircling its wrists, reminding me of a bracer strapped to a homing pigeon's leg, and wondered if this beast had a master who had tamed him, who would miss him if he failed to fly home.

Another bullet ripped through the dragon, and I leapt to my feet. Quickly, I emptied the chamber on the shotgun, then tossed it to the ground. I figured the risk of it going off on impact and hurting someone ranked higher than the super gator coming back for seconds. That done, I shimmied down to the end of the third section of the climbing sticks and let myself hang until I shut up the panicked voice in my head. I let go, hit the ground hard and rolled with my momentum. My ankle twisted, and I cried out from the pain.

The dragon, who appeared more confused by its wounds than afraid, snapped its head toward me. With a stunted roar, he flicked his tail at the officer and sent him flying before advancing on me. Tucking me against the warm scales shielding his chest, the beast climbed up the tree, past the canopy. Cinching his shorter forearms around my middle, he leapt from his perch. His pearlescent wings snapped out, saving us from freefall, and he pumped them until his speed caused my eyes to water.

I clung to him until my fingers went numb with cold and fear. The rush of altitude made my head spin, and I gulped down my rising panic. An inquisitive rumble all but asked if I was all right. I opened my mouth, tasting bile and Thai in the back of my throat, and my answer came out in great, wet heaves.

I really, really hoped no one was down there. Thai just wasn't the same the second time around.

A tickle of dread in my already tender middle was all the warning I received that a landing was imminent. The dragon flattened me against him and tucked his wings tighter against his sides. He dove, and I crushed my eyes shut. I didn't want to see. But I couldn't not look, so I stared up at the sky full of stars that appeared close enough to touch. Seconds later, he snapped open his wings, and we jerked hard as they caught wind and slowed our descent. Made clumsy by his burden, he grumbled a steady hum of irritation as he overcorrected his flight path. The sound of his claws scrabbling on wood made me giddy, and I stumbled out of his grasp, drunk on relief.

I'm alive. Don't know for how long. But it counts!

"Let's never do that again." My butt hit the decking before I realized my knees had buckled. As it turned out, my spine had also liquefied during the flight. I flowed backward until my head thumped on the wood, and I lay spread eagle, one knee half-cocked to the side. "Never again."

"Oh, I don't know," a familiar voice drawled. "It looked kind of fun to me."

Santiago leaned over me, sizing me up as though I were the real threat and not the freaking dragon who shoved him stumbling back with a pointed jab from his tail.

"Yeah, I get it." Santiago wobbled on his feet. "She's yours." His eyes narrowed. "What the—?"

The dragon's front legs wobbled, and then he collapsed. He lay half on top of me, and my bones creaked beneath his weight. The angle of my right knee was all wrong. Not broken. Torn. Impact had thrust it sideways to escape the pressure and ruptured the muscle.

"He was shot," I panted. "His chest."

"Damn it. Why didn't you say so?" Santiago stuck two fingers in his mouth and loosed a shrill whistle. "Bring the pliers." He looked back at the dragon. "And a knife."

Miller appeared with a toolbox in one hand and a machete in the other. "Luce." His eyes rounded, and he swung his head toward Santiago. "What did he do?"

Thom landed with a thud inches from my cheek. "He brought her home."

I might have asked what the holy hell all this meant, but Thom lifted my wrist and sank his teeth into the bone. I thrashed until he pinned down my shoulder. The bite hurt, God it hurt, but I didn't scream. Not until fire raced through my veins and left me nothing but ash.

CHAPTER SIXTEEN

———◆———

Vibrations under my left butt cheek drew a low growl of irritation from me. "Hello?" I waited but no one answered. Oh. Yeah. That only worked after I swiped. I reached under me, wiggled the phone out of my pocket, smeared my fingers all over the screen, then pressed it against my cheek. "Yeah?"

"Luce? Where are you?" Rixton barked. "I have thorns in places that have never seen daylight, a tick burrowed in my navel, and a rash resembling the Easter bunny on my throat. Me and thirty of our closest friends spent all night combing the woods behind your house. What in God's name happened? Where the hell are you?"

Hazy memories solidified into a nightmarish tableau that snapped open my eyes.

"Buck was attacked. He emptied a clip before backup arrived, but whatever bled out was gone when we got there. He sustained a head injury and his leg is broken, not that you asked. Now I'm going to ask one more time. Where. The. Fuck. Are. You?"

"I'm ..." I squinted against the sunlight pouring over the foot of my bed. No. Not my bed. "I'm ... hold on." The head rush as I sat up left me reeling. "I don't know where I am. I don't recognize this place."

"Luce?" Miller entered the room holding a soda, his gaze zeroing in on my phone. "Tell him you're fine and that you'll be home soon."

"Are you insane?" Stockholm Syndrome had not set in, if that's what he was hoping for, and no way was I telling my lifeline to call back later. I was clinging to Rixton until Miller pried him from my cold, dead fingers. "Where am I? Why am I here? What is that poking me in the—?"

Cole. I was in a bed. Cole's bed. He was stretched out beside me. Naked. A wall of hard, male flesh.

I shielded my eyes before they dipped past his navel. Okay, fine. So his happy trail dragged my gaze a skosh lower than his outie. The heat sparking low in my belly chilled to glacier coldness when I dragged my attention higher. Bandages covered his chest, and fresh blood seeped through them.

Cole slept with his head at the foot of the bed, and his wide palm wrapped my ankle in sleep. His watch and wristband had gone the way of his clothes, and both his wrists were bare. Thick scar tissue ringed each, and when I shifted my leg a fraction, dragging his hand into the light, a single rose gold band glittered in the valley created by the raised skin.

The first thought that balled tires through my head left me giddy. *Cole is like me, like Jane.* That meant he must have answers. The second slammed on the brakes. Hard. Cutting out the metal worked for a few days. I had no blemishes where the doctors had removed their test section on my upper arm. Regeneration had taken three days? Four? How many times must he have bled to earn those ridges? Over and over and over again. The third thought sat idle as I worked through the ways this could have happened. No matter the scenario, I came to the same end conclusion. He hated those bands. That's why he kept them covered, why he kept digging them out of his skin. Knowing I had seen them would leave him feeling exposed. Of that I felt certain.

A thrumming rattle moved through his chest as he resettled, the noise as close to a purr as human vocal cords could produce.

"*Luce.*"

Rixton's snarl snapped my focus back to him. "Give me two hours." I challenged Miller with my timeline, and he nodded agreement. "I'll meet you then and explain everything," I promised my partner. "Just don't rat me out yet."

"Your dad is pulling out his hair, and he didn't have much to start with. I can't keep this from him."

I made a fist in my lap. "Two hours."

He ended the call first.

"The dragon was real." I pointed out the fist clamped around my ankle, remembering the solid weight of a coiled tail doing the same. "*That* is the dragon."

"*That* is Cole." Miller offered me the drink. "You need the sugar. We don't need shock to set in again."

Again? "How do I know you're not trying to poison me?"

The stupidity of that statement heated my cheeks. They had a dragon. Cole was a *dragon*. He could swallow me whole and there would be no evidence left behind. Who needed poison with a *dragon* on the payroll?

Miller popped the lid on the can, took a long drink, then opened his mouth and stuck out his tongue to prove he'd swallowed.

"That's gross, and I'm not drinking after you." I scratched a red welt on my wrist, and another memory popped into the forefront of my brain. "Thom bit me. What the hell is wrong with you people? Who are you?"

"We're your people," Thom said from the doorway. "I'm sorry I entered your *me* space, but my saliva has a narcotic effect. You were in pain. I helped."

Nope. Nope. Nope.

I changed my mind. I couldn't accept this. Too much crazy too fast. Dragons that shifted into men, okay. I owned a Kindle. I read paranormal romance. I could get behind non-people-eating-dragons. But men with narcotic saliva? Men who drank out of other people's drinks? That was the last straw, no pun intended. Gah. *Gallows humor strikes again.* Apparently I wasn't yet convinced I wasn't going to die horribly at the hand of these . . . whatever they were.

"I was in a car accident a few days ago, and I sustained a head injury," I informed them. "For all I know, none of this is real. I probably cracked my skull like an egg, and my brain seeped out on the pavement before the EMTs arrived. A coma would explain why I'm living a paranormal romance novel."

Miller and Thom exchanged the look that men gave each other when a woman was being difficult. Well boo-hoo, guys. Cry me a river. It must be so terrifying to wake up and realize humans were real. Oh wait. Flip that around. This was happening to *me*. Except with more terror and more dragons.

"Would you feel more comfortable outside?" Miller pushed open the door, and blue sky beckoned. "We can sit on the deck and talk, and then I'll drive you to meet your partner."

"All right." I gave my leg an experimental tug, and Cole growled under his breath. "What do I do about him?"

Thom held up a finger, darted from the room and then returned with a plush orange pony in his hand. "It's not mine." He tipped up his chin. "It's Portia's." He crossed to me, set the toy aside and pried open Cole's hand. "Do the honors?"

I wedged the pony under Thom's hand, its head smooshed

against Cole's palm. Thom let go and, like a bear trap springing closed, Cole clenched his fist and resumed sleeping.

"Healing takes its toll," Thom said when he noticed I hadn't stood yet.

Nodding, I eased off the bed. The ankle that had gotten me into trouble in the first place bore my weight without so much as a twinge. I bent my legs, testing the knee the dragon—Cole—had crushed, but it flexed without aching. Confident my legs wouldn't collapse under me if I had to make a break for it, I escaped out the door, Miller and Thom at my heels.

Beyond the curiosity factor, the one quirk of my biology that got me in the most trouble was the fact I healed fast. Really fast. So fast doctors salivated at the idea of poking me full of holes, cutting me, hurting me to test my limits. Never had I healed injuries to this extent in such an abbreviated timeframe, but, then again, Thom's saliva might have boosted my already hearty immune system.

The exit leading from Cole's bedroom opened onto the massive deck from last night's fiasco. I walked backward, admiring the rest of the structure. The design reminded me of articles I'd read on the Winchester Mystery House, with doors that opened onto air and staircases that terminated mid-climb. "What is this place?"

"It's home," Thom answered from his position behind a chair he had drawn out for me from a wrought-iron table. "This is where we live when we're not working."

"All of you live here together?" I sat and allowed him to push the seat in for me since it weighed a ton. "Are you all … dragons?"

"We're a coterie, so yes. We all live together," Miller said, joining me while Thom crouched where a third chair might have gone. "None of us are the same as Cole, or the same as each other for that matter, but we are all charun."

"Demons," a smug voice grated out behind me. "The closest approximation for you is to say we're demons."

Leaning forward, I spotted Santiago floating in the water near the edge of the deck. Most folks don't do morning laps in swamp water, but I guess he wasn't most folks. Or even a folk since he wasn't human.

"There was nothing demonic about Cole." Infernal? No. Ethereal? Yeah. That I could believe. I shifted my hips to keep Santiago in sight. "Is he right?" Miller seemed the sanest of the bunch. "Or is he being an asshat?"

A tight smile curled his lips. "Both."

"That thing we saw in the swamp the night Jane Doe was discovered, that was one of you too?" Having been on the bitey end of the super gator, I had no trouble believing it had clawed its way out of hell. "It's a person too?"

"Hear that, boys? Cole is a swoon-worthy dragon. The rest of us are just *things*. We're *its*." Water splashed, and Santiago heaved himself onto the dock. Snorting, he shook off like a wet dog and sprayed us all. "Some things never change."

Thom hissed at the spattering droplets, or maybe the posturing was meant for Santiago. "She doesn't know any better."

"Stop defending her and grow a pair, Thom. She doesn't care about you or Miller or Portia or me." He advanced on Thom, leg cocked like he might kick sense in to him. "It's Cole. It's always Cole. It's always been Cole. It'll always be Cole."

"What is your problem?" I demanded. "So what if I like Cole? How is that any of your business?"

Peeling back his lips over his teeth, Santiago snarled, "You asked him out on a date."

"It's her right—" Thom began.

"Fuck her rights," Santiago snarled. "What about our rights? What about what we want?" His lips curved into a cruel smile.

"Or what we don't want. He walked out on you, didn't he? Given the choice, he left you. Unless you force him, he'll always leave you. Gods, you two make me tired."

Thom hissed a warning at Santiago, and Santiago grabbed him by the throat until Thom's face purpled.

Bolstered by a surge of pissedoffedness, I shoved out of my chair and stalked over to them.

"Back off, or me and you are going to have a problem." Forget reaching the end of my rope. I was seconds from losing my grip on reality altogether. Bullies were bullies regardless of species it seemed. "This is between us. Leave Thom out of it."

"Standing up for the weak link. That's different." Santiago cocked his head and pursed his lips, forgetting Thom for the moment. "No, I don't believe the act." He leaned forward, his nose almost brushing mine. "You don't fool me."

A fluid conversation sparked between Miller and Santiago in a language beyond my comprehension. Done with playing human, Santiago huffed and walked away from all of us, tensing his muscles at last moment before he reached Cole's door. As easy as breathing, he sprang up to one of the second-floor rooms, climbed in through the window and slammed it shut behind him.

"I should go." I jiggled my leg, anxiety pushing me to run as far and as fast as possible. "Can you drop me off at the hospital?"

"Do you want to check on Jane?" he asked carefully.

"No. I want to check in." I shook my head. "I need an alibi for last night, and this is the only believable one. You drop me off, I stumble in, folks scramble. I'll tell them a Good Samaritan found me walking the road and left me at the portico. They'll admit me, and the tests will begin." A shudder rippled through me. "I'll tell them I don't remember what happened after I jumped through the window to escape the super gator. They'll assume I hit my head when I landed or jiggled my brain again."

His jaw slackened. "You hate hospitals."

"That's why Dad and anyone else who knows me will believe it's the truth." I offered him a weak smile. "Rixton will need convincing after that phone call, but I can make it work. I don't lie. People don't expect it of me."

"You could tell them the truth." He put it out there with an air of expectation I would out them.

"I've seen enough movies to know how that ends for you guys. Torches and pitchforks." I frowned up at the window of Santiago's room before zeroing in on Cole's door. "Cole saved my life last night. The way I see it, he could have let that thing—that demon—kill me, or he could have eaten me himself. Instead, he got hurt protecting me and brought me here, to his home. That kind of trust . . . I can't repay him by betraying him or his family."

A light filled Miller's eyes that suspiciously resembled hope. "We all need to sit down and talk once Cole is awake. You must have questions."

"Only a million or two." First and foremost . . . *Am I one of you?*

"We've got a lead on the Claremont girl." Mischief sparkled in his eyes. "Are you interested?"

"Yes!" I was desperate for a distraction, and I couldn't shake the feeling Maggie's abduction was linked to her disappearance. "Spill."

Miller caught me up to date on White Horse's findings on the drive to the hospital. Thanks to Super Gator Fever, a cutesy nickname coined by the media, dispatch had been fielding calls left and right. When I asked how he knew this, he just smiled and chatted about the weather until I caved and let him keep his secrets.

According to his sources, amid the frenzy of reported sightings and pranks, one solid lead had trickled through. "A man who lives in the Dunleavy Apartment Complex claims to have witnessed a car run over a small animal from his balcony. He figured a cat. A girl, a teenager by his estimation, saw it happen, then rushed over to check on the injured creature. The driver, an older man with a shiny spot on top of his head, pulled over and joined her. Together they bundled the animal in a shirt the girl removed from her backpack. From there, the girl got in the car with him and they drove, he assumed, to the vet clinic."

"Why didn't he report this sooner?" The similarities between that incident and the one Mr. Hendricks, the school teacher, had relayed to me through his classroom window the night Maggie vanished got my blood pumping. The urge to ditch the hospital and say *screw it* to an alibi kept my thoughts pinwheeling, but the memory of silken scales beneath my palm hardened my resolve to cover my trail, and Cole's. "It's been all over the news."

"The caller's job sent him out of town for a few days. When he returned home and heard about a second disappearance, he called the tip line." Miller flicked on his blinker and made the next to last turn. "The Claremont girl was taken on a Friday. It's football season. There's a pep rally in the gym every week before the game. The caller didn't sweat the pickup because the guy who hit the cat was wearing a polo in school colors. He figured the driver was a teacher and that's why the girl trusted him enough to get in his car."

A balding teacher with a penchant for committing vehicular manslaughter on strays?

"Robert Martin." Heart drumming against my ribs, I wriggled in my seat, unable to hold still. "A license plate number from that distance is wishful thinking. How about a description of the vehicle?"

"About that—We have a small problem. The SAC was notified, and he's pinched the lines of communication we were monitoring closed." He grimaced. "We've bumped heads with Special Agent Kapoor a few times. He's young and hungry. We can't expect him to discount the caller as a crank. He'll pin him down and interview him, and we'll be left picking up the crumbs."

"Can you beat Kapoor to him?" The white box of the hospital loomed ahead, and I gripped the door handle hard enough the plastic groaned. "Get ahead of him?"

"Not sure." Rather than turn under the portico, he pulled into the pharmacy parking lot next door. "We have certain resources at our disposal. Santiago is tapping into those as we speak." He passed me a card with digits scribbled across the back. "You can contact any member of the crew for updates."

I added that card to the one already burning a hole in my pocket.

"Kapoor gave me his number." I couldn't leave without making the offer. "I could—"

"We can't afford to draw attention to ourselves." Miller cut his eyes toward me. "We stay safe by keeping a low profile."

"I'm hardly low profile," I argued. "And he approached me."

"Kapoor is smart, and smart humans are dangerous humans. He sought you out for a reason, and until we know what that is, I don't want you anywhere near him." He drummed his fingers on his thigh. "We've researched him, but his record is clean. Spotless. I don't trust it. You don't make it where he is without getting your hands dirty."

"You think he's not who he says he is?" A chill whispered up my spine.

"None of us are who we say we are," he said on a laugh. "Why should he be any different?"

And I thought I was paranoid.

"Cole . . . " I hesitated remembering Santiago's anger when the dragon toppled. "He's okay, right?"

"He's survived worse." Miller's lips hitched to one side. "He's almost as tough as he is pretty."

A surprised laugh burst past my lips. "How does he feel about being called pretty?"

"He broke Santiago's jaw two weeks ago for painting his claws with this holographic nail goop Portia uses. He ought to know better than to fall asleep sunbathing on the deck. It's too much temptation." He chuckled at the memory before sobering. "The rest of us . . . not all of us are like him. Not all of us are . . . pretty."

"As long as you don't try and eat me when you're being your other self, I don't care how you look." I had a sneaking suspicion the same rule of thumb I applied to people might hold true for demons too. "Beauty is a reflection on the genetic soup we got served. It says nothing about your character or personality. Pretty is just that. Pretty. Substance is what matters. Clichéd as it sounds, it really is what's inside that counts." I unbuckled my seatbelt. "As long as what's inside isn't me in your belly, we're cool."

He scanned my face. "I can almost believe you mean that."

"Believe it." I studied him right back, curiosity a prickle under my skin. "Can I ask you a personal question?"

Miller popped his neck, limbering up, before he nodded for me to go ahead.

"How did you end up here?" In this town, this country, this world. I left the scope of his response up to him. "How did you end up with the coterie?"

"I . . . " His expression twisted before he rearranged his features with careful blankness. "I was born the nameless son of a prince. Nameless because my mother, a slave who worked as a laundress, dared give me nothing of his." His inhale pained him. "I was born hours before his wife gave birth to a daughter, their third. Males inherit in our culture, and even being bastard-born made me his heir.

"The prince's wife learned of my existence when I was nine and ordered me drowned in the river where my mother did her washing. Mother stood against them, and they slit her throat. Her death ... unleashed a terrible power within me. I killed them, and the darkness within me grew. And then I killed my father, his wife, their children—my half-sisters—and any who stood in my path. I was a scourge upon my people until the day ... " He tugged down the white T-shirt beneath his polo, exposing an inch-thick band of stacked rose gold rings encircling his neck. "Joining this coterie saved my life, and swearing fealty to a master who was stronger, who could put me down if I crossed those lines again, saved my sanity."

"A master?" The word tasted bitter and strange.

"Each coterie is led by a high demon. The groups vary in size and species, but the only true limit is how far their master's control extends."

Cole. He must be talking about Cole. Their leader, their master. No wonder he went to such lengths to protect them and their secrets.

"Don't pity me," he said softly. "I don't regret my choice."

The enormity of what Miller had confided didn't stick. Overflowing with new and dangerous information, my brain was Teflon. He might as well have been summing up the latest science fiction blockbuster. His story didn't feel real, but the pain in his eyes was genuine. What had I gotten myself into with these people? What sort of power did Cole wield that he controlled such powerful beasts?

"Thank you for telling me. I won't betray your trust." I heaved myself out of the SUV and plucked at my muddy pants and tattered shirt. The pavement seared my bare feet, and I hopped from foot to foot. "At least I look the part."

"For what it's worth," he said, voice raw, "I'm glad to have you back."

I huffed out a sigh. "I have no idea what that means."

"Call when you're ready to find out." A shadow crossed his face. "Then we'll talk."

Miller refused to budge on his *keep-Luce-in-the-dark* stance, so I shut the door and hotfooted it to the rear of the hospital. Walking through the front doors invited too much attention with me muddied and my clothes torn. I didn't want folks thinking I was auditioning for a *The Return of Swamp Thing* revival. That meant I had to be sneaky.

Fewer people smoked on the job these days, which was a relief for my allergies, but made the move I planned to execute dicey. I located a nice patch of hedges and squatted behind them then checked the time on my phone. I had thirty minutes until Rixton blew a gasket and my cover. I wasted twenty of those waiting in the bushes.

A harried nurse shoved through the emergency exit and kicked a brick between the door and the frame. I waited until she tucked herself into the alcove that would hide her should anyone pop their head out the door, then texted Rixton where to find me, ran across the lot and ducked inside the building.

I imitated the zombie shuffle so popular on television these days, and it didn't take long for a nurse to do a double take and ask if I was all right. She attempted to support my elbow, and I recoiled. That's when her eyes sparked with recognition, and I released an inner groan. Not her again.

"Hey, I know you."

Careful to keep my gaze distant and out of focus, I mumbled nonsense syllables.

"You're Luce Boudreau. I don't know why I didn't put it together sooner." Her eyes sparkled with mischief. "Must have been that nurse uniform that Valerie Burke is swearing got stolen from her locker. That girl . . ." She clicked her tongue. "Let's just say she lies like a rug and most folks walk over her like she is one."

She reached for her phone, and I cringed imagining tomorrow's headlines and photo accompaniment. *Wild Child Boudreau returns to her swamp woman roots. Shows up caked in mud and dazed at hospital. Is history repeating? Find out tonight at six.*

"I go to church with Nancy and Harold Trudeau. That's why I recognized you. He came by earlier flashing your picture and checking to make sure you hadn't been admitted. The poor man's beside himself."

"Uncle Harold," I said softly to assure her I was lucid.

"You poor thing." She scanned the hall, then snapped her fingers in the direction of an open door. "There we go. We just discharged this patient. We don't keep rooms empty for long around here, but you'll have a few minutes while housekeeping comes in to spruce things up for the next occupant." She showed me to a chair since the bed was rumpled. "Sit tight, and I'll call Harry."

The nurse, Ida Bell, made the call at my elbow as though afraid I might toddle off or tip over if she took her eyes off me. She snagged a coworker from the hall and asked him to bring me a soda from the vending machine, then pulled the curtain in the ceiling around to shield me from prying eyes in the hall.

Five minutes later, she poured me a Sprite over ice chips in a foam cup and offered me a packet of peanut butter and honey crackers from her pocket. "Thank you." I toyed with my straw, but I knew without trying the food and drink wouldn't go down and stay that way, not after the night I'd had.

Ten minutes later, Dad barreled into the room and yanked me out of the chair and off my feet into a spine-cracking hug. Uncle Harold was on his heels and thanked Ida for her kindness. Fifteen minutes later, I had laid out the story and agreed to a few tests to reassure Dad my brain hadn't detached and wasn't bouncing around in my skull. Twenty minutes later, I had been checked into my own room.

News of my disappearance must have spread. No doubt the house had been staked out and all my known associates trailed in the hopes of catching a whiff of story. How fitting would it be for the swamp girl to die at the jaws of an alligator first spotted in the same waters where she had been rescued?

Exhausted from the past twenty-four hours and cold from the clinical surroundings, I pulled the paper-thin sheet up to my shoulders and pretended I wasn't back wearing the same flimsy hospital gowns I recalled from my last stint as the resident lab rat. Fatigue blanketed me until twitching my toes required herculean effort, but I couldn't turn off my brain, and sleep evaded me.

Maggie was still out there. Alone, maybe hurt, definitely terrified, while the worst that could happen to me was I get served lime Jell-O with my next meal instead of cherry. Okay, so maybe that wasn't the *worst*-case scenario. I did still have to figure out what to do about Cole and his coterie. Those fears melded with the others, and their combined weight pushed me under. Shivering, I dreamed of pearlescent scales and dragons who ate doctors for breakfast.

CHAPTER SEVENTEEN

———◈———

Two hours ticked past before Rixton marched into my room, pale and shaken, with the cause of his late arrival hooked on his arm. Sherry waddled beside him, a woman on a mission dressed in an open-backed gown to match mine, and arrowed toward me. Elbowing her husband, she blazed a trail for the only chair in the small room. Dad couldn't hop out of his seat fast enough. She almost collapsed in his lap and then scowled at him for making her wait.

"Do you know how long it took me to escape the maternity ward," she snarled. "Do you? I told them my friend was here, that she was hurt, and do you know what they told me? That I should focus on my breathing. That I couldn't get in to see you anyway. That I— Damn it. I stopped listening at that point."

"Sherry." Rixton approached her with caution. "Baby."

"Don't you *baby* me, mister." She gripped the armrests of her chair until the old wood creaked. "This is all your fault. All of this. Your fault." She grunted a pained sound. "Never again.

I am never having sex again, and that means neither are you. I hope you're happy. You've ruined my one and only hobby."

"Mrs. Rixton," Dad began.

"No." She hissed at him. "Keep your man bits over there. Don't get them near me."

"I'm going to get some sweet tea from the cafeteria." Dad inched toward the door. "Does anyone else . . . ?"

Smart man, my father. That's why he didn't wait for an answer. He bolted for safety. Lucky dog.

"Is this the real deal?" I aimed the question at Rixton. "Is the baby coming?"

"Why are you asking him?" Sherry roared. "I'm the one having a baby. Oh, God. A baby. A small person. I'm about to fire a tiny human out of my birth cannon."

"Birth cannon," I echoed, nodding. It seemed safest to agree with the pregnant lady.

"Okay, enough about me and my impending vaginal pyrotechnics," she panted. "What happened to you?"

"Well, as best I remember, it's like this." I rattled off the story I had concocted about the Good Samaritan finding me stumbling across the road and delivering me to the hospital's doorstep. I wrapped up my tale with a cutting scowl I didn't have to fake as I raised my left hand. "Next thing I know, I've got a needle in my arm, and I'm on a stretcher being wheeled down to radiology."

Mesmerized by my tale of derring-do, Sherry hadn't cursed Rixton's anatomy in over sixty seconds. Rixton, however, gave me his flat cop stare. He wasn't buying it, not all of it anyway. Nowhere in my story had I mentioned speaking to him earlier or explained why I'd needed those two hours. By not calling me out, he extended me a smidgen of trust, chose to believe I had left out critical facts for a reason. But he would find me, soon, and I'd better have the right answers when he sat down to chat.

"Oh, great." Sherry's voice cut into my thoughts. "Now I've peed myself."

"Uh, Sher?" Rixton's eyes swallowed his face. "I think your water broke."

Unsure what that entailed, I resisted the urge to lean over and investigate. I wasn't that bored. Yet.

"Luce, I'll check on you once . . ." His voice trailed off into a dazed kind of mumble. "Later. I'll be back later."

I waved them off, and then sank back against my pillows, sending up thanks to the Wi-Fi gods for their bountiful connectivity. Uncle Harold had made a supply run out to the house and returned with Dad's tablet for my Netflixing pleasure. When I'd asked him why he hadn't brought my laptop, he informed me it was toast. When the super gator—demon gator?—tromped through the kitchen, its lashing tail seemed to have sent the old girl sailing into a wall where she shattered.

A buzz on the nightstand had me checking my phone for texts. So far Miller's attempts at tracing the tipster had led nowhere. Must have to do with the whole anonymous crime hotline being *anonymous*. But the guy had given enough details I had no doubt Special Agent Kapoor would soon have his people scouring the apartment building, even if that meant going door-to-door.

The only question was—would White Horse beat him to the punch?

Adopting the no-news-is-good-news mantra, I set aside my phone and powered up the tablet. After opening a new tab, I did what I should have already done and ordered a balloon bouquet for Buck that I signed from Dad and me. It would be a while before I could visit him in person. At least this would let him know he was on my mind. I owed him more than a few plastic sacks of helium for his attempt at saving my life.

With that done, I cleared the browser and started digging. Curiosity had been gnawing on my bones since Miller's big reveal this morning, and so I put off bingeing on *The Great British Bake Off* in favor of doing research on demons. The lore varied from religion to religion and from region to region. Until I sat down with the group as a whole and got their side of the story, I was reluctant to side with Wikipedia articles over first-person retellings of their history.

But demons? Real, live demons? Try as I might, the word conjured only little horned men dancing around in red tights and carrying pitchforks. Cole as a dragon was easier to swallow, but it made me wonder how the others in their crew—their coterie—looked beneath their human veneers.

Over the top edge of the tablet, I noticed the quality of light in the room change. The door swung open, but I kept reading to the end of the page before adding a bookmark. "I was starting to think you got lost. Was the cafeteria that crowded? Or did you wait for them to brew fresh tea to avoid Sherry?"

"Officer Boudreau."

My head snapped up, and I dropped the tablet. "Chief Timmons."

The man was about a decade Dad's junior, but he'd gone white-headed young and passed for older. He was built like a bulldog. Squat and muscular with a thick neck. When he sank his teeth into something, he didn't let go. I ought to know. I had enough bite marks to last a lifetime.

"You gave us all quite a scare." His gaze darted to the door, then he sauntered up to the bed and braced his forearm on the railing. "Your father called me at the house last night and explained the situation."

There was no love lost between my dad and the chief. For the life of me, I couldn't picture Dad dialing the guy up and inviting him to stick his nose into our lives. "We both had a rough night."

"Rough week," he countered, fidgeting with an American flag pin on his lapel. "First Jane Doe, then your friend goes missing, you were involved in an accident and now this."

Apprehension tingled over my nape, a warning prickle as impossible to ignore as the fact Dad hadn't returned yet.

"The thing is this." For the first time since entering the room, he made eye contact. "Your face has been splashed all over the news. That kind of coverage is a blessing and a curse. The kind of social presence you have could draw attention—both good and bad—to both cases." He leaned closer, almost like he wanted to slide his arm behind me and across my shoulders. "The department can help you channel that presence, focus it, so that the real issues aren't lost in the shadows of the spotlight."

A bump against the door urged me up higher in bed. What was going on out there?

"Your case summoned a tsunami of media attention upon our small town when Officer Boudreau found you in Cypress Swamp, and again when you graduated the academy, proving that a girl with no past can have a bright future." He puffed out his chest at that zinger. "But there comes a point when all the publicity starts affecting your work and the ability of your fellow officers to do their jobs. People love a good mystery, and that's what you provide for them by refusing to be interviewed or to sit for photos of your unusual markings. The public has questions. Sate their curiosity, and they'll move on to the next oddity." He projected all things honest and noble, ignoring he had just called me an oddity. "Give them what they want, and they'll give you peace. They'll give Jane peace. Don't you want that? To help her? So that she doesn't have to endure the same hurtful speculation and objectification you've endured?"

Ice licked up the walls of my rib cage and crackled like hoarfrost over my heart.

"Sir, no offense, but I'm not interested in feeding the media frenzy. I want to be left alone to live my life." The temperature in the room seemed to drop as my words permeated his thick skull. "Jane deserves the same opportunity, but feeding the journalists isn't the way to end this. Once they see my birthmarks, they'll want to see hers for comparison, and she's in no condition to give consent. After they listen to my story, they'll expect to hear hers. They'll play us off each other based on our similarities and invent fictions to generate the most profit."

"It has been implied—not by me, you understand—by other, concerned parties, that CPD's association with you is detrimental to the department as a whole. It puts our officers and our records under the microscope of public scrutiny. We are a small department with limited resources, and the bright lights can be blinding. Canton knows this better than most small towns. For those reasons, the others espouse that severing ties with you might be in our best interest."

Careful not to tip my hand, I pretended to give the matter serious consideration while mashing the intercom button wired into the bedrail. "These *others* are willing to look the other way if I agree to an interview and photography session?"

"Your cooperation would go a long way toward smoothing ruffled feathers, yes." He pinned on an earnest smile. "You've proven yourself to be a tribute to your father and your department. I'd hate to see you throw away your career on a whim. What other department would take you on knowing the baggage you carry?"

"Let me get this straight." I crossed my toes that someone, somewhere was hearing this and that help was coming. "Either I conduct interviews and allow photos of my bare upper body to be taken and published, or you and these *others* will fire me? You are aware that's blackmail, correct?"

"Must you be so crass?" He clamped his jaw shut. "I am simply telling you how it is, *Miss* Boudreau."

"I'm not selling my soul, not even one tiny piece of it. Not for you, not for the department. Not for anyone." I raised my voice over the commotion leaking in from the hall. "I think you should leave, *sir*."

"Franke," he called out in a voice that had carried over many a shift meeting.

Franke? My bad feeling got worse when the door swung open.

Sure enough, Moses Franke stumbled into the room as though he had been pushed with a sleek camera hung around his neck. The dull roar of raised voices followed him. He aimed his new toy, pointed and clicked. Done. I reared back in horror at the picture we must have made. Chief Timmons leaning on my bed, his arm inches from burrowing under my pillow in his effort to sling it around my shoulders. The chief had come prepared, and I had been outwitted by an old politico determined to get the last shot at my expense at any cost.

"Got it." Franke lifted his camera in salute to the chief. "Nice doin' business with you." The shutter whirred again, capturing my mortified expression. "Tell your boyfriend I'll send him a copy. Free of charge."

The photographer slid through the crack in the door, and the chief watched him go. I yanked on the tubing in my hand, about to rip out the IV, but Franke was long gone. I couldn't catch him without creating more of a spectacle by flashing my bare butt in hot pursuit of the photojournalistic equivalent of an ambulance chaser.

"Get. Out." I pointed at the door. "*Now.*"

"All this could have been avoided if you had taken my offer." Chief Timmons spun on his heel with military precision. "You and I will talk about disciplinary measures once you've been released to return to active duty."

I bet we would, and I imagined his pet photog would be lurking under his desk to chronicle the ordeal too. Releasing the intercom button, I startled when a crisp voice came from the speakers. "Miss Boudreau, this is Ida. Are you all right?"

"No." I slumped against the pillows. "I'm really not."

I barely managed to zip my lips before tacking on *I want my Daddy*. I was a grown-ass woman. It was time to—not cut the apron strings. What was the father/daughter equivalent? Toss the spent shell casings? Whatever. Doesn't matter.

"I'm on the way," Ida assured me, and I nodded though she couldn't see.

Sick to my core, I drew my legs up against my chest and cinched my arms around them like that might somehow hold me together. I rested my forehead on my kneecaps, and warm tracks wet my cheeks as I purged the anger.

Never had I felt so violated. Exposed. To borrow from that rat bastard, *objectified*.

I was a person, damn it. Not a *thing*. Not an *it*. I wasn't a commodity to be exploited. Huffing out a pitiful laugh, I wiped my nose on the scratchy bedsheet. I got it then. I understood why I wasn't running scared of the White Horse coterie. And I laughed even harder.

This right here, this dehumanization, had primed me for the startling discovery that something *other* existed. I'd known it all along, deep down, hadn't I? All they had done was given me proof. Now I knew that, while I might not be normal, I wasn't alone either. There was comfort in that. So much so that fresh tears spilled over my cheeks.

Miller had no idea how parallel our paths ran. Then again, he had let me go without extracting any blood oaths or mind melds, whatever the demon equivalent was to I cross my heart, hope to die, stick a needle in my eye. Maybe he saw more than a human Cole had entrusted with their secrets. Maybe he saw a kindred spirit too.

The door swung open, but I didn't raise my head. It weighed too much. The betrayal stung too fresh, sat too heavy on my shoulders, for me to care who had entered or what they wanted.

"I brought you a present."

I raised my head slowly, not believing my ears. "Cole."

"Here." He placed a sleek red camera at my feet as an offering. "Thought you might prefer this to flowers or a get-well balloon."

I wiggled my toes. "How did you know?"

"The police cordoned off the hall to give you and the chief privacy. Or so they claimed. Me? I'm not convinced. Seems if that was their goal then they would have been more careful sharing your personal information since the door had no name or chart to identify its patient due to security concerns."

I didn't want to know who had betrayed me for a pat on the head from the chief, so I didn't ask the question in his eyes.

"I was on my way to see you and got sidelined," he continued when I remained quiet. "I was content to wait my turn until I saw that little shit strut right into your room. The uniforms didn't bat an eye, so I figured he must have been given permission to violate your privacy from someone higher up the food chain." Cole stood there, tapping his fingertip on the lens until I expected it to crack under the strain. "He strolled out with that camera in his hands and a smirk on his face." He still refused to look at me. "I asked him nicely to show me his last few shots, and, when he did, I convinced him to part with the camera without forwarding the files to his computer."

"You're right." I hauled the expensive camera into my lap by its neck strap. "This is so much better than wilting flowers or a lame balloon."

Not many people used dedicated cameras instead of snapping pics from their phones, me included, so it took a minute to locate the memory card slot and remove the black square. Thin as it was, I folded it in half and relished the crisp *snap* before moving on to wiping the camera.

"Have you seen my dad?" I asked when the silence lingered.

"I spotted him when I first arrived, but he was called to handle a commotion at the nurses' station." His lips seesawed before settling into a half smile higher on one side than the other. "It seems a patient was being blackmailed by her boss and had the good sense to activate the intercom. The nurses, upon identifying the speakers, whipped out their phones to record the entire exchange. It ought to be making the rounds by now." He flicked his gaze up to mine. "Just don't break Twitter. Portia goes into withdrawal when the robot pops up instead of her timeline."

"I didn't think." Groaning, I flopped back on my pillows and kicked out my feet. "I reacted. Probably overreacted. I was so pissed off at his gall, I couldn't think straight."

At the time, I had been running on instinct. It hadn't occurred to me that the reason why the nurses hadn't chimed in sooner was due to operator error. As long as I depressed the button, they couldn't speak to me. They had to wait until I dropped my hand to do what the blockade had prevented them from doing in person and check on me.

"Don't beat yourself up over it." He gripped the rail, used it to haul himself closer, as though fighting against a fast-moving current to reach me. "You did what you had to do."

"So." I tipped my head back to ease the strain on my neck from gazing up at him. "I had the most vivid dream last night." I pursed my lips and studied him. "You were there."

"A dream, huh?" Metal whined, and the railing caved under the pressure of his fingers.

"Parts of it were scary," I admitted. "Kind of terrifying, really." The tubing gasped as he crushed it flat in his fist. "Other parts . . ." I rested my hand on his until his fingers unclenched. "You're pretty amazing." I shrugged to downplay the awe even I heard in my voice. "Dream you, I mean."

"We need to talk." He turned over his hand, sliding our palms together, the effort to be gentle with me a conscious one. Perhaps it had always been this way, an endeavor on his part not to break me. Well, I saw him now. I saw the others too. Perhaps, for the first time, I began to see myself as well.

Eyes wide open, Luce. All the best mistakes started with a conscious decision to make them.

"Not here." Cole glanced around and then up, as though remembering the story I'd once told him about the photog in the ceiling. "Come home with me?"

Answers. He was offering me what I had always wanted most. I wet my chapped lips and nodded. "Okay."

Eyes wide open.

CHAPTER EIGHTEEN

⟞⟞⟝⟝◉⟞⟞⟝⟝

Sneaking out of the hospital proved more challenging than anticipated. Thanks to the chief all but bussing in the high school's marching band to parade him to my room, I had kissed my anonymity goodbye. Security had cleared the halls after people lost their damn minds over the recording the nurses had made of the chief's bullying tactics, but a guy dressed in scrubs that didn't match the color nurses wore on my floor had been hauled out of my room by Dad seconds before Cole's meaty fist closed around his throat. That had been fun. For me, I mean. I had no sympathy for vultures. But one only had to peer out the window to see news vans circling the lot like they smelled a fresh carcass.

"Okay, let's do this." I had signed myself out against medical advice and changed into the spare clothes Uncle Harold had brought me from home. "What's the plan?"

Cole's gaze drifted toward the ceiling. "How are you with heights?"

See, he said *heights*, but I heard *flying*. "Other than the vomiting and the tears, good."

"It will be easier to go up than down." His hand rose to his chest, and he scratched, an absent gesture that reminded me of his injury. "We can arrange for a pickup in town if you'd rather not fly the whole way."

"Are you up to it?" Every time I asked, he dodged the question. "You're picking at your bandage again."

"It itches," he admitted, lowering his arm. "I'll feel better after I get out of this skin."

I blinked at him, ears ringing. *Out of this skin* implied humanity was a suit he put on before leaving for work in the morning. I might be patting myself on the back with one hand at how well I was adjusting, but the other was clutching the trash bin in a death grip.

I steered us back on track. "What about Dad?"

"Convince him I'm the best chance you've got at getting out of here undetected." His hand lifted, fingers brushing his pectorals. He noticed me watching and dropped his arm. "He can run interference while we escape and buy us some time to put town behind us."

"That's a tall order." For once I wasn't poking fun at his height. "Dad is not a big fan of yours."

"Get him over it." Cole growled low in his throat. "I'm not going anywhere."

A thought occurred to me. "Is discovering the existence of demons like joining the mafia? Once you're in, you can never leave?"

"Something like that," he agreed.

"Does this mean you'll hang around and keep an eye on me?" I smothered the hope buried in the question before it surfaced. But answers. He had answers. I couldn't let him go until I had learned all he knew and maybe not even then. I didn't want to be alone again. "Make sure I don't spill the beans?"

"Luce," he growled. "You don't know what you're asking."

"I would if you told me." I set my lips into a mulish line. "What's wrong with wanting to keep you around?"

Cole prowled toward me, and my hindbrain screamed I ought to be running in the opposite direction, but I buried the instinctive panic beneath a layer of ice. He slid his hand under my hair, his watch tangling in the strands, and wrapped his palm around my nape, pinning me to the spot. Not that my knees would have bent now had I begged them.

Good thing we had already established the whole *this can't happen* thing, or I might have been nervous.

"The reasons are infinite." He lowered his head, his lips a whisper from mine, and I forgot how to breathe. Forgot all the reasons he'd given and wished I could wipe them from his mind too. "You are my personal torment. How the gods must laugh at me." He stared at my mouth like a man starved. "This time will be different."

"I don't understand," I breathed, our exhales mingling.

"I know." He released me, turned his back and paced to the window. "I would prefer we kept it that way."

Not a chance. These demons and their cryptic one-liners. What I had gleaned from my time among them was Cole and I had a history. That wasn't as crazy as it sounded considering the first decade and change of my life was a blank slate. Had the papers been right about me all along? Had I been part of a demonic cult, emphasis on demonic? Had I been lost to my people until the night I crossed paths with White Horse? Was I a foundling yet again? Another sobering thought had me wrapping my arms around my center. On the off chance I was a demon, what had happened to my parents? To me? Had they wanted me? Or had they discarded me?

Cole glanced over his shoulder. Really, I had no idea how long he had been watching me execute my complex mental acrobatics. He didn't say a word. He didn't reach for me again either. I wasn't sure which disappointed me more.

"I'll get Dad and get started convincing him." I spun on my heel and headed for the door. Cole didn't let my fingers close over the knob before he was there, his presence warm at my back, his breath hot at my ear. Breathless expectation sucked the air from my lungs. "Yes?"

A soft rumble poured through his throat, and I recalled his leonine dragon's face in such exacting detail it was as if I had gazed into those crimson eyes of his for all of eternity instead of a brief hour.

"We need to leave soon." His nose traced the column of my throat as he inhaled my scent. "The beast in me is rising."

Chills dappled my arms, and heat flared low in my stomach. Not his intention. I grimaced and said a little prayer that those shifter romances I popped like candy were wrong about the part where the hero could smell the heroine's arousal. That was just plain unfair.

"Are you staying for this?" The urge to lean against his strength had me locking my knees. "He probably won't swear. Much."

"I'll give you two some privacy." He reached over me and levered the door open. I stepped back to keep him from introducing my face to the wood and found my back pressed flush against him. His heart beat through my spine, and I had to focus when he spoke. "Don't keep me waiting long."

I wish Maggie was here.

The thought had been reflexive, but the guilt surged all the same. No matter what simmered between Cole and me, what secrets he might share and what fate unfolded for me, Maggie was the priority, and I was a worthless friend if even the promise of knowledge made me forget that.

Pissed off as Dad was about the chief, about the entire situation, I expected more resistance when I suggested using Cole as my exit strategy. But he was onboard with the plan without me breaking out the puppy eyes or the classic lip tremble. Exhaustion lined his face. Black smudges darkened the skin under his eyes. He hadn't slept last night. He was used to working third shift, from ten at night to six in the morning, so the strain wasn't as bad as it otherwise might have been. That didn't change the fact he was edging toward having spent twenty-four hours on his feet. He was ready to tap out, even if that meant Cole stepped into the ring.

We hashed out the details in a three-man huddle in my room, Dad and I hugged, and then I got handed off to Cole.

"Crash at Uncle Harold's when you get out of here." I squeezed Dad's arm. "I don't want to think about you out at the house with all those holes and a super gator on the loose."

"Call when you get settled," he countered, then faced Cole. "Take care of my baby girl."

"You have my word." His voice carried the weight of a solemn vow. "Luce, we should go."

Aware of the tension coiling in the lines of his body, I hustled out the door and led the charge to a bank of elevators. Neither of us spoke on our ride to the top floor. We located the roof-access door squirreled away behind the staff lounge and there we encountered our first hurdle. We had no key, and using force meant triggering an alarm. It said so in bold, red letters right on the sticker plastered at eye-level.

"There's a camera in the corner." Cole tipped his head in that direction. "That hands them evidence we were here."

Forget demons. Invisibility cloaks ought to be real. "So we might as well plow through the door and keep going?"

"Come here." He walked me back into a corner until my shoulders pressed against the wall. "Stay put. No matter what you see or hear, don't move until I come for you."

"This sounds fun." About as fun as having teeth pulled without anesthetic.

Turning away from me, he positioned himself in another alcove and shut his eyes. Our positions must have hidden us from the security cameras. Whatever he was about to do, I guaranteed it was *not* something he wanted caught on film.

At first nothing happened. I had been staring so hard at him, I missed the first swirl of gauzy fog twining around his ankles. Icy condensation nipped my fingertips, and I flattened my spine as the haze thickened and climbed higher. Soon the entire room spun with white mist, and the drop in temperature set my teeth chattering.

Pop. Pop. Pop.

The rapid fire sounds in the room reminded me of the way ice crackled when plunged into room temperature water. All too easily I imagined the sentient cold shattering objects that piqued its bitter curiosity.

I swallowed a scream when Cole appeared in front of me. The fog had reduced visibility to about six inches, and he was almost standing on my toes. Frost spiked his hair, and his skin glittered with a fine sheen of icy crystals. I examined my hand and found my fingers blue-tipped but lacking the snowflake lace that clung to him in delicate patterns. It hurt to behold him, and I glanced aside. His was a stark and elemental beauty that burned.

"Take my hand." Plunging my arm into a snowbank would have stung less. "I won't let you fall."

A biting coldness prevented my lips from moving except for involuntary tremors. I toddled after Cole, who had but to touch the door for it to shatter. That ... was not going to be easy to explain later. Flinching at the screech of sound as the alarm raised, I rushed out into the humid air that sucked away our cover.

"How long do you need to—?" The words died on my tongue.

In the time it had taken me to fill my lungs with thawed air, he had slid from one skin into the next. The dragon and I exchanged no soulful glances this time. Using his delicate snout, he shoved me against his shoulder. I landed on his bent arm, and he hoisted me onto his back. I ducked to avoid his antlers and sank my fingers in the silky strands of his mane.

"This is not what I signed up for, Cole." I couldn't get down. He wouldn't let me. I was stuck, and he was almost to the edge of the building. "I'm going to fall, and I'm going to die horribly on impact. When I come back as a pancake ghost, I'm going to haunt you for all eternity."

A rumble worked through his chest. Laughter. He was laughing at me.

To make him pay, I fisted my hands, yanking on his hair, and squeezed my thighs around his sides until they quivered. The tip of his tail cracked against my hip, more sound than hurt, and I yelped. "Why you little—"

He rocked forward into a vertical lunge. Over the side of the building. No wings out. No parachute. *Jumped.*

"*Coooooole.*"

The ground rushed up to greet us, and I prayed harder than any maybe-demon had a right to while yanking on his mane as though pulling up his head might lift the rest of him.

Snap.

His wings opened wide, arching over my head, catching the air and slowing our descent. With forceful strokes, he climbed back into the sky and sailed over town. He veered toward the swamp, and I paid attention this time to roads and landmarks. The first time I'd flown Air Cole, I had been in a blind panic and hadn't paid attention. Even when Miller drove me into town later, I had been shell-shocked and hadn't absorbed much after our chat on the deck.

"This is going to come back and bite you on the ass," I yelled near his ear. He turned his head and snapped at me. I nudged his jaw with my foot. "Eyes on the road, buddy." He huffed another laugh, and I debated the wiseness of kicking my trusty steed while several hundred feet in the air. "People can *see* you."

The dragon behaved the rest of the trip, and he landed as light as a feather on the deck of his home. He shook out his shoulders, and I slid down before he managed to dislodge me. The second my feet touched the planks, I caved to the irresistible urge to scratch under his chin and rub his round ears. His back leg kicked as I got my nails involved. Cole or no Cole, the dragon in him was every bit as beautiful as I remembered.

"Aww." Portia popped her head out of a second-floor window and framed out a heart with her fingers. "You guys are so effing cute I could shoot rainbows from my eyes."

Cole cracked his incredibly long tail against the wood, and the tip snapped inches from her nose.

"You could have just asked if you wanted privacy." She sniffed. "You didn't have to get all rude about it."

"You go change." I crossed the deck, dropped into one of the heavy chairs and shot Dad a text to let him know the eagle had landed. He wouldn't get the joke, but it amused me all the same. "I'll wait for you here."

Cool mist formed dense whirls around the dragon's ankles and rolled over his back. A hot breeze gusted it away seconds later, and Cole stood there. Fully dressed. Huh. I told myself I wasn't disappointed. Then told myself that talking to myself wasn't healthy. Especially not where he was concerned.

"You're wearing clothes." I made a rolling gesture with my hand. "I figured you must lose them when you shift since, you know."

That's how it worked in the books I read. How else could the heroine keep accidentally getting an eyeful?

"I was too injured to hold them." He joined me, teasing his chair out with his toe. This furniture didn't moan or groan under his weight. I bet it had been crafted with him in mind. "Usually it's not a problem."

"You look calm for a man who exposed himself in public today." I folded my arms, lips set in a firm line.

"Santiago was at the hospital. I texted him before we left, told him to wipe their systems."

"He can do that?" Doubt sat heavy in my voice. "He's capable of being useful?"

Hearty feminine laughter drifted down, confirmation Portia was eavesdropping.

"He has a degree and everything," Cole said dryly.

"Huh. No wonder you haven't killed him yet." I fluttered my hands in an approximation of wings. "That doesn't help the airshow you performed."

"No one saw." He worked his jaw like he was chewing over his answer. "My scales are coated with a metallic metamaterial. I channel electromagnetic waves from the atmosphere to charge their surface, which deflects light in all directions and gives the illusion of invisibility."

"I would have remembered riding an invisible dragon. There would have been screaming."

His bisected eyebrow arched.

"Okay, there would have been *more* screaming."

"Contact with me nulls the effect." He shrugged. "Riders can see me, but they aren't cloaked."

"Please tell me no one saw me sailing over downtown Canton."

"No one saw you sailing over downtown Canton." Cole extended his arm toward me, and a curl of mist spun on his palm. A flick of his fingers sent a baby cumulus cloud drifting across the space between us. "I cocooned you in a shroud of vapor." His eyes met mine. "Cloaking is a science my people developed, but the affinity for water is a gift born into all those of my line."

"A single cloud rocketing across the sky." I caught the puff only for it to disintegrate in my hands. "That's not suspicious at all."

"Humans will write it off as an atmospheric phenomenon." He rubbed condensate between his fingers. "Or maybe there'll be a rash of UFO sightings."

"UFOs?" I snorted. "Is that the best you can do, Spin Doctor?"

"You can believe in demons, but not in other forms of extra-terrestrial life?"

"Aliens," I murmured. "That sounds so much cooler than demons. People always hope aliens will be benevolent, but they'll always assume demons are malevolent. Maybe charun should overhaul their brand."

He grunted a noncommittal noise, then got lost staring off into the swamp at my back.

"Do you regret revealing yourself to me?" I pitched my voice low to keep the question private.

"How can I?" He zeroed in on me. "You would have died if I hadn't intervened."

"Thanks for that, by the way." I ducked my head. "I owe you."

A brief silence lapsed where *you're welcome* might have fit, but he countered with, "Can I ask you something?"

"Sure." His earnest tone set my nape tingling. "Fire away."

"What is your earliest memory?"

I didn't have to search hard to find it. "A roar, bright light, men screaming."

Cole relaxed a fraction. "Go on."

"A fisherman spotted me running naked through the swamp and reported it to the police. They organized a search and rescue, figuring I must be a runaway who got lost. They swept this massive spotlight back and forth until they spotted me. I froze, total deer in the headlights." I laughed softly. "The boat engine was so loud. The light so bright. And then all these men started screaming and waving their arms at me."

"You must have been frightened."

"That's one word for it." I bit the bullet and admitted the rest. "No one knew for sure how long I had been out there on my own, but they figured several years at least. I could talk, but the sounds I made—they weren't English or any other known language. The shrinks figured I had made up my own." I scratched a nail over a raised flower pattern on the table. "The funny thing is, after about a week, I started talking just fine. Whole sentences. Complete thoughts. Perfect English."

He made a thoughtful sound in the back of his throat.

"After that, they theorized the trauma of living in the wild had caused me to regress to a primal state." I had bitten the hand of the first rescuer to reach me, one Edward Boudreau. "My cognitive breakthrough was attributed to a positive response in my change of circumstance. Mostly being among people in a civilized environment, and my dad. They called what happened imprinting. All I know is he made me feel safe.

He took care of me. He stopped them from ... " I swallowed hard. "He didn't let them hurt me.

"They learned to wait until he left for work to get curious about my arms. One day they wheeled me into surgery, and I screamed for him until they shot the contents of a syringe into my IV port. The drugs didn't take, not all the way, and I woke up with a surgeon leaning over me, a scalpel in one hand and pliers in the other as they pulled a strand of metal from the skin above my elbow."

Cole sucked in a whistling breath through his nose. "What happened next?"

"One of the pediatric nurses called Dad. He'd left his number with a few of them by that point. She tipped him off to what was happening, he rushed up to the hospital, and they put a stop to the procedure." I ended on a bright note. "After that, he never let me out of his sight. He took me home with him a few days later, and I lived with him for about ten months before he came home and slapped a folder on the table at dinner. He said the papers inside made me his daughter, and that no one would ever hurt me again."

And Edward Boudreau had proven as good as his word.

"There's nothing else?" Cole bit out each word. "You have no memory prior to the night you were found?"

"Nope." I could be flippant about it after so many years of being asked the same tired question. "It's like I was born in that moment and nothing came before it."

Meltwater eyes peered straight to my soul, measuring what he saw there, weighing that against an undefinable variable he had yet to share. With a nod, as if confirming what he had long suspected, he sat back in his chair. "That's because you were."

CHAPTER NINETEEN

———◆———

"Come again?" I sputtered a chuckle and shook my head. "I don't think I heard you right."

"You were born into this world fifteen years ago," he said slowly. "Your body is fifteen in human years."

I let that settle. Okay, I *tried* letting it settle. Who was I fooling? "You are pure T-certified crazy. People don't just pop into existence." Though Sherry, who was probably firing her birth cannon as we spoke, might disagree. "Not at that age and not at that size."

"You're not human," he enunciated clearly. "You don't follow their rules. None of us do."

"How?" I pounded my fist on the table, and dull pain rocketed up my arm. "Where did I come from if not here?"

"A world so distant from this one you would die of old age if you tried reaching it as you are now."

More than a hundred years from here, now.

A dull thump announced Portia's arrival. She had leapt

through her window and strolled toward us with an onion in her hand. "Humans dig visual aids," she informed Cole. "Here, sweetie," she said to me. "Let me show you how it works. "This onion represents all the layers in all the worlds." She took a knife from her pocket and sliced it in half. "See all those rings? Each one is its own civilization. We call them terrenes. The kernel in the center is Earth." She took one half and chucked it into the water, then she halved the remaining piece again. "Okay, so. For today's lesson, we're only going to focus on your origin as it pertains to your current location." She tapped the knife's blade at the kernel. "This model shows your world as the top, the cream of the crop, and that's somewhat true." She indicated each of the lower layers until she got to the bottommost one. "This is what humans would consider Hell." She smiled up at me. "That's where you came from, princess."

"I was born in Hell?" I lifted the other discarded quarter of the onion and picked at the outer layer with my thumbnail. "I'm *that* kind of demon?"

"Yes. And, well, no." She pursed her lips. "Hell is a concept spawned by a religion that doesn't exist outside this terrene. It's not even called Hell, technically. It's Otilla. It is the lowest 'hell', the highest court in the land, and the origin of our species."

"Okay." I kept picking apart the crisp, white layers, the pungent smell an anchor to prove this was real. Our conversation was happening. "The princess jab, that part wasn't real."

Santiago had called me princess too. I hoped for my sake it was a term of endearment.

"Otilla's ruling family is related to yours, Czar Astrakhan is your cousin once removed, but no. You're not royalty in that sense." She laughed like I had been silly to imagine I might find out in one day that I was both a demon and a princess. I bet Disney would have loved optioning the rights to that story.

"You're something much worse." She leaned her hip against the table. "You're one of Otilla's elite, a member of the Czar's cadre. This world's lore paints them as the four horsemen, which is totally sexist I might add. Most cadre are women. Few males make the cut. Female Otillians are the most vicious gender, you see."

"Four horsemen?" The onion made a hard thump when it rolled from my hand and thudded onto the planks. "As in *of the apocalypse?*"

"Yep. The very same. Minus the men. And the horses. For one thing, they don't exist in Otilla. For another, if they did, they would be eaten. Not ridden." She patted my cheek. "How does it feel learning you're a horror so feared that word of you has spread throughout all the known terrenes?" She sighed. "Great, right? It must feel amazing. Barely anyone in my terrene knew my name. Mostly they got me confused with my sisters. We were all spawned from the same clutch, and—" She frowned at me. "Why are you so pale? You're not going to vomit again, are you?"

Metal scraped, and then Cole was there, his strong arms sliding around me, his deep voice resonating within me. My whole world narrowed to his face, his lips, but if he was still talking, I was past listening.

Soft sheets, plush mattress, a warm male body stretched beside mine. My senses fed me that information before I opened my eyes. The dark behind my lashes was comfortable, safe. I decided I liked it there. "I'm not opening my eyes until you tell me what just happened was a dream."

"The fainting part or the history lesson?" Portia chirped.

"Portia," Cole growled, "find Luce something to eat."

Her bare feet slapped on the polished wood floor, and a door slammed behind her.

"Are we in your bedroom?" I patted the material beneath me,

certain I was back where I had started my day. "We must be. Otherwise the headboard I feel behind me would be smacking the wall every time you moved."

"Do you mind?" came the dangerous question.

My eyes opened slowly, and sure enough. Cole's room. Cole's bed. Cole's face inches from mine. His nearness gave me the strength to ask, "Am I really some kind of demonic boogeyman?"

"Yes." His gaze never wavered. "Humans named you Pestilence, Breaker of the First Seal. But I have always known you as Conquest, the fierce warrior who crushed terrenes beneath her heel."

"You don't sound as thrilled about the world crushing as Portia," I noted.

"I called you Conquest, and I was your first."

A knot of dread tightened my middle. "What do you mean?"

"Each of us comes from a terrene you and your sisters claimed for the glory of Otilla." Bitterness seeped into his tone. "We are your trophies, your spoils of war, your *pets*. You indoctrinated us into your coterie by force, and we have crossed worlds to fight at your side."

"My coterie?" I pushed up onto my elbows. "I thought these were *your* people."

"Only Otillians are strong enough to bind so many against their will." Fury hissed and crackled in his tone. "I've cared for them in your absence. That's all."

Bind so many against their will. Miller had sounded grateful but . . . no wonder Santiago hated me. No wonder Cole . . . the backs of my eyes stung, and I wished I could blame the onions. "That's why you don't want . . . " *Me.* "You bailed on our date because of what I am. That's why you said we couldn't happen. Are we not . . . ? Compatible?"

Cole searched my face, as he so often did, and exhaled softly. "I want you," he bit out at a clipped pace as though he might somehow outrun his admission. "The fiction of you. So much I slip up sometimes and forget this person, Luce Boudreau, doesn't exist." He traced the curve of my jaw. "She's a shell, a skin Conquest wears and will one day outgrow."

"Don't say that." I shoved him away and rolled to my feet. "I'm *me*. I'm not Conquest. I'm Luce."

The predator in the bed across from me sat up and stared. "You came back wrong."

"Wow. Thanks." A single laugh burst out of me. "Always with the compliments."

"All terrenes are created with inborn defenses meant to insulate them against threats from above and below them. No demon, not even one as powerful as you, can rip a hole between planes and step through. They must be *born* into a world so that they belong to it. The act requires immense power. Few are capable of breaching a new world, but once that seal is broken, others can follow. The more seals that are broken, the more demons can enter a given world." His gaze swept the room as though he saw beyond the walls. "Earth is the core. It's the highest any demon has ever dared climb. This world, so full of soft creatures, has defenses the likes of which we have never encountered."

Until my shoulders brushed the wall, I hadn't been aware I was backing away from him. "Breaching a new terrene?" Grateful for the support, I leaned against the sturdy paneling. "You're saying Earth gave birth to me? And she—what? Dropped me on my head after delivery?"

"It took days for us to transition after you opened the way and days more for us to locate you." He picked at his watchband. "You had been taken in by the humans at that point. We thought that because your skin must be so fragile you meant to live among them and learn from them for a time. You had done the same before, so we created a base in the swamp and waited for your return." He dragged his focus back to me. "Except you never came back for us."

"Not on purpose." I threw up my hands. "I had no idea you existed. I thought I was a freak. I thought I was alone. Do you think I wouldn't have come running had I know there were others like me living so close?"

"I know that now." He studied me, his favorite pastime. "In other terrenes, in other lives, you came back the same. An adult. You belonged to the native culture, but the bands marked you as Otilla's own. You spent months submersing yourself in the local cultures, absorbing information so that when you struck, it was fast and hard and there were no survivors."

Acid burned my throat, and I shook my head until my brain rattled.

"This time you came back as a child. An innocent. You bore the markings of Otilla, but that was all." His lips turned down at the edges. "I thought at first it must be a trap of some kind, a new means of toying with your prey. Years passed before I began to believe the act might be real, to suspect this terrene might have finally bested you by warping your mind and flesh to assimilate you, to create its own champion from the essence of its enemy.

"Part of me still expects betrayal, welcomes it, because that I understand. I dream of you here, in this room with me as you are now, with that soft look in your eyes." He swallowed hard. "I imagine you clawing away the delicate flesh from your bones to expose the demon at your core. I picture you laughing in my face at my horror, kicking the pile of flesh I knew as Luce aside, and mocking me for my weakness." His voice deepened as he stood. "Conquest might have broken me, but I have survived her." He walked past and yanked open the door. "You, Luce . . . you wield the power to shatter me until I am dust, and even that is blown to the four corners of this earth and forgotten."

Cole walked out onto the deck and transformed in the blink of an eye. Massive head bowed, his antlers brushing the planks, he flung back his head and roared, leaping for the sky, and that piercing blue canvas enveloped him in one of her clouds.

"I brought you a Coke," Portia said from outside the room. "The food was a lie. I don't cook. Cole just wanted me out of what little hair he has."

I joined her on the deck, and that was as far as I made it before my knees buckled, and I sat down hard. "I'm a demon."

"Pretty much." She popped the top on the can and drank from it before passing it to me. "What? I don't have cooties, and besides I saw you and Miller do this earlier. Do you know where his mouth has been? No, you don't. While I, on the other hand, brushed my teeth for you. I even gargled with Lysol."

I accepted the can, because it gave me something to do with my hands that wasn't pulling out my hair. "Listerine."

"Sure. Whatever." She sat beside me so close the fabric of our shirts brushed. "It's not so bad, is it? Being one of us?"

"No." I wriggled the tab. "It's just that I've been searching for where I belong my whole life."

"And you didn't expect it to be here." She stretched out her long legs and crossed them at the ankles. "I get that. It's just nice." She nudged me with her knee. "Having the gang back together. One big, dysfunctional family."

"Why don't you hate me?" I glanced up at her. "How can you be so . . . nice?"

"Life was a misery before you arrived in Cael. As the youngest daughter in a family of thirty, and a runt to boot, I had no value. I was a piss-poor fighter, I had never killed anyone of note in battle, and I had no reputation to shield me.

"My father sold me into marriage three years before you arrived. My husband beat me, shared me with his men, and—you can imagine the rest. I might have let him live had he not crushed my eggs as I laid them. Those were my children, regardless of who their father might have been, they were *mine*. And I failed them as I had been failed.

"When you arrived, when you unleashed Cole and Miller. Gods, *Miller*." Her eyes gleamed with the memory. "You promised me vengeance in exchange for fealty. I bent my knee to you, and we razed my little corner of the world. We hunted each lover that had been forced upon me, and we slaughtered them. And months later, when at last I located my coward of a husband, I ripped out his primary heart with my claws and fed it to him in strips. The secondary I gifted Miller while it was still inside his carcass." She raised her pant leg, and a thin band of rose gold shone at her ankle. "I was already a slave, but when I left with you, I chose my master. I have never regretted the bargain we struck, and I never will."

Words caught in my throat. Horror at what she had done, the reckoning I had helped unleash, shriveled my gut to the size of a raisin. But what had been done to Portia . . . to her unborn children . . . that was so much worse. The acts so vile I had difficulty dredging up the guilt that ought to be choking me.

Later. I would process all of this later. Alone in my room, in the quiet, when I could look inside myself and wait to see what stared back. That's when I would shatter. Not here. Not now. Not when so many others depended on me to keep putting one foot in front of the other. For Maggie I would not stumble.

"There are worse fates," she told me. "This life—at least it's not boring."

"What about the others?" Santiago had no love for me. Cole ... I smacked down that thought so fast I gave myself whiplash. But Miller didn't seem to mind me and neither did Thom. "Are they here willingly?"

"No, sweet cheeks, they're not. Not all of them. And don't waste your breath asking me for the scoop. Each of us deserves the chance to tell you our own story the way we remember it. Maybe not the way you do."

"How is this possible?" I held out my hands and examined the lines and scars and creases. No hint of claw or scale showed. What kind of monster was I that I could hide so well in plain sight? "I'm a cop. My job is to uphold the law, to protect innocents. Not enslave them."

"Irony, am I right?" Portia ground her knuckle into the skin over my heart. "Some part of you must be aware of Conquest deep down. That kind of demon can't be contained forever. That you've managed this long—*if* you've managed this long— is miraculous." More confirmation that no one believed I was who I said I was, which, I guess, was fair considering I had the same problem believing them when they claimed I was who they said I was too. "Who knows? Maybe this incarnation is about atonement." Sudden laughter exploded from her, and she doubled over holding her stomach. "Phew, boy. That was a good one. The Remorseful Conqueror." She wiped tears from her eyes. "The upstanding citizen shtick, acting like you care for your fellow man, that's what makes this all so unbelievable."

"Me as a mass murderer you believe," I said, stunned, "but me as a cop—that's suspicious to you?"

"When you've known Conquest for as long as we all have, yes. It is. She doesn't turn over new leaves. She crushes them in her fist just to hear them crinkle, then sets the tree they fell from on fire after chopping it down and marking all the acorns from its line for death by boll weevil. That's a thing, right? No? Maybe I'm thinking about cotton."

"I can't absorb this." I tossed back the sugary soda, hoping the caffeine might kick my brain into gear. "There's a tiny voice in my head that's screaming and running in circles."

"You do appear to be mostly human," she mused. "Maybe we should have been more strategic when dropping our truth bombs."

The rumble of an engine and the sound of gravel crunching under tires announced we had company.

"Who goes there?" Portia called. "Luce and I are bonding over old war stories. Mostly hers. She doesn't even remember them, which is heartbreaking when you reflect on it. I mean, that's her lives' work gone. Poof. She could live and die as this skin sack she's wearing, and all that history would be lost."

When no smartass response was forthcoming, I got a bad feeling and pushed to my feet. Portia rose beside me, and together we crossed the deck and circled around to the parking area where five SUVs sat, one of them idling.

"Thom." I recognized him first, blood smearing his cheek, and broke into a run. "He's hurt." Portia beat me to the SUV and yanked open the door. He spilled out into her arms, and she lowered him onto the ground. I dropped to my knees and checked his pulse. "Thom, can you hear me?"

His eyelids fluttered, and a string of rasped words impossible for me to untangle eased past his lips. Portia didn't have that problem. She launched into a fluid glide of conversation while I sat there worse than useless. Who could I call? Not the paramedics. Not even Cole. Dragons didn't carry cellphones.

A moan rose from the darkened interior of the SUV, and I ducked in to check the backseat.

"Portia," I called. "Santiago's on the bench." I killed the

ignition, slid out, then yanked the rear door open. "Hey, asshat. Open your eyes if you can hear me."

He cracked his lids a fraction and growled. "Hands off."

"I'm certified in first aid, CPR and AED." Touch was unavoidable, so I tugged my sleeves down over my palms and pinned them in place with my fingertips. Hooking my arms under his, I hauled him out and then eased him onto the ground. "Show me where it hurts."

Santiago grimaced and curled in on himself. "Nothing hurts." He hissed at me. "Get lost."

"Stop being a dick," Portia snapped. "Let her help."

Snarling at us both, he exposed his stomach and the ropes of intestines spilling through his fingers. "Do *not* vomit on me. I'm already pissed off as it is."

Grateful as I was when that frost crackled over my heart, and the panicked voice shrieking in my head silenced, I questioned for the first time if it was—as I had always assumed—a byproduct of my training, or if it was a remnant of Conquest's battle-hardened personality embedded so deeply into my psyche I could wrap that calm around myself like a blanket.

"How fast do you heal?" I gripped his shoulder and pushed him flat on his back. "I can stuff this back into you, but I need to know if it's going to take. Do I need to sew you shut?"

"Fast," he snapped. "I might heal ... before I can ... "

"Bite down on this." I leaned to the right and hauled a dead limb closer, then snapped off a fat stick. "Scream if you feel the need."

Teeth flaking bark into his mouth, he growled, "I'm not going to—"

I sank my hands into the slimy wet lengths of his innards, shoving them into the bulging gash across his lower stomach, and his eyes rolled back in his head. I packed it all in and pressed my palms end-to-end to hold his guts where they belonged. As I watched, his skin knit together, fusing in an angry red line. I had a fingertip in the wound below his navel when the flesh began mending, and when I withdrew, it nursed on my nail.

The icy calm might have admired his rapid healing ability, coveted it even, but I suppressed a disgusted shudder. Even cocooned deep within myself, I had limits. Santiago had been right to worry I might lose my lunch on him. With him out of danger, I jerked out of that headspace and gave myself a minute to get used to the rush of heightened emotions around me again.

"What did you do?" Portia asked in a quiet voice. "Where did you go just now?"

"I locked down my panic at seeing a man's guts writhing like worms on the ground, and I handled the situation." I sucked in a few more breaths, grateful for the humid air warming me from the inside out. "How's Thom?"

"Better off than Santiago." She scratched her nails over his scalp. "It's hard to take down Thom. He's our medic. Most of his bodily fluids can be used for medicinal purposes." Her eyes danced when she caught me wrinkling my nose. "You should see your face right now. You're wondering how you healed from your injuries so fast, and which of his body parts donated the miracle drug."

"What could have done this to them?" I asked, knowing full well the answer.

"Another demon. A higher demon." She glanced back at the SUV, but I assured her it was clear. "We need to touch base with Miller."

"This morning he was working on the Claremont case." It had been hours since his last update, which I had taken to mean good things since the alternative sucked. "Where would he go?"

"Anywhere with strong brew and quick refills." Portia frowned at Santiago, reaching out to ruffle his hair. "He's such a bastard."

"No argument here." I read between the lines. "He's your friend."

"Yeah, I guess I'd piss on him if he was on fire." She thumped him on the head. "Just don't tell him about the friends thing, or I'll never hear the end of his proposed benefits list."

"My lips are sealed." I couldn't bring myself to look at my hands. "Let me wash up, and I'll call Miller for a check-in." I got to my feet and decided swamp water would have to do. I didn't want to leave gore on the doorknobs while I searched for a bathroom. Assuming these demons used the facilities in the same sense as me. "Will you need help bringing them in?"

"Nah." She crossed her legs and sat in the gravel. "I'll wait for them to wake. It shouldn't take long. An hour or so. Thom worked some mojo on Santiago, or he'd be dead right about now. They need rest, and I don't want to risk moving either of them."

Nodding, I set off to the water's edge and knelt to scrub my hands clean with grit from the silty bottom. I risked a glimpse at my wavering reflection, but she only stared back at me. I blinked first, too afraid of what might emerge if I watched her for too long. After wiping my palms dry on a clean part of my shirt, I dialed Miller. He answered on the first ring. "That was fast."

"I was expecting a call from Santiago." Irritation spiked his voice. "He was doing a wipe job at the hospital and promised to get back with me—"

"Damn it." Shocked by the guys showing up wearing their insides on their outsides, I had overlooked a serious problem. "Jane is at the hospital without a guard."

"Come again?"

"Santiago and Thom were attacked." I blotted my knuckles long after the skin dried. "They're in bad shape, but Portia says they'll recover. Both of them will be out of commission for a while, though."

"Meet me there?" he said a beat later.

"Like you have to ask." I ended the call, jogged to Portia and filled her in on what few bits she hadn't caught with her super hearing. "Can I borrow a car?"

"Take number three. She's usually mine, so she's full on gas and not overflowing with takeout garbage." She tossed me a set of keys from her pocket. "Stop waffling. Miller needs backup. I can cover these two."

"What about Cole?" I closed my fingers over warm metal. "Do you have a way to warn him?"

"He never stays gone long," she assured me, a heaviness in her gaze. "I'll fill him in when he gets back. Be careful out there."

"You too." I climbed in the berry-scented SUV, cranked up the AC, then spun gravel in my haste. Juiced on adrenaline, I almost ignored the ringing of my cell, but I couldn't afford to miss an update. Not with so many irons on the fire. "Boudreau."

"Dougherty," the detective grunted in response. "Thought you'd want to know we traced the call Maggie made at the emergency vet clinic to Justin Sheridan. Turns out he routes his calls through an answering service during his business trips. The phone system went down the night before Maggie disappeared, and their rep says when the service is interrupted, messages accumulated during that time don't automatically resend. Sheridan had no idea there was an issue until we contacted him."

"Did you hear the message?" The air whooshed from my lungs. "What did Maggie say?"

"There were two, actually. The first one came in around seven on the morning she disappeared. She mentioned leaving her phone at your house and told Sheridan to call the school if he needed her before four. In the last call, the one from the vet clinic, she confirmed she was with Robert Martin and apologized for running late for dinner. She promised to be home soon." He hesitated. "We've issued an APB on Martin. I'll let you know when we have him in custody."

"Thanks." A lump clogged my throat, and I couldn't swallow past my guilt. Had I returned her phone, she could have called for help. We might have tracked her cell signal. But I hadn't prioritized her, and I might not get the chance to correct that mistake. "I appreciate the update."

"Anytime, Boudreau." He gentled his tone. "I'll do my best for your friend."

"I know you will." And because it was my fault his workload had just doubled, I forced out, "I'm sorry about Buck. I heard he's expected to make a full recovery."

"Bastard just wanted a vacation if you ask me." He huffed, trying to sound miffed while concern thickened his voice. "His sister is going through an ugly divorce. She moved in with her three kids, all under five, and his house is a zoo. He probably broke his own leg to escape."

I shared a laugh with him because he seemed to need one and signed off with my thanks.

Thanks to Maggie, we had a lock on Robert Martin. Now it was time to nail his ass to the wall.

But first I had to meet Miller and secure Jane. Even if choosing them felt like letting Maggie down. Again.

CHAPTER TWENTY

———◆———

Hungry vultures kept watch on the hospital entrance, so I cruised around to the pharmacy where Miller had let me out the first time and parked. We must have been surfing the same wavelength, because he joined me a minute later. His first point of business was removing the White Horse magnets from the sides of his SUV and stowing them in the trunk. He slapped logos that read Thom's Plumbing on each of our vehicles then slung a laptop bag over his shoulder and met me on the sidewalk.

"Do you have a way in?" He adjusted the strap while he scanned the area for roosting cameramen.

"Follow me." I led him around back, waded into the bushes then hauled him along behind me. "Sit tight. We could be here awhile."

Fifteen minutes later, a tall man with a vaporizer pen between his fingers emerged. The door hadn't closed before he was sucking down lungfuls of aerosol and expelling white

curls of mist through his nose that managed to remind me of
Cole's dragon. After the first several huffs, he exhaled with
relief then wedged the brick into place and moseyed over to
the usual alcove.

I gestured for Miller to follow, then led the charge through
the back door. This time Ida wasn't around to run interference,
and we had to flash badges to assure the nurses who stopped
us that we had a right to be in this section of the building. We
zipped up to the fourth floor and eased into the hall. Three
steps later, Miller stiffened beside me.

"Blood." Chin tipped back, he breathed deep. "Santiago and
Thom's . . . and Jane's."

My feet wrested control away from my brain, and I bolted for
her room. Miller caught me by the wrist and almost dislocated
my shoulder hauling me a safe distance from the door.

"Let me go." I snapped my hand up, applying pressure
against his thumb and breaking his grip. "She's hurt. We
have to—"

"She's the threat, Luce." Pity filled his gaze, and his voice
came out raw. "Think about it."

Portia had told me only a higher demon could have savaged
Thom and Santiago. Well, apparently, it didn't get much higher
than me. And Jane's markings were a carbon copy of mine.
Hers weren't singularities like the others in the coterie but the
full treatment. Meaning she must be from Otilla too.

"I'm an idiot." I rubbed my forehead with the heel of my
palm. "She's like me, like Cole, like *us*." I had known about
demons for twenty-four hours, and my brain had been the
consistency of oatmeal for a large portion of that time, but I
couldn't blame either of those for my willful ignorance. "The
bruises. Goddamn it. Why didn't I see this sooner?"

Better make that two months of brushing with bar soap.

"You didn't know sooner." Miller let me work it out on my own while keeping me corralled. "None of this is your fault."

"All this time it's been her." From what I had observed of demons, they all cloaked themselves with humanity. Jane was the skin. The gator was her true face. Jane was the gator. The gator was Jane. *Jane tried to kill me.* "That bitch." Fury crackled through my veins. "She punched holes through my house. Five minutes earlier, and Dad would have been home." The demon had almost been too fast for me. He never would have made it across the field. "She could have killed him. She *would* have killed him."

"We should have told you last night, but you were so hopeful." He bowed his head. "We had no idea if Jane had been reborn the same blank slate as you. All we could do until we had proof was wait and watch. It's the only reason Cole accepted the commission from your father."

"The same as me," I echoed, shoulder blades hitting the wall as that final puzzle piece *snicked* into place. The size of my hurt couldn't be contained. It bled from my pores, a vicious ache that shattered me on a fundamental level. Family stood together. Family stuck up for each other. Family loved one another. Those were the lessons I had learned during my short human life, and she had blown them all to smithereens. "Jane is one of my sisters."

"No." Miller brushed his fingertips under my eyes to dry the tears I hadn't noticed falling. "She's one of Conquest's sisters. War. Breaker of the Second Seal." Preoccupied with the liquid on his fingertips, he sniffed them and then tasted the salty residue. "These are heart's tears. They taste of pain and betrayal."

"Does that mean you believe me?" I sniffled, unable to articulate what it would mean for at least one person to believe I was real, that I was Luce. "Cole called me a fiction, but I'm not. I'm me."

"Cole has earned his right to bitterness where Conquest is concerned, and you may never outstretch her dark shadow with him. Perhaps that means his opinion of you, *Luce*—" he emphasized my name over hers "—is not the one you should hold closest to your heart."

I offered him a watery smile, certain any demon cred I had was ruined. Not that I minded all that much. I'd take blubbering human over stone-cold bitch any day. "You're a good guy."

His lips quirked. "For a demon?"

"Did you hear a qualifier?" He flushed and glanced away as an unsavory thought occurred to me. "If Jane is my sister, and she's also the super gator, does that mean Conquest is a spring-loaded fish trap too?"

"No." He dragged a hand over his mouth, as though unsure what or how much to tell me. "Jane mated the former general of Czar Astrakhan's army, a Drosera by the name of Thanases. Otillians are chameleonic. It's how they infiltrate the other terrenes with ease, how they spread their genetic material throughout the worlds, but there are limits."

Chameleonic implied I was a shapeshifter of some kind. After Cole that shouldn't surprise me, but it did. Maybe Cole was right. Maybe Luce was my skin suit. Maybe that's why I didn't identify with the woman in the mirror. Perhaps my truest self was the one invisible in this form.

What a terrifying thought.

"Each Otillian can possess only one core identity. Usually, they take the shape of their mate, and once the bond is permanent, they're no longer able to shift to their birth form. War took Thanases's form so they could . . ." red splotches mottled his cheeks " . . . procreate. He joined her coterie and travels with her."

Demons wearing people suits. Demons wearing alligator suits. Sure. Why not? At least the latter was more palatable by human fashion standards.

"The super gator who almost bit off my head, the one swimming around Jane—*War*—that was him? Thanases?"

"He was protecting her." Miller tilted his head. "Aren't you going to ask what your true form resembles?"

Honest curiosity burned in the question, and I sensed its answer would render me to cinders.

"No." I shook my head. "I'll be able to sleep knowing I'm not going to shift into some villain from *Peter Pan*, and that's good enough for me."

The amusement dancing in his eyes hinted at pleasure over keeping the secret. I wondered if he thought I would enjoy the eventual revelation. I hated to burst his balloon, but if birthdays had taught me anything, it was that I didn't deal with surprise well.

I nudged him aside with a gentle sweep of my arm. "The crime scene isn't getting any fresher. Let's go."

After a lingering assessment, he nodded and let me take point. Having Miller at my back gave me the courage to grip the doorknob and wrench it open onto a bloodbath. Crimson smears covered the walls and floor. The sheets were soaked, and red tipped the glassy teeth of the shattered window.

"Let's clear the room." I checked the hall to ensure it had remained clear. "I go left. You go right."

We entered together. I jerked aside the curtain hanging from the ceiling while Miller checked behind the door. We cleared the bathroom as a unit, as though we had worked together for years instead of minutes, then shut ourselves in the suite while I made the call down to the station to report Jane's disappearance.

All the while, I wondered if it was smart leaving demon blood smeared across so many surfaces, but the cherry on top of today would be getting charged for evidence tampering by a pissed off police chief champing at the bit for revenge and a means of salvaging his career.

The first cop arrived less than five minutes later. He'd been one floor down, sitting with Buck's sister while he was in surgery. The doctors were inserting a metal rod through his shattered femur, and I winced when he mentioned screws. Buck might never walk without a limp, and that was on me.

Shoving that guilt, that regret, down until I could breathe again, I focused on making an exit.

The lies I told the officer came easier. Maggie had been wrong about me. It turned out I was a good liar after all. Was my demon heritage to blame? Or was I simply getting better with practice? I didn't want to think too hard about either option.

I told the officer I'd bumped into Miller in the elevator. I claimed he'd been on his way up to relieve Thom, that we had discovered the scene together and called it in immediately. After promising to fill out a report and fax it over from my shared home office—I wasn't tempting fate by stepping foot inside the department today—he released us to get serious about locating Jane without thinking to ask where Thom had gone.

Figuring there was safety in numbers, I ditched Portia's SUV and called shotgun in Miller's. I had to move a tablet and a stack of papers out of my way first. The FBI logo winking up at me gave me pause, as did the six-by-nine copy of Robert Martin's yearbook portrait and the candid shot of his vehicle. I climbed in and balanced the pile on my knees while I fastened my seatbelt. "How far did you get with the Kapoor situation before I called?"

"I got in and got out with what we needed before he cleared the first-floor residents." Miller smiled like the cat who ate the canary. "Turns out the apartment complex has been undergoing renovations. The day the incident was reported, only one section of balconies was accessible. The lower floors had all been sandblasted and repainted. Their balconies were covered in plastic sheeting and taped off besides. That left the fourth floor as the only viable option. All I had to do was beat Kapoor there and canvas the residents with apartments facing the road. I found Mr. Arnold Brashear on my second knock."

"Smart," I praised him. "Very smart."

"I was prepared to tell him I worked for White Horse and that we had taken on the Claremont case, but he was happy to invite me in and chat me up without me flashing my credentials." He tapped the photo. "He positively ID'd Robert Martin and his vehicle."

"Kapoor won't be far behind. Once he catches wind of the APB out on Martin, he'll want to seize control of Maggie's case and tie them together as tightly as possible." Miller rolled his hand, waiting for me to elaborate. "Turns out Maggie made a call the night she disappeared. She left a voicemail IDing Robert Martin as the man who drove her to the clinic. Proof he was the last person to see her." Not that we'd had much doubt about his involvement. What we lacked was motive. "What are the odds Jane is involved in these disappearances?"

"High," he said without missing a beat. "Chances are good she's been studying you since her breach. That explains how she knew to go for Maggie, but not why she chose the Claremont girl."

"I have a theory about that." I massaged my aching forehead, each thought a shard of glass embedded in my temples. "War recreated my—breach?" He nodded that I had it right. "She wanted to draw me out, see what makes me tick."

"Okay, I'm with you so far."

"Think about it. As well documented as my case was, she had step-by-step instructions. The Claremont girl was bait. War used the high-profile disappearance to catch my attention." She and Angel shared a similar build and hair color. That must have been intentional. "All she had to do once Rixton and I were assigned to the case was dunk herself in the swamp that night, ensuring no one could tell more than she was a female in distress. She was hedging her bets. Between the case and the link to my past, she was guaranteed I would show up or hear about it and hunt her down afterward."

"Initiating first contact allowed her to manipulate the circumstances, ensuring a favorable outcome," he murmured.

"I was so desperate for answers that I welcomed her. Heck, my dad hired a security detail for her." A chill settled in my bones, and I had my phone in hand and his number dialed before Miller's lips parted. I held up my finger and didn't breathe until his voice came on the line. "Dad?"

"Hey, baby girl." A television blared in the background, the sports announcer's voice familiar. "Hold on." He covered the mouthpiece and called, "Harry, turn that down. Luce is on the phone."

"You're with Uncle Harold?" I melted into my seat with gratitude he had taken my advice. "Good. Stay put. Don't go home yet. It's not safe."

"What aren't you telling me?" His voice went stern. "Where are you?"

"I'm following a lead on Maggie's case. I'm with Miller, from White Horse. There was an incident at the hospital. Jane is missing." His shouted *what* made my eardrum ring. "We have people on it. There's no reason for you to get involved at this juncture. I called the station, and Miller called Cole. We've got the situation covered."

"Where is Cole?" He heaped a whole lot of suspicion into three little words.

"Not here." I sank my nails into my palm. "I haven't seen him for a few hours. Listen, that doesn't matter. All you need to know is that I'm fine, and I've got someone watching my back. Just stay with Uncle Harold, okay? Don't go out after dark, and it wouldn't hurt my feelings if y'all finished watching the ballgame with a couple of shotguns on the table next to the pita chips and hummus." A twinge hit me as I remembered I had no idea if mine had been retrieved. I was attached to that gun, damn it. "Promise?"

"I don't like this," he grumped. "You *will* explain yourself. I'll give you twenty-four hours, and I expect contact every eight hours, or I'm coming after you." He made it an order. "Understand?"

"Yes, sir." I couldn't fight my smile. "You've got yourself a deal."

We each ended the call before the other heaped on more ultimatums.

Miller cocked his head, staring at the phone with curiosity. "You really love him, don't you?"

"He's my dad." I let him hear my fierce pride in the man who had raised me. "He's the best man I know, and I would do anything to live up to his expectations."

After absorbing my declaration, Miller pulled out of the parking lot. "What's our next move?"

"We go after Robert Martin." It was the only option available to us that made sense. "He's in this up to his neck, and War needs a safe haven to run to while she recovers from her injuries. As chewed up as Thom and Santiago were, there's no way she slipped past them without sustaining damage."

"I agree on all points." He picked up speed. "You mind doing the legwork to pin him down?"

The urge to call in and ask for backup twitched in my fingers, but this wasn't my case. The department, and soon the FBI, would be searching for Martin. Thanks to our pit stop at the hospital, they had gotten a head start on the manhunt. Meaning we might be picking through their sloppy seconds or even thirds.

"Not at all." I dialed up the front office at the John W. Rosen Elementary School and waited for the secretary to answer. "Hey, Megan. It's Luce Boudreau. Can you do a favor for me?"

"The police are here," Megan blurted. "They're in a meeting with Principal Higgins."

That right there was why I made her my first call. Small towns do love their gossip.

"I'm calling in relation to that." Sort of. "Can you tell me if Robert Martin is on the campus?"

"Sure thing." She pitched her voice low. "The police already had me check his records. He's been absent for the last two days. It's odd because he otherwise had perfect attendance. Five years, and he never called in. He didn't this time either. He just didn't show up for his class." She hesitated. "Should I be telling you this? Are you sure you wouldn't like to talk to one of the officers?"

"I wouldn't want to interrupt." I thumbed through the stack of papers on my lap and found what I needed. Martin's home address was on the second page of the file Miller had compiled. "Thanks for your help."

I ended the call before I got caught buttering up the staff.

"He's not at work," I told Miller. "Looks like we're making

a house call." Martin's neighborhood was part of the beat I shared with Rixton. I could have navigated there with my eyes shut. Since Miller didn't stop me, I flipped through the rest of the materials on my lap. "What's this?"

"A copy of the crime-scene photos from where the severed leg was recovered. Took me longer than expected to gain access to those files." His turn-of-phrase had me thinking his methods might not be exactly legal. Oblivious to me mentally sticking fingers in my ears, because I did not want details, he continued, "I was printing the set when you called. I brought them along just in case."

"You're hoping I can ID it if it's Maggie's." I thumbed the yellow tab and reached for that calm, cold place in my middle. Pulse steady, I turned the page and studied the image. "No jewelry, birthmarks or—wait. There's mud on the toes, but see this? They're painted."

"Okay." He sounded unconvinced. "What does that matter?"

"Maggie is allergic to the dibutyl phthalate in regular nail polish, and she can't sit still long enough to apply water-based polishes. They're more, well, watery." I tapped the image. "These toes are painted, that means they aren't hers."

The grim set of his jaw told me he had followed that information to its logical conclusion. "Then there's a good chance it belongs to Angel Claremont."

The cold, rational part of my mind agreed, and it wasn't bothered by the butchery. Emotion was required before regret or disgust or sorrow could manifest, and I had yet to shrug back into that frame of mind. As I thawed, I found no scrap of happiness over Maggie being spared. A young woman had, at best, lost a limb. At worst, she had lost her life, chopped up for spare parts War sprinkled like breadcrumbs in a trail I was meant to follow.

"Do you think she's alive?" I forced myself to ask him. I trusted his gut more than mine right now.

"Yes." His thumbs kneaded the steering wheel. "War will have done her homework. She'll know there are tests that can determine if the victim was alive when the leg was severed. She'll want you to hope."

I braced my head against the window and zoned out while he drove. All these years, I had pined for answers. Ignorance had been bliss, but I'd had tunnel vision and hadn't enjoyed that window of happiness. Thanks to history lessons with Portia and Cole, I possessed more information than I could process. My brain rebelled against the volume I had absorbed, the knowledge so foreign and impossible as to be alien.

Be careful what you wish for, you just might get it.

Miller parked on the curb in front of a modest house in an older subdivision that fit with what I knew about Robert Martin. No crime scene tape clung to the doorway, and I spotted no signs of forced entry. The Feds must not have breached the house, hoping he might return here. Or perhaps they might have temporarily dismissed the location after learning he'd had two days in which to disappear. Maybe they knew something we didn't. Probably a lot of somethings, actually. The quiet street might also indicate a dispute over where the department's jurisdiction ended and the FBI's began. Maggie was still Canton PD's case, after all.

Whatever the reason for our good fortune, we planned on making the most of the opportunity.

"Sit tight." Miller claimed the laptop. "Let me email Cole our coordinates and attach the Martin files."

Used to covering my and Rixton's bacon with dispatch before exiting the vehicle to answer a call, I sat tight and scanned the area for signs one of the harbingers of the apocalypse was bedding down in the nondescript house, that a super gator might be prowling the backyard or that kidnap victims might be held inside, but the blandness of the neighborhood made it impossible to imagine anything so extraordinary might occur here.

War had chosen her mark well. Given her name, I assumed strategy was her strength, and she had certainly flexed those muscles so far. She had fooled us. Me most of all.

"Ready?" Miller muted his phone, and I did the same. We got out, and he circled around and opened the SUV's rear hatch. He lifted the flap covering the tire well and withdrew handguns from a padded case for each of us. "Here's an extra clip."

"I can appreciate a guy willing to share his toys." Grateful as I was to be armed, my fingers itched for my service weapon. "I'll circle around back and—"

"No." He slammed the hatch and paced up the sidewalk. "We go in through the front. Together."

I caught up to him. "We do that, and we risk her slipping out the back."

"We don't do that, and we're toast. Cole is the only one of us who can take on a daughter of Otilla and live to tell the tale." He deferred to me. "Unless you're willing to unpack Conquest?"

"That's not an option." I hoped I was telling us both the truth. I wanted her buried so deep nothing short of my death would unleash her. "We'll do this your way. The victims are our primary concern."

"Wrong." He edged in front of me when we reached the door. "Staying alive is our primary concern."

Live to fight another day was solid advice, and I couldn't argue against his logic even when a part of me hissed running was cowardice.

"You want to do the honors?" He glanced over his shoulder

while pounding his fist against the door. "People respond better to pretty women with badges."

Unsure I believed him on either point, I lifted my badge and held it up to the peephole. "Officer Luce Boudreau with the Canton Police Department." I gave it a full minute. "Mr. Martin, we need to ask you some questions. Open the door."

Miller paused his banging and leaned closer, pressing his ear against the wood. "I hear movement. No footsteps. Scraping." His nostrils flared as he pressed his nose to the seam in the door, and his pupils dilated. "I smell old blood."

"Check it." I trained my weapon on the door at chest height. We didn't get lucky with the lock. It was engaged. That meant we couldn't fudge our way inside by claiming it had been open when we arrived. Odds were good we weren't the first to give it a spin, but we would be the last. I turned Miller's earlier question around on him. "You want to do the honors?"

"I thought you'd never ask." He used his shoulder as a battering ram, and wood splintered. "It's coming from over here."

The interior was as bland and tidy as the exterior. Standing in the living room, I couldn't hear or smell what had set Miller on high alert. I let him lead with his keen nose and sharp ears while covering us from the rear. Ambush was a popular wartime tactic for a good reason. What some might view as cowardice, others considered the best use of resources, even if the supply expended was human life.

After clearing the house, we entered the garage. The space hadn't been converted structurally, but pegboard covered the walls, and interlocking foam squares cushioned the concrete floor. Tools hung from hooks, and a large workbench occupied the center of the space. Next to that Martin had peeled up a four-by-four section of foam, and under that we discovered a hatch set into the foundation.

I spat out a curse. "It's an in-ground storm shelter."

"That's a thing in garages?" He squatted and tested the latch then ran his finger over a keyhole. "This unit is new. The man-ufacturing date and brand is printed right here on this sticker."

"From what I remember, these units run larger than typi-cal shelters. The capacity is around eight to ten people." He quirked up an eyebrow. "Dad went through a baby proofing phase after my adoption was finalized. Part of his upgrades to the house included us sitting through a presentation on these things. They're usually added-on after construction, and that jacks up the cost." I toed the edge with my shoe. "The install-ers cut through the slab with a diamond blade wet saw, use a backhoe to scoop out all the dirt then lower the unit into place and bolt it down. All without wrecking the garage."

"What I'm hearing is this will require finesse."

"Finesse. I like that." I shot him a grin. "How good are you at safe-cracking?"

The house creaked behind us, the protest of old floorboards under new weight, and I whirled toward the door, raised my gun and waited. A full minute lapsed before my arms got shaky. Taut with nerves, I had reached the edge of my endurance for the day. I was about to suggest we sweep the house again when a boxy tomcat with lush midnight fur strutted out with a smirking twitch of his whiskers. His tail, what was left of it, pointed straight up in the air. Scars crisscrossed his face, and his eyes gleamed emerald in the low light. All of that I could overlook except for ... *those*.

"Miller?" I kept the gun trained on the demon cat. "Is this a friend of yours?"

"*Meow.*"

"Think about it," he said, a smile in his voice. "It'll come to you."

"Me-ow."

"That's what I'm afraid of." The cat gazed up at me in expectation. "What does he want?"

Almost on cue, he tensed his hind legs and leapt. At the midpoint of his arc, delicate black wings unfurled from his back, and he flapped with feline laziness, expending only the exact amount of effort required to perch on my shoulder. Much to my surprise, he weighed about as much as the cockatoo who had once failed Maggie's audition as class pet due to her allergies.

"Thom." It hit me in a sudden rush. "Thom the Tomcat. Funny."

First Cole's leonine dragon and now a feathered kitty cat.

Obviously Conquest had a type. Great. My terrifying inner demon was a crazy cat lady.

"You look well enough." I rubbed his ears. "Portia was on the nose about how fast you'd heal."

How she'd earned that information made my gut twist, so I locked those thoughts away for later examination too. All the while wondering how many skeletons my mental closet could hold before exploding.

"Thom's the most resilient of us," Miller confided. "He's had about nine thousand lives and counting."

Despite Miller's grim warnings about their demonic forms, there was nothing terrifying about the demon cat. He was kind of adorable in a rough and tumble way. Even Cole, whose dragon awestruck me, didn't inspire the same urge to cuddle.

"You're a cute little fella," I cooed at the kitty, who purred back and butted his head against my jaw. Cole must have forwarded Miller's email to the others, and they had dispatched Thom, the demonic equivalent of an EMT. "Thanks for coming to lend a paw."

Miller, who had set about attempting to pick the lock, let the tools go limp in his hand. He watched me scratch under Thom's chin, his lips set in a grim line. He ducked his head when he caught me staring and resumed his task. The muscles in his shoulders tensed, and something told me not to press him.

"What are our options for getting the hatch open?" Normal shelters weren't built with these kinds of exterior locking mechanisms. They were constructed with the understanding the people inside would be the ones sliding the bars or flipping the latches into place. Screwing up my courage, I asked the question I hadn't braved since entering the garage. "Can you still hear them?"

"Yes." He traced the seam with a fingertip. "It's not sound-proof." His eyelashes lowered. "I can hear a heartbeat."

"Singular." My heart plummeted as fast as a stone hurled down a well. "Not plural."

"The blood scent is freshest here. One of the victims bled out, recently." He lifted a mat and peered underneath. "He was neat. Kept his mess contained, his workstation tidy. He messed up with the concrete. It's porous, absorbs like a sponge, and he didn't seal the raw seams."

"So either one of them is . . . " I couldn't say the word. "Or one was moved to a separate location."

"I can rip it off the hinges," he offered. "It'll be hard to explain to the Feds later."

No harder than explaining what we were doing here or how we got in through the ruined front door.

"Do it." The victim was in imminent danger. That was all the permission my conscience required to act. "What do you need?"

Miller angled his face away. "For you to step inside the house and shut the door."

"There's plenty of room." I backed up a few steps. "I'll just hang over here out of the way."

"I'll have to complete a partial shift." Turn his head any farther, and it would pop right off his neck. "You don't want to see that." He shook his head. "*I* don't want you to see that."

"I'm not afraid." I stood my ground. "I trust you, Miller."

A shudder rippled through him as though my words had broken him. "No." He hesitated. "I value our friendship too much for you to see what I really am."

Sharp claws pierced my shoulder as Thom kicked off me and fluttered to the ground. Stubby tail up, he yowled imperiously until I followed him. At his urging, I shut the door and left the man I was starting to consider a friend alone to deal with his personal demon.

CHAPTER TWENTY-ONE

———◆———

Thom planted his butt in front of the door to prevent curiosity from overtaking me. Smart move for a cat, even a demonic one. I was human enough to admit—okay, so I wasn't human—but I was still willing to own up to my failings. Yes, I wondered what the big deal was about Miller's demonic form. And yes, some part of me burned to prove to him I could handle his truth.

But a niggling voice whined in my head. What if he was right? What if I couldn't handle another major shock on top of all the others? He would read any fear as rejection. I would hurt him, and that was the last thing I wanted to do. He deserved better than that from me.

"Someone ought to write one of those dummy guides on how to befriend demons," I told the cat.

Thom rustled his wings, and a feather drifted to the carpet. Tail flicking, he pounced on it, batting it in the air and kicking his hind legs to keep it in play, chomping on the vane when it tickled his nose. When at last he had sufficiently murdered it, he spat the wet clump out on the floor then started grooming himself.

A heinous grinding noise caused Thom's fur to stand on end. Metal screamed. The ground shook. A low reptilian hiss slithered under the door, tickling my hindbrain, and I inched back a step on instinct. The cat glared at me as if to say *See? This is why you weren't invited to the party.* Properly chastised, I resumed my position and waited. A perfectly human Miller opened the door not too long after, pale and shaken, his chest rising in hard pants.

"I can't be in here." The raw, deep voice he projected belonged on a man five times his size. "The meat is too ... fresh."

The blood drained from my face in a cold rush. "Go wait in the car," I snapped out the order to refocus his attention, which kept skipping from me to the gaping hole. He wet his lips, hungry, his fist clenching on the doorknob until it crumpled in his palm. "I'll check out the shelter, and Thom can watch my back."

"Mmmrrrrpt," the cat said in agreement.

I exchanged places with Miller and shut the door behind him, waiting until his footsteps thumped past the closed garage door before unhooking a battery-powered lantern from the pegboard and braving the opening. Even built to hold up to a dozen people, the space was compact. I didn't have to step down to see inside, and what I found curdled my stomach.

Angel Claremont sat strapped to a wooden chair borrowed from the kitchen. Her pink-rimmed eyes rolled in her head. Duct tape restrained her arms behind her back, the wide silver bands wrapping across her stomach for added security. I brought my wrist up to my nose, but it didn't help. The reek of urine, feces and rot caused my eyes to water. A mass of soiled bandages wrapped her hip where her left leg should have been. Blood and other fluids mingled on the floor under her. Her right leg bounced up and down, up and down.

"Angel?" I called to her, fumbling my phone out of my pocket and dialing 911. "Can you hear me?"

A whimper escaped her mouth, the only part of her left unbound. No. I saw the shine of tape around her throat. She had chewed through her gag at some point. The noises she made were inhuman, the wildness in her eyes pure animal instinct.

"911, what's your emergency?" a cheery voice asked.

"This is Officer Luce Boudreau. I've located Angel Claremont. I need an ambulance dispatched to this location." I rattled off Martin's address. "The girl's case is being handled by Special Agent Kapoor with the FBI." I paced while wrapping up the pertinent information then ended the call as wailing sirens grew louder. "I'm going to meet the first responders," I told Thom. "You need to be gone when I get back—" I turned a slow circle. "Thom? Where did you go?"

Spry for his size, even without the use of his wings, the big cat leapt out of the shelter onto the foam square where I stood. His fur was too dark to show stains, but his muzzle was damp, and he was licking his chops. That was when I noticed the girl had stopped crying. Thom's narcotic saliva had dosed her so well her head hung forward, chin resting on her frail chest.

"Thanks for easing her pain." I tasted acid in the back of my throat when I leaned down and patted the tip top of his head, careful to avoid the blood. "She's earned her rest."

Leaving the cat to let himself out, I placed my borrowed weapon on one of the work benches, sent up a prayer that the firearm was properly registered since it was covered in my fingerprints, then gripped my badge. I walked to the front door with my hands held up at shoulder level, ID visible from a mile away. A dusty patrol car screeched onto the curb and spilled out two officers with their hands on their guns. Their wary expressions melted at the sight of me, and they jogged up the walkway.

"The house is clear." I waited three or four more seconds, until an ambulance screamed into the subdivision, before guiding a tour through to the garage. "Angel Claremont is down there, and she's in bad shape. I'd let the EMTs handle her." The cops examined the buckled metal, and their eyes rounded. "I had to—" I fumbled for a believable explanation, "—use the winch on the front of my Bronco."

Neither asked too many questions after that. Not where I had parked the Bronco, or why I was at Martin's house in civvies. Or why I was there at all. There was too much work to be done, and I had never given them a reason not to trust me. When I finally extricated myself from the bustling scene, turning it over to the senior officer, it was to text Rixton and then Dad updates. Acting casual, I moseyed to the SUV and let myself in on the passenger side.

Miller glided away from the curb in silence, navigating through the parked vehicles and rubberneckers.

"Are you okay?" I asked once it became clear he had no intention of initiating conversation.

"It will pass. It always does."

The ghosts in his eyes kept me from prying further.

"The lab emailed their findings while you were inside." He indicated a slim laptop wedged between the seat and the console. "I don't know how much good the results will do us at this point."

He turned onto Peace Street and parked in the lot of a boarded-up fast food restaurant.

"Martin and War are MIA. We need to catch a break. Maybe this will be it." I wiggled the laptop free then set it up on my thighs. "Password?"

"Your birthday."

I punched in the numbers, and sure enough, the lock screen dissolved. "Any particular reason why you chose those digits?"

"Sentimentality," he replied. "The date represents more than your rebirth. It marks ours as well. We've had fifteen years of freedom, of peace." He drew in a long breath. "It was a good day, one worth remembering."

"Peace seems unlikely with someone named War on the loose," I said gently. "Freedom—that's your right. Slavery was abolished here. It hasn't existed in my lifetime, and I'm not about to usher in the second coming. You're free. You all are. Live your life on your own terms."

The look Miller turned on me was fond, if indulgent. "You are unique in all the terrenes, Luce Boudreau."

"Aww." I twisted my finger in his chest. "You're not so bad yourself." A grin slipped his leash, and I patted myself on the back for lightening his mood. "Let's see what we've got here." A few clicks downloaded the preliminary reports. "The blood Cole found on the sidewalk at the school is a positive match for Maggie." I released a shuddering exhale. There was knowing, and then there was *knowing*. "There's a second attachment here."

The samples taken at the dump site were moot at this point. The leg had belonged to Angel Claremont.

"Looks like the sand Portia scraped off Jane's heels matches the sand Cole and I collected at the Upton house. There were traces of nitrogen, potassium and phosphorus." I clicked over to Google and double checked my memory. "Those are common fertilizer components. Makes sense. The Uptons laid new sod a few weeks ago. They basically offered to show us their *baby's first fertilizer* pics while we were there."

"The tracks already linked War to the property," he reminded me.

"The blood samples I scraped off their driveway must still be baking." The chances of those results breaking new ground were slim too. "The odds are high the prints were made with her blood. She attacked us in her base form while we were in the SUV, Thom creamed her, then she limped off to lick her wounds. She must have cut through the Upton's yard on her way to the marsh."

"That never made sense to me. A head-on collision with an SUV wouldn't kill War, but it would still hurt like hell. It was careless. I see no benefit." He gazed across the road, lips pinched in thought. "The bruises had already alerted us to the high probability she had breached in full possession of her faculties. Why keep up the act?"

As opposed to me, who had been suffering from brain damage since "birth".

"Traipsing through the subdivision was foolish and flashy." I had to agree with him there. "What if the reason why it doesn't fit is because it wasn't part of her calculated strategy? What if the accident was her attempt at causing a distraction?"

"You think she kept two caches?" he wondered aloud. "One for each victim?"

"It's no different than when dealers hide their product in multiple locations to lessen the chance of one police raid robbing them of their livelihood." Minus the fact we were talking about living, breathing people. "We found Angel Claremont, and maybe War didn't care at this point if we did. She had time to move her and didn't bother. She had to know once we uncovered Martin's involvement, his home would be searched.

It makes sense she would hide Maggie in a more secure, less obvious location."

"Any theories on why she's escalating now?"

"I failed her in some way. She was testing me with the Claremont girl, with Maggie, and I didn't pass." I shut the laptop. "She'll take her disappointment out on Maggie if we don't find her first."

Miller gazed out the window, lips mashed into an unforgiving line as he sorted through the evidence.

"The leg was a taunt. She wanted me to wonder if it belonged to Maggie." Had I not known my best friend so well, it would have worked. It *had* worked up until I saw the pictures. "She would have kept divvying up Angel until she ran out of parts or the DNA results came back."

"Why abandon the charade?" Miller glanced at me, scratching his chin. "War must have spent months learning about you to pull this off, yet she burned her identity as Jane within days of initiating contact."

"Her injuries were the tipping point. She had to know those would raise questions, and she couldn't play Sleeping Beauty forever. Yet she still risked returning to the hospital one last time." I kept circling back to the night of the crash. Maggie had just gone missing. So why would War . . . ? "Maybe we're giving her too much credit. The more people involved in a plan, the greater the risk of it going wrong. What if she had to choose? Maintain her Jane identity or cover her tracks with Maggie?"

"If those were her only remaining choices, that would mean she hid your friend nearby." He let his head fall back against the seat and uttered a disgusted noise. "This is not good news, Luce. It means she's been here longer than any of us realized. The only way that gambit could succeed was if she provided the distraction while someone else secured Maggie."

"Robert Martin is still at large." I mirrored his position. "It seems unlikely he would handle both victims at both locations, though. It would double his chances at being caught. What about her husband? Where does he fit into the hierarchy?"

"War wouldn't waste a powerful resource like Thanases unless she had no choice. He's her right hand. That means there are more of them than we realized." He angled his chin toward me. "She must be growing her coterie."

That sounded decidedly *not* good. "How does that work?"

"Conquest is a collector. The rarer, the more beautiful, the better." His gaze sharpened. "War cares only about brute strength, cunning and skill. With the exception of Thanases, her coterie are all lesser demons. Most of them are her offspring with Thanases. They can't manifest in the flesh the way most of us do."

The *most of us* qualifier didn't stop relief from gliding through me. "Not manifesting sounds good."

What kind of monster bred her own demon army? How could War, my blood sister, view her children as expendable when Portia had sold herself to Conquest for the promise of vengeance for her unborn babes? Clearly, not all demons were created equal. Not that I'd had many illusions about my sibling to dispel at this point.

"The atmosphere in many foreign terrenes is toxic to non-native demons. That's why we take on skins. We study the wildlife, determine the hierarchy and then emulate the highest tier of life. If her coterie isn't strong enough to manifest their own skins, they'll bargain humans out of theirs."

Meaning a deal had been struck. Martin was no longer fully human. Or he might not be in there at all.

CHAPTER TWENTY-TWO

———◆◎◆———

A hard tap on the window made me jump. "Sunday witch." I
shot Miller a dirty look for not warning me we had company,
then composed myself before lowering the window. "Cole."

Dressed in a White Horse security uniform, he cast off all-
business vibes. "Luce." He nodded to the other man without
taking his eyes off me. "Miller." He braced his forearm in the
opening and dropped his voice. "I shouldn't have walked away
from you."

"I get why you did." I wasn't going to punish him for my past
misdeeds. "We're good. Don't sweat it."

"I brought you this." He passed me a manila folder. "To make
amends."

"You didn't have to do that." Though a part of me fluttered
that he had as I thumbed it open. "It's the test results on
the blood taken from the Upton's driveway." I pushed out a
slow breath. Afraid to read any lower, I studied him instead.
"Strange how all the results arrived at once."

Cole stared right back at me, grumpy apology written all over his face. "I might have given the lab incentive to prioritize them."

A trip to the lab would explain his absence for the past few hours. I should have known he wouldn't sulk or shun me. Well, at least not for so long. Pouting wasn't Cole's style.

Unable to put off the inevitable any longer, I broke from him and lifted the paper. "The blood used to make the prints was human." A lump clogged my throat. "Maggie's."

The small puddle on the sidewalk was one thing. But the blood had to have been fresh at the time the tracks were made. Human bodies only contained so much of the stuff. At the rate she had been bleeding . . .

"We're assuming War was directly involved in Maggie's disappearance because of the car accident, and she might still be but . . . " I worried my lip between my teeth. "It makes more sense that a person assaulted Maggie. Had the super gator been responsible, it would have had to drag the body across the road and into the subdivision. There would have been smears, more bloody tracks, something." I double checked my memory of the scene. "There were none. The sidewalk and surrounding areas were clear."

Cole grunted in the affirmative that the trail had ended where it began, and I trusted his nose enough to believe his assessment.

"Martin could have driven Maggie to the subdivision and met Jane there," Miller pointed out. "That would place War in the area at the right time to initiate the accident."

"Maggie bled out on the sidewalk," I argued. "He must have driven her from the vet to the school, not the subdivision."

"We're missing a step," Cole murmured. "Or we have the sequence of events wrong."

"Maggie left work, witnessed Martin back over the dog and ran to offer help. She ended up volunteering, or being pressured into assisting, and got in his car." That's where things got muddy. "Dog or no dog, she would have required medical assistance had her injury been sustained at that time. Since she made the trip to the vet's office without incident, we can assume she was well up to that point." I mulled over the final clues. "Maggie would have expected Martin to drop her off at the school and for them to part ways. The blood proves she was returned, but why?"

"Martin had her in his car, under his control. Orchestrating her kidnapping required a lot of effort, and he botched it when she bled out. They left no traces behind at the Claremont scene. This was messy by comparison." Miller brought up excellent points. "Why complete the errand once he had her in his car? Why bring her to the school and provide her with an opportunity to escape?"

"We need to get another look at the Upton's property." I thumbed through the report in my lap. "It's the last known link between Martin and Maggie we've got left."

Cole gave a tight nod and joined us in the SUV. The vehicle rocked under his shifting weight. I didn't have to turn my head to know he had settled in behind me. The sudden urge to lean across the console toward Miller in order to feel balanced told me that much.

"How's Santiago?" A cat had Thom's tongue the last time we'd met, so I hadn't gotten an opportunity to check on the other injured party. "We saw Thom earlier, so I'm guessing they're both fine."

"Santiago is resting. He'll make a full recovery thanks to Thom's quick thinking." Cole's heavy, warm hand landed on the back of my seat. "And your cool head."

"I'm glad to hear it." Santiago wasn't my favorite person, but I didn't want him to die. "Any word on how Jane got the drop on them?"

"Santiago reported finding her in an unusual position on the bed when he relieved Portia. Jane was curled around a pillow that hid half her face, and the covers had been pulled up to her ears. He figured since she had been waking for short intervals, she had made herself comfortable and let it go." Cole's breath warmed my neck, and I shivered recalling his steak-knife teeth. "Thom took the next shift, and he performed his own inspection. That's when he noticed puckered scarring above her cheek—on the opposite side of her face from her previous injuries. He bent down to get a better look, and she attacked."

"I shot the super gator in the eye the night Cole saved me," I said in case they hadn't already known. "Why would War go back to the hospital at all? The bruising after the car accident, okay. By playing possum, she managed to drag out that inquiry and buy herself time." Though we still had no idea why she felt returning had been worth the risk of discovery. "But a missing eye? That's kind of hard to explain away. No one is going to believe 'Oops. The patient rolled off the bed, landed on a spoon that fell off her lunch tray and scooped out her eye on impact.'"

The men snorted in stereo, but I was serious.

"War must have known by that point you had no affiliation with us," Miller said in a thoughtful voice. "No idea of your true identity or ours."

"She went to great lengths to play off your empathy." Cole picked up the speculative thread. "This incident would have been a second strike on our watch. Maybe she hoped to turn you against us by convincing you we were abusive toward her. With us out of the way, she could have had you to herself."

"She tried to kill me." So much for sisterhood. "It doesn't sound like she cared all that much about combining forces."

"Unless she planned on using your ignorance against you. Conquest would make a powerful ally for anyone who could control her. All War had to do was win your loyalty as Jane, then she could have given you the answers you wanted, filled your head with talk of monsters and blamed her actions on us." The steady growl rumbling from the backseat turned my chair into a vibrator. "War is clever. Eventually, I have no doubt she would have asked you for a favor—as her sister—and extracted a vow of allegiance from you."

"That sounds bad." And irreversible if Cole's agitation was any gauge.

"Cole." Miller spoke his name in a soothing tone.

Cole was not to be soothed. "A handful of words, a few drops of blood, and she would have owned you." He snarled. "She has no use for us. She would have used us up, then killed us or left us behind to rot in the charred wasteland that is Earth's future."

"Cole." This time Miller let the word ring with warning. "Don't push her mind so hard, so fast. Humans are breakable."

A grumble from the rear resembled *She's not human*. I took the high road and pretended not to hear. World domination didn't happen overnight. Empires weren't built or leveled in a day. I had time to educate myself and form a plan to stop whatever chaos War was brewing. But Maggie's was running out. She had to be my priority. Besides the fact my head was so full of new information, I sloshed when I walked. I had reached my saturation point. I had to digest what I'd been taught before I could absorb more.

"You're saying the gloves are off now." I picked up the strand of our earlier conversation. "I can't expect her to show mercy. Not to me or to Maggie."

"She'll use Maggie as leverage. Prepare yourself for what concessions you're willing to make." Cole left no room for doubt. "She's counting on your love of an old friend to outweigh any loyalty you might feel to us."

Cole's clipped delivery conveyed his belief I would sell them out to save her. No defense sprang to my lips. There wasn't much I wouldn't do to save Maggie.

The rest of the short trip to the upscale neighborhood where the Uptons resided passed in a quiet so thick scissors might be required to cut myself out of the SUV. We parked at the curb one house down and sat there, surveying the cul-de-sac. The Uptons must have pressure washed their driveway with hydrogen peroxide to restore its pristine condition. The sand hill was gone, leaving nothing but a yellowed patch of sickly grass across the property line as evidence the tarp had been there. Their lawn, however, grew thick and lush.

This was why I could never survive suburban living. The temptation to irk my snooty and self-important neighbors would drive me to adopt a large dog from the pound for the sole purpose of allowing it accidentally off-leash to fertilize their yard with fist-sized poo bombs. A dog deserved better than that. I wasn't yet convinced the Uptons did, considering their casual disregard for their neighbor's property.

"Do we go with the direct approach?" I'd almost expected my voice to echo in the cavernous silence.

"Can you get us inside?" Cole shifted, leaning over the console for a better look, and the SUV rocked forward. "Or buy us time to search the yard?"

"I guess we're about to find out." I popped my seatbelt. "How close before you can hear or smell Maggie?"

"About the same distance as what we encountered at the Martin house, depending on where she's being held." Miller wet his lips and glanced away. "Blood helps. I can find her faster if she's bleeding."

I locked down my instinctive shiver before it rippled through me. "Let's do this."

We all exited the vehicle. Or I thought we had. Miller still sat behind the wheel taking slow and even breaths, lips moving in soundless words, as though psyching himself up for what came next. Cole crowded me, his shadow engulfing mine. I waited for him to find the words he wanted to fire at me.

"You're kind to him." He made it an accusation. "He cares about you, about your opinion of him."

"Miller's good people." I couldn't decide if he didn't trust my intentions toward Miller or if he was jealous there was no friction between us. We worked well together. We got along. Both of us knew what page the other was on. I had none of that certainty when dealing with a certain finicky dragon. "He was in the lead for my favorite," I teased, "until I saw Thom's demon form. If you can even call it that. I'm starting to think Miller's overreacting with his paranoia about me glimpsing his dark side. So far, all I've seen out of you guys are cuddle-worthy creatures straight out of every little girl's fantasies."

A sharp glower cut his mouth. "I am not cuddly."

"Of course you're not." I patted his chest. "And the next time you shift, I won't be tempted to scratch behind your wittle ears out of respect for your manliness."

The steady rumble might have cowed another woman. Heck, I would have swallowed my tongue a week ago had it been aimed at me. But I was learning to decipher The Many Growls of Cole, and this one smacked of masculine displeasure at the perceived slight to his machoness rather than a genuine threat.

I would never admit it out loud or to his face, but I *liked* him growly. Maybe there was something to this inner demon business after all.

Miller joined us a few minutes later, his bottom lip chewed ragged. "I've got a handle on it."

I took him at his word and set off up the driveway. Cole and Miller lingered near the garage, no doubt hoping to discover if the Uptons shared Martin's fear of inclement weather. Heads bowed together, they conferred about a topic that scrunched their foreheads into matching furrows. Leaving them to it, I knocked on the front door and waited. I didn't stand there long.

"Oh, hello again, Officer Boudreau." Cheeks flushed, Mrs. Upton must have jogged from deeper in the house to greet me. "I want to thank you for handling our situation with such delicacy."

Delicacy was not the word I would have chosen considering how Thom had mangled their sod. "No problem."

"My husband managed to transplant a fresh sod square over the one your *associate* removed. We insisted on planting a small patch in the backyard for just such an occasion. Grass can be so temperamental." She clicked her tongue. "It's all for the best. There was so much blood, and what with the iron—"

"I'm glad to hear your sod has recovered from its ordeal," I rushed out before my brain hit snooze on our conversation. "The transplantation process sounds fascinating. Would you mind showing me?"

"Not at all." Her eyes brightened. "Wait there, and I'll slip on my shoes."

I shot the guys a covert thumbs-up while she slid on her flip-flops. Cole was rubbing his nose, and Miller, who seemed the more sensitive of the two, had launched into a sneezing fit.

"I thought I heard . . . " Her bright façade crackled. "Oh. You didn't tell me you brought friends."

"You remember Mr. Heaton from my last visit." I indicated Miller with a sweep of my arm. "This is Miller Henshaw."

"Why are they here?" She frowned at them and their proximity to her garage door. "This is a police matter, surely."

"Yes, ma'am, it is." I guided her away from them. "Their security firm is working a case that overlaps mine." What used to be one of mine anyway. "We were in a meeting nearby, and it occurred to me I ought to follow up since I was in the neighborhood. You haven't seen the gator again, have you?"

"Goodness no." Her eyes widened. "We would have reported it if we had."

The next ten minutes passed in mind-numbing slowness while she explained more about sod than any sane person ought to know unless they were in the business of carpeting yards with the stuff. While I ran interference, the guys snooped around the side of the house. I don't know how far they got before a violent sneezing fit alerted Mrs. Upton. She set off at a clip, and I rushed to keep up with her.

"Have you gotten a chance to use your new patio yet?" I eased in front of her, and she had to stop or bowl me over. We almost both went down. "I see you finished with the sand. It's messy, right? Gets everywhere, and stray cats treat the stuff like it's a litterbox."

"What are they doing?" She rose on her toes and peered around me. Her mouth gaped at what she saw. "*What are you doing?*" Twisting away from me, she ran straight for them. "Stop that right now. Those pavers were just laid."

Cole held one of the red bricks in hand while Miller knelt and sifted sand through his fingers.

"Guys?" I put the question to them. "Want to share with the rest of the class?"

"She was here." Red rimmed Miller's eyes, and water steadily trickled down his pale cheeks. His nose had been rubbed raw from his shirtsleeve, and his upper lip glistened. "She might still be here."

"Mrs. Upton." I caught her upper arm when she inched away from us. "I don't suppose you have a storm shelter?"

"N-no." She wriggled like a fish on a line in my grip. "I don't."

"Forgive me if I would like to verify that with my own eyes."

I marched her back to the garage, and she pressed a button that caused the mechanism to purr to life. The segmented door rolled back and exposed a smooth slab stained with faded oil splatters from an old leak. Boxes lined the walls, and junk stood in the corners. Not what I would have expected from two perfectionists, but perhaps they cared only for outward appearances. Somehow that seemed fitting.

"Mrs. Upton, I'm going to be blunt. I'm working a missing person case, and I have reason to believe the victim, Maggie Stevens, was brought to this location at some point after her abduction. She was injured and bleeding. It was her blood that made the prints in your driveway, not the gator's. Think long and hard about that before you say another word."

"You don't think that I—that we—?" Her hand flew to her mouth, and her knees wobbled. "Oh sweet God in heaven."

I looped an arm around her waist before she collapsed. "Mrs. Upton?"

"He built me a wine cellar for our anniversary. That was weeks ago." Tears sprang into her eyes. "It was almost finished when he—he told me we lived too close to the swamp. He said the land was marshy and water kept seeping in, so he had it filled." Limp as she was, she slid through my fingers. "He installed the sod instead and set pavers over the top. He bought

me a set of lawn furniture I wanted since my gift was ruined."
Her lip trembled. "The cushions are due to arrive next week."

"Are you sure he had the cellar filled?" I squatted in front of
her. "Did you see it done with your own eyes?"

"He oversaw the construction while I was at work." Her
voice quavered. "I came home hours after he told me about the
standing water, and it was all done. The yard had been raked
down to the dirt. The sod arrived the next day."

Cole prowled up to us. "Where is your husband now?"

"He's at work." She pressed her back harder against the wall
the closer he got. "He won't be here until five-thirty."

"How did you plan to access the cellar?" Miller sounded far
away. He hadn't entered the garage.

"We decided to have an addition made to the kitchen. Just
a door that opened onto the stairwell." She regained a smidge
of color. "I planned a rose garden, a hedge, to cover the new
construction so it didn't clash with the lines of the house."

Miller joined us at last, but he stood apart. "Mrs. Upton,
would you mind if we removed a few pavers and dug down to
see if anything is there?"

"My company will cover any damages and pay for any necessary repairs," Cole offered.

"We've been married ten years." She mopped her blotchy
face. "You can't hide your true self from someone for that long."

None of us had much to say after that. So much of my life
was a lie. So much of my true self remained hidden, even from
me. How well did we ever really know another person? My gaze
slid to Cole and stuck as though magnetized, and I had the
oddest sensation he had been thinking the exact same thing.

"This will go a lot faster with your permission," I told her
gently, but I would secure the paperwork if she forced me to
circumvent her. "Maggie is my best friend. Please, if you think

there's any reason your husband might be involved, help us save her."

"Lipstick on his collar. That's where it all started." Her finger tapped the side of her neck. "I told myself it was a midlife crisis. I didn't push. I didn't force. I let him work it out of his system." Her shoulders rounded. "The cellar, our anniversary ... I thought he was apologizing for the late nights and the perfume on his clothes."

"Mrs. Upton," I prompted.

"Do whatever you want. I don't care." Fat tears pooled in her eyes. "I'm calling my mother to come get me. I'm going home like I should have done the first night he came home smelling like beer and *sex*."

"Get started," I ordered the guys. "I'm going to help Mrs. Upton into the house."

As much as I wanted to raid the gardening shed for a shovel and dig in to help, I trusted Miller and Cole. What I didn't trust was Mrs. Upton's story. I wanted to believe she was a jilted wife. It was a mundane and simple excuse, and I craved those things. But nothing had been simple since the night Jane Doe entered my life.

I sat with Mrs. Upton while she dialed up her mother and listened for any hint she might be calling her husband instead, but nothing about the weepy exchange struck me as odd. I trailed her to her bedroom and watched over her while she packed a suitcase full of clothes and an overnight bag of toiletries. Again, she did and said nothing out of the ordinary. She drifted through the routine of packing up her life as though it had been choreographed, and perhaps that's what caused my skin to itch.

"Luce," Cole bellowed.

"Stay here," I ordered her. "I'll be right back."

Mrs. Upton nodded and sank onto the foot of her bed in a dejected heap.

"Cole, can you—?" I inclined my head in the direction of the house. "I don't trust her alone."

He hesitated the barest fraction of a second. "Be careful." He was staring at Miller, who had broken out in a sweat. "Call if you need me."

I jutted out my chin. "Same goes for you."

With a grimace certain to terrify Mrs. Upton, Cole strolled into the house, and I turned my attention on Miller and the undisturbed patio. "Well?" I toed the one paver they had removed, the one Cole had been holding when Mrs. Upton started having heart palpitations. "What did you find?"

"A small room, cinderblock walls." He sucked in air over his tongue. "Blood. Fresh blood." A shiver wracked his body. "She was here, and not long ago."

"We missed them?" I growled with frustration. "How was he accessing the cellar?"

"Through a rough tunnel that comes out in the shed. Found it when I went looking for a shovel."

Miller stared with rapt attention at his fingertips and the clumps of dirt under his nails that must have contained blood. I made myself busy while he cleaned them with his tongue and suffocated the wailing voice in my head so she would shut the hell up for five minutes. I could have a nice psychotic break later, maybe pair that with a trip to one of the nicer casinos in Biloxi for a long mental-health weekend.

I stormed the gardening shed to escape the panic chasing its tail through my thoughts.

Demons exist. Monsters are real. Dragons? Flying cats? Also a thing. And Miller—what the hell is up with him? He calls people meat. I am not hamburger! He finds human blood tasty. I'm a walking blood bag. He's going to pop a straw in me and slurp me dry. Slurp, like a soda. Sluyuuurp.

Sadly, it turns out you can't outrun your own crazy. It just keeps pace with you.

The gaping hole in the earth built a strong case against Mrs. Upton. Gardeners require access to their tools, and she would have fallen in the tunnel had she not avoided it. The couple who mulches together, murders together, I guess?

The hairs on the back of my neck lifted, and I had to lock my knees to keep from running when Miller entered the shed behind me, blocking me in a confined space with a demon skirting the edges of his control. I anchored my hands on my hips, which put a heavy-duty pair of shears within reach. "There's no way the missus missed this."

Miller's low voice grated against my nerves. "I won't hurt you." His fists clenched at his sides. "I won't."

"You don't sound all that convinced." I skirted the wall and exited the small building. "Let's not tempt fate, shall we?"

Fresh air improved his color, and soon he breathed easier. "I have to return home." Apology rang through the words. "I've reached my limit. I might hurt your friend if I found her while I'm like this."

"Can you send Thom?" I let understanding soften my tone. "Preferably on two legs?"

A tight nod that popped cords in his neck was all Miller offered before setting off at a run into the copse of trees at the back of the Uptons' property. The swamp was a good twenty-minute run for the average human, and the marshy land would make the trek difficult. But he wasn't human, and I got the feeling very little could stop Miller. I bet he made it home in half that time.

Feeling oddly exposed standing in the yard alone, I let

myself inside the house. I returned to where I'd left Mrs. Upton to find Cole face down on the floor, the room otherwise empty. I dropped to my knees, wedged my hands under him and shoved. I could have been attempting to roll an elephant up a hill for all the good it did me. I gave up on moving his body and worked on angling his head to clear his airway.

"Cole?" I shook him gently. "Hey, big guy. Naptime's over." I checked his pulse, found it steady. "You're scaring me here." Never had I imagined Mrs. Upton capable of taking down anyone, let alone Cole. "Wakey, wakey."

Fingers shaking, I dialed up Miller. He couldn't turn back, but maybe he could light a fire under Thom or send Portia. He didn't answer. Where was the card? The one with the coteries' numbers? I checked my pockets and came up empty. I didn't know what to do, who else I rely on for help. The only person I trusted with any of this was Dad, and I didn't want him involved. Dr. Norwood was an option, but I had no way of getting Cole to the SUV in order to drive him to the dilapidated clinic. I was stuck.

"Luce," a gentle voice drifted into the room. "Tears won't fix this."

"I'm not crying. I have allergies." I bit my tongue before tacking on *to cats*. Me being spiteful was about as useful as my blubbering had been. "Can you tell what's wrong?"

"I spoke with Miller. He has the second-best nose, and he couldn't smell the blood until he got his hands dirty." Thom assessed Cole in an altogether peculiar manner, leaning down to sniff his breath then his hair and ears. "I checked the yard and the shed first. There are several bags marked fertilizer that have been opened and mixed with chemicals designed to cause head blindness."

"Head blindness?" I considered the Uptons' fanatical lawn

care. "They used the new sod as a cover. The fertilizer compound masked the blood and demon scents." I sat back on my haunches. "That's why Cole didn't smell Maggie the first time we came out to the Uptons' property."

This proved the Uptons were part of War's coterie, meaning they had used the chemicals to hide from us in plain sight.

A coterie of at least four also explained the water phenomenon we experienced the night Jane Doe was rescued. Three massive demons easing into a pocket of swamp was more than enough to raise the water level.

"I picked up traces of human blood that day." Thom mirrored my stance. "They were so faint I wrote it off as the tracks being fresh. I left with a headache, but I blamed it on—" he pretended interest in a stain on the floor "—something I ate."

I let the subject of his dinner drop with an audible thud. *Don't ask, don't tell.* That was my new favorite motto when dealing with demons.

"Does that mean this will clear up on its own?" I noticed I hadn't stopped petting Cole and flushed. "Will fresh air help?"

"She must have given him a concentrated dose. An aerosol spray is my guess. He wouldn't have let her get close enough for an injection, and he's too smart to have ingested anything she offered him." Thom angled his head. "He's too heavy for us to move. We can open the windows and turn on the fan." He mulled over some inner debate. "I'll bite him to be safe."

"You do this." I pointed at Cole and then the ceiling fan. "I'll do that."

The room had two windows, and they were set into opposing walls in the far corner. Opening them provided decent cross-ventilation, so I skipped the fan. The biting portion of Cole's treatment was finished by the time I returned, and I sank onto the carpet to wait for him to wake.

"What I don't get is why the Uptons called in the gator sighting in the first place." I scratched Cole's scalp lightly with my fingernails to calm my nerves. "Why draw attention to themselves even with preventatives in place?"

Thom watched my fingers with a heavy-lidded gaze like he was recalling them scratching between his ears. "Maybe they didn't." He settled into a crouch a few feet away. "Did you check the 911 call record?"

"No," I admitted. "There was no reason to." With time to kill, I pulled out my phone and texted Uncle Harold to ask if he could finesse the answer while leaving my name out of things. Until the chief cooled off, I was happy to avoid the station. There was also the teensy tiny issue of me slipping away from not one but two crime scenes. The cops from Madison Memorial and the cops at Martin's house would be eager to nail down statements I wasn't ready to give. Dad would be pissed I wasn't asking for his help, but he was more of a blunt-force weapon while Uncle Harold was in possession of a silver tongue. "We should have an answer soon."

"Miller mentioned you showing interest in his history." Thom spread his fingers the way a cat might flex its claws. "Is he special to you?"

Santiago's taunts about the others not mattering rang in my ears. "Not in the way you mean." I glanced over at him. "Miller is easy to talk to, so I asked him for his story first." Thom began examining his nail beds, and I took the hint. "Would you like to tell me how you joined the coterie?"

He cocked his head, appearing bored as he scraped imaginary dirt from under a nail. "Why do cats do anything?"

Everything I knew about cats I'd learned from reading Internet memes. "Because they want to?"

"Precisely."

And that was that.

Grinning smugly, Thom prowled off to inspect the rest of the house.

Well, okay then.

"Luce," Cole rasped.

The phone slipped from my hand. "Hey, sleepyhead."

Cole swung out his nearest arm, wound it around my hips and hauled me against him.

Pressure coiled tight in my chest as he revved up a purr that vibrated our bodies and caused my bones to melt. I was too weak to push him away even though everything I had learned about our history told me that was the only way to protect him from me.

Five minutes, I allowed myself.

I sat there for ten before I started the clock.

CHAPTER TWENTY-THREE

———◈———

Cole's head cleared before the five minutes, the timed ones, ended. And he didn't look thrilled to wake with me in his arms. He and his subconscious clearly had issues to resolve between them. Once our team was ready to go, I called the station and turned over this scene for processing. Cowboying was not looked upon favorably by the brass, but I had resources at my disposal they didn't, and a best friend to find before it was too late.

"I'm open to suggestions." I paced the Uptons' bedroom, which served as our command center while we each routed and rerouted calls, answered emails and sent texts. We traded information to try and bring the bigger picture into focus, but the best we managed was a fuzzy outline. "The only location still on the table is the dumpsite for the leg."

"It's too exposed." Thom rested in his customary crouch near the door. "The swamp beyond perhaps."

"What's the point of using Maggie as bait if War doesn't put her on the hook?" I hated sounding eager. I had ideas of what War might do to her. I was a cop. I had lost my innocence lost ago. But I had never witnessed anything like this. "Where else would she go?"

A melodic chime rang out, and we all jumped.

"It's Miller." With a few taps of his fingertips, Cole grunted at his phone's screen. "Robert Martin doesn't own any other properties. Neither do the Uptons. Their houses are the only deeds in their names."

"War sank months of prep work into those locations," I said. "She must have stocked a bolt hole too."

"The other locations doubled as food storage," Thom agreed then picked at the carpet. "I shouldn't have said that."

Food storage. "You're saying the shelter and cellar held more than two victims?"

Thom sneaked a peek at Cole, who sighed and confessed. "It's impossible for us to determine how many, but I would guess between ten and a dozen between the two locations based on the scents."

I sank down on the edge of the bed. "Why didn't anyone tell me?"

"To avoid this." Cole glared daggers at Thom. "The scents were old, and I doubt there's anything left to find if the storm shelter and cellar were used as—" he bit off the same phrase "—cells to keep their victims." He crossed to me and hooked his finger under my chin, forcing me to hold his gaze. "You can't help what was done. Right now you need to focus on the person you can save, not the ones who are already lost." He cut off my snarl. "Later, there will be time for forensics and searching databases. I'm not saying you have to abandon them. I'm just saying Maggie needs you more."

"You're right." The lost would want me to do for Maggie what hadn't been done for them. "Thanks for putting it into perspective."

Cole looked like he wanted to say more, do more, but he did neither and withdrew.

"Do we think it's worth mounting an effort to search the swamp?" I wondered out loud.

"Portia's been at it for a half hour." Cole tapped his phone against his palm. "No news yet."

He must have been setting that up while I was chatting with Uncle Harold. The Uptons had not, in fact, made the 911 call. At least not from their private cellphones or places of employment. Brilliant man that my uncle was, he had done one better and also reported back on the security footage pulled from the cameras at the elementary school. The initial accident was documented, but Martin's subsequent return with Maggie wasn't recorded. Whatever had gone down on that sidewalk, he had been careful to obscure the result.

The idea someone else might have arranged a surprise inspection for the Uptons made about as much sense as the couple calling attention to themselves in the first place.

Thinking of Uncle Harold reminded me I hadn't checked in with Dad in a while. He must be good and fuming by now. "I'm going to get some air, clear my head."

"Stay close," Cole warned. "We don't know when War will strike next."

No, we didn't. That was the whole problem.

The chemicals in the fertilizer didn't bother me, so I soaked up sunshine while standing in the driveway. I dialed Dad's number and got ready to rumble. Better to face his wrath now than let him simmer all day.

"Luce," a feminine voice purred.

Despite the temperature being in the low nineties, a sudden chill lifted the hairs down my arms. "Who is this?"

"You named me Jane," she said, amusement ripe in her voice. "I rather like it, to be honest. It's so delightfully *human*."

There was no way to underplay what I had to ask, so I spat it out. "Why are you answering my dad's phone?"

"Really, Luce, the things you say." She chuckled softly. "He contributed nothing to your genetics."

"He loves me. I love him. That makes us family." Hiding the depth of our bond wouldn't work if the guys were right and she had been studying me. She would have seen the movie nights, the game nights, the late nights sitting on the porch and talking shop. "Cut the crap, War. What do you want?"

"I want you, sister dear." Rustling noises filled her end of the line. "I was going to trade this Maggie person for your vow of fealty, but she won't live long enough for you to make the trade, and I can't afford for you to balk. Your caretaker will do well enough, it seems."

Maggie. Maggie. Maggie.

With her name a steady chant in my head, I begged, "Release her as a show of good faith. Call an ambulance. Help her."

"No. This one is dying. She might as well do it here and get it over with." She closed that topic and opened another discussion. "Now then. Your caretaker, on the other hand, is very much alive. I haven't even let my darlings have a taste."

"Understand me, *sister*." The threat frosted on my lips as the cold place numbed the burn of acid rising up my throat. "I will kill you if you harm him."

"For thousands of years you've been trying, and yet I'm still here." The noise in the background increased. "Hmm. How about a trinket of equal value? Would you trade? The archduke for your father?"

An instant *yes* clashed with a persistent *no*, and all that came out was a gasp of air.

The archduke. Cole. It had to be. The others had noticed how drawn I was to him, so would she.

"Gods, you're pathetic. After all this time?" Her voice lowered to a sultry purr. "I can't say I don't see the appeal, but really. Aren't you tired of him yet? Toys do get so worn after centuries of play."

I bit my tongue to keep from tripping up worse than I had already. This conversation convinced me as nothing else had that War was my sister. Siblings always knew what buttons to mash, and she was jumping up and down on mine.

"Humanity has done nothing for you." Her sigh heaped on disappointment. "It's time for the prodigal daughter to return home."

The call ended.

Home.

War was at my house.

Spots danced in my vision. I sucked in air and fumbled my phone with limp fingers. I tried and tried, but War let my calls collide with the voicemail box Dad had never set up despite my nagging. I almost dialed Uncle Harold. Dad should have been with him. He should have been safe. But all War had to do was threaten my uncle or his wife, and Dad would have sacrificed himself for them. That's what family—real family—did for one another. I stumbled back into the house without seeing where I was going, and then Cole was there.

"Luce?"

The words launched into the air. "She took Dad."

"Where?" He cupped my face and forced me to look up at him. "What did she say?"

"She wanted to trade." I gripped his wrists, and his strength was all that kept me standing. "But she said Maggie is . . ." I didn't finish, couldn't finish. "So she took Dad." My nails sank into the meat of his forearms. "She wants you too. She offered me a trade. For Dad."

Cole stared down at me. "Take it."

"*No.*" I wrested free of him and bumped into Thom. "You and Dad and Maggie— You're people. Not things. Not toys. Not belongings to be traded. *People.* We don't play her game."

A feral gleam lit Cole's eyes, but Thom whirled me out the door and onto the sidewalk before I could understand what I had done to upset him. He hauled me to the SUV faster than was comfortable for a woman of my height being dragged by a man of his stature.

"I'm not trading him or anyone else," I told Thom.

"I know," he said, releasing me at the vehicle. "He knows it too. That's the problem."

"Why is that a problem?" A cold stone dropped into my stomach. "No. He wouldn't. Thom, tell me he isn't going to face her alone."

"I wanted to believe otherwise. I hoped this time would be different." Thom's expression shuttered. "You can't help but ruin him, can you?"

Even without the subtext they tended to forget I didn't remember, I understood enough to panic.

"Give me the keys." I held out my hand. "Thomas, the goddamn keys."

He handed them over, and I slid behind the wheel of the SUV. I didn't wait to see if Thom made it inside. He had wings. Let him fly for all I cared. Why, oh why, hadn't I driven? I had an interior lightbar mounted in the Bronco along with a hundred-watt siren. Oh well. This wouldn't be my first ticket, and I doubted it would be my last. If they could catch me.

Pedal, meet metal.

Thom, who it turned out had made it inside, hissed at the high rate of speed as we blasted out of the subdivision. Or maybe it was the combination of so many of those fancy maneuvers I'd learned during a tactical driving course I'd taken last year. Plastic groaned, and I glanced over at him. Thom had claws tipping his fingers. Actual claws. And he'd sunk them into the plastic of the dash in an effort to hold on.

As a teenager, I had become a pro at racing against curfew to get home. I called on those memories, taking every shortcut and avoiding the known speed traps. I squealed into the driveway and hopped out almost before I threw the SUV into park. Thom poured out the door onto the gravel beside me, and a dull thud sounded as his phone tumbled from his pocket. He bent as if to scoop it up, wobbled on unsteady feet, and then fell in behind me as I marched up to the front door.

Robert Martin opened it before I reached him, his expression sharp and hungry. There was nothing human in his gaze. Nothing merciful. None of the light or joy or humor I had glimpsed in my own coterie showed on his face. What more had War done to stamp out even a glimmer of what I hesitated to label humanity in hers? They were not human, but my coterie, I was relieved to finally understand, were not monsters either. Though how much credit I could take for that after a fifteen-year absence remained to be seen.

Martin allowed Thom to join me in the foyer, then returned to his position guarding the door. Mr. Upton prowled forward to greet us, a vicious smile playing on his lips, and I marveled that he had aped being a frazzled human so well. He ushered me into my own living room where Cole sat in Dad's recliner with War sprawled across his lap. A tall man with the cold, unending universe in his eyes stood behind them, black hair framing a pale face sculpted from glorious nightmares. A blade filled his hand, its razor edge drawing blood against Cole's throat while War nestled against him. She grinned at me, happy as a lark, her regenerating eye a red welt on her face, mucus dripping onto her cheek.

No sign of Portia, Miller or Santiago. That was good news. No sign of Dad either. That was the not-so-good news.

"I'm here." I walked right up to her, fisted her hair and hauled her off Cole's lap. The man behind her didn't so much as flinch. "Where's Dad?"

"Still like it rough, do we?" War punched me in the solar plexus, and her knuckles must have brushed my spine. The edges of the man's lips curled at that, but I didn't have air to hiss at him. "Where are you hiding, Conquest?" She waited until I hit my knees, coughing and wheezing, before wrapping my ponytail around her fist and yanking my head back until my neck threatened to snap. Our gazes clashed, and her lips pursed. "I don't see you in there at all." She jabbed my cheek with a finger. "This skin suit is quite convincing."

"My name—" I gulped another lungful of air "—is Luce."

"Release her." Cole spoke against the blade, though it drew fresh blood. "I've agreed to your terms."

The black-haired man sank his weapon deeper, and fresh blood dripped down the strong column of Cole's throat.

"Sadly, Conquest owns you to the marrow of your soul, beautiful one. You might have hoped to find a kinder mistress in me, and I do so hate to disappoint, but you are hers. There is no salvaging you." Sparks ignited in her eyes as she swept her gaze over the black-haired man. "Besides, my beloved is the jealous sort. It's probably best we not tempt his rage." War turned back to me, leaning down until our cheeks brushed, and her lips tickled my ear. "Even *I* don't go to such lengths to secure my coterie. What have you done to the poor archduke? I've never seen the like, and I have seen much."

"I've done nothing to him," I snarled.

"Nothing? You destroyed his family, his homeland. You enslaved him. I was there when you bound him as the first member of your coterie. I would not call that nothing." She cocked her head. "You must remember. Everyone remembers their first."

The moisture wicked from my tongue, and I couldn't stop the sidelong glance at Cole or the chills from the fraction of a smirk on the lips of the man I realized must be Thanases.

"Tell her the story, Archduke," she purred. "Explain why you love and hate her so much."

Cole set his jaw, his lips pressed into a bloodless line that didn't flinch when Thanases applied more pressure.

"Oh fine, I tell it better anyway." War strolled over to him and ran her palm over the stubble covering his scalp. "Once upon a time, the man you know as Cole Heaton was an archduke, the son of an emperor. Isn't that how all the human fairy tales begin?" She scratched lightly with her nails. "His terrene fell first and hardest. We were young and vicious then, and Convallaria was to be our proving ground.

"You met him on the battlefield that first day, and you wanted him as you had never wanted in your existence. But he was noble and kind, and you were deceitful and cruel, and he denied your advances." A smile teased her lips. "You took it as a challenge and brought him to his knees, and then you offered him a bargain. Bow to you, accept you as his master, and you would spare his kingdom from the horrors we had planned for the wider world. His honor was such that he agreed, and yours was such that you betrayed him within hours of the bond setting."

"Cole?" I rasped out his name. This was no story of rescue, no reprieve from a worse existence. This had been a massacre. I had let myself hope that when he finally confided his story in me that . . . I would somehow not end up the villainess.

I had been a fool to doubt the icy fury crackling in those meltwater eyes.

"We butchered his family and his friends," War continued into the silence, "felled his entire kingdom and burned it to ash you scraped into an urn to present him. You said, 'There. I have spared them. They will not live to see what becomes of their sweet archduke or their precious Convallaria.'" She stroked his head once more then sighed. "He's been your loyal second ever since. The bond ensures he must remain in close proximity to you, or he'll die. So will the others for that matter. All those stolen touches, all those kindnesses, all a lie. A means of loosening the chains that bind him to you. He will protect you until his last breath, because you are his master and have commanded it so, not because he cares whether you live or die. He will always crave you, but you will never sate him. Any capacity he had for love, you have burned from his heart. Lust is harder to stamp out, but you don't carry his scent in your skin.

"Is this new persona of yours chaste? Or is she simply cruel? In any case, I applaud your newfound restraint." Her razor-sharp laughter should have drawn blood. "Poor male. Denied even that much pleasure, if bedding your mortal enemy could be called such. Perhaps that's what appeals. Do you see your death in his eyes while you rut like beasts? Is that why you've bound him so close? Why you can't let him go?" She drew a pattern on his scalp with her nail. "He would raze this world you've embraced as your own if he ever slipped his leash. What a wonderfully dangerous game you play."

The room spun around me, and bile rose up my throat.

"Give him an order," she invited me. "Any order. See for yourself. He will break himself to obey."

"No," I breathed through the knot in my chest. "Cole is free to do as he wishes."

"This nonsense again?" She rolled her eyes. "Must you go on? I understand this production has had a fifteen-year run, and you're comfortable in your role, but aren't you tired of playing human? Aren't you ready to welcome our sisters?"

There was no convincing her the only person in this body was me.

A rustling noise coming from the kitchen had my lips moving in silent prayer that White Horse had arrived. But the person who stepped through the doorway was as familiar as her appearance was unexpected.

Ida Bell.

"Luce." The nurse's expression shifted from curious to amused. "I'd offer you a drink or a snack, but I wouldn't want to step on your toes. This is your house, after all."

"Well, that explains a lot." Her offer broke open a detail that had been pestering me. "All those foam cups were your handiwork, I assume. That's how War got past the guards when she left the hospital. Those nights you slipped in something extra the soda masked."

"I'll admit I was surprised how easily I tamed them to my hand. Playing human has softened them if they accept food and drink from strangers, even ones wearing uniforms." Ida swept her gaze over War, a flicker of concern tightening her face. "Did you really believe we would leave our mistress unguarded?"

"A girl can hope." Especially when I hadn't known any better.

"Hope," she mused. "When have prayers ever saved anyone?"

I clamped my jaw shut to keep from agreeing with her.

"Poor Ida sold her soul at a mere fraction of its worth after her youngest suffered a tragic accident in the pond behind their house." War chuckled, relishing the memory. "I had hoped seeing me incapacitated might rouse your killer instincts and end this charade, but not even a second chance prompted you to act. Your sympathy for my injuries only served to prove how very weak you've become."

Plots within plots within plots. The hospital had been a test. Win me to her cause or wake the monster in me. She seemed fine with either outcome. Too bad she was getting neither.

"I'll tell Harold you said hello the next time I see him," she said, joining War on the rug, a respectful step behind her mistress. "Nancy and I have that big church bake sale to organize."

A fringe of ice encased my heart, and my chest burned from the cold. "I'm ready to see my father."

"Bring the human male." War snapped her fingers, and Mr. Upton jogged up the stairs. "Have a care with him, would you? Humans are so fragile, so brittle, at that age."

"Where's Maggie?" I demanded when she made no mention of retrieving my friend.

"Who? Oh. That." She flipped her wrist in the direction of the backyard. "I told you she was dying. That was what—twenty minutes ago? Surely she's finished by now. There wasn't much left of her in the first place." She cooed in Thanases's direction. "My beloved gets so hungry, you understand."

Without me seeking it out, the calm and cool place where I retreated when emotion might otherwise get me killed surfaced all on its own. I sank into its chill embrace and kept my position kneeling on the floor. Meek. Mild. Meaningless.

I projected those things and bided my time. I had infinite amounts of it.

Mr. Upton reappeared moments later, the missus in tow. She nudged Dad ahead of them, the shove sending him tumbling down the last few steps. He landed with a grunt of pain and blinked up at me through a swollen face marked with dried blood and purpling bruises.

"There." War gestured to him. "See how well he is?"

Gritting my teeth against the coming pain, I made a fist and swung with all I had, right in her lady business. She screamed and covered the tender area with a hand. Her grip loosened on my hair, and I jerked to my feet. It cost me a clump of ponytail, but I made the sacrifice willingly. Once I got my legs propped under me, I staggered over to Dad and smoothed my hand across his brow.

Thom joined me and bent his head to mine. "Be ready."

My lips parted as the dropped phone flashed in my memory, and I got it. He'd activated his GPS and left it out there as a beacon in case War patted us down for electronic devices. Thom's attention flickered past my shoulder, and I understood the message. I couldn't afford to turn my back on War or her coterie. Drawing her attention from Dad, I circled nearer Cole. "Hope you and Thanases weren't planning on spawning."

War had recovered her composure, but her lips peeled away from her teeth. "You will regret this once you're mine."

"Is that what this is all about?" I cocked a hip and anchored my fist there. "You want me to join Team War?"

"My heart," Thanases purred in a velvety rumble. "She doesn't yet understand."

War absorbed his words, and a calculating smile swept across her lips. "Your coterie has run wild for fifteen years. I imagine the taste of freedom soured in their mouths when I made my grand entrance. They haven't told you, have they? Perhaps they want to spare you, or perhaps they only want to spare themselves."

The urge to ask what she meant was a tic in my cheek.

"Czar Astrakhan wishes us to conquer this terrene and explore that which lies beyond." She rubbed a thumb over one of the bands at her wrist. "You were bred for this. You're a conqueror, my *sister*, not a sack of meat and bones that will turn to dust in the blink of an eye."

"I won't help you," I rasped, horror tickling up my spine on spider feet.

"Your newest skin will crack when the right amount of pressure is applied, and when it does, we'll laugh about this. All four of us. Together."

I stood firm. "No."

"You asked for this, remember that." She examined her nails. "Kill them."

Thanases carved a gaping, red smile from under Cole's left ear to his right, and his snarl dissolved into wet gurgles. A yowl stopped my heart from beating as I whipped my head toward Thom and found him slammed against the wall, a knife in his gut. Mrs. Upton twisted the blade while her husband ripped open Dad's shirt and stroked the fragile skin above his heart with sickle-shaped claws.

"Stop!" I screamed, rushing for Dad. "Let him go. Please. He has nothing to do with this."

Martin scooped me up around the middle and hauled me back to my spot on the faded rug.

War lifted a hand, barely more than a flick of her wrist, but her coterie stilled. "What will you give me in return?"

Time. I needed more time. Ours was running out. "What do you want?"

"I want you. On your knees. Kissing my feet. Begging my forgiveness. Pleading for my mercy." She dipped her fingertips in Cole's blood, then licked them clean, all while holding my glare, throwing my helplessness in my face. "I want this farce ended. Fifteen years. Fifteen years to prepare for my coming, and what have you done? Nothing. You have raised no armies, won no allies, done no research on the inborn defenses of this realm. What sort of conqueror hides behind a speck of metal and a uniform?"

The kind who didn't know she was a conqueror was my best guess, though I kept my snark to myself.

"You were firstborn, and each new world is yours to behold with fresh eyes," she seethed. "I want that honor, I want you to shred the veils between realms at my behest, for you to stand behind me as I enter a new world and claim the glory of its downfall as my own."

All this death, this ruin, so I would play interdimensional can opener for her when I didn't even know how.

The ground rumbled under our feet, the pictures rattling on the walls, and the room held its collective breath. Thom was grinning like the cat that got the cream, and Cole had gone predator-still. Help was coming. All I had to do was hold out until it arrived.

"Let them go," I demanded, ripping War's attention back to me. "Release them, and I'm yours."

Cole snarled behind the blade still sheathed in his throat while Thom sank claws into his attacker's forearm.

"Is that all?" Her smile was imitation-maple syrup sweet. "Then you have it."

CHAPTER TWENTY-FOUR

———◆———

No, that was not all. I wanted more. More time to explore who I was, what I was, what this all meant. I wanted to meet Ezra face-to-face, just once, and ask him why. Why the calls? Why spare me from that all-consuming pain yet leave me to this? Why build me up to watch me fall? Or had he been patching me together in order to set this chain of events into motion? Who was he to me? To War? To any of us? And what did it matter? He was never where or when I needed him. Tonight would be no different. We were on our own.

"You sell yourself cheaply," War sighed, bored of me already. "But who am I to complain?"

A snippet of memory niggled at me. Her story about how Conquest had spared Cole's family and yet damned them with the same twist of phrase had me amending my request.

"I want to hear from your own lips that you will release them, and no, I don't mean *release* as in death. I want them to live. Call them each by name and swear to me that you will not harm them or theirs. I want vows from each member of your coterie as well." On and on I kept going, praying our rescuers wouldn't arrive too late, expounding until I could see no possible loopholes, adding in the names of all those I wanted safeguarded while knowing that by excluding others, I damned them. "Give me those assurances, and you can have me."

"Very well," she agreed with a huff of annoyance. "Is there anything else?"

First, before I bargained my life away, I checked in with Thom. Dad was banged up, but he was conscious and alert. Confused. Afraid. Pissed. But he was mostly okay.

"Tell me what happened at the school the night you took Maggie." Closure was a pathetic substitute for bringing her home, but it would provide her family with answers, and that was all I had left to give. Even if taking this deal meant leaving White Horse to convey what my obedience had bought. "We tracked her to the vet clinic. Why did Martin return her to the school?"

"You are a curious thing, aren't you?" War deliberated over my request. She must have decided there was no harm confiding in me. "His orders were to lure your friend into his vehicle, then transport her to the subdivision where Thanases and I awaited them, but your Maggie didn't take her kidnapping well. Martin refused to pull into the faculty parking lot, and she flung open her door and rolled out of a moving car, rather than wait and see where he took her."

Pride so fierce it burned filled my chest. She had fought back. Had she been up against humans rather than demons, she might have succeeded in saving herself. "Why take the dog to the vet? Why not have Martin bring Maggie straight to you?"

"I'm not without soul." She bristled with genuine offense. "Dogs are fiercely loyal creatures. Of course I saw to its care."

She glared daggers at Martin. "Was it so much to ask that you use another cat?"

Yes, by all means let's get offended over War's minion harming an innocent dog rather than the kidnapping and mutilation of human beings. The cat dig wasn't lost on me either. She must have planned on using Conquest's affinity for felines to rub salt in the wound.

I cleared my throat to cut off his pitiful attempts at justifying his choice of sacrifice.

"Okay, so that explains the blood we found on the sidewalk." Martin must have scooped up Maggie, injured or dazed from her stunt, and stuffed her back in his car. "Why attack the SUV?"

"I had no choice." Another cutting glare left Martin cowering. "Martin called for backup when your friend proved difficult, and I was closest. He recovered Maggie after her rather unfortunate antics just as I arrived, but I scented you upwind of me and hid to observe you.

"At that point, I had no idea if you'd realized Martin was responsible for the Claremont girl's disappearance. You might have been there to question him, arrest him. Or you might have been there on behalf of your friend. But she hadn't been gone long. A few hours. You might not have noticed her missing yet. And if you hadn't, well, I wasn't about to let you pick up her trail while it was so fresh. So I was forced to provide a distraction while Thanases and Martin secured her."

That explained why there had been no demon blood mixed in with the sample we took from the Uptons' property. Thanases hadn't been injured. He must have carried Maggie on his back while in his demonic form to make hauling her through the tunnel easier, and her blood had become ink for his footprints.

Done indulging me, War arched her eyebrows. "Anything else?"

I had but one question left, and I relished the asking of it. "How's your eye?"

"Much better after a good meal. Thank you *so* much for asking." War smoothed a finger over the afflicted lid. "I would ask you to pass along my apologies to your partner, I do hate adding to the poor man's workload, but alas, your association ends tonight. He will have to muddle through his burdens alone."

The petty victory I'd exacted by reminding War I had hurt her evaporated, leaving her the clear winner.

Another life destroyed to satisfy her taste for chaos. Another soul never laid to rest. Another family whose cries for justice would go unanswered. Choosing my own family, my own friends, over her nameless, faceless victims made me complicit in her crimes. But my decision had been made, and there was no backing down now. I wouldn't even if she gave me an out. I might be going to hell, but at least I was selecting my own handbasket.

"Any other pesky matters of conscience?" War prompted me.

Yes. More than I could voice in a lifetime. "No."

"Good." She clasped her hands together. "Let's begin."

The entire process stretched for over an hour during which time no cavalry arrived. Confident I had protected my family, friends and coterie to the best of my ability, I prepared to rest my neck on the chopping block. Conquest had yet to make an appearance, even to save her own hide, so I fully expected War to set about torturing me once the air cleared of our agreement. I also fully expected her to kill me to get to her sister. Mortal bodies break, and Conquest seemed attached to mine.

"Luce, you can't do this." The rasp of Cole's voice from his mangled throat jerked my attention to where he sat in a chair now upholstered with his blood. "Conquest is too dangerous for War to control." His wide palms gripped the armrests of Dad's chair until they splintered. "You condemn this terrene with your actions."

"Earth was condemned the second I woke, according to you." I was no savior. This terrene would fall the same as all the others. At least this bought them time. At least this severed their ties to me. They would live free for however short a time. "Watch over Dad for me?"

The frustrated growl pouring from his mouth put my worries at ease. Dad was in good hands. The best.

War hooked her arm through mine, lifting me to my feet, forcing me to lean on her to regain my balance. Thanases settled his black gaze on me, but it flickered to Ida seconds later. She bobbed her head and exited the house through the kitchen without another word, returning to her post I assumed.

"Soak it in," she urged me. "This is the last time you'll see this place or these people."

The old house had seen better days. The tarp covering the ruined bay window resembled a black hole flapping in the soft breeze. The pictures on my lifetime achievement wall hung at odd angles. Mud had been tracked in, and the scent of rot blotted out the usual gun oil and burnt toast smell of the house. I lingered on Dad, memorizing his features, knowing she would refuse me a last hug for the simple reason I wanted one. I smiled at Thom, who had, at some point, bitten Dad if his dazed expression was any indication. *Thank you*, I mouthed. Better if he slept through this next part. Cole I saved for last. His fury was a palpable hum in the air, bathing my skin in chills. That he cared if I lived or died humbled me. I didn't deserve his consideration. Not after what I had done to him, his family, his entire world.

"Now that protocol has been observed," War said, "I must ask if your conditions are satisfied."

Having endured the protracted spectacle that was the consummation of a demon bargain, I got how she might have thought creating Jane and using that nascent bond of sister-hood to coax me through the steps would be simpler than all the arm-twisting it otherwise required.

"I am satisfied." Not happy, but no one had it all.

"Repeat after me." She linked fingers with me. "I do so swear fealty to my most beloved sister . . ."

The swearing-in ceremony lasted twice as long as it had taken me to extract vows from her and her entire coterie. I doubted that was a coincidence. At the end of the proceedings, I felt the exact same as I had at the beginning. The binding must have worked, though, because War kissed me on both cheeks and hugged me close.

"We are going to have *so* much fun," she promised. "Starting with your archduke." Her eyes gleamed with feral intent. "Finish what my beloved started."

"You swore," I spat, recoiling from her.

"I own you. You own him. Therefore, I own him by default. That means he is mine to do with as I see fit." Oh, she was pleased with the trap she had constructed. "He is a distraction, a weakness. Just look what you bargained away for him. *Your* life. As though you were equals." Her nails bit into my skin. "I want him gone."

"No." I set my jaw. "Take your broken oaths and stick them where the sun don't shine."

"I ordered you to end him." Her glee morphed into startled disbelief. "Why aren't you ending him?"

"She is not bound." Thanases pursed his full lips. "Her aura has not changed."

This crackpot saw auras? I smoothed my hands down my sides, feeling the same as always.

"On. Your. Knees." War pointed an imperious finger at the floor. "*Now.*"

The order slid off me, the same as if I had never taken the oath to serve her.

"No." I blessed Thom again for sending Dad into a deep sleep, even if he might not reawaken if War went nuclear. "You're a liar. I can't trust you to keep your word. You broke your oath, and in so doing released me from mine."

War let her gaze go distant. "I see it now. A single thread of compulsion." War flexed a finger in the air as though plucking a harp string. "Delicate work. Very fine. You are owned, sister." Her teeth clacked together. "But not by me."

"Then who?" Cole demanded.

War blinked the room into focus. "That is the question, isn't it?"

The grim news drained the color from Cole's face; even his ice chip eyes dulled. Thom hadn't fared much better. Had he been in his demonic form, his nub of a tail would have been twitching.

"This is a most unfortunate discovery. I don't much care for surprises. The introduction of new players so early in the game ..." Despite her words, her voice lilted with pleasure. The idea appeared to pique her interest more than her present company. "This will require an altogether new strategy." She meandered toward the kitchen and the gaping hole punched through the rear of the house, trailing her fingers down Thanases's arm in passing. "Kill her caretaker, incapacitate the others, and burn the house down around them. We must keep applying pressure until she breaks. She's no use to us until she regains her senses." She clapped her hands. "Make it quick. We have preparations to make before Famine arrives. At least I can count on *her* to make this interesting."

A bellow that rattled the stars pulled her up short, and the blood drained from her face. Miller. It had to be. War snapped her fingers, and Mrs. Upton leapt from the stairs and trotted to her side, too brainwashed to care if she was cannon fodder.

"We'll continue this discussion once you're more yourself," War tossed over her shoulder.

The two exited through the flapping tarps sealing the ruined kitchen from the outdoors.

Blocking out dread over what else might be prowling in the night, I tore after her. A sharp yank snapped my head back and forced me to stop or scalp myself. Martin. The little weasel.

"Your friend cried your name when I tasted her." He grinned at me, his teeth rows of dagger-sharp blades in an all-too-human mouth. "Sweet blood these mortals have, and you smell so very like them, mistress."

I sank my elbow in his gut and stomped on his instep. He grunted but held firm. I had to get free. I had to reach the closet. Panic edged my vision, and I sank into the cold place on reflex. The details of the room sharpened as the chill embraced me. I reached over my shoulder, cupped the back of his skull, and raked the side of his face with my fingernails. This time, he howled with pain and loosened his grip enough I could break his hold while sacrificing another fistful of hair. I was going to have serious bald spots when this was over. I just hoped I lived long enough to need Rogaine.

I ran full-tilt down the hall. I passed Thom, who crouched protectively over Dad, and spared a glance for Cole, who was locked in battle with Thanases.

Spinning the combination on the gun safe required time I didn't have with Martin barreling after me, so I altered my course, looped through the kitchen and aimed for the staircase. Mr. Upton had leapt the bannister in an attempt to circle behind Thom. I darted out of his reach, leapt over Dad and scrabbled up the steps. Martin landed almost on top of me, and I mule-kicked him. He smacked the floor on his back but sprung up like a jack-in-the-box. I gripped the railing, hauled myself up and ran to the second floor. I skidded into my bedroom, slammed the door shut and locked it, then ran to my bedside table and removed my service weapon from the top drawer.

The door exploded inward as I flipped off the safety. Martin lunged for me, and I emptied an entire clip into him. He hit his knees, blood pouring down his shirtfront, but he kept crawling after me, and the bastard was healing before my eyes. I jogged over to my duty belt and unsnapped the handcuffs. I doubted they'd hold him long, but they'd work for now. I snapped one bracelet on him and dragged him out into the hall. After looping the chain through a thick post on the staircase, I clicked the other in place.

With one demon down, I rocketed down the stairs to assist the guys with theirs and discovered they didn't need my help after all. Thom, winged and furry, sat on Dad's chest. Having read an article once about a cat suffocating someone that way, I shooed him off before asking a favor. "Can you get him out of here? Take him to Uncle Harold's, please."

"Mmmrrrrpt."

Leaving Thom to his change, I advanced on Cole. The bodies of Mr. Upton and Ida Bell lay side-by-side on the carpet before him. Mr. Upton's head was missing, and Cole was making quick work of hers.

Decapitation. Why hadn't I thought of that? Oh yeah. Normal

people used carving knives for things like turkey or ham ... not human esophaguses. Clamping a hand over my mouth, I excused myself onto the back porch where I emptied my stomach on the lawn.

That's when I spotted her—them. Portia stood over a shadowy lump with a delicate sword in one hand. I wiped my mouth and joined her. The last tingles of cold had faded, and I couldn't summon that calm a second time. Not when I was staring down at my best friend. What remained of her.

"Maggie," I breathed, knees caving without my permission. "Oh, God."

"I'm sorry, Luce." Portia sheathed the blade in a leather holster that hugged her spine. "Santiago pinged me after Thom activated his emergency beacon, but I was deep in the swamp and—"

Maggie's skin was cool to the touch. I fought my instinctive recoil and forced myself to check her pulse. A tear had splashed against her skin before I accepted there was no flutter beneath my fingertips.

"Luce." Portia rubbed her hands together as though they ached. "I can't make any promises, but there might be a way to bring her back."

"How?" Suspicion honed my voice to a razor edge that matched her sword. "I can't deal with zombies being real too."

"Do you remember when we first met, I mentioned how I was going to miss this body?"

Now that I knew demons wore human suits, I had an idea of where this was headed. "No." I cut my hand through the air. "I remember, but no."

"I'm different from the others. I can't manifest my own skin. My people are symbiotic. We require cohabitation with another organism in order to survive."

"Maggie is not going to become a skin suit like Martin and the Uptons." I stared back at the house, thinking of the corpses within that once claimed humanity before striking their bargains. "She is—*was*—my best friend."

"I don't take skins, Luce. I live within a host, like I'm doing now." She thumped her fist against her chest. "This woman is alive. She bargained with me for the use of her body." Anticipating my next question, she added, "We agreed to a five-year term, and that contract ends next month." She must be psychic, because she guessed my next one too. "She had breast cancer. I cured her. That was the trade. Five years in exchange for a chance to live into her golden years."

"Maggie is dead."

"Try her wrist." Portia tested each, then showed me where to put my fingers. "It's not much, but it might be enough."

A whisper of a pulse, so faint I might have imagined it, had me asking, "What are the terms?"

"Three years is the best I can do. Less than that, and I won't survive the transfer to a new host."

Hope really was the worst thing that could happen to a person. "You can heal her?"

"Yes." She touched Maggie's swollen cheek. "With Thom's help, I think we can save her."

"What will it mean if she's your host?" As though I had any right to ask for clarification, to even contemplate this deal.

"We'll share her body. Usually one of my stipulations is full control of a host. Her mind would sleep through the term and awaken when I leave. Her memories will be intact up to that point, and she'll have no knowledge of my actions." She peered up at me. "For you, I'm willing to attempt to share. It may not work. It might prove too much for Maggie. Human minds are delicate. She might have to be put in stasis in order to preserve her sanity. I can't make you any promises."

"I can't make this decision for her." I balked from the magnitude of what Portia offered. "She has a life, a career—friends and family. She has a fiancé. She's getting married in five months."

"I can fake it with her family. Probably. I'll have access to her memories, and that gives me a template to build on. She probably wouldn't thank me for sleeping with her man for three years, so that's out. Teaching is also not my gig. I don't do kids. I just ... I can't be around young." Portia sighed. "Honestly? The best thing for all those involved is if she drops off the face of the earth. Three years from now, she wakes up and picks up her life where she left off."

Except her dream job would have hired someone new. Her fiancé might have found someone else. Or maybe worse, he might not have let her go. Her family would have grieved until even her miraculous return might not heal all the wounds her absence inflicted. Her whole life would be packed up in dusty boxes in a storage building somewhere.

Maggie would lose everything. No. Maggie had already lost everything.

Portia was offering a means of giving it back. All I had to do was sign away three years of her life.

"This is all my fault." I wrapped my arms around myself and rocked. "She never would have been targeted if not for her friendship with me."

"We're almost out of time," Portia murmured. "You have to decide."

The vibration in my back pocket gave me an out, and coward that I was, I took it. "Boudreau."

"I'm a father." Rixton's joy soured my mouth. "I'm holding seven pounds and eight ounces of Annette Marjoram Rixton."

"Congratulations." A veil of tears curtained my vision. "How's Sherry?"

"Tired. Gorgeous. Snoring." Pride beat at me across the line. "She's the most beautiful thing I've ever seen."

"Annette?"

"No." He got choked up on his next breath. "My wife."

A sob broke free of my chest, a reminder the cycle of birth and death were intertwined, and I wiped my cheeks dry. "Call me when you're ready for visitors, okay?"

Lost to the cooing sighs of his brand-new baby girl, he didn't find my sniffles odd or notice the catch in my voice.

"You can be the first non-relative to hold her," he promised. "I'll save you a spot in line."

On a watery laugh, I signed off before the sorrow arrowing through my chest pierced his bubble of perfect happiness. Maggie and I should have been fighting over dibs with a mean hand of paper, rock, scissors. But I would never lose to her again. Unless . . .

Portia could save Maggie's life, give her a future. She could wind back the hands on the clock. Make things like they used to be. Almost. But wasn't almost better than nothing?

Hating my weakness, knowing what I did next was an act of pure selfishness, I croaked out, "Do it." I wobbled to my feet, unable to sit there and watch. "Save her."

In my haste to escape what I had done, I backed into a warm wall of muscle. Cole. I turned in his arms and pressed my face against his chest. Santiago had been right about me. Thom too. I broke the people I loved. I ruined them. I couldn't seem to help it. And worst of all, I was too weak to let them go, to force them to let me go too.

Cole didn't yell at me or absolve me. He didn't tell me I'd done the wrong thing or the right one. He held me to keep me from flying apart, and he shielded me from the scene playing

out behind me. His strength anchored me, and I leaned on him as I faced Portia and the consequences of my actions.

"Miller and Santiago dispatched the other members of War's coterie. Nineteen in all. She must have laid a clutch and waited for them to hatch as part of her preparations. That explains the delay in her confronting you." And the reason why we had heard Miller's bellows, but he had never materialized. "Santiago's wounds were reopened in the skirmish, but Miller walked away unscathed."

"And War?" I hadn't seen where Thanases had gone. "Did she get away?"

"Portia arrived in time to intercept her, but War tugged on her bond with Thanases before she sustained much damage. He bolted from the living room before I could finish what he started. Miller's already gone. He carried Santiago back to our base while Portia stayed with Maggie."

"What about Mrs. Upton?" Hers had been the only corpse missing from among the lower demons.

"Miller" was all he needed to say.

"Can you get Portia and Maggie to your base?" I couldn't bear looking at Cole. I was too afraid he would condemn me for the choice I had made. "Shit's about to hit the fan. You guys need to be gone before that happens."

"Luce."

"Please don't." I sucked in a shuddering breath. "I can't deal with you hating me right now."

"Hate comes easy." He traced my jaw with his fingertip. "This doesn't feel easy."

"You should go." I withdrew from his touch. "Get somewhere safe and stay there."

"You really have changed," he murmured before shifting into his sleek dragon form and lifting the women in his gentle claws.

Before tonight I might have crowed my victory in establishing my own identity with him, but grief had tightened my throat, and I didn't feel like talking anymore. War had landed some deep blows that might not heal as fast as the bruising on my ribs. She had called me a shell, believed that enough pressure would shatter my human façade, and as much as I wanted to call her a liar, tonight . . . tonight might have given me my first cracks.

CHAPTER TWENTY-FIVE

———◆———

I didn't bother standing to open the door when the authorities arrived to secure the scene. I was sitting in Dad's recliner, what was left of it, kicking off the floor with the tips of my boots. When the knock came, I called, "It's open" and waited for the swarm to descend. Except that's not what happened. Not at all.

"I was hoping to hear from you," Special Agent Kapoor drawled as he strolled into the living room, "but I was thinking we'd start slow. With coffee. Maybe a muffin." He surveyed the room. "Even if this is what it took to get you pick up the phone, I'm glad you called."

I peered around him, first at the decapitated corpses and then up the stairs where Martin snored under the influence of Thom's bite. "You are?"

"Do you mind if I sit?" He gestured toward the couch, which had survived the ordeal unscathed. "I have a proposition for you."

"Knock yourself out." I kept rocking, waiting for the other shoe to drop. "Forgive me if I'm too tired to stand on formalities tonight."

Not that we did in this house even on good days. And this was decidedly not one of those.

"Ms. Boudreau, let me begin by saying I've followed your life with great interest."

My foot hesitated above the floor, and I shoved into an upright position. "How's that?"

"The organization I work for specializes in the neutralization of charun insurgents." He held up a hand when I balked at his job description. "Our department has watched over you since news of Edward Boudreau's discovery hit the national papers. We're impressed, Ms. Boudreau, not only by your service record but by your commitment to protect and serve humanity." He shared a conspiratorial smile with me. "We are well versed in your origins, and we have been made aware of your situation. We are familiar with your siblings as well, including the woman formerly known as Jane Doe."

"How did you know?" I doubted my coterie had cozied up to him. "I only found out days ago."

"You are not the first Otillian to climb the rungs and set your cap at Earth. Others have come before you. More will come after you, I'm sure. Always in sets of four. Always endowed with a set of complementary skills." He treated demon invasion as casually as I handled drunks after a football game. "Charun strong enough to survive the dissolution of their coterie, those who uphold our laws and conform to our way of life, are allowed to remain as long as they submit to close monitoring and sterilization. As we have no means to return them, those unwilling or unable to conform are destroyed."

The harshness of his proclamation stunned me, but after

meeting War and her coterie, what choice did humanity have except protecting itself using all available resources?

"How did you know who I was based on a news article?" I had copies of most, if not all of them, and I had found no such magic key to unlocking my identity.

"The markings on your arms. A tech noticed the rings and flagged your file. Later, we were able to recover photographs taken in a hospital environment documenting your sleeves. It was the first time we had ever seen the entire *rukav*. We integrated that information into our program and used it to track other possible Otillians, including Jane Doe." He treated the violation of my privacy with an air of apologetic necessity. "We have a team dedicated to researching peculiar incidents in the media, which is how you were singled out in the first place."

"*Rukav*." I trailed a finger over the ribbed texture of my arm. "I didn't know the bands had a name."

"All our information on you and your kind comes direct from the source."

Meaning they had a demon, he hinted an Otillian, on the payroll who could help me understand my heritage, my purpose, my past, and how to keep history from repeating. "What's the catch?"

"We want to recruit you." For the first time since arriving, he spared a glance for the bodies. "This case will gain you even more exposure. That's a dangerous prospect for a demoness of your reputation, considering you can't access your powers."

"You're offering me protection in exchange for my cooperation." Why did that sound so familiar? Considering the trail of destruction left in my wake the past few days, it was a better offer than I might have expected, and it came from the lesser of two evils. "What about my coterie?"

"Given the bonds you've formed with them, and your

ignorance as to the depths of those bonds or their origins, we are willing to extend immunity to them." The hard cast to his features gave away his agitation. "The creatures you brought here with you are lethal. Had they not proven loyal to you, we would have put them down. We will still neutralize them if there comes a point where you can no longer control them. Miller, in particular, is a concern of ours."

Tempted as I was to ask him what the deal was with Miller, I wanted Miller to trust me with the truth more than I wanted a clinical explanation from this guy.

"The government is recruiting a demon army." Somehow that didn't shock me as much as I expected. "To what end?"

"We prefer to think of it as a taskforce," he corrected me. "And the answer to your other question is—to no end. That's the whole point. You're here to destroy this world." He spread his hands. "We're here to make sure that doesn't happen by using any means necessary."

Even if that meant recruiting the very beings who had painted a bullseye on Earth in the first place.

"What about all this?" I gestured around the carnage. "Does this go away too?"

"Yes and no." His lips quirked into an almost smile. "Every case receives two official sets of paperwork. One we release to FBI headquarters, and one we keep in our personal files. The first will outline in detail how Robert Martin kidnapped Angel Claremont using his position at the school as a gateway to selecting victims. The Uptons and Ida Bell will be painted as his accomplices. Given other disappearances reported in the area, the story will be spun with a sex trafficking angle. Maggie is older and doesn't fit the profile of the other girls. As far as anyone needs to know, she was taken after asking too many questions of the wrong people."

"It fits." I had to agree. "It's close enough to the truth to be believable."

"We've been doing this a long time." For the first time, he sounded tired. "We've had a lot of practice."

"You can sweep the hospital surveillance footage and Martin's garage incident under the rug too?"

"Already done." He lifted one shoulder then let it fall. "Humans aren't ready to know about the charun yet, so we do our part to conceal their more unlawful activities."

"How have you hidden from my coterie this long?" They considered him a thorn in their sides, but they must not be fully aware of how deeply he was imbedded in their lives. "I don't know them all well yet, but they're good at what they do."

"They are, but so are we. Plus, we had the advantage in knowing who and what they are, what to guard against. We took measures to protect our interests from being discovered prematurely."

"I'm sure there's more I ought to be asking, but this has not been my best week," I admitted. "I'm still trying to make sense of it all."

"We have councilors available if you feel that might help." He linked his hands in his lap and rubbed his thumbs together. "I see one regularly, have since I joined." He shrugged off the vulnerable moment. "Our brains aren't meant to perceive these creatures. We aren't equipped to handle the actuality of them without fracturing our reality."

Figuring it didn't hurt to try, I pressed, "Can I have time to consider your offer?"

"No can do, sorry." He shook his head. "How you answer determines how we spin this incident."

"I figured." People had died, had had their lives changed forever, and justice would be served. Kapoor was leaving it up to me if my head would be dished up on the platter next to Martin, Ida and the Uptons or not. "Either I'm the new recruit with a kill and a capture under her belt, or I'm a cop who went vigilante after her best friend was kidnapped and hacked up the two people responsible in her living room?"

"Your timing did save me a lot of effort drafting a recruitment speech."

"In that case, count me in." I slumped back in the recliner. "I doubt I'll have a job after today anyway. The chief is pissed at having his dirty laundry aired."

"Chief Timmons is facing harassment charges," Kapoor told me. "The media he's so fond of is about to crucify him, and you handed them the nails. He won't be chief much longer."

I perked up at that. "What does that mean for me?"

"It means we'll leave you embedded in the CPD to weather the storm for at least the next thirty days. You need time to acclimate to your new worldview and to get your affairs in order, and we can't afford for you to drop off the face of the earth after this. Not yet. Once the brass gives us the thumbs-up, you'll resign from the CPD and enroll in our academy. That way you'll fall under our auspices, and we can better protect you and yours." His hesitation raised all kinds of red flags, but he barreled forward. "All charun are required to spend one month at a medical facility of our choosing where you will be expected to give blood, tissue and bone marrow samples."

One month. Thirty days. Seven hundred and twenty hours. For medical testing.

All my nightmares, it seemed, had chosen to manifest on the same night. But I had glimpsed beneath War's mask in this room, and I had beheld Thanases's honed brutality. I had witnessed the cruelty her coterie was capable of—and I had two sisters yet to meet.

Embrace my heritage or cling to my humanity with every ounce of strength left in me. I was a weapon, and studying me would help this shadow organization arm themselves for who and what came next. Even if what came next was . . . me.

The answer was easy in the end.

"Normally, we'd ask you to submit to a hysterectomy as well, but Otillians are bred to spread their genetic markers throughout their conquered lands. Your reproductive organs would regenerate over time. So we're asking you to agree to the insertion of an IUD that will be calibrated to your unique physiology."

Given how War reproduced at will, I almost thanked him for ensuring that even if Conquest reemerged, she would be bound to my morals regarding the use of offspring as weapons for as long as Kapoor remained in the picture.

"I can't believe you guys run a spay and neuter program for demons." I might have laughed, but I seemed to have forgotten how for the moment. "Bet that's not on your official business cards."

"No." He chuckled softly more to humor me than because he found me amusing. "It's not.

"The other members of your coterie will be evaluated as well, and the best course of action will be determined upon a review of their medical records."

"That's their choice." I dared him to challenge me with a look. "Their bodies, their choice."

I would find a way to protect them whatever decisions they made, the same as they had protected me.

"You'll have to take that up with management. What you're asking is above my paygrade."

At the reprieve, I let my eyes shut and expelled a slow breath. "What happens next?"

"Next I make this all go away." Kapoor stood, crossed to me and offered his hand. "Welcome to the team, Luce Boudreau."

"Thanks," I said, shaking his firm grip, "but I was thinking in more immediate terms."

"Give me a quick and dirty statement. I'll fill out the paperwork this time." He pulled out a slim, black device and rattled off the date, time, our names and location before pausing the recorder. "After this, you're free to go."

Words tumbled out of me in a semi-cohesive ramble that Kapoor would have fun untangling later. Good as his word, he let me leave after that. I passed four black-clad agents on my way out and spotted movement in the tree line that suggested more remained hidden. I didn't care. I hopped in my Bronco and roared out of the driveway headed for the White Horse bunkhouse.

Used to flying Air Cole, I got turned around more times than pride allowed me to admit. The pitch darkness and lack of street lights didn't help matters but, after a few false starts, I retraced the twisting single-lane roads I'd driven a grand total of once until I snugged my Bronco among the fleet of SUVs.

The house stood silent and dark, and I had about made up my mind to come back in the morning when movement in the water drew me to the edge of the pier. Santiago leveraged himself onto the wood and sat there panting a moment while he recovered from his exertion.

"Should you be swimming?" I folded my arms across my chest, ready to haul him to his room. Though how I would scale the wall, I had no idea. "Does anyone know you're out here alone?"

Rather than snap at me, he patted the plank next to him. Figuring I might not get a second offer, I joined him. "I doubt you saved my life," he began, "but you did stuff me like a turkey with my own entrails, and that means something to me."

I read between the lines. The print was small and difficult to parse, but it was there. "You're welcome."

"Portia is still out cold in case you came to see them," he offered. "She said they're going to leave for a while."

Part of me exhaled with relief that I could escape facing what I'd done for that much longer while the rest called me a coward. Maybe I could get Santiago's help painting a yellow stripe down my back. That seemed like something he'd enjoy.

"I'm not here for them." I kicked off my shoes and stuck my toes in the warm water. "I hope being a woman down won't put you guys out much."

"She was scheduled for host leave next month." He rolled his shoulders. "We'll bump it up and adjust."

I swished my feet and nodded. "How's Miller?"

"Detoxing out in the swamp. Probably making a dent in the local deer population. The hunger strikes him harder than the rest of us." He pinched the skin on the top of my hand. "Human flesh is so tender. Melts like butter in your mouth. Plus, their hair is strategically placed. You don't even have to skin them."

"Stop trying to scandalize me," I chided. "I'm numb from the heart up at the moment. Save your anecdotes for another day, and I promise I'll act properly shocked and maybe even barf on you for your troubles."

Seeming amenable to this, Santiago let the matter drop. "You've been collecting our stories."

"I'm hoping to understand who I was so that I can prevent myself from becoming that person again."

His quiet laugh called me ten kinds of fool, but he slanted his eyes toward me. "Don't you want to hear mine?"

"Only if you want to tell me." I was too tired to pry it out of him, and I wasn't sure—after Cole—that I could handle the reason for his hatred. "It's your call."

"I was a farmer, and my wife, Cassandra, a former priestess." His voice softened. "Our property straddled the border between her clan's lands and mine, a compromise that pleased both our elders since our mating was meant to bring unity to our people." He quieted for a moment. "A great drought swept through the valley during that first year, and some thought that marked our union as cursed by the gods she had once served. They didn't know—I didn't know, not until much later—it had been Famine at work. Those same villagers who had tossed petals at my woman's feet the day of our mating ceremony tried to take her from me to bring the rains, and I slaughtered them."

I could see where this was going, and it was nowhere good. "They came for you again."

"And again, and again. Until I was too weak to fight back, too wounded to defend our land." His voice broke. "They killed her, fed her blood to the earth. They would have done the same to me if you . . ."

I barely dared to breathe as moisture gathered in his eyes.

"You and your coterie cut your way through them. You spared me when all I wanted was to die. Cassandra's blood hadn't yet cooled when you breached the next world, right there in my fields, while I cursed you and swore vengeance." He wiped a hand over his mouth. "Sometimes I think you believed you were doing me a favor or paying a debt for using my field, knowing it would attract the attention of your sisters and that I was unlikely to survive their crossing." He showed me his wrists, his ankles, his throat. "I'm not bound to your service, but I'm trapped all the same unless I decide to remain in one of the terrenes, but there is nothing for me there. There is nothing for me anywhere, so I might as well live so that when I die, I have stories enough to fill my eternity with Cassandra."

"I'm sorry." It was all I had. It wasn't enough. Not nearly enough.

"Now you understand." He palmed the boards under him. "Let us never speak of this again."

"All right." I owed him that much. "Truce over."

He snorted an amused sound and lingered when I had expected him to rise and leave.

"Thom make it home okay?" Unable to stomach the water—or maybe it was the conversation—I curled my legs under me. "He called after dropping Dad with Uncle Harold, but that was hours ago."

"He's not out catting around if that's what has you worried." He glanced at a darkened window. "His tank is on E. He'll sleep like the dead for the next forty-eight hours if we don't pester him."

"Good." Thom had earned his sleep. "Did the, um, host make it off okay?"

"Why don't you ask what you really want to know?" He dared me with only a hint of his usual malice. Poor baby, he really must not be up to full strength yet.

"I'm not sure I want to know anything," I admitted, knowing he had expected me to ask after Cole. Well, I wasn't falling for that trick. Not with him. "I had a shitty day and a crappy week, and I just didn't want to be alone."

Okay, make that a case of soap and a month of brushing with suds.

Santiago, who appeared to prefer spending time on his own, digested this.

"I have a couple of cane poles and some sliced hotdogs in a baggie if you're game." His muscles tensed as though in preparation for a strike, and he dared me with a belligerent, "Well?"

"Fishing sounds perfect." I was tired and bloody and wanted sleep more than my next breath, but he had offered, and I wasn't about to say no. "Let's make this interesting. Loser has to clean the winner's fish."

"I don't mind the crunch," he informed me, shoulders easing when I didn't raise a hand against him. "How about the loser has to clean the winner's vehicle?"

I wrinkled my nose. "I'm going to regret this, aren't I?"

"Yep." Santiago's grin, the first real smile he'd ever given me, blinded. "Don't worry. I have a detailing kit, and I stole Miller's toothbrush last week. You're all set. I'll even let you pick the date."

"Hey," I complained, "I haven't lost yet."

"*Yet* being the operative word." He glided to his feet in a fluid motion. "Be right back."

The guarded look he cast over his shoulder cracked my heart. Hands in his pockets, bare feet leaving wet tracks on the wood, he reminded me so much of the tough boys Maggie taught who couldn't expose their hurt without it costing them their pride.

Maggie. Oh God, Maggie. What have I done?

I didn't budge from my spot, too afraid any small movement might send him storming off again, but I couldn't stop from craning my neck to glimpse Cole's bedroom window once Santiago rounded the corner. The urge to walk up to his door and knock, let him invite me in so I could outline Kapoor's offer and use his steady presence to postpone the guilt over Maggie eating up my middle, almost won. I had my feet under me, ready to stand, until Santiago emerged with two poles gripped in one hand and a cooler held in the other.

"You coming?" He threw the question at me and didn't wait around to see if it stuck.

"Right behind you." Rubbing my neck, I resisted the urge to glance back one last time and gave Santiago my full attention. "So, do hotdogs really catch fish, or do you just like fondling wieners?"

"Play your cards right, and you'll soon find out."

Laughter tickled my throat, and I decided maybe one day I might actually like Santiago.

We fished for hours in companionable silence, and I drove home afterward without glimpsing so much as one ivory scale.

The agents had left the house by the time I returned and taken the bodies with them. The bloodstains remained, as did the busted furniture and gaping holes in the exterior walls. I rubbed my hands down my face and spun on my heel. Staying here tonight was out of the question no matter how much I pined for my own bed and my own room, a slice of normal in a life gone paranormal.

I had one foot on the bottom stair, determined to pack a bag and join Dad at Uncle Harold's, when I heard it.

Briiiiiing.

The urge to dash up the stairs never manifested. I was tired, sore, peppered with mosquito bites and smelled like fish and hotdogs. I clomped up to the second floor, entered my room and listened. For years, I had willed that phone to ring. I had prayed for the caller to think of me outside my found day and dial me up for an actual conversation. He never had, and I had believed he never would.

Briiiiiing.

I gripped the heavy plastic handset, took a breath then lifted it to my ear.

"Luce," the familiar voice growled. Tingles still danced over my skin, but they saved their pirouettes for Cole these days.

"Look, Ezra, it's late, I'm tired, and you want something from me after giving me exactly nothing for as long as I've known you."

The ambient noise in the background hummed.

"This is what I'm willing to offer you." I sat on the edge of my bed and started unlacing my boots, which were soaked through and mud-covered, and let them thunk to the floor. "Take it or leave it."

"I'm listening."

"Let's rewind to last week. Pick up where we left off." I lay back and curled on my side, too drained to shower, change or even pull the sheet over me. "Can we do that?"

"Happy birthday," he said in answer, proving he was a quick study.

"Thank you." I yawned hugely and mashed my face into the pillow. My eyelids dropped like weights had been tied to the ends of each lash. Exhaustion thickened my voice, turned it as husky as a whisper. "Stay with me."

I fell asleep listening to the static whir of box fans in my ear. And when I teetered on the edge of unconsciousness, about to tumble over, I thought I heard him murmur, "Always."

EPILOGUE

———◆———

The rooftop creaked under his weight, but no one was awake to hear, and even if they had been, the inhabitants had long ago assigned any noises he made to the house settling. Rolling his shoulders, he loosened the tension from waiting for Luce's tired breaths to taper to the quiet huffs that indicated true sleep. Unready to sever their mental connection, he maintained it as he shook out his three sets of wings and stepped off the edge.

Hovering outside Luce's window, he drank in the sight of her, parched for more despite having contacted her only days earlier. Faded jeans molded to her lower body, wrapping her full hips in a loving embrace. Mud drenched the cuffs and black smudged her bare feet. The skintight top she wore had rode up, exposing a gap of creamy skin between her belt and hem. Her arms remained covered, as always, as did his mark upon her. He regretted her modesty almost as much as he applauded her caution in flashing the heritage embedded in her skin.

Fingertip pressed to the glass, he traced the gentle curve of her spine. Caressed the soft brown hair with red highlights spilling around her shoulders. Her face pressed into the pillow, robbing him of a chance to catalog her features. The full curve of her bottom lip, the slight arch of its counterpart. Her delicate nose with its upturned tip. Expressive brows. Sharp, blue eyes that held the weight of eons in their depths yet retained their open curiosity.

Luce Boudreau was a paradox of his own creation, and though he ought to be her master, he suspected she had made him her slave.

A slight vibration in his pocket had him palming his phone. He had loaned his preferred ringtone to Cole, who had blamed the switch on Santiago, for the sole purpose of watching Luce remember him each time the other man's phone rang. He would have to pick another, less distinctive one later. For now, he flicked the green icon with his thumb as he rocketed into the night sky. "Special Agent Kapoor."

"We have her." Kapoor vibrated with glee. "She's joined the team. She'll be fully active within six months."

Six months. What was that in the span of the one hundred and eighty such months he had already endured? Or the thousands that came before time was measured in such increments? "Excellent."

"Calling in that tip about the Uptons was a masterstroke. You led her right to us." Kapoor hesitated. "I don't think her coterie has put all their cards on the table. They may not trust her yet. Miller—"

"Miller is hers," he assured the harried agent. "They all are." *We* all are. "She can control him."

"If she can't?" he persisted.

"Then I will neutralize him." Conquest would have mourned

the loss of such a wonder as mortal eyes had never beheld, but his stubborn Luce would brand him a traitor for the execution of a man she considered a friend. No. He would hold that option as a last resort, and only consider it then because if Miller slipped her control, this world would end in the cradle of a serpent's belly and Luce with it. "Let me worry about Miller Henshaw."

"She'll want to meet you," he pressed. "What should I tell her?"

He pretended to consider Kapoor's request then answered in a calm, measured tone. "Tell her yes."

After all, he had fifteen years' worth of belated birthday gifts to make up to her. Why not start by giving her what she wanted most?

Him.